Linda Sealy Knowles

JOURNEY
TO
HEAVEN KNOWS WHERE

Linda Sealy Knowles

ISBN-13: 9781092570190

With Love

To my daughter, Kelli von Eberstein, for her love and encouragement And to my granddaughter, Rachel von Eberstein, who is my biggest supporter and fan.

Acknowledgements

My undying thanks goes to my eight-year-old granddaughter, Lauren von Eberstein, whose knowledge of grammar and spelling is well beyond her years.

To my sister and dearest friend, Hope Summers Coaker, whose personality influenced the characteristic traits of my youngest character, Hope.

To Adelaide Blades, my dearest pal. She gave me the desire to move forward through her sweet words of encouragement.

Chapter 1

Texas
September 1892

After boarding a big red stagecoach in Junction City and traveling for two days, Rae Rogers and her three-year-old sister, Hope, were finally on a journey to heaven knows where. Rae sighed in relief knowing that no one was chasing the stagecoach and trying to drag them back home. She felt that she could finally breathe.

With her stepfather's demands and threats, Rae had known that she had to take action and get as far away from him as she could. She had purchased two tickets that would carry her and Hope at least one hundred miles away. Rae wished that she had had more time to form a plan and secure funds to cover expenses for the trip. At the last station stop, she had used the last of her coins to buy breakfast for her sister. Rae had not eaten since yesterday, and her body was beginning to feel the result of being hungry.

For the first two days of travel, Rae and Hope had been the only passengers. Having the coach to themselves had been nice. Hope, being an active little girl, climbed from seat to seat, window to window, without disturbing anyone. Now, she had to sit still and be quiet.

At the last stop a short, fat, middle-aged man got aboard and sat across from Rae. He wore a three-piece suit with a stiff, white collar that was too tight for his pudgy neck. The man kept running his finger down into the collar and pulling on it, never taking his beady eyes off Rae. Noticing that his eyes kept glancing up and down her body, Rae straightened her bonnet, stiffened her back, and sat straight up. As she pressed her nervous hands down the front of her skirt, she looked directly at the little man, 1 never blinking an eye. She stared him down, causing the man to feel uncomfortable. He immediately turned his focus to the scenery.

Rae gathered Hope onto the seat beside her with instructions to sit as still as possible. Hope was getting restless after traveling so long over rough, rocky terrain. There were miles of low, flat, treeless plains as far as an eye could see. Rae pointed out a herd of cattle or a stray coyote, but that didn't make Hope happy.

The stage came to a quick stop and a tall young man tossed his saddle onto the back. He jerked the door open and climbed aboard, sitting beside the little fat man. Tipping his hat at Rae and addressing the other passenger with "How are you?" he quickly slid down into the seat, covering his eyes with his big brown Stetson hat. As the stage pulled away, Rae glanced out the window and saw a man driving a buckboard wagon away in the opposite direction.

During the long ride, Hope whined that she wanted to change seats and sit where the little fat man was sitting. Not giving Rae a chance to reason with her, the little man immediately moved onto the seat next to Rae, giving the baby what she wanted. "No problem," he said. "I don't mind changing seats." As Rae watched Hope play with her dolly, all she could think about was how hungry she was. *Lord, how much longer will it be before we get to our destination?* she prayed silently. She knew that she would have to trade a few of her personal belongings for lodging and food, but she really didn't have a choice. Her stomach had started making growling sounds. Thank goodness the noise from the bumps and grinds of the stagecoach helped cover up some of her body sounds, she thought.

"Mama, can I sit there? I want to see!"

"Yes, darling, climb up and you can sit in my lap and look out the window."

"No, you have a growling bear in your tummy! I want to sit there. Tell him to wake up and let me sit there," she demanded as she pointed toward the stranger's side window.

After listening to the child whine about every little thing, the tall stranger reacted by saying, "Tell that kid no!" Th ere was no room for him to get comfortable. The leg space was very inadequate for his long legs, and his knees kept brushing up against Rae's skirt. She had moved as far away as she could, but every time they hit a bump, his knees would slide over and touch her again.

The stranger couldn't help but grin under his large Stetson because the little lady was sitting so straight and stiff . One thing was for sure, he thought as he looked at her. This was the most beautiful girl he had ever seen. She had the biggest brown eyes and golden blonde hair peeking out from under her bonnet. Her skin was very fair with just a spray of freckles across her nose. And her lips, goodness, they were as pink as a rosebud in the spring.

"I want to sit there now," whined Hope. "Please!"

In an instant, the stranger lifted Hope from the floor to his lap. He told her to sit still, be quiet, and look out the window. After looking at Rae and the other passenger in the coach, Hope slowly put her thumb in her mouth and sat very still.

Lord help me, thought Rae, *she is finally behaving herself.* Most of the time Hope was a very good child, but she was just tired from this long journey. Looking at the stranger, Rae mouthed a "thank you" and he just lowered his eyelids and went right back to sleep. After what seemed like hours of watching Hope sleep comfortably in the arms of the handsome stranger, the stagecoach driver yelled, "Folks, we're almost home!"

Home would have to be Limason, Texas, as Rae had spent the last of her funds, and there was no other money to travel further. She would already have to trade some personal things to get money for food and lodging. Sighing, Rae felt safe. At least they would be about a hundred miles from Herbert. Leaving Rosedale, Texas—the only home and town she had ever known—was the hardest thing she had ever done. Th ere was no choice—they had to leave.

"What's this town like?" Rae asked, finally deciding to talk to the little fat man sitting next to her. He had tried several times to start up a conversation.

"Oh, we have a wonderful town. Growing every day with cattle drives passing out from us a few miles. I own the general mercantile that carries most of the supplies the people need to refi ll their chuck wagons. We have one bank, several saloons but of course, you wouldn't be interested in them." The little man pulled at his collar and blushed after making that statement. He was very pleased with himself now that he had this lovely girl's attention.

"There is a rooming house, which is always full of wild cowhands, a blacksmith, a church that has a traveling preacher once a month or so, a schoolhouse in the church—but well, we have no teacher now—a horse stable and corral, and we have a doctor. He's a young man straight out of medical school, but no one is interested in using him because he's so young. Anyway, I am sure he will be moving along to a bigger town soon."

"That is too bad. Everyone needs a chance, and a town certainly needs a doctor," Rae replied.

The stranger, who had been playing possum, lifted his eyes up at Rae and asked, "Are you in need of a doctor?"

"What? No! Of course not. Why would you even ask me that? Go back to sleep. No one is talking to you." *Of all the nerve! That big ox has no* business asking about my person, *she thought.*

The stagecoach began to slow and suddenly the horses came to a stop, but the cabin kept rocking and swaying. Rae felt lightheaded from the movement that she was thankful the men finally got the horses under control.

"All out, folks. Welcome home to those who live here, and a mighty big welcome to those folks that are just visiting."

"I gotta go to the outhouse, Mama! I got to go now," whined Hope.

"Please be good." Rae whispered in Hope's ear as she glanced out of the window at the town. This looked to be a very nice place. *There is very* little traffic on the street, *thought Rae.*

The tall stranger pushed open the door and jumped down without using the three steps. There, standing in front of him, was Hank, his ranch foreman. "Gosh, Hank. It's great to see you."

"Are you kidding? Jess, your horse arrived at the ranch without you last night, and I came into town to see if anybody had seen or heard anything about you. Rider went off looking for you in the other direction! We have been so worried."

Jesse turned around and could see that the young lady was struggling to get out of the stagecoach with her child. "Here, give me that brat! Be careful getting down because those steps are wobbly," he explained.

Before Rae could refuse his help, the stranger grabbed Hope out of her arms and held on to her like he was holding a sack of grain.

For gosh sakes, what a pig! As Rae started down the wood steps, everything in front of her went out of focus. She felt lightheaded. Shutting her eyes, she thought, *oh my, I am going to swoon.* She never got to finish that thought because everything went black.

"Gosh almighty. She fainted! Hank, get me some help," Jesse shouted as he struggled with the kid in his arms. "Darn kid!" he said. "You've wet all over me. Here, take this baggage while I see to her mom."

"What will I do with her?" asked Hank, holding up his arms while jumping backward. "Golly, Jess, I've never been around babies, much less held one. I gotta go get the doctor." Hank ran as fast as his old legs would carry him.

"Mama, Mama," screamed Hope at the top of her lungs. "I want my mama!"

"Sit down on this boardwalk, kid, and stop the waterworks. You have been enough trouble as it is." Jessed flopped her down on the rough boardwalk and gave her a stern look as she wailed.

A crowd of people had begun to gather around and ask questions.

Finally the doctor came running with his new shiny, black bag. "What's the problem?"

"This little lady has fallen out of the stage in a dead faint and hit her head on the boardwalk. She is bleeding, but I don't think it is too bad," Jesse said as he removed her bonnet.

The young doctor picked up Rae's small right wrist to feel for a pulse.

His own pulse was racing because he was so excited that he finally had a real patient. He reached into his black bag and took out a soft, white towel.

After applying pressure to the wound on her forehead to stop the flow of blood, he laid his head on her bosom to listen to her heart.

Several of the townspeople started whispering, and the women were making *tsk* sounds as they watched the new doctor place his head on the lady's chest. Each one was thinking, *whatever is he doing? Shameful!*

"From all the noise coming from her stomach, I would say that she has fainted due to hunger. No telling the last time she's eaten a decent meal," stated Jesse.

"Let's get her to my office so I can examine her," instructed the doctor.

"Place one hand under her back and one under her limbs as you lift her. Don't drop her," the doctor ordered as he led the way to his office.

"She weighs less than a sack of oats," mumbled Jesse. "Hank, grab up that youngster and bring her along. Don't hold her too tight 'cause she is wet all the way through."

As they entered the doctor's office, Jesse couldn't help but notice how neat and clean everything was. The last doctor they had smelled of rotgut, and his office was so messy a person really had to be almost dead to want to enter the door.

"Place her in the back room where I have a table prepared for my patients. I have to get a cold cloth to place on her head to slow down any swelling that may occur."

The doctor came back into the room with a wet cloth and wrapped it around Rae's head. "Fine, now let me roll her over and see if I can loosen some of the ties she has on this undergarment she is wearing."

"Don't you think we should get a woman in here to do this for you?" Jesse whispered as he looked around the room.

"I am a doctor. Besides, do you see any womenfolk? They won't come near this office, much less offer to help me in any way. I am too young and 'ain't got no sense.' If you don't believe me, ask any one of them," replied the doctor in a very sad voice.

"Well, let's get those ties loose so she can breathe, then we have to get some food in her. Do you have anything here to eat?" asked Jesse.

"There's some soup on the stove in the back that I cooked earlier. Ask your friend Hank to warm it while we try to get her to wake up."

"Hank, please heat the soup in the back. Maybe you can find a cracker or biscuit for the brat."

Hank looked up and rubbed his long, gray beard, hitched up his overalls that barely fi t over his barrel belly, and grumbled, "Do this, do that! Now I am a cook and nursemaid. Gosh almighty, just let me get back to the ranch."

"All right, Doc, I will slip her out of the jacket and let's flip her over and untie her corset. Watch her head. She will be fighting mad at us, but that can't be helped," stated Jesse.

"All right, now the jacket is off , so turn her over easy," said the doctor.

"Can you loosen the strings on the corset?"

"Damn, my fingers are so big for these silly ties," exclaimed Jesse as he grabbed for a sharp instrument next to the bed. With one cut, all the ties were undone and a sigh came from the patient.

"Good," said the doctor. "Lay her back down on her back while I replace this cool cloth on her face. Look, I believe she is coming around."

Rae was groaning and trying to sit up, but her head hurt and she was drowning in a lake of dark memories of her past ...

*****

Rae was trying to get away from Herbert. He was holding tight, hurting her arms and trying his best to kiss her. She had tried to bite his hands to make him turn her loose. She used her knees to hurt him, but they had no effect on his punchy body.

"Don't fight me, baby," Herbert was saying. "You know that you want me. I've seen the way you look at me, and now that your mama has passed away there is no reason we can't be together. I want you. You will be mine.

Just the two of us together always from now on."

"Never!" she screamed as she rolled her head side to side. "I'd rather be dead than let you put your filthy hands on me."

Herbert towered over her with his fi ve-foot-ten-inch, 250-pound frame. Most of his weight surrounded his middle from lack of physical work. His face was blood red, which matched his reddish goatee.

"No one else will have you, Rae. You will be mine and mine only. If you choose not to marry me, you will be disgraced in this country for miles, and not one decent young man will have you after I get through ruining your reputation."

She finally got away from him and moved across the room, closer to the door, but he stepped in front of her to block any chance of escape.

"How can you ruin my reputation? Everyone knows me. Th ey know that I have always been good and took care of my mama until she died. You can't hurt my good name." insisted Rae.

"Yes, I can. And your little sister, my precious off spring, will help me." He threw back his head and laughed like he was sharing a joke with someone. With a sneer on his face, he said through his teeth, "I will tell everyone that Hope is your child and not Claire's. I will tell them that you came into my room one night and climbed into my bed to help comfort me because your mama couldn't do it any longer. I will say that I thought you were Claire until it was too late. You never went to church or into town before Hope was born, and people hadn't seen you in months.

"Even Amelia stopped coming out to visit before Hope's birth because I told her you were in love with the boy she planned to marry. So you see, my precious Rae, it will be very easy to say that brat is yours. Everyone knows that she calls you "Mama" already, and you never correct her. So, just start making plans to be my wife. I will give you two weeks to mourn the loss of your mama, and then we will go into town and see the minister.

It would be better for your reputation to live out here as my wife than my stepdaughter. People are so easy to convince." Herbert laughed as he strolled slowly out the door, murmuring under his breath.

*****

Struggling to wake up from this nightmare, Rae could feel tears running down her cheeks onto her neck. She must leave—escape now with Hope. Run as far away from Herbert as possible. Never marry him …

Rae lay very still. Her head felt heavy, almost like she had been drugged. Someone was wiping her face and speaking softly to her. She couldn't make out his words. She could tell that she wasn't lying on the hard ground. The words that she could make out sounded like a doctor.

She slowly lifted her eyelids to get a peek at her surroundings.

There, right in front of her, was that beast of a man from the stagecoach.

This is a nightmare, she thought. *Oh! Where is my baby? Where is Hope?*

Please, Lord, help me, she prayed. "I believe she is coming around now," Jesse said.

Rae sat straight up and demanded, "Where is my baby?" It surprised the men and made Jesse and the doctor jump back.

"Hey little lady, everything is fine. Your baby is in the kitchen with Hank, and you are in my office. Do you remember what happened?"

Rae eased herself back down onto the table and said, "I must have swooned for some reason. I have never done that before."

"How long has it been since you have had anything to eat?" demanded the beast, thinking he was looking into the face of an angel. Damn, this is the most beautiful girl I have ever seen.

"Must you be here? Go away … leave me alone," wailed Rae. "Oh, my head." She reached up to feel a soft, wet cloth wrapped around her forehead. "I am none of your business, and I can take care of myself," she said very softly.

"Look, Mama, I got a biscuit, and I'm wet! I told you I had to go! I'm sorry," she said as she lowered her chin to her chest and put her thumb in her mouth.

Rae sat up to reach for Hope. When she did, she noticed that her jacket had been removed and the back of her dress was loose and open because a cool breeze hit her bare skin. With a shocked look on her face, she stared at the two men standing at her bedside. "My Lord, my clothes! What have you done? You miserable …" she said, her eyes never leaving the beast called Jesse.

"Wait, little lady," cried the doctor. "Please stay calm. We had to get your garments loose so you could breathe. You were kept very decent, believe me. I will get someone to go and fetch your luggage from the stagecoach office."

"Please, Hank," gestured Jesse with a nod of his head pointing toward the door. "This baby needs a change of clothes, too."

"Please, miss, just lay back down until I can get you some soup that Hank warmed for you. With some food in your stomach, I bet you'll feel better soon. I don't think you will need stitches in your face, but I will need to place a good bandage over it," said the young doctor.

After the doctor left the room, Jesse reached around and grabbed a chair, turned it backward, and straddled it. He looked directly at Rae and asked as sweetly as he could, "Now, miss, who will be meeting you? Who do I need to tell that you are here in the doctor's office?"

Jesse was running out of patience. He was hungry, tired, and smelled like pee. He wanted to get this woman and her baby on their way with her relatives or friends. After seeing them settled, he could go to the livery and rent a wagon so that he could gather his supplies and head on home to his ranch. He was already running behind schedule. He had only planned to be gone three days. Will, his younger brother, would be biting at the bits for having to do most of the chores. Ollie, his old black nanny who raised him after his mother died, would be standing on her head with worry too.

He had told them both that he was going over to McBain, a town that was only about twenty-fi ve miles away. He wanted to check on a bull that he had heard so much about from men on the last trail drive that passed by his spread. He had been planning on purchasing a bull to help increase his small herd. After completing the sale and arranging for the delivery of the bull, a rainstorm came up and he was forced to stay the night. The

thunder and lightning was so bad that his horse had bolted, then jumped the corral fence and headed home without him.

Mr. Thomas's foreman loaded Jesse's gear in his flatbed wagon and drove him out to the road where the stagecoach traveled to Limason. He was able to fl ag the coach down and hitch a ride back to town. He was sure that some of the men who worked for him would be in town looking for him when his horse showed up at the ranch with no rider.

"Now tell me, who you are meeting?" demanded Jesse. Rae could tell that this man called Jesse was rapidly running out of patience with her. He was smiling even though he was gritting his teeth, and his beautiful blue eyes were now dark as storm clouds. He wanted answers, and he wasn't leaving until he got her settled.

"Here we go, missy. Good, hot soup if I might say. I know the cook," said the doctor with a big smile that showed the deep dimples in his cheeks.

Slowly Rae sat up and leaned against the pillow that was propped behind her back. "Oh, it smells so good. Thank you so much. I am sure I will be f ne in a little while after I get dressed and out of your way. I have caused you so much trouble." Jesse got up and strolled around the office, looking out the window.

Several people still stood around the outside hoping to get a glimpse of the young woman who had been carried into the doctor's office.

"Your baby has on a pair of Riley Parker's short britches. I had to lance a boil on his bottom last week and with all his screaming, Mrs. Parker wrapped him in a blanket and left quickly, leaving behind his soiled clothes. I had them washed, but she hasn't been back into town to retrieve them. She won't mind the baby wearing them for a little while," said the doctor.

"Thank you," whispered Rae as she was trying very hard not to look at Jesse. She could tell that he was very determined to get answers out of her, and he was trying so hard to be patient with the young doctor because he was giving her more attention than Jesse thought necessary.

"Now, miss," said Jesse, "please tell me who you are meeting. Doc and I have other matters waiting our attention, and we want to see you and your child settled with your relatives."

Slowly Rae placed the soup bowl on the table next to her and finally decided that telling the truth was going to be the only way out of this office and away from this stubborn, tall stranger who had decided to make her plans his business.

"Well, actually, I am not meeting anyone. I am alone in this world except for my baby. We needed a fresh start, and I have decided that Limason looks like the perfect place for us to live," answered Rae.

Jesse's mouth dropped open. He couldn't believe what he had heard her say. She had traveled a great distance, from God knows where, without two pennies to her name and with a baby for gosh sake! He stuttered for a second and finally asked her, "Where did you get on the stage? Where are you from and what happened to your husband?"

His eyes instantly flew to her wedding finger where she wore a simple gold band. How could her man allow her the freedom to travel alone like this? Was she running away from him? Something wasn't sitting right with him, but he was going to get some straight answers if it took the rest of the day.

"Mr. Jesse ... whoever you are ... none of my affairs are your business. You may take your leave! I don't need or want your help."

Jesse felt his face turning red, and he had to get a hard grip on the back of the chair and restrain his voice to speak in a civilized tone.

"Listen to me, little lady. I don't want you saddled around my neck. I don't care what you do, but since you have that brat—I mean baby—to care for, you can't just start walking up and down the boardwalk. Since Sheriff Murphy is out of town, I don't know anybody who can or would be responsible for you. "You can't just get up and leave without a place to go. I happen to know that you don't have two pennies to your name! Th is town doesn't have a decent rooming house for you to stay, and there is only one place of business and one bank for you to get a job—and both of those places have help. How are you going to feed that youngster come dark?"

Rae couldn't help the flow of tears forming in her eyes or stop them from trailing down her face. "I don't need someone to be responsible for me. I am a grown woman," Rae said through choked tears. Who does he think he is? She didn't need a man bossing her around. She had enough with Herbert scaring her and making demands on her body every time that she was near him. She was going to stand on her own two feet and not allow a perfect stranger to control her life.

"Well, you do need help. Think of your child, if not yourself." Staring her down, Jesse said after sighing, "I guess I will have to take you out to my ranch. There is not one person in this town who can take you in. The Smiths that own the store are the only family that lives in this town that could afford to take you in, but they have two bedrooms up over their store and three kids. "I have a big house," and remembering how hungry she seemed to be, he continued, "and there is always plenty of good food. You can stay and help out around the place until you can make some plans for your future."

Rae looked at him like he had lost his mind, and before she could get a word in, he interrupted her.

"Oh, don't get riled up again. You will have a chaperone. I have my nanny who lives with me. Her name is Ollie. She will be thrilled to have some help, and she will dote on your baby. The baby will be rotten to the core in a week with all the attention that she will receive. You need to get your strength back, and eating a few of Ollie's meals will make you better real soon. My younger brother, Will, also lives in the house, but he can move out to the bunkhouse with the other men I have working for me.

"Let me go and see what Hank has done about getting me a horse and wagon, and get your bags rounded up. I won't be long, so try to finish that soup the doc has prepared for you."

"But I haven't said that I would go with you. I don't even know your name." Jesse stopped with his hand on the door handle and turned to look at her.

"My name is Jess Maxwell." He looked at her and then waited a moment as if to say something. He changed his mind and headed out the door.

Rae watched him disappear. Jesse seemed to have calmed down. He had made decisions about her future without her consent—like it or not.

He just expected her to get up off this doctor's table, redress, get Hope ready, and be at attention when he returned. Well, just who did he think he was giving orders to? He could go jump in a river as far as she was concerned.

After sitting up and trying to adjust her clothes, Rae's head was still a little dizzy. Everything was spinning around but a lot slower. Placing her face down into her hands, she thought, what am I going to do? He is right, the brute. I don't have two pennies or even one. I do need lodging for Hope and me—a safe place to hide away for a while. Gosh, I need real food. I am not thinking straight. Th is man is a perfect stranger, and I am going to his ranch. I have to be crazy.

"Mama, are you better? Does your head still hurt? I am so tired. Can I lay down on your bed now?" Hope asked, as she was pulling on the sheets trying to climb up on the bed.

"Of course, darling. Come on up, and I will hold you for a minute."

She reached for Hope as she started climbing up on the bed. "Stop fussing, and come and give me a hand with the girls. I want to get home before dark and get them settled." Rae could hear Jesse talking to the man called Hank.

I don't even know one important thing about this man, she thought.

Jesse and Hank entered the office to find Rae sitting on the side of the bed, patting the baby's back with one hand and trying to hold the back of her dress together with the other. "I can't get up like this," mumbled Rae as Jesse took in the problem she was having.

"Just a minute," he said and left the office for just a moment. He came back in carrying a soft, baby-blue shawl that she had packed for the trip.

Oh my goodness, this man is impossible. Now he is going through my personal things in my trunk. What's next? Rae thought.

"Here, wrap this around you, Hank, pick up the baby and lay her on the blankets that I have placed in the back of the wagon." Hope had gotten comfortable and fallen asleep on the bed with Rae. Jesse was giving orders to Hank as if he was a first sergeant in the army.

The doctor appeared out of the back room, and Rae noticed for the first time how really young he was. He couldn't be more than thirty. He had sandy brown hair that wanted to fly away when he moved his head.

When he smiled, he had the sweetest dimples in his cheeks. And those crystal-clear blue eyes. A girl could lose herself in them. He was taller than her, and he had the nicest way with words. Rae was sure that if she stayed in town, they could become very good friends.

The doctor reached out to Rae, holding her bonnet. "Sorry, it has some blood on it."

"Thank you so much for your help, Doctor," Rae said, taking her bonnet and looking it over. "I shall always remember your kindness. When I get a job, I will pay you for your services to me."

"Please do not fret over any payment," said the doctor. "I enjoyed taking care of you, and Jesse has already seen that I was rewarded for the treatment that I gave you. I tried to tell him that I didn't want any payment, but he wouldn't listen to me. I will ride out to see you in a few days to check that cut on your head. Try to keep it dry. Maybe we can have some tea and a nice chat when I come out."

Jesse looked to Rae and then to the doctor as they exchanged comments and for the first time, he felt a spark of jealousy come over him. *Now, where in the heck did that come from?* he thought.

Hank had placed Hope on a soft bed of blankets and covered her in the wagon. Jesse stood on one foot and then the other as he waited for Rae to finish talking to the doctor. Finally, Rae came up to the side of the wagon. Jesse stood to take her hand and help her up onto the seat. Seeing the bonnet in her hands, he said, "You better put that on."

Hank mounted his horse as Jesse got himself settled on the bench next to Rae. "Finally," he murmured to himself, "we are on our way."

Chapter 2

As the wagon moved slowly out of town, Rae was sitting as far away from Jesse as she could with her back as stiff as a board.

"I know that we have gotten off to a bad start with each other, but I am not going to bite you. If you don't get comfortable, you are going to bounce off this seat. We should be home in less than an hour and have you both settled in," said Jesse.

Rae could tell that this tall stranger was trying to be nice and helpful.

"I do apologize for my actions back there, and I thank you for your help. I want you to know we will not be at your place long. I intend to get a place of our own and a job."

"Look, miss, I don't even know your last name, where you are from, and how you came to want to settle here in Limason."

Rae sat silently, giving herself some time before she answered. She began looking at the beautiful blue sky and the open range surrounding them as they passed by. It was a very sunny afternoon, and she was glad that she was wearing her bonnet. Looking over the land, Rae was surprised that the grass was so green and the landscape was flat. Th ere were only a few clusters of trees every so often and a stray cactus. Bluebonnets were still blooming close to the trail. This was beautiful country.

Finally she said, "I don't know anything about you either, and here we are, two strangers thrown together."

"All right," replied Jesse. "I will go first. My name is Jesse Maxwell. 'Jess' to some. I have a small ranch that my brother and I inherited from our pa, who passed away three years ago."

"Oh. I am so sorry. How did he die?" Rae knew that this must be very hard for him to talk about. She still couldn't even think of her mama's passing without crying.

"He was thrown from his horse, and we found him back up the trail in a small ravine. He had a broken neck. Will was only twelve, and I have been trying to take care of him ever since. It has been hard because he feels like he is a grown man. My mom passed away shortly after he was born.

"Ollie is an old cantankerous, sassy Negro woman who has lived with us as long as I can remember. She practically raised me and Will while doing all the cleaning, cooking, and teaching us to be good human beings.

We couldn't do without her, but I could never tell her that," Jesse said as he chuckled to himself. "She is having a little problem getting around, so she finally has allowed me to hire a lady to come out once a week to help with the laundry."

Giving the horse a little pull to slow him down, he asked, "Now Rae, do you have a last name?"

"Of course." She studied him for a minute, biting the inside of her mouth as she was trying to think of a common name. Something simple that wouldn't jump out to anyone looking for her. "Rae Rivers is my name. I'm from Russellville, Texas."

Rae Rivers? Huh, thought Jesse as he gave her a side glance. "Rae Rivers," he repeated. "Nice name. Rivers is a very common name." His tone of voice and the way he repeated everything let her know that he didn't believe her at all.

"Russellville is only about a hundred miles away. Why leave there?" quizzed Jesse.

"I needed a change. My husband passed away a few months ago, and Hope and I needed to move out of our home that we had let so let's talk about something else, please," she said as she wiped at her eyes. She needed more time to think of a good story about her past life. More believable details, she thought.

Jesse thought to himself, *A widow? Sure. If she is a widow, I am a rodeo champion.* "So," pausing to appear concerned, "why aren't you dressed in black widow weeds?" Jesse asked, waiting for another lie to come out of that beautiful mouth.

Caught off guard with that question, she replied, "I didn't have the money to purchase anything or material to make a black dress. ... Please, please let's talk about something else."

Jesse gave her a look that said that this conversation wasn't over, but he would let things go for now. "Sure," he said. *Maybe I will get the truth next time she tells me her life story.*

"I will be glad to help out around the homestead for room and board for Hope and me. I promise she won't be any trouble. You won't even know she's around." *Please let this be the truth,* prayed Rae silently.

"How old is your brother? And you?" Sheepishly she let that question slip out. *Now he will think that I am interested in him.*

"Will is fifteen, and like I said earlier, he thinks he is a grown man. I am twenty-eight. ... And how old are you? Let me guess," and before she could answer, he said, "You must be at least twenty-five?" He laughed as he knew he was being funny.

"No." She grinned. "I am twenty."

Jesse glanced at Rae as she smiled for the first time. *Gracious, this little lady is just too pretty for her own good,* he thought. "A child bride with a child. My, my, there had to be some hard times."

"There you go with your smart remarks about me when you don't know anything." She bristled inside over the way he was questioning her.

"Just don't ask me any more questions if you're not willing to believe me. You can turn around and take us back to town." He had her so flustered, she couldn't think straight, and being hungry didn't help either. *I have to concentrate and keep my story straight to help keep Hope safe.*

"All right, calm down and get off your high horse. We aren't getting anywhere with that hair-trigger temper of yours. When you get ready to tell me the truth about who you are, where you came from, and who you are running from, I will be here to listen."

Oh! He had the audacity to grin while he was calling her a liar.

"Mama, Mama, I am hungry and I gotta go." Rae turned around, and there stood Hope in the wagon, hanging on to the back of the seat for dear life.

Jesse slowed the wagon down as Rae reached behind the seat and lifted Hope onto her lap. "We are almost to Mr. Maxwell's ranch, darling."

Hope reached her small hand up to touch the bandage on Rae's head and asked, "Does that hurt, Mama?"

"I have a headache, but it will be fine in a while."

Hope looked around at the man who had manhandled her earlier and whispered to Rae, "I don't like him, Mama. Make him go away. I like *him.*"

She pointed and wiggled her little finger at Hank.

"Sweetheart, Mr. Maxwell is a nice man. He was just excited and a little upset when he saw me fall out of the stagecoach. He really didn't mean to yell at you. Isn't that right, Mr. Maxwell?" asked Rae, looking over at him with her big brown eyes.

Jesse looked at Hope, and he felt so bad that he had made her afraid of him. He guessed she had a right to be a little unsure of him because of the way he had been acting. After looking at the baby's face for the first time, he saw a beautiful child with big, doe brown eyes and long, golden blonde curls. She had the tiniest pink lips with a flush to her smooth cheeks. How could anyone mistreat this lovely creature? God, he was a heel, and he realized that he had a lot of making up to get in this child's good graces.

He reached out his hand to cover Hope's, and she jerked her hand back and placed it around Rae's neck. "Hey, squirt," he started, "I am sorry that I lost my temper and yelled.

If you give me another chance, I promise not to do that again. I want us to be friends while you are staying at my place. You know what? My old nanny—Ollie is her name—will give you something really good to eat when we get to my ranch. We will be there in just a little while.

"Hank!" yelled Jesse to his foreman, who had been riding alongside the wagon, "Ride ahead and tell Ollie and Will that we are coming, and there will be two more mouths to feed. Tell her I've got two hungry young ladies, and one of them would love to have a few of her special cookies!"

"Cookies," whispered Hope to Rae.

"Let me tell you this, sweetheart, if Ollie doesn't have any cookies tonight, I bet my boots she will have them tomorrow. I can promise you that. When I was a youngster like you, Ollie always kept the cookie jar filled." He could tell the baby was already warming up to him by the way she was listening and hanging on to every word he said.

As they neared some open range with a tall cactus looking out of place, Jesse said, "There it is, home," pointing his finger toward a very lovely house surrounded with a white board fence.

Rae looked to where he was pointing, and her lips formed and said

"*Oh.*" Jesse felt very proud that she was pleased with what she saw. Ever since he and Will had inherited the ranch, he had worked day and night to build it into one of nicest small spreads in the state.

As Jesse pulled the wagon up to the porch, Rae noticed that the veranda wrapped around three sides of the white house. Her first thought was this was a nice place, but the yard could use a woman's touch. Th ere were no flowers. There were swings on each end of the screened front porch, and several large, comfortable rocking chairs. *Just maybe Hope and I will be safe here until I can make better plans for our future,* thought Rae.

"Goodness, Mr. Jess," came a voice from the side of the house. "I have been so worried about you. Who you got with you, Mr. Jess?" quizzed Ollie as she was trying to catch her breath. She was trying her best to get a good look at Rae and Hope. "Mr. Hank said you were bringing home some hungry folks," she said with a big smile.

After getting a glance at Hope, Ollie was very excited. "Hurry, hurry, and get that baby down so I can get her into the house. Mr. Jess, you done brought company home, and all I got cooked is some soup and corn bread.

I do have some bread pudding. Lawdy, Lawdy me."

Jess couldn't help but laugh at his old nanny as she flapped around them, waving her long, white apron that tied at her waist and went all the way to her ankles. He stepped in front of her and grabbed her around the shoulders, giving her a big bear hug as he lifted her feet off the ground and kissed her on the side of the face.

"Did you miss me? You haven't said anything about me being back. You just want to know who I brought with me." He laughed at Ollie as she tried to push him away and wipe away tears forming in those big brown eyes of hers.

"Oh, you big baby. You knows I've missed you, and I have been worried sick until I heard Hank come in the yard a bit ago with news you were on your way home. We have all been about crazy with worry since your horse came in here last night with no saddle or bridle," said Ollie as she continued rubbing Jesse's arm.

"I will tell you about my trip and my new bull when we get these two settled." He turned to lift Hope down, but her little feet never touched the ground. Ollie scooped her out of Jesse's arms, saying, "Oh my, oh my, what a beautiful child. Come with me, honey child. Old Ollie will take good care of you. I haven't had a babe in a long, long time to care for." Ollie was in her glory now.

"Jess, you bring her mama along so I can make them comfortable and feed them some of my hot soup. Be sure to get their things and put them in Will's room. It has two beds. Open the window and let some fresh air come in," ordered Ollie.

Rae had fallen silent and was taking in her surroundings. She felt a smile on her face and appeared to be relaxing. She had never seen such a black woman. Ollie's skin was as dark as molasses, and her short, white hair was covered with a solid red bandanna. She had the biggest brown eyes and the whitest teeth Rae had ever seen on anyone. Her eyes seemed to sparkle when she spoke to Jesse.

"Let me get you down from there and inside before Ollie comes back looking for us," said Jesse, shaking his head and softly laughing. "Old Ollie is happy now that she has someone to fuss over."

As they entered the house, Hope was telling Ollie that she needed to go pee-pee. Ollie laughed and led her into the front room. "Don't you worry none about this child, old Ollie has her now," yelled Ollie out of the kitchen.

Rae was standing in the kitchen taking in the wonderful smell of home-cooked soup and fresh baked bread—her stomach growled. She smiled. What a wonderful room. Rae glanced in a full circle as she looked around at Ollie's kitchen. Everything was in order. Nothing needed to be straightening or put away.

Hank brought in Rae's trunk and carried it into the front bedroom where Ollie had Hope behind a screen, which she called the water closet.

Ollie opened the trunk and got some pantaloons and a white muslin gown out for Hope. She rushed into the kitchen and got the teapot of hot water and poured a big bowl full so she could wash Hope up a little. Tomorrow would be soon enough for a full bath.

After completing Hope's toilette, she took her to the kitchen and fed her a small bowl of vegetable soup with some corn bread in it. Hope was so tired she could hardly hold her eyes open. After giving Hope a sugar cookie, she gathered her into her arms and walked into the big front room and sat in a rocking chair. She reached down and pulled the bottom of her apron up around Hope's shoulders. Hope's head laid on Ollie's big bosom with the cookie in one hand, and with her other hand, she placed her thumb in her mouth. Soon she was sound asleep. This is the way Rae

found them. Ollie rocking and humming a religious tune with Hope sound asleep, nestled into Ollie's body. Safe and secure.

Rae's emotions were getting the best of her. She took her hand and placed her palm over her mouth. It was all she could do not to cry. She was so tired and hungry herself, but to see Hope all clean, fed, and asleep nearly made her lose all the emotions that she had bottled up inside.

Jesse came into the room and took in the scene himself. "Here, Ollie, let me have the baby. I will place her in the bed that you have turned down."

Watching Ollie as she handed Hope to him, Rae said, "Thank you so much, Ollie ... may I call you Ollie?" whispered Rae.

"Yes, ma'am, please do. Now you come with me and let me dip you up some good hot soup and corn bread. Don't tell me you ain't hungry. I know better. I need to look at your head before you get in bed. Th is food will help any old headache go away. Your baby done told me that your head hurts," said Ollie.

After Jesse came out of the bedroom, he took in Rae all settled at the table, eating some of Ollie's good food.

"I have to go out to the bunkhouse and see Will and the other men. Ollie will take good care of you, and I will be back for some of that soup too." He smiled at Ollie, and she nodded.

Jess headed to the door and reached over to the hat rack to retrieve his hat. As he turned, he nodded to Rae as he thought to himself, *she looks like she already belongs here. Then he caught himself.* Heavens, where did that thought come from? For gosh sakes, she will be leaving soon.

Before Jesse could get halfway to the barn, Will came riding into the yard, jumping off his brown-and-white pinto horse.

"Gosh Jess, it is so good to have you home. We have all been worried sick about you."

The two brothers hugged each other, and then Will jumped back away from Jesse and slapped him on his back a couple of times. *Real men don't hug. They slap on the back,* thought Will.

"Come on into the bunkhouse, and I will tell you and the others what happened, and about our new bull that will be delivered in a few days. I'm really proud of it. Oh, and thanks, Will, for taking care of things around here while I was gone. I'm sorry to have caused you any worry."

As Rae watched Jesse leave, she looked around at her surroundings in the house for the first time. Sitting at the long pine table that could easily seat eight to ten people, she noticed Ollie stacking small logs into the fireplace, which covered the back wall of the living area. The wall was covered with rustic river rocks that had been smoothed to perfection. All the rocks were a beautiful brown and sandy color with a little black rock woven into it. The mantle looked as if it took at least ten men to hold it in place while it was being constructed into the rocks. It was a six-inch rustic plank that had been smoothed to a glossy shine. Many hours of hard labor had gone into building this wall.

Ollie looked up and noticed Rae staring at the masterpiece of river rock and said, "Master Jake, Jess's papa, done built this wall with his bare hands. It took him almost a year or more to complete it. After this here wall was up, then he built the rest of the house around it. Jess's mamma shore loved to sit right here and rock her boys.

"We try to keep this fire going most all the time during the fall and winter months to keep the chill out of the house," said Ollie as she was sweeping up the twigs that had fallen onto the floor. "This being September, we still have some mighty hot days, but the nights are getting cooler."

Rae had finished her soup and gotten up to carry her bowl over to the dishpan to wash it. Ollie hurried to her side and said, "Oh no, you don't have to do that tonight. I know you are plumb dead on your feet."

Ollie told Rae that she had laid out her gown on the bed next to her baby. There was a bowl of steaming hot water and some clean linens already in the room. She hurried Rae off to bed, telling her that they would have a long talk the next day about how she came to be here. "You can tell old Ollie everything."

Rae turned to Ollie and looked into her sweet face, and before she could catch herself, she stepped into Ollie's arms and put her face down on her shoulder and wept like a babe for the first time in weeks. With all the loving care that Ollie had showered on her and Hope, Rae lost all control of her emotions.

"Now, now, child, go into your room and get settled. I will be in to see about your head."

"Thank you for everything," mumbled Rae, embarrassed that she had cried on her shoulder. She hurried into the bedroom and closed the door. She glanced over the room to see Hope still all curled up and sleeping peacefully. *This is a nice, comfortable room,* thought Rae. It had two beds that resembled large bunk beds, but they were not stacked. The dresser was built out of soft pine that also had a shiny finish. Someone certainly knew how to work with wood. The floor was covered with a colorful, braided rug and the window covers were a dark green gingham material. *Th is must be Will's room,* she thought. *I need to thank him for giving it up to us.*

A fire had been built and was burning bright in the corner of the room. A large rocker had been placed in front of the fireplace with a cozy, brown pillow. Rae walked over to the rocker and touched the back of it thinking what a cozy room this was. Her home, before mama married Herbert, had been warm and cozy like this. A yawn escaped her, and she realized how tired she really was. She really needed to thank Jesse for his hospitality, but morning would be soon enough. She couldn't figure this man. One minute, he was beastly and snapping orders. Th e next, he was nice. Yes, that's it. Nice.

After using the water closet and washing her body as much as she could, she gathered up her brush and took out all the pins that were holding up her hair that had been twisted into a bun. The blonde curls tumbled down her back. Her mom would tell her often how blessed she was to have thick, long hair. Her hair was one of her best qualities. With the brush in her hand, she walked over to the window to look out. This room was at the front of the house, and she could see three men standing near the corral. The tall, lean man looked like Jesse, she thought.

Closing the curtain, Rae walked over to the bed and turned back the warm-looking quilt. She sat on the bed and gave it a slight bounce. So soft. She stretched out under the covers, and that was her last thought before she drifted into a deep sleep.

Sometime during the evening, Hope had managed to get out of her bed and crawl under the quilt with Rae. This is the way Ollie found them a little later. After banking the fire, she turned to tiptoe out of the room and ran into Jesse who was standing in the bedroom doorway.

Jesse glanced at Ollie and saw in her face many questions to be asked. "Please get me something to eat, and I will tell you all I know about our two houseguests."

After finishing his dinner and settling back in his chair with his second cup of coffee, he told Ollie how he came in contact with the girls. Ollie had only a few more questions to ask, and it was "What now?" and "What are you going to do? Wait 'til she tells you the truth about herself?"

Sighing and running his hand through his hair, he said, "I don't know what else I could have done. I couldn't leave her in town with the baby, with no money. There she was, lying on Doc's bed, hurt, no place to stay, with a child. Gosh Ollie, this was the last thing I wanted to do. I know practically nothing about her and her past." He looked at Ollie as if to say, "You do understand?"

"I thought or hoped Rae—I guess that is her real name—could help you out here for a little while. It is getting colder, and you know how the cold weather affects your old bones … okay, okay," Jesse said, laughing.

"Really, I can't let her just lay around here. This is a working ranch and everyone has to pull their weight. I don't know how long she will be here anyway.

"Will can meet them in the morning. I have a feeling she is going to be an infernal nuisance. Hank has Will and the other men all excited about meeting the most beautiful girl in the county."

*****

Rae was so exhausted that all she could do was toss and turn. Disturbing dreams of her mama and Herbert wouldn't allow her to rest. Rae's mama had married Herbert Summers four years ago. Their lives were supposed to be better. Herbert was a successful banker and acted like he loved Mama. After Mama had a beautiful baby girl that she named Hope, she continued to have weak spells and had to lay in bed all the time. Rae had to do all the things that Mama had always done. The cooking, cleaning, and washing were now her responsibilities. She had lost her childhood.

Herbert said that she had to quit school and take care of Mama and the new baby. Mama said that when she got well, things would be better for all of them. But Herbert changed. He started hanging around the house more and was always watching, trying to catch her alone. She couldn't have any friends. Every young boy who came calling on her was sent away with a threat that Herbert would kill him if he ever set foot on his porch again.

Rae had threatened to tell her mama if he didn't leave her alone. He would only laugh. After almost three years of struggling and trying to get her strength back, Mama got a bad cold. Th e cold quickly turned to pneumonia and took her sweet life. She made Rae promise before she fell into a weak slumber that she would always take care of her precious baby. Rae promised her mama that she would care for Hope like she was her very own.

*****

The morning seemed to arrive way too soon for Rae, but once she was awake, she couldn't go back to sleep. She was as tired this morning as she was yesterday. She kept dreaming of Mama and Herbert. *Lord, please don't let him find us,* she prayed.

A cup of coffee sounded like a good idea. She moved Hope over to her side of the bed and eased out, trying not to wake her. After hurrying to the water closet to take care of her personal needs, she opened the door of her room and peeked into the kitchen. The sunlight was trying to shine into the wide kitchen window, but no one was stirring about. Rae walked softly over to the stove and felt it. It was cold.

Looking around, she saw a box of small pieces of wood with some kindling pieces cut. She reached up on the shelf of the stove and got a match. Lifting the cast-iron lid, she placed some wood and a piece of kindling into the stove. She struck the match and the wood flamed up in a few seconds. Rae could almost smell the coffee while she was placing water in the blue coffeepot. After placing the pot onto the back of the stove, she reached up and got herself a white mug that was hanging on a hook. She turned and ran into Jesse's hard chest and dropped the glass mug.

"Ouch!" said Jesse. The mug had landed on his big toe, and he jumped back, hopping on his good foot and reaching for his bloody toe.

"Goodness, you scared me half to death," Rae whispered.

"I'm sorry. I did say good morning," Jesse said, or he thought he had. He couldn't believe his eyes. In the dim sunlight in the kitchen stood a goddess. Her lovely blonde, tangled curls were hanging down her back. She wore a simple, white gown trimmed with a cotton lace at the neck. Never had he seen such a lovely creature. Standing with the sunshine, casting a glow on her thin gown, he could see her small, curvy frame. He had been spellbound until the mug came crashing down onto his toe.

"Stand still! There is glass on the floor, and we are both in our bare feet," said Jesse.

She bent down to pick up the pieces of the mug, then she remembered that she didn't have on her wrapper. Jesse stopped hopping around as he was taking in the sight of her.

"Here, let me do that."

Before she knew what he intended, he scooped her up in his bare arms and sat her on the corner of the table.

"Sit still while I get the broom and pail," he whispered as he limped off to the pantry.

Rae could feel her body beaming bright red from embarrassment.

Never had she been this close to a man. She couldn't help but hold on to his arms as he lifted her. *Those arms ... my,* she thought, *those arms of his are as solid as an oak tree. So fi rm and muscular.* As she glanced down his bare chest, she could see a hard flat stomach with curly black hair just below the front of his waistline. She couldn't move. She wasn't sure that she even liked this man, but his touch just made her feel weak all over.

Before she could say anything, he had gathered her foot into his big hands and starting wiping it with a soft white cloth.

"Please, I'm fine," she stuttered. "Take care of yourself." He reached for her other foot and gave it a good swipe with the cloth, and then he declared that she didn't have any broken glass on the bottom of her feet.

As Jesse swept up the broken mug, Rae slipped off the table and headed straight to her room and closed the door, nearing melting to the floor. She was sure she heard him laughing softly as she was retreating.

Heavens, whatever was she going to do? She nearly melted into a dead faint every time he touched her.

Going to her trunk, Rae gathered up a day dress and shook it, trying to remove some of the wrinkles. As she selected her other personal items, she thought what she would give to have a long soak in a tub bath and be able to wash this hair of hers.

Quickly dressing as fast as she could, she stood in front of the mirror and brushed her wild curls. She noticed movement from under the quilt.

Tiptoeing across the room, she ran her hand under the quilt to tickle Hope.

"Oh my, Rae-Rae! You make me laugh. I'm hungry. Can I have some of my new friend's cookies?"

Laughing and hugging the baby, Rae asked, "Who is your new friend?"

"Ollie, Ollie, Ollie! She's nice," exclaimed Hope.

"Well, come on, sweetheart, let's get you out of that bed and dressed for breakfast. I bet Ollie will have something wonderful for you to eat," said Rae.

While Hope was trying hard to get her socks on, Rae was trying her best to contain her hair into a tight bun. "Leave it down, Mama! I like it 'oose," said Hope.

After spending more time than she should have, she agreed with her.

"Down it will stay for now. Get your shoes on, and I will buckle them for you," said Rae.

"Come on, let's go help Ollie with breakfast." Down from the bed and running as fast as her little legs would carry her, she opened the door and entered into the kitchen like she had always lived there.

Ollie had come back into the kitchen carrying a basket of fresh eggs and found Jesse sitting at the table drinking coffee. "Goodness, Jess, when did you start making coffee? What happened to your foot?"

"I didn't make this. Rae had put it on the stove right before she dropped a coffee mug on to my toe," he said, laughing. "Mighty fine coffee, too." He turned at the sound of running feet and warned, "Watch out, Ollie! Here comes the baby, and you are her target."

Hope ran straight to Ollie with her arms raised over her head. She gave Jesse a glance as if to say *go away*, but refrained from doing so.

"Well, look here. My new precious baby girl. Come here, honey child, and give old Ollie a morning squeeze."

Ollie reached down and grabbed Hope up and smacked a big kiss on both sides of her face. "How about some good biscuits and jam? Good morning, Miss Rae. Did you sleep well? Thank you for putting on the coffee. My, don't you look pretty."

Rae glanced over to see Jesse giving her a special look. She felt her cheeks burning. She was blushing like a young schoolgirl getting her first compliment.

"Sit yourself down, Miss Rae, and I will have your breakfast in just a bit," ordered Ollie.

"Please let me help you. I am a pretty good cook if I do say so myself. At least let me cook the bacon and eggs. I can start the bacon, and when the bread comes out of the stove, I will scramble up the eggs."

Ollie gave a Jesse a look, and he nodded his head to say it's all right, let her.

"So, Ollie, do you think six eggs will be enough?" asked Rae.

Jesse coughed and nearly spit his coffee out onto the table when he laughed. "Golly girl! You are feeding real men here, not some city slickers.

Cook at least two dozen. Will is coming in soon with the milk, and he will be starving. He is a growing boy with two hollow legs."

Embarrassed again at her stupidity and trying desperately to hold on to her anger, she started breaking eggs into a bowl; then she added some milk and a good pinch of salt. She beat the eggs into a golden froth. At home she never cooked more than three eggs at a time. Herbert never ate eggs, so she cooked only one apiece for herself, Mama, and Hope. *Who is going to be eating all these eggs?* she thought.

As Rae was removing the eggs from the big hot skillet, Will came bursting through the door carrying a pail of fresh, warm milk. "Morning every—." Will stopped speaking in midsentence when he took in the sight of Rae standing at the stove. *Gosh! Hank wasn't kidding about her,* he thought. Never had he seen such a beautiful girl before.

"Come on in, baby boy, and shut your mouth before you catch flies," said Ollie, chuckling at the expression on Will's face. "Sit down—sit here next to our little houseguest."

As Will eased onto the bench next to Hope, Rae said a soft hello to him.

"The eggs will be ready in just a minute." As she was cooking the eggs, she couldn't help glancing over at Will. What a handsome young man, she thought. He was tall, almost willow thin, and with straight black hair pulled back with a leather thong. He wore a checked shirt covered with a soft leather vest and low-riding jeans. His youthful face had a few fresh pimples on his forehead and a handful of scattered black whiskers on the chin. The eyes that looked up at her were just like his brother's.

"Are you Ollie's baby?" asked Hope. Will looked down into Hope's face and smiled for the first time since entering the room.

"I can't believe she asked me that," said Will as he glanced around the room at everyone.

"Hankie, my Hankie," yelled Hope as Hank entered the room, removing his boots at the door. Will snickered and nearly choked on his coffee. Hope nearly fell backward off the bench trying to get down. She ran to Hank and grabbed him around the leg. "You gonna show me them puppies now?" Hope whispered loud enough for all to hear.

Hank reached down and picked Hope up into his arms and gave her a pat on her rump. "Let's eat breakfast first, sweetheart. I could eat a horse!"

"When did you start playing with babies?" Will asked Hank, giggling under his breath.

"When did you give up shaving off that peach fuzz?" Jesse said as he was staring at Will with his shaggy appearance.

Will immediately stopped his kidding of Hank and gave Jesse a hard stare, but he didn't respond. Rae could feel the friction between the brothers as they looked across the table at each other. *Sad,* she thought.

"I've got a lot to do to prepare for the arrival of our new bull. I will be in at lunch, and we will have a discussion … a talk about your plans while you are here, Rae. Can I do anything or is there something you need this morning before I leave?" asked Jesse.

"Hope and I could use a bath if that is possible." She spoke so soft that Jesse could hardly hear her. "It has been a while."

"Will, when you finish eating, grab those buckets outside and fill them with water. At least four and bring them into the house. Hank, you get that big tub out of the bunkhouse and place it in Rae's room—set it in front of the fireplace. Our houseguests need a bath!" said Jesse.

Oh, that beast … he makes me sound like a royal pain in my backside. Oh my, what language coming from my mouth. Rae sighed.

"Miss Rae, I will take this sweetheart with me to the barn to look at the new puppies, and then I will get the tub. I will watch after her real good," said Hank. He couldn't believe how fond he had gotten of this lovely child and so quickly.

After everyone had left the kitchen to get their chores started, Ollie and Rae sat at the table with their first real cup of coffee. *What a morning,* thought Rae.

Chapter 3

Rosedale

Herbert stood at the open window in his office at the bank in Rosedale.

It had been six days since Rae left with his baby. He couldn't believe that girl had the nerve to sneak off the place and take Hope. Not that he really cared about the little whiny brat. He never wanted a baby, much less a girl child. On the second day after Rae had run away, he walked up to the livery stable where he kept his horse and wagon while at work. Mr.

Jefferson from the livery stable called out to him.

"Rae rented this here rig yesterday morning. A boy from Junction Creek brought it back a few minutes ago and said that Rae had given him a dollar to return it for her to my livery. Yesterday, when she rented this rig, she told me when she returned it that you would pay for her outing.

So, banker man, you owe me two dollars, since she kept it for most of two days."

Herbert was pondering what old Jefferson was telling him. So, that is how she got away from him. She got on a stage in Junction Creek where she wouldn't be noticed. *I will have to make a trip over there and see where she said she was headed. She will never, ever escape me!*

"Hey, man, did you hear me?" shouted Jeferson.

"Of course, Jefferson," said Herbert reaching into his pocket for the two dollars and giving it to him. "Let's keep this little business between us, old man, if you know what I mean?" His voice had a threatening tone.

"Whatever you said, banker man, whatever. Ain't no never mind to me," Jefferson commented as he drove off , leaving Herbert standing in the street chewing on a well-used cigar.

So the little gal ran away on the stagecoach! I will drive over to Junction Creek and fi nd out which stage she took and where it was headed. She can't be far. I know that she had very little money because I never gave her mama any, and Rae had no way of earning money herself.

When I get her home, she will be my bride, and she will be very, very sorry she ran from me. Herbert laughed wickedly to himself.

The next day, Herbert was sitting behind his desk when his bank teller knocked softly on his door. "Come in, Sawyer!" yelled Herbert. "What do you want so early in the day? You see how busy I am. Speak up, man!"

Sawyer was very young, timid, and scared to death of Herbert. He had finished college and was very knowledgeable about the banking business, but he was afraid of what he had to tell Herbert. It could mean his job, but he had to speak up about this problem.

"What is it, man? Speak up. We don't have all day," shouted Herbert at Sawyer, making him tremble that much more.

"Well, sir, it has come to my attention as I was balancing the books for the end of the month that we, I mean the bank, are short of funds."

"What the hell do you mean? Short of funds? Have you been dipping into the till? Where do you think the money has gone, and how much money are you talking about? Short of funds. Th at is crazy talk. Get back out there and redo the numbers again and balance those books or you will be put in jail. It is only you and me who handle the money here, and if any money is missing, it has to be your fault. Understand me, Sawyer?"

Herbert's face was blood red, and the veins in his neck were throbbing.

Sawyer started backing up and bumped into the door handle. Reaching behind him, he opened the door and ran out into the bank. Th ere stood

Mae Flowers, a young lady whom he had been courting. *Lord, I pray that she didn't hear any of that conversation,* thought Sawyer as he straightened up his vest and tie.

"Good morning, Miss Mae. How nice it is to see you this lovely morning," said Sawyer, trying hard to appear very calm.

"But it is raining, Sawyer. Not lovely at all. Are you all right?" She was looking at his flushed face.

"Oh, sorry about the weather. I have been very busy, and I haven't had time to even look outside. What can I do for you this fine rainy day?" He gave her a big smile as if teasing her.

"I just came by to see if you were going to take me to the church picnic this Saturday. I will have a basket to bid on, and I was hoping that just maybe you might be the highest bidder on mine. It will have a large yellow ribbon tied on the handle."

"Yes, I want to take you to the picnic. I have been so busy, I have forgotten about it. I hope you don't think for one minute I will allow another fellow to win your basket."

Before she could respond to his teasing, a loud voice was overheard from Herbert's office. She glanced toward the office door, then whirled around and ran out of the bank.

Well, this morning hasn't been a total loss, Sawyer thought to himself.

Chapter 4

Limason

"After you and honey child get your bath, I will show you around the inside of the house, and Jesse will be in for lunch. Afterward, maybe he can show you around the grounds."

"Oh, I am looking forward to being clean all over and washing my hair. But Jesse doesn't need to show me around the ranch. I can explore the place by myself," said Rae.

"I'm sure he will want you to meet the ranch hands. They are nice men

and hard workers. It's a job keeping them all fed. So, I've got to go down in the cellar and get potatoes and carrots to go in the stew that I'm cooking for lunch," stated Ollie.

"Oh, let me go down with you this morning to see the cellar. Afterward, I can go down there for you while I am here."

"Honey child that will be good. My old legs don't do too well on them stairs. Come on in, Will, and place the water on the stove," Ollie said to Will as he was standing at the screen door with two pails of water.

"Thank you, Will. Please put the water down, and I will place them on the stove. Hank will be bringing in the tub for me. ... Oh, here he comes now," Rae said. "Goodness, Hank that has to be heavy. Let me help," said Rae.

"I got it," muttered Will, blushing a bright red as he rushed over to give Hank a hand instead of allowing Rae to do it.

Rae looked behind Hank and glanced out of the door, looking for Hope.

"Hank, where did you leave Hope?" asked Rae.

"She's right behind me," yelled Hank from the bedroom. Hank came out of the room and looked around, expecting to see the baby. "We were looking at the new puppies, and I told her to come with me to the house."

Rae gave him a nod and raced out of the door, running to the barn.

She could hear a dog barking as she pushed open the big, red double doors. There stood Hope with a shiny, newborn puppy. Her little hands were holding the tiny creature by the neck. It was hanging limp like it was dead. The pup's mama was going crazy with barking and jumping. She was pulling at the hem of Hope's dress, trying her best to rescue her baby.

Hope started spinning around and yelling at the top of her lungs, "No, no, it's mine, it's mine!"

Betsy the milk cow was mooing and swaying around in her stall. With all the commotion, she started kicking up her back heels and knocking the boards loose on the back wall of the barn.

Hank ran ahead of Rae and grabbed up the mama dog from behind, tapping her nose hard to make her turn loose of Hope's dress.

Will tried to take the dangling pup out of Hope's hands. She had a death grip on the poor soul's little neck, spinning around out of Will's reach. Rae got down on her knees in front of Hope, pleading with her.

"Oh, baby, please give me the puppy so its mama can take care of it."

Then she heard Jesse yell, "What in the hell is going on in here? Will. Get a hold of that cow before she knocks down this barn or hurts herself."

Rae was still kneeling in the hay, begging softly to the tearful baby to give up the puppy. She was praying that the poor little thing was still alive. When she looked up to see Jesse, he was giving her an infuriated look.

"Hope, give your mama that puppy *now!*" Jesse said with a disgruntled look.

She looked up at the tall stranger with tears streaming down her hot, dirty face. Slowly she reached out to Rae and gave up her most prized possession. "It's mine," she said, still crying softly. "Hankie gave it to me, didn't you Hankie?"

Rae passed the newborn puppy over to Hank, and he carried it along with the pup's mama back to their bed.

"The little fellow is all right," said Hank. "The mama is settling down, sniffing and licking her baby all over." He laughed, trying to lighten the mood of the situation.

Rae had gathered up Hope in her arms, whispering sweet phrases for her ears only. She was trying to make her understand about the mama dog and her baby puppy.

Jesse had walked over to Will to check on the cow. She had kicked one board loose from the wall. "Hank, get this wall repaired first thing," yelled Jesse.

Walking over to where Rae stood holding the baby, Jesse gave both of them a stern look and said, "Hope, you are not to come into this barn by yourself. Is that understood, young lady?"

For an answer, Hope turned her face away and placed her head on Rae's shoulder. Not getting the answer he wanted, he stormed off repeating to himself, "She will be no trouble."

"Come on, baby. Let's go into the house and get cleaned up. Hank brought in a real big bathtub, and it will be filled with nice warm water. We will get all clean again and smell good. You like a bath, don't you?"

For an answer, Hope sniff ed a little and said, "I want my puppy. Please Rae."

"Oh, honey, you have got to let that puppy grow a little. We can come out to the barn every day and visit the little fellow. Maybe, when it gets bigger, you can hold him some. How's that?" Hope had to think about that for a minute, and finally she shook her head *okay*. She threw her arms around Rae's neck and hugged her tight and said, "I love you, Mama."

When Rae and Hope entered the house, Ollie was coming out of the bedroom carrying two empty pails, and Rae hurried over to her. "Oh, Ollie, I didn't mean to make more work for you. I am so sorry that you carried all that water in to the tub."

"Oh, missy, it was no bother. It is all ready for you two to take a nice, long bath. I am here in this front room, and I will keep them men folks out."

Rae couldn't help but smile. *I couldn't be safer with Ollie around,* she thought as she entered her bedroom for a long-awaited soak.

*****

By early afternoon, Jesse had not come back to the ranch house for lunch or the discussion he planned to have with Rae. She occupied herself by inspecting the cellar with Ollie and carrying up some vegetables to prepare for dinner. After peeling what seemed like ten pounds of potatoes and a pan of carrots, she cut them up and placed them in the pot on the stove where pieces of beef had been simmering most of the morning. Ollie dropped in some seasonings and placed the lid on the pot. "Now we will just let that cook. Have you ever made piecrust, honey? Th ese here men like their sweets, so I have some fresh peaches that will make a wonderful cobbler."

Rae could almost taste the cobbler. Her mama used to cook the best pies in the county, and she had taught her to make them too.

"Oh, Ollie, I love to make sweets. I will be glad to prepare the cobbler for you. Let me check on Hope, then I will peel the peaches and let them simmer with some sugar while I will make the crust."

After all the screaming and crying, Rae had bathed Hope and given her a little jam on a slice of fresh bread. Hope was still upset over the ordeal with the puppy. Rae gathered her up in her arms and sat in the rocker and rocked and talked to Hope until she drifted off into a peaceful sleep.

"She is sound asleep," said Rae to Ollie. "She just wore herself out crying over that puppy. I know Hank meant well, but I wish he hadn't told her the puppy could be hers. We won't be here very long. I don't believe that when we leave I can handle Hope and a new puppy," said Rae.

"Now don't you fret over leaving right away, Miss Rae. You've got to get your strength back. Why don't you sit a spell and let me put a new bandage on your head."

As she was speaking, she was pulling down a box with all types of bandages. Rae sat on the bench at the table, and Ollie removed the old bandage and said, "This cut looks better already. In a few days, you can leave this off and it will be just fine."

"I will be the judge of when she can leave off that bandage. Here, let me see before you replace it with a clean one." Surprised to hear Jesse's voice, Rae and Ollie both jumped.

"My Lawd, Mr. Jess, we didn't know that you was even on the place, much less here in the kitchen."

"Sorry, I wasn't wearing one of Betsy's bells around my neck," he stated sarcastically.

Ollie was surprised at Jesse's tone of voice. She gave him a stern look. "Now you listen to me, sonny boy. I won't have no disrespect coming out of your mouth," stuttered Ollie. "I ain't too old to get my wooden spoon after you." Ollie wobbled across the room, putting space between herself and Jesse. She was still talking under her breath as she gathered up a soft white cloth and poured cool water on it.

Jesse blushed from the dressing down that he just received from Ollie, which he knew he deserved. "I'm sorry. I have had a rough morning and afternoon. I'm hungry. Didn't mean to be so harsh with my words." Jesse shrugged, looking over at Ollie with a grin.

My goodness, thought Rae, *his grin could turn my knees to water.* She was glad that she was sitting down. And those beautiful blue eyes. Whatever was she thinking as she watched the exchange of words?

"That's better," said Ollie as she folded the cloth that she was going to use to clean Rae's cut and gave it to Jesse. "What do you think about the cut on Rae's face?"

Jesse lifted Rae's hair back away from her forehead. The brush of his hand, just barely touching her, sent chills down her spine and turned her face a blushing pink.

"It looks good, but it still needs to be covered for a few more days."

After wiping the bruised area, he took the bandage and smoothed it over the cut ever so gently.

Jesse walked over to Ollie and placed his arms around the back of her waist and whispered in her ear, "Do you think I could have some leftover roast beef on a sandwich? I don't believe I can wait until dinner. Please, pretty please."

"Oh go on with you," slapping her dishrag at him and laughing. "Sit yourself down, and I will get it for you."

Rae knew that she should have volunteered to make his sandwich, but she didn't think her legs would carry her across the room. His presence had made her head feel off balance. *I am going to have to get away from this place soon,* she thought.

"Move down to this end of the table so I don't have to shout at you," said Jesse, giving Rae a curious look. "Are you feeling all right? Does your head still hurt?"

Rae got up and moved down the table as Jesse had instructed, while Ollie served her a fresh cup of coffee. She poured Jesse some to go with his sandwich.

"Oh, Ollie, you don't have to wait on me, but thank you so much."

"Oh you just hush, honey, and have a little rest. You've been working all morning."

Jess took in the conversation between Ollie and Rae. "So, it seems that you have already started helping out."

Ollie looked up and said, "She shore has, Mr. Jess. There ain't a lazy bone in this one. No sir!"

"That's mighty fine. We have needed an extra hand around the house for a while. Now, Rae, after dinner, you and I need to have a long talk about what plans you have for yourself and the baby. You are welcome to stay here for a period of time. Well, we will continue this conversation tonight. I have more fence to see about. Our new bull should be arriving in a day or two, and I need to have a place for him."

Jesse walked to the door and stopped to reach for his hat. He turned and said thanks to Ollie for the delicious sandwich. Looking at Rae, he gave her a nod and was gone as quick as he had arrived.

Chapter 5

It would seem that supper time at the Maxwell's was almost like a party.

The long table was covered with a soft white cloth. All the plates and silverware were set with a large coffee mug for each person. A small jar of wildflowers had been placed in the middle of the table.

Rae had helped Ollie place all the bowls of food in the center of the table with a large spoon in each one. A basket of warm corn bread was at one end of the table, while a platter of hot biscuits was placed at the opposite corner. Covered crystal bowls with soft butter sat beside the bread with apple butter and fi g preserves. Jesse had been telling the truth when he said that his place had plenty of good food.

Ollie stepped out onto the screen porch and rang the dinner bell.

The dinner bell was placed chest high on a shelf beside the back door.

This bell was used only to call the men into the house for meals or for an emergency. The ringing of this bell was taken very serious by all who lived on the ranch.

Will and Hank were f rst to arrive with their faces and hands cleaned and the front of their hair wet. Both of them took their seats at the table while the three ranch hands came in looking all clean and ready to eat. Jesse followed the three men into the kitchen, and one by one, he introduced them to Rae. John was the oldest of the men and had worked for Jesse's father many years and stayed on to help the boys with the ranch.

Joseph was about forty and had been on the ranch five years. He was engaged to be married to a lady in town. Rider was the youngest man. He was a tall drink of water with a head of blond curls. He got his nickname "Rider" because he had won a few horse races in town during the Fourth of July celebration.

After the introductions were completed, the men took their places at the table. Everyone was eager to begin eating, but they waited patiently for Jesse to be seated and ask grace.

"Heavenly Father, thank you for this ranch, our family and new friends, and this wonderful food. Amen," mumbled Jesse.

As the men ate their supper, very little was said about work. Jesse mentioned that tomorrow they were all going to build a covered shed for the new bull, with a roof and three sturdy walls. Later, they may build a front wall with double doors. Closing it up completely would depend on the winter weather.

Limason was located in the southern part of Texas where they didn't get much snow, but the wind could be mighty fearsome. The wind was strong enough at times to blow a man down.

The men continued to eat and nodded their heads to let Jesse know that they had heard him. Rae couldn't help but smile as she watched the men enjoy the food. Hope sat next to Hank and ate two biscuits with apple butter. She was being a very good girl.

Rae eased out of her seat and walked over to the stove. Th e men did not raise their heads, but every eye was on her movements. She got the pan of peach cobbler and the pitcher of heavy cream and brought them over to the table to serve. Big smiles were on each man's face as they passed their plate to her with a nod and a hearty thank-you.

After the dinner was over, Rae jumped up and started cleaning up the dinner table. Ollie wobbled over to the stove to cover up and store the leftovers, which were very few. Rae joked to Ollie that these men really had big appetites. It didn't take long before all the dishes were cleaned and put away. Rae swept the kitchen floor and hung her apron up on the kitchen hook.

She walked over to Hope, who was playing with her doll in front of the fireplace, and took her hand. "Come with me, darling, and let's get you dressed for bed. I need to talk to Mr. Maxwell tonight, and I want you all ready to be tucked into bed."

"You get her changed, Miss Rae, and I will let her play a little. I might even tell her a story before she goes to sleep. I will put her to bed for you," said Ollie with a smile in her voice.

After taking care of Hope and leaving her in Ollie's care, she walked to the end of the screen porch and sat in the swing.

The sun was down, the crickets were singing, and the sound of laughter was coming from the bunkhouse. Her eyes were adjusting to the dark, and she could see a man walking from the barn to the house. She knew it was Jesse.

Jesse opened the screen door to the porch. He stopped and slipped off his boots before continuing to walk to the swing where Rae was sitting.

"May I sit beside you?" Jesse asked very softly.

Rae's heart was racing fast, but she answered him with a sweet, "Yes, please do."

"How is your head this evening?"

"Fine, just fine. It doesn't hurt much like it did before."

"Good, I'm glad," whispered Jesse as he was looking at her bandage.

Rae's nerves were jumping to the beat of the screaming sounds of the crickets and katydids. She was trying to appear calm with him so close.

"Now, Rae," said Jesse with a sigh, "I feel like I need to have some truthful answers from you. Please," he reached out to take her arm as she attempted to get up, "let's talk about you and your problems without running away. I only want to be your friend, not your judge."

Rae felt cornered sitting beside Jesse. She knew she had to come up with some very convincing answers. Her hands were shaking, so she slipped them under the sides of her skirt.

"What do you want to know that I haven't already told you? You know my name, where I came from, and the reason I left. What part of my story do you not believe?" She knew that she had messed up the minute she said the word "story."

"That's just it, Rae. I feel like what you told me is just that, a story. Something you have put together to cover up the real reason you were on that stagecoach. Are you running from someone? Let me help you," he pleaded. "If you don't want me to help, tell the truth to Sheriff Murphy. He should be back in a few days. He had to go to Frisco City on business."

"Why do you think I am running from someone? I have nothing more to tell you. Just allow me to stay here a few more days, and I can go into town and see if I can get a job—maybe help the doctor—somewhere I can earn money so I can support my baby."

Jesse lifted his left leg and placed it over his right knee and leaned back into the swing. With a big sigh, he put his hands over his eyes and rubbed them hard. "Are you joking? The doctor can hardly support himself." Jesse was trying hard to not show the anger that ran through him when she mentioned letting the doctor help her. Why did he care who helped her?

"All right, since we aren't getting anywhere, and you are in need of money, let's make a deal. Ollie needs help here. She is ready to accept help, and she likes you and your baby. We have the room. There is plenty of work to be done around the house, and the new fall garden always needs attention."

Thinking for a minute, Jesse said, "I'm willing to pay you forty-dollars a month with room and board. Let's say after two months, if you aren't happy here, I will not stand in your way if you want to leave. Two months of pay should help you get a start somewhere. Maybe, just maybe, during your stay here, you will learn to trust me."

Jesse raised his left arm and placed it on the swing behind Rae's back. He slowly lowered his hand down to lightly touch her shoulder and patted it. A tingle ran down her neck, and she caught her breath. *Please don't touch me again,* she silently prayed.

"Well, what you think of my job offer?" he asked quietly.

Rae could hardly think straight with his leg touching the side of her skirt. His touch was like shock waves running up and down her spine. Finally she said, "Could I have tonight to think over this very generous offer?"

"Sure, take all the time you need."

"Well, it has been a long day, and I better go check on Hope. Good night Mr. ... Jesse." She practically sneaked out from under his arm, then stood up and walked into the house. *You can keep your secrets for now, missy,* thought Jesse as he watched her walk in the back door.

As Rae lay in her bed, she could not get Jesse's words out of her head. *He said that I could trust him. How do I know for certain? Would he contact Herbert? Not everyone will understand why I took Hope with me. Th e sheriff will say that I kidnapped my baby sister. I am old enough to leave home if I wanted to, but not take Hope away from her father. Th ey will never understand that I had promised Mama that I would care for Hope. Mama gave Hope to me. She's mine now.* She turned her face into her pillow and cried.

The morning rooster was calling the beginning of the day too early for Rae. She had tossed and turned all night, trying hard not to think of her past and what would become of them. She had to get up and get ready to face Jesse with her decision. There was only one decision that she could make and that was to take his job offer. *Why not?* she asked herself. *This is a wonderful place. There are good people here. And I feel safe. Hope is safe.*

"Good morning, darling," Rae said to Hope as she was crawling out from under the quilt. "Why don't you stay in bed a little while until I get dressed?"

"All right, but hurry. I've got to go see my baby puppy."

"Now you remember that you cannot go out to the barn without me or Hank? You know that Mr. Maxwell will be very upset with you if you aren't a good little girl."

"I don't like him. He yells all the time and makes funny faces when he's mad, like this," Hope pulled at her mouth and started wagging her tongue. Rae couldn't help but smile, and she tried very hard not to laugh.

"Please be a good girl and try hard not to make him mad," she said as she grabbed her clothes and went into the water closet to dress.

After Rae and Hope dressed and readied themselves for the day, they entered the kitchen to find Ollie at the stove making biscuits.

"That coffee sure smells good, Ollie. What can I do to help you this lovely morning?"

"My, my, someone feels good today. Come and set the table and break me two dozen eggs to scramble. The men are all excited today. Mr. Jess's new bull is arriving sometime after lunch. He has waited two years to buy that bull, and it is a grand day for its arrival," said Ollie.

The men all came through the door one at a time, laughing and talking about the new bull. This seemed to be a day of celebration.

Rae poured their cups with piping hot coffee, and after grace was spoken by Jesse, the platters of eggs, bacon, and hot biscuits were passed around to each man. It seemed that the men were too excited to eat, because they all finished quickly and went out the door with chores to complete.

Jesse lingered behind and nodded his head at Rae to take a seat at the end of the table near him. "Well, Rae, have you reached a decision about staying here on the ranch for a while? I have a lot to do today, and I would like to get this business with you settled."

Lifting her chin and glaring at him with her big brown eyes, she replied, "I don't mean to be a burden to you, Mr. Maxwell."

"Stop that crap now. My name is Jess or Jesse, whatever you prefer to call me, but not Mr. Maxwell. That was my father's name," said Jesse, daring her to give him an argument.

Rae turned red in the face, but after taking a deep breath, she answered slowly, "Yes, I have decided to stay for at least two months—if that is still the deal. After that time, I should be able to move on and take care of myself and Hope." Looking shyly at him, she said, "Thank you for your offer of a job and opening your home to us. I will work hard and—" Jesse held up his hand for her to stop talking.

"I'm sure you will hold up your end of the bargain. Just keep a close eye on that baby of yours to keep her safe. A ranch can be a dangerous place for a small child."

"Oh, don't worry about her. I will watch her every minute!"

Jesse rose up from the table and thanked Ollie for the good breakfast. He grabbed his hat from the hook beside the door and said that he would see them at lunch.

"Well, Ollie, you heard. We're staying for a while, and I will be helping you out as much as possible. I don't want to hear any fuss out of you," said Rae as she was pointing and wagging her finger at Ollie's smiling face. "Now, let me get busy and start earning my keep. Let me get this kitchen cleaned and ready to cook a big delicious lunch for that bunch of overgrown boys."

Rae laughed as she walked around in the kitchen. She felt like a big load had been lifted off her shoulders—for a while anyway.

"Mama! I want to go see my puppy now. You said after I ate my breakfast, and I eat it all, see! Let's go now," said Hope, grabbing Rae's skirt and pulling her toward the door.

"Let me place these dishes in the dishpan and pour water over them. Wait, honey, stop pulling on me. Please stop!"

"Here, Rae, let me finish this, and you go on and take the baby outside. Go on with yourself. Scoot, I can do this," said Ollie, fanning her apron at her.

"Well, all right. Come on, Hope, let's go check on that puppy!" Rae laughed as she reached for her little hand.

In the dim light of the barn, Rae could see Hank and Joseph looking at a small colt. Hank was kneeling down on one knee, running his hands over the colt's front leg. *He sure is a beautiful animal,* thought Rae.

Hope saw Hank and ran to him yelling, "Hankie, Hankie, I come to see my puppy!"

The colt sidestepped and kicked his hind legs right into Joseph's left side, knocking him down.

"Dammit," yelled Joseph as he was falling backward onto the barn floor, turning over two buckets of feed.

"Whoa, boy," Hank said, speaking calmly to the colt.

Rae raced over to help Joseph get up off the floor while he was holding his left side. "Are you hurt badly? I'm so sorry. I didn't know that she was going to be so excited to see Hank."

Joseph had a grin on his face as he was trying to stand up straight. He said, "You mean 'Hankie' don't you? I'm fine, Miss Rae, really. Just got me when I wasn't looking."

Rae turned to speak to Hope when she noticed that Will had come into the barn and was holding her real tight, begging her not to cry. *What a surprise,* thought Rae.

She walked over to Will and tried to take her baby out of his arms, but Hope was latched on to him for dear life.

"I will show her the puppy while they get the colt settled down," he said as he walked toward the bed of puppies. Hope had a big smile on her face because no one was yelling at her and she was going to get to hold her puppy.

Will was whispering into Hope's ear about how to hold the squirming pup, and he was telling her why she should not yell or run in the barn.

"Miss Rae, I will watch her for a while and bring her back to the house," Will said softly.

"If you are sure, Will. I know you all have a lot to do today. I don't want to get you in trouble with Jesse."

"He is not my boss." Will said vehemently.

Rae was surprised at his tone of voice and sighed. "All right then. I do have work to do this morning. Thank you." She turned and walked back to the house.

As Rae strolled out of the barn toward the house, she couldn't help but notice the front steps leading up on the screen porch. There wasn't a flower or pretty blooming plant in sight. This place really needed a woman's touch outside. She would plant some blooming bulbs and bushes that stayed green all year long in this climate. *Something to help cheer up the front of the house and make it more inviting,* she thought. Ollie had the inside of the home so clean that a person could eat off her floors. The place always smells so good with fresh baked bread and sweet desserts. Yes, a few flowers outside would be the finishing touch to this nice home.

After entering the house, Rae couldn't help but be concerned about the tone of voice Will used when speaking about Jesse. Will certainly has growing pains or there is something wrong with the brothers' relationship, *she thought,* but I have enough problems of my own. I'm not going to interfere in theirs.

"I'm sorry Miss Rae, but I had to bring Sweetheart back inside."

"Sweetheart?" Rae smiled at Will.

"Yes ma'am, that's what Hank calls her, and I guess it's catching on.

She seems to like her new name." He laughed as he stood her back down onto the floor.

"Bye, baby boy," said Hope, giggling as she raced across the room to scoop up her dolly that she had left by the fireplace.

Ollie laughed while thinking to herself that everyone would have a nickname to answer to soon! What a joy this child was to have around.

"Come on, Miss Rae. Get Hope and let's go to the smokehouse and get some meat to cook for lunch. It is filled to the brim with sausages, smoked hams, bacon, and big pieces of meat to be cut into chops and roast. This here is a rich ranch when it comes to good food. Yes madam."

After the three returned from the smokehouse, Rae cut up some Granny green apples for two pies for supper.

Ollie had taken a big slab of meat and cut it up into cubes and placed it on the stove to boil until tender. She said that she would make a big pot of dumplings for lunch with some fresh baked bread and serve it with some wild strawberry preserves. That should hold them until supper!

Rae decided to take Hope outside for a little while. They would scout out the rest of the homestead in walking distance, away from the corralled animals. The fresh air would be good for both of them. They walked around the back of the house and up a little hillside that was lovely.

Turning to their right and down the hill a piece was a small fenced area that was the family cemetery. It was so beautifully cared for. Th ere were several graves. Each one had a headstone with carving. Th e beds of the graves were covered neatly with small rocks. Each had a bouquet of fresh flowers laying at the bottom of the headstone. *So lovely,* thought Rae.

"Mama, is this where my mama is sleeping?" asked Hope.

Rae was so surprised with that question that she was almost speechless. "Oh, darling," she said as she kneeled down next to her on the ground. "Don't you remember where we placed Mama? Her body is where we lived before we came here. Her spirit, the part of Mama that loved you so much, is in heaven. I know it is hard to remember, and we do miss Mama so much." Rae was talking so softly that it was like a whisper coming from her. She was trying hard to hold back tears.

"I talk to Mama sometimes, and she talks to me too. I want to see her," whined Hope. "Tell her spir't to come back down here and see me, please. I want her to see my new puppy." Hope's bottom lip was quivering, and the tears were dropping down on her cheeks. "I want … I want my mama," she cried. She buried her little face into Rae's lap and wept until she was limp.

Oh, my love. I wish I could bring her back to us, too, thought Rae, choking back tears. Rae was sitting next to Jesse's mother's grave while Hope was settling down. She looked up to see Ollie walking down the hillside toward them.

"So, this is where you got off to. Oh, my, why has this baby child been crying?" Before Rae could speak, Ollie took Hope out of her lap and gave her a big squeeze, not waiting for an answer.

"Come with old Ollie, and let me give you a nice big cookie and fresh milk. You can help me make the dumplings for lunch. Would you like to do that, honey child?"

Hope moved her head up and down on Ollie's shoulder while letting her carry her toward the house. Ollie called back over her shoulder, "You finish your walk, honey, and don't fret about this here baby. I'll take good care of her."

Rae reached up and touched her head to adjust the bandage. She should be able to remove it tonight. Watching Ollie walk up the hillside with Hope, she pushed herself up, dusted off her skirt, and decided to continue on past the cemetery. She wanted to see what was on the other side of the house.

To her surprise, there were several beautiful apple trees. The trees were so big and healthy. *This area of the ranch is so pretty.*

Continuing on a little further, she came upon the new fall garden that Jesse had mentioned to her earlier. The rows were planted with different vegetables that had a painted stick stuck in the ground at the end of each row. She would have to remember to ask about the sticks. The rows were swept so clean that a weed wouldn't dare grow in this garden, she thought.

"I will have to work in this garden a little every day to keep it this way," said Rae out loud.

Walking a little further, she came full circle back to the front of the house. The men were all gathered at the corral, talking about the new bull. From what she could hear, the bull would be arriving in a few hours.

Jesse noticed Rae as she was coming from around the house, and he never took his eyes off of her. He liked the way she walked, almost like she was floating, so light on her feet. Rae turned to look over her shoulder before she entered the house, and their eyes connected. She stood frozen in place for a split second and then moved on into the house.

Lunchtime was an exciting event. A messenger had ridden in with a note. Mr. Thomas from McBain had put the bull in a wagon, and it was on the way. It should arrive after lunch. After delivering the message and declining lunch, the rider headed on his way. Th e men were so full of chatter about the bull that they were eager to eat and get back outside.

Rae couldn't help but laugh at how fast the dumplings and fresh bread disappeared from the table.

"Rae, when the bull arrives, it is going to be hard for all of us to handle him. We will drive the wagon into the corral and let the bull out in the fenced area, but he is going to be one mad son of a b—gun. Please keep Hope in the house. After we get the bull settled down, then I will come and get you both so you can see him. Will you do that for me?"

"Certainly! I will be putting her down for a nap in just a few minutes. You don't have to worry about us."

Hope was playing in the corner of the kitchen, but she could hear them talking about her and a bull, whatever that was.

Rae called Hope to come and get ready to take a nap and rest after their long walk today. "Later, we will go outside and see your puppy again."

Hope got up and took her dolly. She walked over to Rae, yawning and dragging her dolly on the floor. She was really tired.

After tucking Hope into bed, Rae came back into the kitchen and started cleaning up after lunch. She made Ollie go and sit down and take a rest too. Ollie had prepared the lunch mostly by herself, and she was ready to sit and put up her feet for a while.

"You spoil me, Miss Rae, you shore do—but I like it." She laughed as she got herself settled into the large rocker by the fireplace.

As Rae raised the kitchen window to let fresh air into the room, she could see the men all gathered around a large wagon that had three sides of long boards built around the bed. The bull had been transferred here in that wagon. Jesse was waving his hands to the driver, giving him instructions as to where to drive the wagon. He had said that he would unload the wagon with the bull into the corral. Th e men were all running around the bull, laughing and talking loud to each. They were like kids with a new toy.

"Jess, this is a fine animal," said John.

The bull was young, but he was very beefy and solid black in color except for one white ring of hair close to his left hoof. He was well-proportioned from his head to his backside, and his back was good and straight. The head was large with short horns above his ears. This bull was a fine-looking animal any rancher would be proud to have.

"Thanks, John. I have waited for a while to get just the right one. I hope this spring we will have calves dropping all over the hillside." Jesse smiled as he watched the bull move around in the corral, kicking up his hind legs and giving himself a good workout after being cooped up for several hours.

"He is something, Jess," said Will. "I can't believe he's finally here. Pa would have liked your choice."

 Thanks, boy," answered Jesse with a knot in his throat. He still missed his pa so much, and purchasing a new bull was one of the things that his pa had planned to do before the accident.

All of the men were gathered close to each other at the fence, watching and talking about the bull. None of them noticed the baby crawling under the fence at the corner of the corral. She was skipping out to the bull with some hay in her hand, singing, "Come blackie come to me, blackie. I have something for you."

"Gosh oh mighty, look there," yelled Rider at the top of his lungs. Th e men looked to where he was pointing. Immediately they all scooted under the fence, running and removing their shirts to wave at the bull to take his attention away from the child. Jesse was the first one to reach Hope.

He grabbed her up like a sack of potatoes and ran to the other side of the corral. There were so many men in the fenced area, the bull didn't know who to chase. Once the others saw that Hope was out of danger, they ran as fast as they could to safer ground. Hank was only one foot faster than the bull. He f ew over the top of the fence and landed on his backside with his right foot twisted under him.

"Oh! Man. I think I busted my foot," cried Hank.

With the window open in the kitchen, Rae heard the men yelling and carrying on so much that she wanted to see what the excitement was all about. Walking out to the corral area, she saw Jesse with Hope in his arms, giving her a good shake. When he put her down, he gave her bottom a good whack. He had her by the hand and was practically dragging her toward the house. Hope had not made a sound.

Rae couldn't believe what she had just seen. Th at beast of a man had beat her baby. "How dare you!" shouted Rae. "Don't you ever beat my baby again. No one, I mean *no one* will—"

Jesse turned loose of Hope's hand. She raced to bury her face into Rae's skirt, trying to hide from Jesse.

"Beat her? One slap on the butt is not a beating," blurted out Jesse.

Rae reached down and grabbed up Hope, ready to give him a fierce tongue-lashing when Jesse started marching toward her with anger in his eyes.

"Get that baby and your sassy fanny out of my sight before I forget myself and turn you over my knee and give you that beating that I didn't give that young'un!"

"How dare you!"

"You said that before. *Now move!* " He pointed his finger toward the house.

Rae was so furious, she was shaking, but she knew she had better get Hope out of his sight. She had no idea what could have made him so mad.

To strike a child?

Ollie was waiting on the screen porch when Rae returned carrying Hope. "I thought that my honey child was taking a nap. What was she doing outside close to the corral and that bull?"

"I don't know, Ollie, but Jesse … my goodness that man makes me so mad I could just spit. Listen, Ollie," said Rae still shaking from her outburst with Jesse. "Will you make sure she stays in bed for a while? Hank got hurt, and I need to see if I can do something to help."

Rae ran to the bunkhouse and knocked on the door. Rider, the youngest member of the trio that worked for Jesse, answered and stepped outside.

"I came to see if I could help Hank. I heard him yell that he had hurt his foot," said Rae.

"Yes, ma'am. He twisted his ankle, and it looks real bad. Joseph has already ridden to town to bring the doctor out here to look at it. I believe he will be laid up for a while. We had to cut his boot off because it had started swelling."

"Have him soak it in some cold well water until the doctor gets here."

Rae was giving instructions to Rider when Jesse opened the door.

"Do as Rae says, Rider, and get a pail of cold water for Hank. Anything to keep the swelling down. *You* ... come with me. We are going to have a talk. I am going to do the talking, and *you* are going to listen. Understand?"

"Yes, master," mumbled Rae, following behind him. Jesse gave her a look that said if she made one more smart remark, she'd be sorry.

He walked past the house and strolled up the hillside and came upon the apple trees. He gestured for her to sit in the shade of a tree as he stretched himself out beside her. He was still shaking, so he didn't say anything for a few minutes.

Finally Jesse asked her, "Do you have any idea what happened out in the corral this afternoon?"

Rae slowly shook her head as if to say no.

"After the bull was unloaded and let loose in the corral, we were all watching it run around kicking and stomping the ground. Rider just happened to glance over his shoulder and saw your baby crawling under the fence. She skipped out to the middle of the corral with a handful of hay, calling to the bull." Jesse stopped talking while shaking his head.

"My heart stopped beating. The others started running toward the bull while I ran to Hope and grabbed her up. She was kicking, hitting me, and screaming to be put down. I was so angry, for just a second I lost control of my temper." Jesse sat up and leaned forward. With a sigh, he said, "I have never been so frightened in my life."

Rae started to interrupt, but he held up his hand so he could finish.

"I have never struck a child. Never have I hit Will even when I knew he needed a good paddling. I am sorry, Rae. Please don't think that I would ever harm your baby or you. I can get my back up pretty good at times, but I am only human," he said as he gave her an incredible grin.

"Now, you can lay into me. It's your turn to talk," he said.

Placing her hands over her face, she said, "Oh, Jess, I'm so ashamed."

She was surprised to learn that Hope had been in so much danger. "I had no idea that Hope was outside the house. She was supposed to be taking a nap. I cannot believe I acted like such an idiot when all of you had just risked your lives to rescue my child. Please forgive me."

Jesse reached up to remove some hair that had fallen over Rae's eyes, and he smoothed it back behind her ear. "I wouldn't say that we were all in danger, but it was scary."

When she glanced up at him, he felt lost in those eyes of hers and couldn't help himself. He leaned into her and brushed his lips over her right eye and then the left one. His kisses were like a butterfly's touch, so light and tender. She sat frozen. Slowly she pulled away from him and kept her eyes locked down toward her hands.

Jesse stood and offered Rae his hand to get up off the ground. "Best get back before that herd of men I have working for me comes with a rescue party looking for you."

Rae laughed. She could just imagine Ollie running up this hill to rescue her with her rolling pin in hand. The two of them headed back toward the house.

When Jesse and Rae had walked off toward the orchard, Ollie settled down with Hope in the rocking chair. As she was rocking her honey child and talking to her about being a good girl, Hope said that she wanted her mama. "Please, Ollie, I want her so much."

"Your mama will be back in a little while. She is taking a walk with Mr. Jess."

"No, not Rae, Rae," cried Hope. Tears had formed in her eyes, and her nose was running.

"Please don't cry, my child."

"My mama wouldn't be mad at me," murmured Hope. "She wouldn't like that mean old Jess," she said, hiding her face in Ollie's bosom.

Ollie was pondering what Hope meant about wanting her mama. *Not Rae? Now, what is this all about?*

Just then, Ollie looked up to see Rae walking over to the rocker. She took Hope out of Ollie's arms and told the baby that they had to have a little talk. "You've got to learn to do as you are told, little girl."

Chapter 6

With all the moaning and grumbling coming from Hank, a person would have thought that every bone in his old body had been broken.

"Hang on a little longer, Hankie." Will snickered. "We will have you tucked in your bed in just a second."

"You better get your young skinny behind out of my sight, boy!" yelled Hank. "If I could, I would kick you across this here ranch."

After Hank was settled in the bed, Rider went to the well house and pulled up a fresh bucket of cold water and brought it into the bunkhouse.

"Miss Rae said for you to soak your foot. It should help with the swelling."

After disposing of Hank's filthy sock, Will told Hank to place his foot slowly into the bucket of cold water.

"You get too close to me, boy, and I will soak your head in this here bucket! One of you better see if that doc is on his way before I die!"

Rider and Will stepped outside the bunkhouse to wait for the doctor.

Just then, they saw Joseph ride into sight followed by a carriage. "Here they come now." said Rider as he watched Joseph dismount.

"That was a fast trip, Joseph."

"I met Doc up the road. He said that he had just delivered a calf at old man Downing's farm. Lucky for Hank that he was so close."

Will called out to the doctor, "Sure glad you are here, Doc. Hank's carrying on like his leg is broken, but his ankle just got twisted a little."

Driving his old rickety carriage over to the barn, the doctor hopped out. "Well, I better have a look. If I remember Hank from town a few days ago, he is not a young fellow."

After examining Hank's foot, he explained that it was a very bad sprain. Hank's shoulder and arm was bruised, too. Just then, Jesse walked back inside the bunkhouse to get the report about Hank's condition.

"This man cannot be moving around for at least two weeks. He is going to need constant care." Looking around the bunkhouse, the doctor noticed that it would be impossible for Hank to remain out here by himself.

After describing the care that Hank was going to need, it was decided that it would be best if he were settled in the house. Ollie, along with Rae's help, could take care of him.

As Jesse and the doctor walked to the house, Jesse was wishing that he had finished the loft room for a fourth bedroom. *Great, Hank will have to bunk in my room with me—but not in my bed!*

Before entering the kitchen door, both men removed their boots. Rae was in the kitchen with her hands full of piecrust. Ollie was cutting some potatoes that she would fry later with some sliced onions for the supper meal. Both ladies were surprised to see the young doctor with Jesse.

"Mercy me," said Ollie. "Come right in here, young man. You must be the doctor." Before he could answer, she went on talking. "Tell us all about Hank—what I can do for him. But first, let me gets you all some coffee and a platter of my fresh baked cookies."

The doctor smiled as he took in every inch of Rae standing at the counter. *She's still as beautiful as I remember her to be,* he thought.

"Yes, ma'am, coffee and fresh cookies sound wonderful. I haven't eaten since early this morning."

Rae hurried over to the dry sink and poured a bowl of water and rinsed her hands so she could get the cups down and serve them.

"It is so nice to see you again, Mrs. Rivers. I will have to look at your head while I am here. How have you been? Any headaches, dizzy spells, or …?" While questioning Rae and looking at her lovely face, the doctor completely forgot what he had been saying.

"I'm fine, really," she said, giving him a shy, sweet smile.

Jesse was standing at the table with both hands on his hips, waiting to be noticed. Rae and the doctor didn't seem to know that anyone else was in the room.

Clearing his throat, Jesse said, "You know, doctor, I have never heard your name. What do people call you besides 'Doc'?" Jesse had a very rude tone.

After realizing that he had been almost in a trance, he said, "Oh, I guess you are right. It seemed we didn't take the time to formally introduce ourselves in town. My name is Tim O'Riley. I am from the big city of Houston."

"Now, that we know your name, tell Ollie and Rae what they will need to do to help Hank get back on his feet. I am going to the bunkhouse. I need to make arrangements to have a bed carried into my bedroom. We need to get Hank settled so he can rest this afternoon, like you suggested," said Jesse to the doctor.

It was like transporting an ornery old mule into the house. First, the bunk bed had to be set up and placed in the room near the window. Hank came next, bellowing like a bull moose and cussing a blue streak at the men who carried him. After some laudanum was forced down his throat, his foot wrapped tight, and the arm placed in a sling, came peace. *What a nice sound,* thought Jesse.

When Jesse came back into the kitchen, he found the table all set. The food smelled so good. Ollie was taking up the potatoes that she had fried with onions in pork grease. The smell of apple pies made his stomach ache from hunger. This was wonderful. Peace and good food.

As he turned around, Tim O'Riley was standing beside him, announcing how much he was going to enjoy this wonderful home-cooked meal.

Ollie had insisted that he stay for dinner. "Nobody leaves my home hungry, no sir. Now everyone just sit down so we can serve up this good, hot meal."

Jesse's stomach tightened into a knot. He didn't want the doctor to stay ... to be here ... near Rae? What was wrong with him? Was he jealous? Who of? Rae and the doc? No! *You idiot! You better get a grip on your feelings, whatever they are,* thought Jesse as he took his seat. Th e others

kept up the conversation, so he managed to get through the meal without having to talk to the doctor.

"Ma'am, I have to say to you and Miss Rae that this is the best supper I have had since arriving in town," the doctor said as he slid his chair back to stand. "Thank you so much for the invitation."

"Go on with your young self!" said Ollie and giggled.

"Now Rae, you go with the doctor and let him look at your head. I know that cut is all right, but I want the doc to say so. Run on! Go sit in the swing and visit for a while. I will take care of the kitchen," instructed Ollie.

Rae didn't know what to do. She knew she should do as Ollie said, but Jesse's behavior toward the doctor was strange. He kept giving the doctor suspicious looks, especially when the doctor's conversation was directed to her.

"If you are sure ..." Rae looked at Ollie and then shyly looked at Jesse.

"Go ahead," grumbled Jesse to Rae. "I will give Ollie a hand with the table." Ollie's mouth fell open, but she didn't say anything. It had been years since Jesse helped her clean up the kitchen.

"Come, Rae. Let me grab my bag out of the bedroom, and I will meet you at the swing on the porch."

Rae glanced at Hope who was lying on the floor on her stomach, looking at a book, and then she went out to the swing.

"What a crazy afternoon you had around here today. I am so happy that your baby didn't get injured by that new bull of Jess's! Hank will heal, but it will take a few weeks. The hardest part of his recovery will be keeping him down. Mercy. Just listen to me. I haven't shut up since I walked out of the house." The doctor laughed.

"You are so funny," said Rae.

"And you are beautiful. Goodness! I was thinking that. I can't believe I said that aloud." He laughed at himself.

"Thank you for the compliment anyway," said Rae.

The doctor opened his bag and took out a soft cloth to wipe Rae's forehead after removing the bandage. After instructing her to hold back her hair, he removed the bandage ever so slowly.

"How does it look to you, Doc? Ollie has been keeping it clean and dressed almost every day," said Jesse as he came through the screen door onto the porch.

Rae and the doctor were both speechless and surprised to see Jesse come out of the house so soon.

"I thought you were helping Ollie," said Rae.

"Oh, we have finished. Everything is put away. Well, what do you have to say about the cut? All well? No more bandages?" *No more visits from the doctor,* thought Jesse to himself.

"Ollie has done a fine job. You do not need a bandage, and I am sure you will not have a scar."

"Thank you so much for everything," said Rae as she stood to go back inside. "I am sure I will see you again when you come to check on Hank."

Chapter 7

Frisco City

Herbert was almost sure that Rae had driven to Junction Creek to catch the stagecoach. After making an inquiry in the stagecoach office, he still didn't know where she was going. The clerk inside said that a young lady with a small child did purchase two tickets for the stage, but he wasn't at liberty to say where she was going.

Herbert realized that he was going to have to let the people of Rosedale know that Hope had been missing for a few days. Everyone thought that Rae and Hope had gone to Claire's sister's home in Peamont, Texas, a few days after the funeral.

Herbert walked down to the newspaper office that also printed reward posters and fliers. He needed posters to place around town, and fliers that he could put on the stagecoach to be carried to other towns.

After leaving a description of Hope, the date she came up missing, and a sizeable reward, he felt like rejoicing. *Now, Miss Rae, it won't be long,* he said to himself. After I get the new fliers on the stagecoach to be delivered to the other towns, you will be back here quick enough.

I better visit with the marshal and let him know how concerned I am over my missing child, he thought. *Maybe I will even shed a tear*. He laughed out loud.

Chapter 8

After declaring that Rae's head injury was all well and seeing that Hank was fast asleep, the doctor took his leave, explaining that he would return in two days. He wanted to make sure that Hank's arm and shoulder were healing, and the swelling in his foot had gone down.

The following morning was to be an example of how the next few days would be. Hank woke up fussing and complaining about someone helping with his personal needs. He claimed that everyone was trying to starve him and that he was bored out of his mind.

Ollie took on the chore of taking care of Hank, while Rae cooked him a special breakfast. Hope took on the job of entertaining him with her storybooks and dolly.

Rae and Ollie cooked delicious meals, cleaned the house, and worked in the vegetable garden. They made a good work team. Ollie enjoyed telling Rae stories about Jesse and Will when they were little. Hope followed underfoot with her dolly, and every day Rae made special time for a visit to the barn to see the puppy.

In the evenings after putting Hope to bed, Rae would sit in the swing on the porch. Jesse never came out to join her. He seemed to be keeping his distance. Rae wished that he would join her so she could get to know him a little better. A few evenings, Rider and Joseph walked over from the bunkhouse and talked for a while. Will spent his evenings in the bedroom with Hank, talking about the events of the day.

Life is good here, thought Rae, using her foot to push the swing back and forth. Thinking back before her mama passed away, Rae never felt safe in her own home with Herbert lurking around every door. Going to bed here was heavenly. No more wondering if Herbert was going to enter her room or grab at her body when she walked by him. *Yes,* she thought as she looked out into the darkness, *this is a wonderful place.*

After Rae had been at the ranch for ten days, Jesse came out on the porch. He did not attempt to sit with her in the swing, but instead he paced back and forth for a few minutes. Finally, he asked, "Uh, I was wondering if you would like to ride into town with me tomorrow. I have got to check on a few things at the bank and get some supplies. Ollie has a long list. I thought maybe you could fill her list at the store and pick up a few things you may need for yourself and the baby."

Rae was so shocked that he f nally had spoken to her. She couldn't believe that he wanted her to go somewhere with him. She just sat and looked at him.

Jesse was looking at Rae, waiting for her answer. Rae wanted to shout for joy. Jesse noticed that she lit up like a Christmas tree with excitement.

"Oh, I would love to go into town with you. It has been months since I have been to a town to shop," said Rae. Since Mama had been so ill, she never left her bedside. Herbert would bring home the things they needed.

Realizing that she didn't have any funds brought a frown to her face.

Guessing what she was thinking, Jesse said, "If you need something, I can give you an advance on your wages."

"Oh, really? That would be nice of you. In that case, I would like to go," she said with excitement in her voice. "I will have to bring Hope. I couldn't ask Ollie to watch her for that long with Hank laid up and with all the cooking. She really is a handful," said Rae very quickly, hoping that Jesse wouldn't change his mind about taking her along.

"Fine, fine," replied Jesse. He wanted to have her all to himself, but he couldn't deny her reasons for wanting to take the child. "We will leave after breakfast," he said and walked into the house.

*****

True to his word, Jesse was hitched up and ready to leave the ranch soon after breakfast. Rae was so excited to be going into town, she could hardly sit still on the wagon bench. Jesse joked that she was going to bounce off the wagon. As they were traveling toward town, they passed a herd of Texas longhorns. Hope clapped her hands and laughed at the funny-looking cows with the long, pointed horns.

Most of the cowpunchers were saddle-weary and lonely. Some had been on the dusty trail drive for months. Several of the men waved as they passed. They looked very dirty, thirsty, hungry, and tired. The herd had stopped outside of Limason and was grazing on the green grass. The cowpunchers would go into town in two diff erent shifts. Most of the men were looking for the same thing; a drink, a hot bath, and the friendly face of a pretty girl.

"There won't be any peace in town tonight," said Jesse. "I hope Sheriff Murphy is back from his trip. Sometimes the cowboys can get pretty wild and shoot up the town. They really don't mean any harm. Just letting off some steam."

"Are they taking the herd to Frisco City?" asked Rae.

"Yep. They will take the cattle to the stockyard, and when they are sold, they will be loaded in boxcars. The train will carry them somewhere up north."

As they traveled nearly a mile, they could still see part of the herd and hear the bawling sounds in the distance. The smell of the cattle still lingered in the air.

"With the cattle drives coming so close to Limason, the few businesses that we have really thrive. They are all ready to accommodate the rowdy cowboys. Without them, I doubt the stores and bank could stay open," stated Jesse.

When they reached town, Main street was bustling with people, horses, and carriages. The cool change in the temperature had brought the farmers and ranchers into town to purchase items for fall.

"Is this small town always so busy?" Rae was looking around at the weathered old signs above the storefronts and the whitewashed boardwalks.

The main street was reddish brown dirt that would turn into a mud pie of sludge when it rained. Tied to hitching posts in front of buildings were horses with fresh manure in the street around them and horseflies buzzing all about.

"There is always a lot of excitement when there is a trail drive nearby," Jesse commented.

"I am going to drop you off here in front of the store. Mr. Smith will help you fill Ollie's list. Tell him to put everything on my account—even the things that you choose for yourself. I will drive the rig down to the livery, and then I have to take care of some business. See you in a little while."

Giving Jesse a small wave good-bye, Rae and Hope went into the store. Mr. Smith, the proprietor, was busy with another customer, but he didn't take his eyes off Rae. He had not seen this little beauty since she had left town with Jesse Maxwell.

Mrs. Smith looked up from her account book and slammed it shut. She knew Rae was the new lady from the stage coach. "My goodness, good morning. You must be the young lady that Mr. Smith told me about. I see the cut on your head is all well. This must be your darling little girl. Gracious, listen to me go on. My name is Judith Smith. You met Mr. Smith on the stagecoach. My husband and I own this store. We are so glad to have you here. What can I do for you today?"

Rae could only nod at Mrs. Smith. *She certainly is a chatterbox,* she thought.

Rae stretched out her hand with Ollie's list, attempting to say that she needed to have it filled. Mrs. Smith grabbed the list, looked it over, and said, "I see Ollie has her list made out ever so neat. I know that Ollie is enjoying having a baby to care for," she said as she hurried off to fill the order.

"Whew," whispered Rae to Hope, "she is like a hummingbird fluttering all about."

Rae had Hope's hand as they circled around the tables of piece goods.

"Hope, look. They have pretty pieces of material. What do you like?" Hope wasn't interested in anything but the candy counter.

Hope pulled on Rae's hand until she finally got free. She walked over to the counter that had jars of stick candy. All colors. She lifted her small hand and touched each jar, saying, "I want this one, this one, and this one.

When Rae did not immediately respond, she demanded, "Mama, Rae, Rae. I want candy. Hurry and get me some candy *now.*"

"Hope," whispered Rae as she stooped down to get her attention. "You know how to use your manners and say please. You do not yell in the store demanding candy."

"Please." Hope hung her head and pouted. "Now, I want the red one."

Rae stood and sighed. "Mrs. Smith, could you please give me one red stick of candy so my baby can enjoy it now? Just add it to Mr. Maxwell's account. I will be picking out a few more things."

"Now, Hope, you just sit right here on this window seat and do not move. Eat your candy while I shop for a few things. Understand?"

Rae busied herself in selecting some tooth powder, a bar of ready-made soap that smelled like roses, and two skeins of pink yarn. She would start on a hat and gloves for Hope before it got to be cold weather. Happy with her selections, she turned to look at Hope, whom she had left sitting at the window, looking out. She wasn't there.

Rae nearly panicked for a minute. Hope was gone. *Be calm,* she said to herself. She started looking around in the store. "Mrs. Smith, have you seen my little girl? She was sitting over there by the window a few minutes ago."

Mrs. Smith and Rae walked around the store in search of Hope.

Neither of them noticed that Hope had slid off the window seat. She had been watching a kitten stroll on the boardwalk toward the store.

"Here kitty, here kitty," called Hope to the pretty black-and-white kitten that she had watched from the store window. Hope was holding out her candy as an offering to the soft, fluff y kitten. "Please kitty, wait for me!" She started running as fast as her little legs would carry her right behind the cat. She wasn't looking where she was going—her little eyes focused only on her prey; the kitty.

Jumping off the boardwalk into the street, the kitten pranced right out in the middle and sat down. When he lifted his hind leg to scratch behind his ear, it gave Hope the opportunity to make a grab for it. Before she could put her hands on the kitty, the long arms of a stranger lifted her and rushed across the road to the safety of the boardwalk. Two cowboys raced pass on down the street.

"Hey, pretty thing, what are you doing out in the street by yourself? Where are your folks?" asked Sheriff Murphy, giving this lovely child a tight squeeze as he held her. Hope was twisting and pushing at him to let her down. "I want that kitty," she cried.

"Sorry, baby, but the kitten has run off ." Putting her down, he said, "Take my hand and lead me to where you left your mama and pa." Looking up the boardwalk, Sheriff Murphy realized that he was going to meet the child's mama in about two seconds.

"Hope, darling, why did you leave the store? I have been scared to death," said Rae, bending down toward Hope and giving her a little shake.

Glancing up from Hope, Rae saw the sheriff 's badge pinned to the chest of the man who had his hand on Hope's shoulder. Clutching Hope's hand tighter than she should have, she gave the man a shy smile.

"I was just bringing her to find you, ma'am. I am the sheriff of this town. I believe you are the young lady that Tim—or Doc as most people call him—told me about."

"Yes, I guess I am. The doctor took care of me when I fell out of the stagecoach and hit my head. I am much better now, and I will be moving on soon."

"Hate to hear that. This town could use some pretty young ladies like yourself."

"Thank you. Come, Hope, let's get back to the store so we can be ready when Jesse returns."

"So, you are staying at the Maxwell's place?"

"Yes, for now," replied Rae.

"How is Ollie? I love to drop by there at dinnertime. That old woman can put on a spread of good food like no other."

"She is well, but one of the men who works on the ranch hurt his ankle real bad. Do you know Hank?" asked Rae.

"Yes, I know him. Gosh, I hate to hear that! I will have to ride out and give him a visit—and I will have to arrive close to lunch or dinnertime."

The sheriff laughed. "Sure good meeting you, Mrs. ....?"

"Rivers, my name is Rivers. I am from Russellville."

"Like I said, nice meeting you, Mrs. Rivers, and tell Hank that I will be out to see him soon." The sheriff tipped his hat and walked on his way.

Rae stood frozen in fear for a few seconds. She didn't think that the sheriff had heard any news about her and Hope. He certainly didn't act like he knew. *Good for now,* she thought as she tried to appear calm.

Jesse had completed his business at the bank. He felt good about being able to pay his property taxes early. There had been a few lean years when he didn't think that the ranch would make enough to cover all their expenses. The ranch was thriving now with the new horses, hay and cornfields. The new calves he had purchased were growing, and the hogs were producing many little piglets. The hogs and some of the hay were his biggest cash crops for now. Later, with the new bull, he hoped that his ranch would be considered a horse and cattle ranch.

As he was walking over to the store to check on Rae, he passed Sheriff Murphy. "Welcome home, fellow. Good to have you back," said Jesse, giving the sheriff a good pat on the shoulder.

"Thanks, good to be home. I like the big cities for a day or two, but that is all. Too many folks. I met your houseguest and her child a little bit ago. Mrs. Rivers? Pretty girl."

"Yes, she is that now. Were you at the store just now?"

"No, I met her on the boardwalk." The sheriff went on to tell Jesse how he grabbed up the little girl out of the street.

"That child is something else. She is little, but she is like a keg of dynamite. At her age, she must be watched every minute. Her mama is a tigress when it comes to protecting that little cub of hers. I gave the child a slap on the bottom, and for a minute I thought my life was in danger." said Jesse with a snicker. "It's kinda funny now, but it wasn't then."

The sheriff laughed out loud at the expressions on Jesse's face as he told the story about the bull, the baby, and Hank's accident.

"Sounds like it has been anything but dull at your place," said Sheriff Murphy. "Tell Hank I will be out to see him real soon," he said as he entered his office.

Jesse went into the store to gather Rae and Hope to head home. Rae looked like she had seen a ghost. Her face was white, and she appeared very nervous. He walked by her and asked if everything was ready. Mrs. Smith was chatting away about the contents of the list. Jesse carried one basket of items out and returned to get the other one. Mr. Smith had finalized his business with the other customer.

"I'm sorry I haven't had the time to visit with you, Mrs. Rivers. Glad to hear that you have recovered from the accident. Tim has been keeping me informed about you. Now, uh," looking over his shoulder before he continued, "if I can ever do anything for you, uh, please let me know."

"Thanks, Smithy," said Jesse sarcastically as he passed by them, carrying a fifty-pound bag of sugar. "My houseguest will not need anything that I can't help her with."

Jesse had made a pallet in the back of the wagon for Hope. It had been a long morning, and he was sure that she would be ready for a nap. As he helped Rae up on the seat, she looked all around and asked, "Does this town have a place for people to go and attend to their personal needs?" She was embarrassed from the tip of her head down to her toes for having to ask such a question.

"You need to go to an outhouse?" asked Jesse, making sure he understood exactly what she needed.

When Rae just stared at him like he had two heads, he stammered,

"Yes, no, I mean ..." Realizing that he had to do something, he looked around.

"I can stop at the rooming house and ask Flo ... anyway it is a nice, clean place, and I am sure she will help."

Once they drove up to the rooming house, Jesse saw Flo sweeping the front walk. "Whoa," called Jesse, and he pulled on the horses until they stopped at the gate.

"My, my, look who's here." Flo said as she walked up to the wagon, patting her silver-gray bun. "Climb on down, young man. Who you got with you?"

"Miss Flo, this is Mrs. Rivers and her child. She just arrived in town."

"Stop right there; I've got no rooms to let. This is a full house."

"Thanks anyway, Miss Flo, but we are headed to my ranch, and these two ladies need to go or use your, uh, outbuilding."

As Jesse strutted over what he needed, Hope's blonde curls appeared over the wagon's side and announced that she had to pee. "Now, Mama, now!"

Miss Flo burst out laughing and motioned with her hand for them to follow her. As they walked around the back of the house, she couldn't keep her eyes off this beautiful child. Seeing this little girl made her miss her five-year-old granddaughter.

Jesse was so relieved that problem was solved. He walked over to a rocker on the front porch and sat down. He wasn't used to taking care of girls.

Out of the screen door, Mary Lou, one of the ladies that Jesse had spent time with, slithered behind him and placed her lily-white hands over his eyes. She said, "Guess who?"

"Mary Lou?" guessed Jesse, praying that he was wrong. Then she moved around the rocker and stood between his knees. "Hello, nice to see you," he said as he looked her over in the flimsy wrapper.

"Where have you been?" Her lips pouted as she straddled his legs and sat in his lap.

Jesse tried to lift her off him as he said, "Please, Mary Lou, I didn't come calling on you. I have a lady and her child with me. They needed to take care of something, and Flo is helping them."

Mary Lou was not giving up, and she attempted to persuade him to stay by placing baby kisses on his chin and neck. Just as Jesse was trying again to remove her from his lap, Flo and the girls came from around the side of the house. Immediately Flo took in Jesse's predicament.

"Mary Lou. Scat on upstairs and get some decent clothes on. You know better than to be out here in public dressed like that. I run a decent place here."

Rae was so shocked to see Jesse wrapped up in the arms of a "woman like that." This man was just insufferable. She walked past him, grabbed up the baby, and practically tossed her in the back of the wagon. Jesse raced over to assist Rae up on the wagon seat. She pulled her arm loose from his touch and climbed up by herself. She sat down in a huff and glared straight ahead, leaving Jesse to give a thank-you to his friend, Miss Flo.

Before Jesse even got in the wagon, Rae's forehead was throbbing from the rage building up in her.

After making sure the girls were settled in the wagon and traveling a few miles toward the ranch, Jesse tried to explain his conduct with Mary Lou to Rae. Rae wasn't having any explanation. All she said was, "Mr. Maxwell, what you do and whom you do it with, is none of my affair. Please. Do not bother to explain your actions to me."

Not another sound was uttered from those clenched lips of hers. Her back was ramrod straight, and her hands were clutched together.

Jesse noted that one good bump, and Miss Goody Two-shoes would go bouncing right off the wagon seat. All that was missing was smoke coming out the top of her head.

Rae's reaction to Jesse as he was trying to give her an explanation about the embarrassing situation had gotten his temper riled. *She doesn't know who she is sitting beside,* he thought. He could handle her cantankerous attitude toward him. *If she doesn't want to talk to me, well fine. Two can play at this game.*

When the wagon pulled up to the front of the house, Rae didn't wait for Jesse to help her. She leaped from the seat to the ground and hurried to the side of the wagon to lift Hope out. The baby had fallen asleep when the wagon started home, and she lay all curled up on the blankets.

Rae attempted to reach the baby when Jess appeared at her side and said, "I will carry her." When Rae opened her mouth to put up a fuss, he gave her a hard, cold look that meant he would brook no argument.

Rae gathered up her skirt and raced into the house, passing by Ollie and Will without speaking. She went into her room and turned Hope's bedcovers back. When Jesse came in carrying Hope, he ignored the couple sitting at the table.

Ollie whispered to Will, "Looks like the trip wasn't a happy time for two people." Will agreed with the nod of his head.

Will went out to the wagon and started bringing in the things that were purchased in town. Jesse came storming out of the house and let the screen door slam. He grabbed up the fifty-pound bag of sugar and carried it down in the cellar.

When he came back up, Will said, "Maybe you should stay down there until you cool off ."

Without looking at Will, Jesse said, "Back off , boy. Leave me alone."

In her room, Rae changed her clothes and put away the few items that she had charged on Jesse's account at the store. She put on her apron and walked out to the kitchen to see Ollie. "What can I do to help with supper?"

Ollie laughed and said, "Maybe you better set the table. It is not good for the food to have a person filled with anger stirring the pots. Food should have gentle, loving hands caring for it."

Rae was so surprised by Ollie's statement that she burst out laughing.

She walked over and placed her arms around Ollie's waist and said, "You make me ashamed of my behavior." This is the way Jesse found Rae and Ollie, all hugged together.

Chapter 9

As Sheriff Murphy entered his office, he couldn't wait to get a good cup of coffee, sit in his desk chair, and relax. He knew he would have mail to sort through, but there was never anything exciting. As he walked in the door, the first thing he saw was Joey.

"Hey, hey, look who's back," said Joey, the young man who watched the office for him while he was away.

"I see you have made yourself at home," the sheriff said, noticing the young pup stretched out in his chair, smoking a cigarette.

"When did you take up smoking?" Joey looked at his cigarette, but before he could answer, the sheriff said, "Put that stinking thing out."

The sheriff looked around his office and was surprised to see that everything looked in order. "Thanks for watching the place for me. Now, get your behind out of my chair. I'm bushed."

Joey got up and gave a big stretch. "Glad to have helped out. You know, the ladies like a man in charge." Tipping his hat toward the sheriff , he went out the door, laughing.

The sheriff got up and poured himself a big cup of fresh coffee and picked up the pile of mail. The first thing he noticed was a wanted poster.

Reward

$500.00

Missing child

Blonde hair, brown eyes
Name: Hope Summers
Age: 3
Please Notify Local Authorities
Child believed to have wandered off or been kidnapped

"Gosh oh mighty," exclaimed the sheriff to the empty office. He just had that child in his arms. Hope? Yes, that is the name her mama called her.

Her mama? *How can this child be missing if she is with her mama?* Sheriff Murphy leaned back in his chair to ponder this situation. He didn't want to jump to conclusions just because the child was called Hope—but the blonde hair? And her age? She looked to be about three. He decided that he had better ride out to Jesse's and find out more about Mrs. Rivers. If he left now, Ollie would be cooking supper, and he could do with a good home-cooked meal.

*****

"Supper will be on the table in about ten minutes, Jesse," announced Ollie. "Did you get everything on my list while in town?" When no answer came from him, she let it go. *I will get to the bottom of what took place on this trip sooner or later,* she said to herself, while looking at Rae and Jesse.

When Ollie stepped out on the porch to ring the dinner bell, a rider on a horse was coming toward the ranch house.

"Jess," called Ollie. "We've got company coming. Come out and greet whoever it is."

The other hands all filed into the kitchen and took their places at the table. "Hey," bellowed Hank from the back room, "when am I going to get to eat? Is anybody out there?"

"Lord have mercy on me," swore Ollie, and she waddled into the room with Hank. "Land sakes, Mr. Hank, we thought you were still sleeping.

Now you just hush making all this here racket before you wake up honey child. I will have Miss Rae bring you a tray." She turned to go back to the kitchen.

Coming in the kitchen door when Ollie entered the room was Jesse with Sheriff Murphy. "Look who came calling on you, Ollie," said the sheriff, giving her a big, teasing grin.

"Go on with yourself, Sheriff . Truth be known, you came hoping I would have something good to eat," she replied, laughing. "Well, you got here just in time. Move down, boys, and make room for the sheriff . He will need plenty of elbow room."

Jesse and the sheriff waited to see if Rae was going to take a seat, but she waved them to sit down. She excused herself, saying that she was making a plate for Hank. She would eat with him tonight.

Hank was so thankful to have Rae's company for the meal. He told her that he was going crazy in that room all day. He needed to get well and get back to work.

"The doctor is coming out tomorrow. Maybe he will let you use some crutches now that your shoulder and arm are better. You could sit in the rocking chair in the front room. Ollie and I can always use an extra hand peeling potatoes," teased Rae.

Once Rae was sure that dinner was over and all the men, especially Jesse, had left the house, she said, "Hank, Ollie will be in to help you get ready for bed in a little while. I better go and help clean the kitchen."

"Did you have a nice trip into town today?" asked Hank as she was leaving the room.

She turned and gave him a crooked smile. "It was interesting."

*****

After dinner, the sheriff and Jesse had taken a walk to the corral with the pretense to see the new bull. Rae glanced out the kitchen window and could see them talking. Whatever they were discussing seemed to have upset Jesse. He was waving his hands and shaking his head.

Placing her hand on her throbbing forehead, she walked back to the table to begin clearing it. She was going to go to bed early tonight.

Outside the barn, Sheriff Murphy and Jesse were still discussing Rae's situation. "Look, Jess, you are going to have to just ask her. If you don't want to question her, I will. I have a strong feeling her baby is the one who is missing. Maybe she's running from her husband. Whatever the case, I am going to give you a day or two to talk to Mrs. Rivers, and then I will have to do my duty," instructed the sheriff.

Jesse looked up at the sheriff. "What do you mean, your duty?"

"I will have to come back out here and question her myself. I have to know for sure."

"I will get to the bottom of this. Thanks for coming out and telling me about this first. I will see you tomorrow with her answers." *With the truth, I hope,* thought Jesse.

Jesse walked into the barn and slowly moved from one animal to another, giving each a pat. He rubbed his horse's nose and gave him a small sugar cube as he was thinking about Rae. He rubbed his horse's right leg, picked up his right hoof, and looked it over. He stood, thinking that he had suspected all along that she wasn't telling him the truth about why she was on the stagecoach. Being a widow? That's bull hockey for sure.

Now, with her as mad as any old bantam rooster, he was going to have to get some truthful facts from her. And get them he would, starting now. He gave the horse one more pat and whispered a sweet word into his ear. With a full head of steam, he started walking to the house.

The men were all walking out of the house, heading to the bunkhouse.

"Hey Jess, what have you and the sheriff been talking about?" quizzed Will.

"Oh, nothing. He was telling me about his trip to Frisco City, that's all. See you boys in the morning." Waving at the men, he went into the house.

Rae was standing at the dry sink with a dishrag in her hand. Ollie was in the back room helping to get Hank all settled in for the night. Hope was in the front room sitting in the rocking chair with a book. Jess took in all the activity going on.

He strolled over to the rocking chair and looked down on the lovely child. "What kind of book are you looking at?" She replied with pouted lips, "Don't talk to me," hiding her face behind the book.

Jesse lifted his shoulders as he glanced over at Rae and said, "I guess she hasn't forgiven me yet." He went into the back room to visit with Hank.

Rae couldn't help but feel bad for Jesse. This wasn't the first time that he tried to warm up to Hope. She was going to have to talk to Hope about her behavior toward him. *And what about your behavior?* She said to her reflection in the kitchen window.

Thinking to herself, she realized that she really didn't have any reason to be mad at Jesse for his display on the porch with that "girl." Whoever he wanted to associate with had nothing to do with her. *He has been very gracious to us. Taking us into his home and giving me a job,* thought Rae. *I can't believe how ugly I was to him this afternoon. What must he think of me?*

"Rae," Jesse called to her as he stood across the kitchen from her.

"My Lord, I didn't know that you were back in the kitchen. I nearly jumped out of my skin," said Rae, looking down at the floor.

"Sorry, I didn't mean to scare you. Listen, I know that you are tired from the trip today, but I must talk with you. Ollie will put Hope to bed. Come out on the porch after you tell her good night." He paused, "Please."

She nodded *yes*, and he went out the door.

Ollie came strolling into the kitchen and took Rae by the hand. "Listen to me, child. I don't know what happened today between you and Mr. Jess, but you are a part of this here family to me. I never let Mr. Maxwell or his boys go off to bed mad with each other. And well, you and Jess needs to settle whatever is eating at you. I can't abide anger and family members being unkind to each other. Understand me?"

For an answer, Rae wrapped her arms around Ollie as tears filled her eyes. She couldn't speak, so she shook her head *yes* as she laid her forehead on Ollie's shoulder. After a warm hug and pat on her back, she turned and walked to her room.

Rae knew that she had stalled as long as she could, so she went out to meet Jesse. He had been sitting in the swing, waiting. He stood when he saw her at the screen door and met her before she could sit.

"Let's go for a walk. I don't want anyone overhearing our conversation." He guided her down the steps and led the way toward the apple orchard.

The moon was full, and the stars were twinkling spots of light. It was a lovely evening. *Sad,* Jesse thought. *We're fixing to have fireworks, and the mood will be destroyed.*

"I know you are wondering why I asked you out here this evening." He turned toward her and leaned back against a tree.

"Yes," she answered so softly he barely heard her.

"We are going to have a "go-to-a-church-house meeting.""

"What?" She was surprised at what Jesse had said and not quite understanding.

"My pa would have a meeting like this when he wanted to get the truth out of me. When he asked me about something and if I told him the truth, then I was forgiven. Most of the time—if you get my drift." Jesse couldn't see Rae's face, but he could feel the tension coming from her.

"All right," she said, gritting her teeth, "start your meeting."

"There will be only the truth spoken. Lies and half-truths are left unspoken. Do I make myself clear?" said Jesse, setting the rules of the meeting. A movement of her head was the only answer he received.

"I can't help you if I don't know what is wrong," he continued. Waiting for a response and receiving none. "Sheriff Murphy had a reason for coming out to see me this afternoon. He found a wanted poster on his desk when he got back in town." Still no comment out of Rae.

"The wanted poster is for a missing child with a $500 reward."

"What does this have to do with me?" asked Rae, getting a little nervous.

Jesse didn't bother to answer her but continued, "Rae, where is your husband? Who are you running away from, if not your husband?" She was still very quiet.

"Is Hope your child?" demanded Jesse. "Remember, I said the truth and nothing but the truth!"

"Why are asking me these questions?" Rae was getting very nervous.

The moonlight shined down on her face and Jesse knew that he had hit on something to do with her past. "I told you everything before. Just because Sheriff Murphy has a poster with a missing child doesn't mean that it is Hope or has anything to do with me."

"The poster says that the child is three years old and her name is Hope Summers. She is believed to have wandered off or been kidnapped." He waited for a reply, but none came.

"Please, Rae, the truth. Confide in me, let me help," pleaded Jesse.

"How do I know that I can trust you?" snapped Rae, surprising even herself that she blurted out a comment like that. Covering her mouth with one hand and picking up the front of her dress with the other, she tried to dart pass Jesse. He guessed her reaction and pulled her to a sudden stop.

"Stand still," he whispered. "Keep your voice down before we have the men coming out here." He turned her loose and placed both of his hands on top of her shoulders. "Rae, why would you think that you can't trust me? Haven't I done everything I said I would for you and your child since you have been here?"

Rae stood as still as the night, not moving a muscle. She seemed to be terrified. Rae's mind was racing with wild, terrifying thoughts. *I don't really know this man or any of these people. They may think that I have no right to Hope. They may feel that I have stolen her away from her father. They might take Hope from me and give her to the sheriff. Oh, I will die before I let Herbert get his hands on my little sister.*

Jess attempted to pull Rae into his arms. He wanted to comfort her, hold her close. She pushed him away and stood with her arms folded around her waist with her fists clenched, fighting back angry tears.

"Listen, Jesse, please allow me to go inside. I will tell you all you want to know about me tomorrow night. Please give me a little time. I am too upset to talk right now."

Jesse could see that she looked like she wanted to throw up her guts.

She hadn't been prepared to have been caught so soon. He knew that something like this was coming and damn, if it didn't upset him, too.

"Well, I guess it will be better to talk when you aren't so tired. But Rae, be prepared to tell me everything. Please remember that you can trust me," he said as he took her arm and guided her back to the house.

Jesse's hand wrapped around the top part of her arm felt like a searing hot poker. She was caught and felt trapped. They knew part of the truth, but she couldn't trust them. She had to leave and find a safe haven far away from Herbert's reach. At least Jesse was giving her a little time to think; and plan.

Entering the house, Ollie had banked the fire in the fireplace and distinguished all the lanterns except one sitting in the middle of the kitchen table. She had gone to bed after tufting in Hope for the night.

The only sound in the house was the snoring coming from Hank. Rae wondered how Jesse could sleep in the same room with him.

Rae got her small carpetbag from under her bed. She packed a few changes of clothes and her personal items. She packed as many of Hope's things as possible, but she couldn't make the bag too heavy. She needed to rest while waiting for Jesse to come inside for the night. She was going to need every ounce of strength that she had to carry Hope and the carpetbag, but carry her she would, even if it killed her.

Chapter 10

Rosedale

A crowd had gathered around the sheriff 's office as he was nailing up the reward poster about Hope.

"Where is Rae?" one of the women in the group yelled.

"Mr. Summers said that she is staying at her aunt's place in Peamont, where the child came up missing. He wanted Rae to be there just in case his child is found and brought back home. They have had a search party looking for her these past three or four days. There's a lot of forest surrounding that home place."

Several of the ladies had their heads together discussing how they could help Mr. Summers. "The poor thing, losing Claire and now his beautiful little girl."

"What about Rae? I know that she is about crazy with worry. Why, that child is her whole life. You know the baby called her 'mama' most all the time," spoke up another lady in the group.

Herbert was at the bank locked in his office. He was filtering some of the money back into the safe so his teller could balance the books one more time. He was going to make his move as soon as the authorities found Rae.

Sawyer will balance the books at the end of the month, he thought. "Then, *I* will remove the cash out of the safe afterward and fly away. I am going on a business trip," he said, laughing to himself, "but never to return. I would love to see Sawyer's face when he finds all the money gone." He giggled like a young schoolgirl.

Herbert had been planning this trip for a while. He had just been waiting for Claire to pass on. Lord, it took her forever to die, even with the special toddy he started giving her. Their secret. Rae didn't know about the health drink he gave her mama to make her stronger. He laughed as he remembered her drinking it and saying how much better she felt. She would lie back and go into a deep, restful sleep. He wanted

71

her gone.

Dead. Damn her. Each morning she would wake up, and he would have to continue to be the sweet, loving husband all over again. Smiling, he said, "Until I got smart and hurried things along."

Coming back to the present, Herbert quickly closed the safe and walked over and unlocked his door.

"Sawyer," he yelled, "come in here."

When the young man hurried into the office, Herbert informed him,

"I am going to have to be gone again for a few days. Again. I want you to try and balance the books. I don't need to be worrying about the townspeople's money and their trust in us. Do I?"

Chapter 11

Jesse was trying hard to unwind from the confrontation he had with Rae. He was mentally tuckered out. The trip to town had started off pleasant and ended in disaster. He still didn't know any more about Rae's troubles. But trouble was in her future, and she was very afraid. He needed to get some rest because tomorrow night couldn't come soon enough.

After Jesse stretched out on his bed, he thought even Hank's snoring would not bother him. And it didn't. He fell into an exhausted, deep sleep.

Rae could tell that everyone in the house was sleeping. The lantern on the kitchen table had been put out, and the only sound coming from inside the house was Hank's snoring. After her eyes had adjusted to the dark, she picked up her carpetbag and, as quiet as a mouse, tiptoed to her door. She opened both doors out to the porch and walked over to the screen door.

Placing her bag down on the top step to hold the door open, she hurried back to her room. Wrapping Hope as tight as she could with a soft quilt, she again made her way across the kitchen and porch to the outside. Hope was so much heavier with the quilt, but it didn't matter. She'd made it without waking anyone.

Now, she sighed as she took her first few steps. She was on her way to freedom. Away from Jesse and the sheriff and all their questions. As she made her way out of the yard, she had a decision to make. The road in front of the ranch would take her to town. *Someone will see us for sure come daylight,* thought Rae. She realized that she would have to travel in the opposite direction and pray that there would be a town close by.

Clutching Hope as tight as possible with one arm and carrying the carpetbag with the other was an accomplishment. *So far, so good,* she thought. "I can do this, and I will," she was repeating out loud to herself as her legs were about to buckle under her.

The sky was getting lighter with each step she took. Having to stay off the main road and walk in the woods was a great feat in itself. Th e branches were slapping her in the face, and briars were pulling on her long skirt, ripping holes in the material. Her shoes weren't made for hiking, and her silk stockings were already shredded from the heavy underbrush. She had to sit down. Finding a spot cleared of weeds, she laid Hope down, tucking some of the quilt under her.

Oh, my back. It will never be the same, she thought. Things will be a little better once Hope wakes up and can walk, she reasoned. She reached for her bag and retrieved a clean cloth to wipe her face and hands. She felt so dirty from fighting all the branches, and her hands were bleeding from several scratches on her palms. She did not have any idea where she was or how far she had traveled. As her eyes searched her surroundings, she couldn't help but think that maybe she had made a big mistake in running away from the ranch.

*****

Someone was shaking and pulling on him. He was chasing a girl … running and breathing hard … he couldn't catch her … what? He said as he stopped running. His hair and chest were wet.

Jesse sat straight up in bed and looked at Ollie, "What's wrong?"

"There's trouble. I just know it. Rae and honey child are gone. They are not in the house or anywhere outside," said Ollie, and she stood wringing her hands.

"Damn, damn it!" yelled Jesse. "I should have guessed that she would try to leave." He was pulling up his jeans and looking around for his boots.

"Oh, Ollie, I'm sorry."

He reached out and pulled Ollie into his arms. "Rae is in some kind of trouble, and it concerns the baby. When Sheriff Murphy came yesterday, he had a poster. It was for a missing child, three years old, named Hope Summers. I questioned Rae last night, and she promised to tell me everything tonight," he said as he pulled on his boots and grabbed for a shirt that was hanging on a peg on the wall.

"Oh Jess, what do you think? Rae is a good girl, I knows that for sure. Something bad has happened in her past to make her run away. You find that child, and you best be gentle with her, you hear me?" Ollie could see that Jesse was boiling mad."

"Being gentle with her is the last thing I had in mind. A good thrashing is what she needs for looking me straight in the eyes and lying to me. Oh. I can't believe she did that." Seeing how concerned Ollie was, he said, "I will find her, Ollie."

Hank was now awake and staring at the two of them. He had overheard them talking and realized what had taken place.

"Jess," said Hank. "Look for her in the opposition direction of town. She's running scared, and she doesn't know this area at all. She has sense enough to stay off the main trail. Go slow. Remember she is probably carrying Sweetheart."

"Thanks for the advice, Hank. It shouldn't take long. Remember, the doctor is coming today, and maybe you can get out of this room." Jesse raced out of the house, running full speed to the barn. The sky was still dark except for deep purple and grey streaks. Ollie had already walked outside and was tossing feed to the chickens. Will was standing outside of the chicken yard talking to her.

"Hey, Jess," Will yelled as Jesse raced into the barn. "You want me to ride with you or look in a different direction?"

Jesse was wiping his horses back before placing the horse blanket on. "Not now, Will. If I haven't found her in an hour, I will be back and we'll form a search party. Ollie is pretty upset. Take care of her and give Hank a hand this morning. Ollie will have enough to do with getting breakfast for the guys."

"You can count on me, but Jess, please find them. I really care about that little girl," whispered Will as he left Jesse to finish saddling his horse.

Jesse figured that Rae had a few hours head start. She had to wait until she was sure everyone was asleep. It was almost daylight now so she couldn't have traveled too far carrying a child and a carpetbag.

He took Hank's advice and trotted his horse a little ways from the ranch and then let him walk. He looked in the woods for any signs of her. He began to notice broken branches. A young scout without any training could follow her trail.

After what seemed like forever to him, he finally spotted her. Sitting off the side of the road on a boulder, she was wiping her face and hands.

He was so damn relieved to find her. A part of him wanted to run to her and grab her up in his arms and place kisses all over her beautiful face. Another part wanted to place his hands around her neck and give her a good shaking.

As he watched, she tucked the quilt around the baby, giving her more warmth, and started humming a lullaby. She didn't seem to be aware of the danger that she was about to face.

All Jesse could remember was how frightened he felt when Ollie said that she was missing. Now, here she sat like she was at some damn tea party waiting to be served. He was so angry at the sight of her, he didn't even think that he could speak, but he did.

"Hello, Rae," he said as sweet as he could.

Rae jumped and stood. She couldn't believe that he had found her, and so quick! "How did you find me?" she asked, but received no answer.

Jesse slowly started walking toward her. She put out her hands in front of herself and said, "Don't come near me!" as the hunter advanced upon his prey.

He stopped and stood with his hands on his hips, looking straight at her. Grinding his teeth and trying hard to control his temper, he spoke to her. "You know, Rae, the worst paddling I ever got from my pa was when I lied to him. Then I ran away. Do you recognize this story?"

Jesse took another step closer to her. Rae stepped back one giant step.

"Well, you see, I thought if I ran away from Pa, that when I was found, he would be so relieved and overjoyed that I would be forgiven. Well, for me, his joy of finding me didn't create the warm reunion I thought it would have. I couldn't sit down for a week." He had taken small steps toward her as he was speaking.

"Don't you dare touch me. Back away or I will scream so loud everyone for miles will hear me."

Jesse could almost reach out and touch her, when he stopped closing in on her. He knew her running for tonight was over. She would never leave the baby, and there was no way she could grab Hope up off the ground and escape.

"You listen to me now," he said, shaking his finger in her face. "I am going to be a little more lenient with you than my pa was to me. I want an explanation as to what you were thinking to drag your baby out of bed in the dead of the night, and carry her nearly four miles in this damp air."

She took a couple of steps backward as she was looking down at the ground, moving her head back and forth, but giving no answer.

"I know you are very afraid of something or someone. Rae, I'm not stupid. But, I am very, very angry at your display of stupidity. Damn it, girl. These woods are filled with all types of wild creatures."

"I know. I'm looking at one," she snapped right back at him.

Jesse glared at her as he walked over and picked Hope off the ground. She didn't even move.

"Don't push me any further. I haven't completely given up the idea of giving you a well-deserved spanking." He recovered his horse and held the bridle tight. "Climb up and I will give you the baby. I will ride behind you both."

"What? Why can't you just lead the horse?"

Jesse looked up at the morning sunrise and prayed, "Don't let me strangle her, Lord."

When all three were settled on his horse, Jesse said into Rae's ear, "When we arrive home, the go-to-the-church meeting will begin. Again."

Ollie and Will were in the kitchen cooking breakfast when they heard Jesse ride up with the girls. Glancing out the door, Ollie said, "Go, go, help them get down and bring them in the house," giving Will a push. Ollie looked up with folded hands and said, "Thank you, Lord, oh my, thank you. My babies are home safe."

Rae came into the kitchen first with Will following, carrying the baby, who had finally awaken. Hope, seeing Ollie, reached her little hand out and wiggled her fingers as if to say, *take me.*

"Come to me, honey child, and let's go get cleaned up for breakfast. I knows you're both starving." She was looking at Rae as she said that.

Ollie's eyes were shining, filled with tears. Eyeing Rae's dirty clothes and her ruined shoes, she only shook her head. "Come on, Miss Rae, let's get you changed out of them there rags."

"Will, bring me that kettle of hot water to Miss Rae's room now," Ollie ordered, "and don't let them biscuits burn."

Jesse came into the kitchen. He had heard Ollie giving orders to Will.

He walked over to the oven and took out the biscuits. Everything looked ready to eat, so he walked to the door and rang the bell for the others to come.

As Joseph, Rider, and John entered the kitchen, they were looking around for the girls. Jesse noticed that they were very concerned. "Sit down. The girls are getting cleaned up, and both of them are fine. I haven't murdered them yet." His announcement about the girls relieved some of the tension, and the men all laughed.

In the back room, Hank laid in his bed listening to Ollie talk to Rae until she pushed the door closed. *At least Rae seemed all right,* thought Hank. Will entered Hank's room carrying a tray of hot food.

"Damn it, boy! That shore looks good. What do you think about those youngsters? You've seen them?" asked Hank as he starting slapping butter on his biscuit.

"Well, they aren't hurt, but Rae's clothes are a mess. I don't think Sweetheart even knew that she wasn't in her own bed. Rae's palms have some bad scratches on them," answered Will.

"How is Sweetheart? Really?" Hank was really worried about Hope's condition.

"She's fine, Hank, I promise. She was fussing about having to change clothes because she wanted to eat. Ollie is getting her out of her clothes because she wants to make sure she doesn't have any ticks on her little body. Remember once, I had a wood tick embedded under this arm, and I was so sick with fever."

"I remember that, boy. You were probably nine?"

"Yeah, something like that. Ollie's going to check Rae too. I will be back shortly. I better go eat before it's all gone."

*****

"I am going to throw all these here clothes in the trash. The bottom of your skirt is ripped bad, and your stockings have as many holes as my milk strainer does." Ollie shook the stocking in the air.

"Wait, please, Ollie. The bodice of that dress is still good. My wrapper protected most of it. I made the dress, and I can sew a new skirt to go on it. Please let me keep it."

ae quickly thought to herself, if I am still here. After this evening, I may be headed back to Rosedale or placed in jail.

Ollie walked over to the rocking chair in the room and sat down. Rae started washing her body all over. She couldn't stop glancing over at Ollie, because she looked so tired and sorrowful.

Rae put on her wrapper and walked over to the rocker. She stooped down next to Ollie's knees and placed her head in her lap. Ollie started rubbing Rae's beautiful hair.

"I'm so sorry that I have come here and brought my troubles," she whispered. "I'm going to have to leave. My heart is breaking. I miss my mama so much, Ollie, but you are so good and kind, just like her. Jesse and Will are so fortunate to have you. Oh, I don't know what's going to become of us. I love all of you so much." Tears were raining down her tired face.

"You even love Mr. Jess?" Ollie asked as she continued to rub Rae's hair around her ear and face.

After what seemed like a long time, Rae whispered, "Yes, but Ollie, he doesn't care for me. I don't think he even likes me." Rae couldn't see Ollie's face, but for the first time since early morning, a big wide smile spread across it.

Ollie gave Rae an extra pat and said, "Now I knows everything is going to be just fine. Get up, honey, and you just lie down on your bed. I knows you are dead tired from carrying that baby and tromping through those woods. You just rest, and I will bring you some breakfast."

Reaching out for Hope's little hand and walking to the kitchen where everyone was having breakfast, Ollie announced, "Look who's hungry."

Will and John both jumped up at the same time to help Hope take her seat at the table. Hope looked around at the others and spotted Jesse.

"I like your horse," she said, giving him her first smile since they had met.

Jesse looked into those big brown eyes with her lovely, blonde curls framing her adorable doll face and melted. He had fallen in love.

Jesse, like the others, was wondering when Rae was going to make an appearance. Finally he asked Ollie, "Is Rae coming to breakfast?"

Looking around at the men's eager faces, she spoke, "I want all of you to know that Miss Rae is fine. She stayed up most of the night, as you know, and she is resting. I am sure she will be joining us for supper."

Everyone seemed to be glad to hear that, but Jesse was very concerned about Rae's emotional state. He pushed back his plate and stood. "I won't be but a minute, Ollie, but I have to speak with her now."

Jesse tapped on Rae's door and when he didn't receive an answer, he opened the door just a crack. He could tell immediately that she was sound asleep. He went over to her bed and looked down at the sleeping beauty.

Rae's hair was fanned out on the pillow, and her rosy lips were parted just a bit. She had a scratch on the side of one cheek, but it didn't mar her looks.

It would heal. He felt an overpowering feeling come over him as he stared down at her. He would protect her with his life. *Whatever her problems are, they are mine now.* After reaching down and pulling the top sheet up over her, he left the room.

Jesse walked over to Ollie and said, "Thanks for all your help earlier. Listen, you go and lie down for a while. I will have Will check on Hank every hour or so. Don't worry about cooking lunch either. Th ere is plenty of fresh bread and ham. It won't hurt us to have a cold meal, and we can all fix our own. I may even lie down later myself."

"I am tired, but my heart is so sad for Miss Rae. You are going to help her, ain't you, Jess?"

"Don't fret. As soon as I know how to help her, I will. Go and rest."

Turning her around and giving her a little nudge, he said, "And leave things to me," as he leaned into her and kissed her forehead.

Will came walking out of the back room where he had gone to get Hank's morning tray and to assist him with some of his personal needs.

Jesse looked up and said, "Give me a hand with these dishes." Will looked at him like he was out of his mind. "Oh, come on now. Ollie is worn out, and I sent her off to bed. Pour water in that dishpan, and we'll let the dishes soak until we come back in for lunch."

Jesse noticed that Hope was humming a song as she was sitting in the rocker holding her dolly. *Last night didn't do her any harm,* he thought.

"Another thing, Will, I need you to lend a hand with Hope until Ollie or Rae wakes up. Watch her good. Take her to the barn to see her new puppy or whatever you can do to entertain her. Just keep her out of mischief."

"Why me?" grumbled Will. "Why not one of the others?"

"Would you rather butcher a couple of hogs? I'm sure Rider will change jobs with you real fast."

"That's all right. The kid and I get along pretty good."

"See you at lunch, if not sooner," said Jesse as he went out without letting the screen door slam.

With the household settled down and everyone doing their chores, no one would have guessed the trouble that had gone on at the ranch last night. Jesse had gone riding on the range, checking on his heifers and looking for new calves, even though it wasn't springtime. His large herd of ponies were running and playing; kicking up their heels and nipping each other on the rump.

John was building a new pen for the sow that was about to have babies, and Joseph was putting new hinges on the back gate of the corral. The store owner, Mr. Smith, had placed an order for a fresh hog to be butchered, so that task fell to Rider.

The sun was up pretty high as Jesse sat on his horse and looked out over his range. He loved this place. The wheat fields and corn crops had all been cut, stored, or sold. His cattle were grazing on a new section of grass, and his new bull was growing every day. The good Lord had blessed all of Texas this past year with good weather and plenty of rain. He had a home that any young man could be proud of. All he needed now was a young wife and a house full of little ones.

Wow! Where did that thought come from? Realizing that it was near lunchtime, he turned his horse around and headed back to the ranch house. The men would be ready for lunch, and he remembered that he had taken on that responsibility.

As he arrived back at the house, the doctor's carriage was parked down by the barn. "Damn it to hell and back," he swore under his breath.

"Why today?" Then he remembered that the doctor was coming to check on Hank.

John had greeted the doctor and taken him up on the screen porch out of the sun. "Hi, Doc, you come to see Hank? He's right where you left him." Jesse grinned as he led the doctor to Hank's room.

As they passed Rae's room, Jesse thought he heard someone moving around. He figured she must be awake and getting dressed.

"Thank goodness you finally got here," boomed Hank, forgetting that he was supposed to be quiet. "I am going stir crazy, cooped up in this here room. I hope you bought me some crutches. Rae said that I could sit in the rocking chair in the front room if I could hop out there."

"Well, it is good to see you too, Hank. I wish all my patients were as happy to see me as you are." Laughing, he pushed the cover back to look at Hank's sprained foot.

"I didn't know you had any human patients, but me."

"Well, a cowhand from the cattle drive needed a tooth pull this week," Tim said. "He didn't smell human, but he was!"

Ollie had woken up, and after refreshing herself, she walked in the room with Hank and the doctor.

"Good day, Miss Ollie," said the doctor. "You have done a wonderful job with Hank. His arm and shoulder are better, so I believe he can try out the crutches that I brought for him to use. You all will be happier if he can get around on them."

"You're sure right about that. Let me go out and see about some lunch. Please stay and eat with us."

"Let me go out and get those crutches, Hank. I will be right back."

Hurrying out of Hank's room, he ran right into Rae, knocking her off balance. "Oh my goodness, Miss Rae, I didn't see you! Are you all right?"

he inquired as he grabbed for her hand to steady her.

"I'm fine, really I am." She laughed for the first time in a while.

Still holding her hand, he noticed the scratch marks on her palm.

"What have you been doing with your pretty hand to get it in this condition?" Before she could offer up an excuse, he picked up her other hand. "Surely Jess doesn't have you working outside ... uh ... like some field hand."

Rae looked over the doctor's shoulder and saw Jesse watching them. If looks could kill, the doctor would be dead. "Of course not," she stammered.

"Why don't you get the crutches, Doc? Hank may like to come in here and visit with the men," said Jesse with a smile that never reached his eyes.

The doctor raced out to his carriage. Jesse looked at Rae. "Glad to see you're up. Come and join everyone at the table. I know that you are starving," he said, giving her a big smile. He reached out to take her hand.

She hesitated. Slowly she placed her palm in his large, rough hand. He took her hand and pulled her close to him and whispered, "The men know that something happened, but they are all glad you are home."

As Jesse and Rae got closer to the table, all the men rose to their feet, giving her a big smile of welcome. These men always made her feel so special.

"Please, take your seats." She looked around, and all the men were watching her. "You know walking four miles can surely make a person hungry, and I am starving!" she joked to break the ice.

Before she knew it, several of the men were offering her their sandwiches. She smiled, but before she could choose, Jesse growled, "Eat your own sandwiches. Rae can make her own." Everyone laughed.

The doctor came hurrying back in the house with the crutches. He glanced over to the table and signaled for Will to come with him. They got Hank up on the side of the bed and stood him up. His large frame was weaving forward, right, and then left.

"Hold him tight, Will," ordered the doctor. "He is still very weak from lying in bed for so long."

"Who is weak?" demanded Hank.

"Place a crutch under this arm. Good, now put this one under that arm. Great," replied Doctor Tim.

"Don't put any weight on your foot," said Will.

"Do I look like a damn fool to you? It is throbbing now. Why would I want to try to stand on it? Get out of my way before I flatten you," said Hank to Will.

Will jumped away from Hank and walked over to the rocking chair, dragging it closer to the table.

Ollie was so surprised to see him hopping on one foot. "My goodness, you will be up and about soon for sure," she said, pushing over a small stool to put Hank's bad foot on.

"Oh, Hankie, can I sit in your lap?" asked Hope, climbing on him without waiting for an answer.

The men all snickered over Hank's nickname, but when he glared at them, they looked down at their food.

"Come and get some lunch, Mr. Tim," Ollie said very sweetly. "I'm not going to call you Doc, like you don't have no name. I went ahead and made you a plate. Sit here beside Miss Rae," she purred.

"Ollie, you are a jewel. I am starving, and this looks wonderful," said the doctor as he was biting into a large ham sandwich.

After lunch, the doctor asked Rae to come sit in the big room with him. "I want to give your forehead one final look, but mostly I want to look at your palms. It is possible that with all your scratches, you may have a splinter or two."

"Oh, I know that they are fine."

"Come on now, Rae, and let the doc do his job," spoke up Hank. "Splinters can be bad if they get infected."

Rae walked slowly over to the couch and sat down beside the doctor as he was digging in his black bag for his magnifying glass.

"Now, give me your hand. Mercy, this must hurt."

He had taken her hand ever so gently and turned it palm side up. Looking through his glass, he saw a big thorn under the skin above the thumb. "This must come out," he said while searching for his tweezers. "This might hurt." He spoke softly while rubbing her hand.

"I'm a big girl. I can take a little pain."

Jesse was sitting at the kitchen table watching the doctor with his patient. He could feel anger rising up in him. If Tim O'Riley rubbed her hand one more time and whispered words that he could not hear, he might not be responsible for his actions.

Hank was watching Jesse. He wanted to laugh so badly. In all the years that he had known this young man, he had never been rude to anyone in his home. He thought, Ollie would say, *the old green-eyed monster done took him over.*

"Ouch! That hurt more than I expected," said Rae.

Jesse jumped up and was across the room in a flash. "Why do you have to hurt her? Be easy or let Ollie take care of her," muttered Jesse, embarrassed that he was acting so stupid. He glanced around the room, and everyone was looking at him.

"I've got chores to do. See you in a little while, Rae?"

"Yes," she answered and then added, "I will be here."

*****

Ollie and Rae had gotten back into their routine of preparing supper for the men. With the sore places on her palms, it wasn't easy to do much.

While Hank was in the rocking chair watching every move that she and Ollie made, asking why they were doing this or that, Ollie placed a pan of potatoes in his lap and demanded, "Peel."

He grumbled under his breath about how a man can't ever just sit and rest, but he took the knife and started peeling.

Hope had fallen asleep on the rug in front of the fireplace with her dolly. "She is a sweetheart for sure," said Hank, glancing down at the child.

"You remember, Ollie, Jess and Will were never sweet and loving as this little bit. To tell you the truth, when she looks up at me with those brown eyes, I could give her the world." Hank chuckled as he reached to rub the baby's back.

Ollie laughed at Hank's remarks and agreed that she felt the same way.

Dinner was well on its way. Will came into the house and helped Hank hop back to bed for a well-earned nap.

Jesse came inside a few minutes later and announced to Rae that it was time for their talk. She slowly got up from the table and walked outside with him.

"Where are you taking me? she asked.

Jesse had hitched a horse up to the small black carriage that he kept stored in the back of the barn for special occasions. It had a single black padded bench seat with a black canvas top. It was a very cozy and charming little carriage.

"I thought we would take a ride. There's a place down by a stream with some nice shade trees where we can have our conversation." He was going to say "have the go-to-church-house meeting" but he didn't want her to be afraid of him.

After what seemed like a short distance to Rae, he stopped the horse and jumped down. Reaching for her hand, he helped her to the ground, but he didn't turn her loose. Looking her hand over, then motioning for her to give him the other one, he asked, "Did the cream that the doc put on your hands help?"

"Yes, they feel much better, thank you."

Retrieving a small blanket from behind the seat in the carriage, he shook it out and placed it down on a grassy spot of ground. "Please," he said sweetly. "Have a seat."

After getting comfortable and glancing around at the scenery, Jesse spoke very quietly. "Rae, I want to be your friend. I think you are starting to like me a little. I have grown quite fond of you and the little rascal. I need for you to trust me. I will be the last person to betray the faith and trust you place in me. Please just start at the beginning. Tell me the reason why you left your home in Rosedale."

Rae's insides were shaking. She was praying that she wouldn't throw up. *Th*is is a good man. I have to trust him to help me. I have no other choice. *Trust him or go to jail.* Her mind was racing with such thoughts. After what seemed like a lifetime to Jesse, she agreed ... on one condition.

"I will tell you everything, but you must promise me that under no circumstances will you let them take Hope away from me," she pleaded.

"Tell me first who 'they' are."

"No! Hope is mine, and I will die before I give her up. Promise or I will run again, and this time I will do a better job of not being found."

Jesse's mind was racing in a hundred different directions. What has she done? Is Hope her child? Can I make that promise without breaking it?

Rae placed her hand on his leg. He looked into her beautiful sad eyes as she moved her lips, pleading with him. "Please, please promise."

"I promise," he said, silently praying to himself that whatever her problems were, he would be able to keep his word to her.

"Now, Rae, please start at the beginning."

Sitting quietly for a moment, trying hard to gather her thoughts, she began. "Mama and I were alone for many years. My papa died when I was very small. Mama struggled and worked very hard to keep food in the house and clothes on our backs. She was a wonderful cook and a seamstress. She taught me to help her make pies and other desserts for the rooming house in town. She made dresses for some of the ladies. I was happy, and I thought Mama was too.

"Then Herbert started coming around. I was sixteen. He was the town banker. Mama said that she would never have to work again if she married Herbert, and he promised to send me to an all-girls school when I got older. He promised her many things. After they married, Mama was so happy. She wanted to give Herbert a child, a son. She wanted to please him in any way that she could.

"After Hope was born, Mama never seemed to get well. She had to lie in bed most of the time. The doctor didn't know why she wasn't getting her strength back.

"Herbert was nice to Mama, but he wanted to be nicer to me. At first I didn't know why he gave me so much attention that I didn't want, but I soon realized. He was always trying to touch me. He wouldn't allow me to go to dances or picnics with my friends. I couldn't leave the house. He made me quit school because Mama needed me. I didn't mind taking care of her, but I felt like a prisoner. Mama wouldn't listen to me when I tried to tell her about Herbert and how he was treating me. She would get so upset that she would have a spell. I stopped trying to tell her.

"I had to take to locking my bedroom door at night. If I didn't, he would come in my room and stand over my bed while I pretended to be asleep. He would whisper things that he wanted to do to me. I was terrified of him.

"When Mama died, my Aunt Katie, Mama's sister, came for the funeral. I told her about Herbert and his advances toward me. She asked Herbert to let me and Hope go home with her for a while, but he refused.

Who would do for him? He needed us because he was so heartbroken over losing his wife. He insisted that my aunt leave sooner than she planned. He told her she wasn't welcome in his home again. So I was left in the house alone with him.

"After Aunt Katie left, he told me that I belonged to him. We would be married in two weeks. I had no choice. It would look better to the community if we were married. If I didn't marry him, he would tell the townspeople that Hope was my child and that I had forced myself on him. I had to leave—I had no choice. I would have died if I had to marry that man."

She looked up at Jesse with tears streaming down her face. "You believe me, don't you?" Before Jesse could answer, she said, "Herbert is insane! I couldn't leave my baby sister. Besides, Mama gave her to me before she died. She made me promise, Jesse. She made me promise to raise her, and I did promise. I will … never … give … her … up." Tears were choking her to the point that she couldn't continue to speak clearly.

Jesse reached for Rae and pulled her onto his lap, rubbing her hair and softly telling her that everything would be fine. "I won't let that man take her away. Please, honey, stop crying. I promised to help, and I will."

"How can you do anything now that he has the law looking for me?" she asked.

"Listen, the law is not looking for you. The poster said that he wants Hope found. He knows that if and when she is found, he will have found you too. I have to go into town and talk this over with Sheriff Murphy."

"No! What if he contacts Herbert and he comes here and takes Hope? He can, by law, because she is his child."

"Something tells me that he doesn't want her. It's you that he's after. And I will tell you something right now. He will never, ever lay his hands on you again!"

Both sat quietly for a while with Jesse holding Rae tight.

As Jesse held Rae, he was pondering about her mama's health. "Is there anything else I need to know about your mama and her health problems?

What do you think kept her from getting better after Hope was born?"

"I am not sure. The doctor was very puzzled over her condition," said Rae. "But listen to me, Jess. Herbert has never held Hope in his arms.

He never gave her any hugs or kisses or played with her. Mama said that he loved Hope in his own way, but that she had failed him by not giving him a son. She wanted to try again, but he wouldn't hear of it. She was heartbroken when he stopped sharing a bedroom with her. He told her that she needed complete rest.

"Jess, Hope is not my child, but I have cared for her since the day she was born. I couldn't love another child more than I love her. She calls me 'mama' most of the time, as you know. Rae, Rae sometimes. She loved our mama, but Hope knows that I am the one who she depends on for everything. Oh, she knew Herbert was her father, but she never ran to him likes she runs to Hank, wanting him to pick her up. She has never had that kind of affection from a man before.

"I'm scared, Jess," she said as she laid her head on his chest.

"I understand why you are afraid," said Jesse. "But I did make you a promise, and I will do everything in my power to keep it. I need to take you back to the ranch. I feel that I must talk this situation over with Sheriff Murphy and make some plans. I may have to go on a trip to your hometown of Rosedale."

After taking Rae back to the house, she went directly to her room to freshen up. Jesse walked over to Ollie as she was placing a platter of fried chicken on the table. He spoke quietly to her that Rae had confided in him about her past, and that he had to go and talk with the sheriff .

"Save me some supper, but for now I am taking this chicken leg and a piece of bread," he said as patted her cheek.

"Go on with yourself, boy, and hurry back."

*****

Sheriff Murphy sat at his desk, rubbing his chin, as he listened to Jesse tell him about Rae's situation and why she had to leave her home.

"Listen to me, Jess. We must keep this quiet for a while. I haven't shown anyone that poster about the baby. Keep Rae at the ranch and don't bring her back into town until we can find out more. Th e less people who know that she is staying at your place, the better."

"On my way here, I was making a plan to go to Rosedale. It is close to a hundred miles from here. This man, Herbert Summers, is the banker there, so he will be easy to fine. Everybody probably knows everything about him, including his life with Rae and Hope. I should be able to travel there in less than three days with two of my best mustang horses and a good packhorse."

The sheriff was nodding his head yes. "Good idea."

"I will leave at daybreak. I will have the boys guarding Rae and Hope in case Herbert shows up. I have a feeling that he will get someone else to do his dirty work."

"What do you mean? Do you think that he will hurt them?"

"From what Rae said and didn't say, Herbert wants her bad. He thinks he can force her to marry. I'm afraid that this is an evil man, probably capable of doing anything to get what he wants."

"I will have Joey helping me to watch out for strangers, other than the cowpunchers who come in town to celebrate a little. Tell your men not to allow any strangers on the place while you are gone. Keep the girls out of sight as much as possible without alarming them."

Jesse rose and walked to the door of the office. "I should be back in a week or a little later. If I see I need to stay on, I will try to get a note to you by way of the stagecoach driver."

"Be careful, son, and good luck to you. I will ride out and check on the girls, but I am sure your men will guard them with their lives."

Chapter 12

Rosedale

Three days before, Jesse had ridden out of the ranch yard with a tearful good-bye from Rae and a loving warning from Ollie to be careful. He had made better time than he hoped. His two mustang horses had held up under the fast pace. He had chosen two young horses because of their speed. Settling them in at the livery, he gave orders for a good rubdown and an extra helping of oats for each of them. The old man who worked at the livery allowed him to store his camping gear in an empty stall. Now it was time to get a room and a good, hot bath for himself.

Rosedale was a larger town than he thought it would be. On Main Street there were several mercantile stores, a nice boardinghouse, several saloons, a bakery, and a café. All the buildings were clearly marked with nice signs above the doorways, and the fronts were whitewashed with a coat of paint. The wide streets were nice and clean. Of course, Jesse noticed the bank right away. After finding the boardinghouse, he set his gear down on the steps and tapped on the door. A young lady answered.

"Yes, may I help you, sir?" she asked, looking him up and down.

"Yes, and please excuse the way I look. I just came into town after traveling on horseback for three days. I was hoping I might get a room for a few days. I have money and can pay in advance."

"I think my mom can help you. *Ma!* " she yelled at the top of her lungs.

"My goodness, Amelia, what is all the yelling about? I was just in the kitchen. Oh, I see," she said when she saw Jesse, a good-looking, rugged young man in the foyer.

Jesse was looking Amelia over. She would be about the same age as Rae. They could have gone to school together, he was thinking.

"Sir!" said Amelia's mother. "Don't be looking at my gal—she's taken. Now, do you want a room or don't you?"

Embarrassed as he could be for staring at the young girl, he answered quickly, "Yes, please."

A good bath and shave made him feel human again, and now for a good, hot meal. He walked in the café, and the fi rst person he saw was a man that had to be the banker. Before he left, he had asked Rae for a description of Herbert. She described him as a big barrel of a man with a reddish beard who always dressed in three-piece suits and spoke very loud.

When the waitress came over to his table, Jesse ordered a big steak and some potatoes. After getting his meal, he asked the young lady if the town had a bank.

"Why, yes sir. You just passed our banker, Mr. Summers, when you came in the door. That was him leaving. The bank is just a ways down that way."

*****

The next morning after breakfast in the café, Jesse decided to go and talk to the sheriff .

"Good morning, Deputy," said Jesse after he stepped into the sheriff 's office. He knew immediately that the sheriff was not in yet. "My name is Jesse Maxwell. I need to talk with the sheriff . Do you know when he will be here today?"

"Sheriff Miller should be here any time now. If you want to have a cup of coffee and wait for him, make yourself at home," the deputy replied, nodding to a chair.

"Thanks. I believe I will pass on the coffee, but I will wait a little while." Jesse was sizing up the deputy without him knowing it. "You lived here in Rosedale long?"

"Just about all my life. I got a little spread a couple miles out of town. I work here to help with the cash flow, if you know what I mean."

"Sure do! Got a small place of my own about hundred miles from here with a few head of cattle. Cash is hard to get and hang on to." Jesse laughed.

"What brings you this far from your home?" inquired the deputy.

"Oh, I'm helping out a friend, and I am trying to gather information about the family. I was hoping the sheriff could help me."

"Hey, Jim!" the sheriff said as he entered the office.

"Morning, Sheriff !" Nodding his head toward Jesse who was sitting in the corner of the office, he said, "This here gent is waiting to see you. What did you said your name was again?"

"Jesse Maxwell, sir," Jesse said to the sheriff as he stretched out his hand for a handshake.

The sheriff nodded at Jesse and said, "Howdy, young fellow, my name is Ron Miller." Then he turned to the deputy. "Jim, you can go on home now. Things are still pretty quiet. Check back in around two."

Jim opened his desk drawer and took out his gun. Strapping it on his hips, he got his hat and walked into the back of the office, heading for the back door. Before leaving, Jim stopped and blended himself into the wall to eavesdrop on Jesse and the sheriff . He knew that the sheriff never shared information with him concerning the townspeople, so he had to find out his own way.

"So, how can I help you?" asked the sheriff .

"Have you seen a poster for a missing child?" Jesse thought that this might be the way to start the inquiry.

"I did see it a few days ago. Mr. Summers, the banker, came in and gave me a few of the posters to place around town. He had been to Frisco City to make a report to the marshal about his missing child, and while there, he had posters and fliers made. Our town doesn't have a newspaper office or any kind of printing press. This was the first time I learned about his little girl gone missing. Lovely child with those blonde curls. "Why do you ask? Have you any information about the child?" asked the sheriff , getting a little excited.

"Before I give you information, I need to know all I can about the banker, his wife, and the child. So, please bear with me and tell me what you know about them."

"You ask and I will try to answer your questions."

"Thanks. First, I want to know how long were they married and how did his wife die?"

"So, you do know something," the sheriff said quietly. The deputy, lurking in the back room, was straining to hear.

"Claire was a lovely lady. She had been widowed for years. She was left with a little girl to support. I never met her man. Claire worked hard cooking cakes and pies for the rooming house and café. She also stitched dresses for some of the ladies. I tried several times to walk out with her, but she wasn't interested in me. Then, one day I heard that the banker man was calling on her. I was surprised, maybe even jealous, but he was her choice."

"How old was her daughter at this time?"

"Now, that's one beautiful young girl. She must have been fourteen or fifteen, I'm not sure. I would see the girl as she was going to school, but afterward, she didn't hang around with the other children. She went straight home."

"So, after they married, what happened to his wife?"

"She had a baby and never got well. She was sick for several years before she died. But, I will tell you something! Her daughter never left her side. She quit school and never came to town. I hadn't seen that girl in a year or more until I happened to pass the house, and she was outside with her baby sister. What a picture those two made. Two beauties."

"When Rae's mama died, did you go to her funeral?"

"Sure! The whole town was there. Claire's sister came and the two girls went home with her over to Peamont. That's where I understand the child came up missing."

"Why would he think the child had been kidnapped?"

"I'm not sure about that. ... Now, it's your turn to tell me what you know about this."

"I don't have any proof, but I think that Herbert Summers may have killed his wife to get to his stepdaughter."

"What! Where did you get such an idea? And what do you mean 'get her'"?

"Sheriff , this is a dangerous situation we have here. Rae and her sister are safe now, but they will not be if her stepfather, Herbert Summers, gets to them. Rae took her sister and ran away almost two weeks ago. She was never over at her aunt's home like everyone was told. She had been living in hell with that man. He was going to force her to marry him even though she told him that she would die first. He had made all kinds of threats toward her, so she had no other choice but to leave and take her baby sister with her."

"Why do you think he killed Claire, and how did he do it?"

"Rae is not sure how he did it, but she told me that he would only spend about thirty minutes with her mom once in a while. He got to acting very strange, talking to himself and going into fits of rage. Most of the time after his visits with her mama, she would sleep for a couple of days. Once she woke up, she would be so weak that she could hardly stand."

"So, that is the reason she took the child with her?"

"Yes. Rae had raised and cared for her little sister, and she really believes that her stepfather is insane. She said that she never knew how he was going to behave when he was around. She is terrified of him."

"Mercy!" said the sheriff as he sat down. "You haven't told me where you came from or where you have Rae and her sister," he finally stated. "I don't know what to do. Mr. Summers has not made any charges against Rae. That is kinda funny, now that I think on it. He had to know that she took his child."

"Look, Sheriff , these girls are safe at my home in Limason." *Oh*

Lord!

I didn't mean to tell him where I live. Jesse continued, "I need to collect as much proof against him as possible. He is an important man in this town, and everyone won't take Rae's word against him."

"You know," said the sheriff very calmly, "I believe you. I have never liked him. Always acting like he's better than the folks around here. I still can't figure why Claire chose him over me," he said sadly. "I will keep your secret. You will keep me informed?" he added.

"I am going to talk to some people I think would know about Rae's home life. She told me that she was practically a prisoner in her own home. He wouldn't allow her to go anywhere. After the funeral, Rae confided in her aunt about the way he treated her. He must have known this because he made her aunt leave sooner than she had planned."

"So, what are you going to do next?" asked the sheriff.

"I am going to ride over to Peamont to pay Rae's aunt a visit."

As Jesse got up to leave, he thought he heard the back door of the office close. He peeked into the back room, and the door was open a crack.

"Do you think someone was here listening to our conversation?" he quizzed the sheriff.

The sheriff glanced over Jesse's shoulder and said, "No, that door is hard to close. A breeze probably blew it open."

*Th*e deputy had left the back room as silently as he could. He rode home with a plan forming in his head. While he was pitching hay down from the loft of his barn, he was building up the nerve to go through with his idea. He had something that the banker wanted: information. If this plan worked, he would never again have to beg for an extension on his farm loan.

How he hated that banker—one sorry piece of fat trash. Each time he had to ask for an extension from him, to give him more time to make a mortgage payment, the man would laugh and say, "You know, Jimmy, my boy, you beg so pretty. You make me want to laugh. One more week, but you better have the money!" The banker would walk away, laughing like a crazy loon.

When the deputy's chores were completed, he had lunch with his wife and two little boys. He told her that he had some business to take care of in town before he could relieve the sheriff for the afternoon.

After arriving back in town, Jim went inside the bank and asked Sawyer, the bank clerk, if he could see Mr. Summers. He didn't want to think about what the banker would do with the information about his stepdaughter and child.

"Tell him I have something very important to discuss, now!" raising his voice to show his authority.

"Mr. Summers said that he will see you for a few minutes, but he is a very busy man," replied Mr. Sawyer.

Jim entered the banker's office and sat down. He leaned back in his

chair and placed his boots on the corner of Mr. Summers's desk like he was a big shot.

"All right, what do you want today?" Mr. Summers was looking at the boots on his desk. "Have you got the money you owe the bank? Is this the reason you are acting so high and mighty?"

Jim removed his boots off the desk and sat his chair on the floor. "No," said Jim, towering over the banker as he sat in his chair like royalty.

"I don't have my payment, but I have something you want very much, and you have something I want. I am here for a trade, you might say."

"You couldn't possibility have anything I want other than that little piece of land you squat on."

"That's where you are wrong," Jim replied, drawing out this statement very slowly. "What about information about a certain missing little girl and her big sister? You must want them back pretty bad to offer such a fat reward."

"What do you want to trade for?" *I may have to kill this idiot,* he was thinking as he tried staring at Jim hard enough to be intimidating.

"I want the deed to my place, signed by you, and marked 'paid in full.'

I will take no less. You have been after my little spread for years, but I am not willing to give up my family's home without a fight."

"How do I know for sure that you have this information you are bargaining with?"

"I got it," said the deputy through clenched teeth. "There's a man

in town looking for you. He's asking all kinds of questions about Rae. I know that you have been planning to marry the girl, you old bastard! She wouldn't have you. That's the reason she ran away and took her sister. This man knows all of this too. He has both girls in a safe place, away from you, but I know where they are," he said as he bent over the banker's desk.

The deputy could see the expression of fear in his eyes, and he was loving every minute of this confrontation. Th is was just a little payback.

The banker had made him beg several times for an extension on his loan. He always felt worse than a failure when he left the bank. But no more!

"Now, are you ready to deal? I don't have all day!"

The banker walked over to the door of his office and opened it.

"Sawyer!" he yelled, "Get me the deed to Jim's place."

Sawyer scurried away and was back in an instant with the paper.

Handing the deed over to the banker, he stood and waited to see what was taking place.

"Leave, you aren't needed anymore," he said while shoving the door shut.

Tapping the deed on the side of his leg, he said to the deputy, "Okay, Mr. Big Shot! It seems you are holding all the cards. I am willing to sign this deed as you requested. I want to know where Rae is hiding with my child, and I want to know now!"

"Sign the deed and give it to me, then I will tell you."

The banker walked back to his desk and unfolded the deed, never taking his eyes off the deputy. He placed the pen in the inkwell and signed the paper. Fanning it slowly in the air, the banker grinned and stretched it out as if to hand it to him.

Jim was watching the banker's every move, not trusting him one second. He was feeling excited but very cautious. Slowly putting his hand out to take the deed, the banker turned it loose and gave it to him.

"The girls are in Limason, about one hundred miles south of here,"

Jim said, being true to his word as the banker was to his. For some reason, the excitement wasn't there anymore. He now owned his home, free and clear, but what price would the girls pay?

"One more thing from you," said the banker. "I am in need of assistance. I must hire someone to go and get the girls and bring them home to me. Who do you suppose I can get to help me with this little job?"

"Go look in the saloons. I am sure there will be a lowlife or two who needs the money, who will be willing to help you," said Jim as he walked out of the bank.

Taking one more look at his free-and-clear deed, he placed it in his vest pocket. He looked up into heaven and said a silent prayer: *Lord, forgive me. Please protect the girls. I know that I have placed them in a dangerous situation.*

Chapter 13

Rosedale

It was late into the evening before Herbert could head for the saloons. He was a prominent businessman, well respected by the community, and he didn't need for some old biddy to see him entering a local tavern. Stopping in front of the swinging doors, he glanced up and down the street before stepping inside. The room was very dim with dirty clouds of smoke floating up to the ceiling and drifting down around the few lanterns on the wall.

How could a man breathe in a place like this? When he wanted a drink, he went to the rooming house. He had a gal there who not only served him his favorite liquor, but anything else he desired. Claire hadn't known how to please a man, he thought angrily. *Now Rae, she will be different. I will teach her how to please me.* He smiled at the thought as he stood in the doorway.

"Get out of the way, you big fat turd!" bellowed the nastiest looking cowpuncher Herbert had ever laid eyes upon. "My pal and I here got some celebrating to do. We are *never, ever* riding behind those stinking cows again. We quit! Bring us two bottles of your best whiskey, bartender, and none of that watered down crap either!"

Herbert was still standing next to the bar, staring at the two men.

It was like he was frozen in place with his mind going in all different directions.

"What the heck you looking at, fatso?" shouted the cowpuncher.

Yes, thought Herbert as a thick silence fell between the two men. *This* could be my man.

The nasty man got up and walked over to the bar, ready to take Herbert and pitch him out of the door that he came in.

"I asked you, old man, who are you looking at?"

Herbert came out of his daydreaming slump. "I am looking at you and your friend, wondering if you would like to make some quick and easy money. I am in need of assistance."

"You hear that, Joe? Mr. Fancy Pants wants to hire us to work for him."

"Please, let's sit down and talk this over, but lower your voice," Herbert said as he looked around to see if he knew any of the men in the saloon. Thankfully, he didn't recognize anyone.

The nasty cowpuncher seemed real interested in making some easy money. "What do you think, Joe? You wanna hear this dude out?"

Joe wasn't as belligerent as his partner. He appeared to be much younger and was certainly cleaner. "Yep, let's hear him out. We are going to need the extra money sooner or later."

Listening to Herbert spin his yarn about needing them to go to Limason to get a girl and then take her to a special location where he would meet them, sounded easy enough. Five thousand dollars would be a nice stake for them to get a fresh start in Old Mexico. There was one part of the deal Joe didn't like. The old man said that the girl wouldn't want to leave behind her little sister.

"Just bring the girl. It's your choice how you dispose of the child." Joe was pondering this deal, but he knew that his partner was all set to head out in the morning. Five thousand dollars made this deal too tempting to refuse.

*****

Peamont

The rain had turned into a steady drizzle and looked like it probably would continue all day. Jesse was thankful that he had remembered to bring along his rain slicker. He had left for Peamont early this morning and made good time despite the rainy weather. Maybe he would arrive at Mrs. Brown's, Rae's aunt, in time for supper. His supply of beef jerky was long gone, and he was hungry. He had gotten used to eating three square meals every day.

Man, he was getting soft. Ollie sure had spoiled him.

Looking straight ahead, he could see a small cottage nestled in a thicket of trees. It was very isolated here with the closest neighbor being several miles away. Jesse could smell the smoke coming from the chimney of the cottage. The quiet of the evening was broken with the barking of a large hound dog. Charging from around the side of the house, with his long ears flapping and his teeth bared, he was prepared to attack. He looked like he could take a man's leg or arm off if he made a wrong move.

Jesse knew that he wouldn't be getting off his horse until someone came out of the house.

"Hello! In the house." Jesse could see the front curtain move a little.

"My name is Jesse Maxwell. I am a friend of your niece, Rae," he shouted.

"Buddy, Buddy! Back, boy. Come! Now!" Buddy, the protector of the home, started walking backward with small, short steps, still growling low.

Jesse glanced over to the small animal shed. An old Negro man was leaning against the wall, pointing a shotgun directly at him.

"Howdy, mister, my name is Jesse Maxwell. I am from Limason, Texas. I need to talk to Mrs. Brown about her niece, Rae. I don't mean any harm."

The old man did not moved a muscle until the front door opened a crack. Jesse could hardly hear the woman's voice as she spoke to the old man. She called him Jeremiah.

"Yes ma'am, if you say so." Pointing the shotgun down toward the ground, the old man waved for Jesse to follow him.

"Jeremiah, I am not here to bring trouble. I want to talk to Mrs. Brown about her sister, Claire."

"You know that Miss Claire is dead now? God rest her soul. So sad."

"Yes, I know," replied Jesse.

After walking into the shed, Jesse removed his rain slicker and hung it on a nail next to the door. He moved his horse into a small stall, and Jeremiah threw a pitchfork full of hay down in front of the animal.

"You can use this old blanket to wipe him down, and place the saddle and blanket over here." He motioned to a table in the corner. "I have got to get a fresh bucket of water for the house. You come on in the side door when you are finished out here. Supper is about ready."

"Mercy me, I hope Mrs. Brown invites me to sit at her table. I am just about to starve!"

"I'm shore she will feed you," said Jeremiah with a laugh.

As he walked up to the side door of the cottage, even with the sun setting, Jesse could see Mrs. Brown's lovely flower garden. Flowers were everywhere. There were yellow and red rosebushes, yellow lilies, and other flowers that he didn't recognize. The sweet smell of honeysuckle was growing near. This place was so lovely, it appeared magical.

Tapping his knuckles lightly on the door, he heard a sweet voice telling him to enter. Once inside the door, Jesse slipped off his wet, muddy boots.

He looked up at the small lady and was totally shocked. There stood before him a vision of beauty. *My gracious,* he thought. *She is an older vision of Rae.* He was speechless for a moment. Petite in stature, with big brown eyes and a golden rope of hair hanging down her back—a storybook princess for sure, he thought.

"Please come in, Mr. Maxwell, and do shut your mouth. You aren't seeing a ghost. I am Claire's twin sister, and everyone says that Rae, my lovely niece, looks just like us."

"I'm sorry to stare at you, Mrs. Brown."

"Now you call me Katie or like Jeremiah, Miss Katie. I haven't been Mrs. Brown in years." She laughed a little. "I understand that you came here to talk about my sister and Rae. I can't believe my Claire is gone, and I am so afraid for Rae," she said, her eyes misting. Doing a quick turnabout, Katie announced that supper was ready, and it was time to eat.

"Please join us for our evening meal, Mr. Maxwell."

Th ank you, Lord. Jesse sighed and looked over at Jeremiah. Both of the men laughed at their private joke about him being invited to eat. "Now, Miss Katie, you must call me Jess or Jesse. I really need to ask you many important questions about Claire and Rae."

"Let's eat our meal first, Mr. ... Jess. We have all evening to discuss them. Jeremiah will bed you down in the shed, and you can be on your way in the morning."

After dinner, Jesse didn't know where to start first with his questions to Miss Katie. He didn't want to alarm her about Rae running away from Rosedale, but she had to know the truth.

"Miss Katie, you said that you were afraid for Rae. What did you mean exactly?" Jesse was thinking he would find out what she knew about Rae and maybe even Herbert.

"I visited Claire several times after she married Herbert. Each time I saw her, she was getting weaker and weaker. She confided in me that her 'sweet man' was making her a special, healthy drink that was making her stronger. I told her to stop drinking it immediately! She wasn't getting better; if anything, she was worse."

"Did you ever tell Rae about this drink that Herbert was giving her?"

"No, Claire said that it was their little secret, and she wouldn't forgive me if I told. So, I never did."

"You mentioned that you were afraid for Rae to stay at Herbert's home alone, just with him. Why?"

"Have you ever met Herbert, Jess?" He shook his head no, and she continued.

"After Claire's funeral, I talked with Rae. I could tell that she never went close to Herbert. If he came in the room, she would find something she had to do in the other room. She tried her best to avoid him in every way. He seemed to torment her with his presence, and he knew this. Finally, I got Rae to open up to me.

"She was terrified. He had been making advances toward her ever since he married Claire. She said that he told her that she belonged to him, and no other man would ever have her. She locked herself and the baby in her room each night. She was living a nightmare with that man stalking her all the time. Right under my poor sister's nose.

"I asked—or let's say, I begged—Herbert to allow Rae and Hope to come home with me for a while. Rae was worn out from caring for Claire, Hope, and that big house. He went into a wild rage! Scared me half to death for a little while until he finally calmed down. He was screaming, talking to himself, and even answering his own questions out loud. I tell you this. His conversations with himself did not require another person.

"Now, he was scary. The next morning before the sun even came up, he shook me awake and told me it was time for me to leave and never come back. I wasn't needed any longer.

"He reminded me of a wild horse that had a crazy look in his eyes. So, I got up and packed. Jeremiah and I left before the girls got up, but I left Rae a note. Also, I just remember! I have Claire's diary. I know that I shouldn't have taken it, but I was in her room going through some of her personal items when I noticed this book tucked under the mattress. I took it. Claire had always written her deepest secrets down as a young girl, and she continued this habit until her death."

Going into her bedroom, Katie was still talking to Jesse as she pulled items out of her large carpetbag. "I have not felt like unpacking some of these items, and I forgot about this book." She held the book up and then clasped it to her heart, hugging it, as she knew that this was a part of her dead sister. Sadly she spoke, "Maybe, just maybe, my sister will speak to us from her grave."

Coming back into the living area, Katie took a seat in her rocker, holding the diary.

"Miss Katie, I have to tell you something. Please don't be too upset, because Rae and Hope are safe and doing very well. After the funeral and your departure, Herbert made demands to Rae. He told her that they were going to get married, and if she didn't comply with his wishes, she would be very sorry. She was so afraid of him that she made a plan and took Hope and ran."

It took Jesse an hour or more to tell Katie and Jeremiah the story about Rae catching the stagecoach to settling in at his ranch. He explained how the sheriff had come to the ranch with the wanted poster for the missing child, not Rae.

"The sheriff promised he would help by not telling anyone about Rae and Hope being at my ranch. Several people know that a beautiful young lady and her baby girl are at the ranch for a while, but that's all. See, Rae changed her name and told everyone, even me, that Hope is her baby. No one has questioned that fact. "I came to Rosedale to see if I could find out more about how Claire died and get information about Mr. Banker Man. Legally, he can get the baby back from Rae if we can't get something to prove he's a bad man ... insane too."

"Rae will never give up the baby to him."

All three of them sat very quietly in the room, listening to the crackling of the wood in the small fireplace. All of sudden, Miss Katie said, "Well, Jess, let's see what my sister had to say about her knight in shining armor."

June 13

Herbie is acting so strange tonight. He gets so mad at me when I call him my pet name for him. He brought me his special health drink, and I told him that I didn't want it. It makes me sleep for hours, and when I wake up, I feel so weak and sick to my stomach. He went wild with anger and started whispering to himself that I was crazy.

He made me drink it. I can hardly write. I feel so sick.

August 10

Rae and Hope came in to sit with me tonight. Rae is tired. She never complains. She isn't sleeping well.

Herbert came in the room and ran them out. He's so short-tempered lately. I try to ask him not to be mean to my babies. He told me to shut my sickly mouth. He made me drink. I cried. He left. He has changed—he hates me.

September 1

I can't seem to breathe. I'm all choked up. I lay down.

I feel like I can't breathe. I can't drink that stuff anymore.

Go away, I told Herbert. You drink it. He laughed. I'm really afraid of him.

"My poor Claire; my poor, poor sister." Misted eyes were looking up at Jesse. "I believe that man was slowing poisoning her. That's the reason he didn't want her to tell Rae or me that he was giving her a 'health drink.' Their secret is what she told me. I wouldn't be a bit surprised if he didn't take a pillow and smother her while she was already struggling to breathe! Oh my ... what do you think?" she asked Jesse, and looked over at Jeremiah.

"This diary tells a lot about the strange way he acted with your sister but—" Jess paused while thinking .

"But what? Surely he is crazy and very dangerous."

"Now Miss Katie, what Jess is saying is that Miss Claire don't write that Herbert actually said he was going to kill her. He acted strange, yes, but Jess needs more proof to have him arrested." He looked at Jesse for approval of his statement.

"You are so right, Jeremiah. I need solid evidence that he caused her death, like, what was he putting in that so-called health drink?"

"It had to be the drink that was keeping her weak and in bed all the time or otherwise, he wouldn't have insisted that she keep it a secret," declared Katie.

"Well, in the morning I am going to ride back over to Rosedale and see if I can find someone who may know something that will help our cause. I did meet a girl named Amelia, who looked about the same age as Rae. She may have been Rae's friend while they attended school. Just a hunch."

"I best go check on my horse, and Jeremiah, if you will show me where to bed down, I will get settled for the night." Jesse walked over to the side door and pushed his feet into his muddy boots and placed his Stetson on his head.

"Good night, Miss Katie. Please don't worry about Rae and Hope. My men are taking good care of them."

Jeremiah got up and limped over to the side door, leading Jesse out to the shed. While getting settled down for the night, Jesse asked Jeremiah how long he had been working for Miss Katie.

"I've been with Miss Kathie for years, but I worked for Mr. Brown first. I was a runaway slave from Georgia. Several of us was on the run for months, and one night we came upon Mr. Brown's campsite. He let us share his fire.

"Later that night, he told me that he could use a good, hardworking man to help him on his farm. So, I came home with him. He had a two-hundred-acre farm and a large house. He wasn't much of a farmer or a hard worker, but he was a nice, kind man. Later he married Miss Katie.

They were married about five years when he got sick with pneumonia and died. I have never left her side. That's probably been thirty years or more. After years of trying to keep that big farm going, Miss Katie sold it, and she bought this place. We both have been very happy here."

Jesse was very impressed with Jeremiah. He was a strong, stocky little man with skin as black as midnight with large, cinnamon brown eyes. His hair was as white as snow. There was no doubt that he was Miss Katie's beloved friend, helping hand, and protector.

The next morning, saying good-bye to Miss Katie and Jeremiah was very hard to do. Their concern and fears for Rae and Hope were very understandable. Jesse tried to reassure them that the girls were safe, and as soon as the trouble with Herbert was over, he would send them a note.

Jesse told them where he lived and said if they wanted to visit, the door was always open. Rae's aunt agreed to wait at home until she heard from him, but if she was needed, she would come running.

*****

Rosedale

Jess arrived back in Rosedale late that afternoon. It had been a fast, hard trip. His horse needed a good rubdown and a clean stall. After checking in at the livery, he gave his horse a personal rubdown, not leaving it up to the stable boy. He checked every part of his prized mustang's body, making sure he was in good condition before he bedded him down with a bucket of fine oats. He headed over to the boardinghouse for a good bath and meal.

"Something sure smells wonderful in here," Jesse told the lady of the house. "I hope there will be room enough at the table for me to join your other guests," he said, giving her his best smile.

"Oh, Mr. Maxwell, you are more than welcome. It is nice to have you back, and your room is still the same one. Did you have a nice trip?"

"The trip was just fine, but it's sure good to come back to this fine supper. Will your daughter, Amelia be joining us?"

"Why yes, but she always helps me put the food on the table and serve the guests." She answered him with her own sweet smile.

"Here comes everybody now. Please take your seats. Everyone! This is our new boarder, Mr. Maxwell. He will be with us for a few days."

Jesse was nodding his head at the ladies, as he looked across the table directly into the banker's eyes. *Well, what a surprise,* thought Jesse as he gave a nod to Mr. Herbert Summers, himself.

"Mr. Maxwell, Mr. Summers is a recent widower. Since he hasn't anyone at his place to cook for him right now, he has started taking his evening meal with my guests."

"My deepest sympathy to you, sir," Jesse said as sincerely as possible.

Amelia came in the dining room carrying a large platter of fried chicken. A young, petite Negro girl followed right behind her with a big bowl of small red potatoes. Both rushed out to the kitchen and were back in a flash with bowls of lima beans, turnip greens, and creamy white gravy.

Hot fluffy biscuits rounded off the meal. Jesse was getting homesick by the minute, because there was no one who could set a better table than Ollie.

Although, this was certainly a close second.

"Please, everybody begin. I blessed this food a hundred times while I was preparing it," said Mrs. Blades with a laugh.

Herbert was serving his plate but watching Jesse the whole time. "Mr. Maxwell, what brings you to our little town?" Before Jesse could answer, he went on to say, "I'm the banker here, and if I can be of any assistance to you, I would be honored. Of course, with banking matters that is." He chuckled at his own words.

"That is very kind of you. Right now, I don't have any business of any kind that would need your attention, but maybe later." Jesse gave him a smile that never reached his eyes.

"Miss Amelia, this is a wonderful spread of good food. Did you help prepare some of this?" Jesse gestured with his fork at the food.

"I'm sorry to say that I didn't, Mr. Maxwell, but I wish I had." She returned his smile with one of her own. *This table is on fire with the heat coming from that young girl*, thought Jesse.

After supper was over and a delicious peach cobbler was served with thick cream, Jesse could hardly move. He had made a pig out of himself.

As everybody got up and moved out to the front porch or exited to their rooms, the young ladies began cleaning off the table. Jesse knew that this would be his chance to talk to Miss Amelia.

"Here. Let me help you lovely girls by carrying this heavy load for you. I'm a great hand in the kitchen."

"Oh my, Mr. Maxwell, you can't do that. Why this is woman's work, and it would be unseemly for you to be in here," declared Amelia.

"Please call me Jesse or Jess, Miss Amelia. After you have finished, would it be possible for you to join me on the front porch to have a little chat?" Jesse smiled and looked straight into her lovely eyes. *Darn, if she wasn't cute.*

Pausing for a second, Amelia cooed at him, "I guess I can, Jesse."

"Great. I will be waiting for you in the swing." When he left the kitchen, he could hear both of the young girls giggling.

Jesse had waited until the sun had gone down. He had pushed the swing back and forth until he was so drowsy that he could hardly keep his eyes open. Since making the hard thirty-mile ride and filling his gut at supper, he could feel himself being lulled into a very relaxing sleep.

"It doesn't look like you are very interested in talking to me," pouted Amelia. "You are almost asleep."

"Come on over here, little gal, and have a seat. It's your mama's fault that I can't keep awake. I ate so much of her good supper that I have rocked myself to sleep like a baby."

Amelia laughed as she sat down beside him, allowing her hand to slide down the leg of his tight jeans. He retrieved her hand and held on to it while rubbing her soft palm.

"Miss Amelia, how old are you? Sixteen, seventeen? Much too young for an old man like me."

"You're too sweet. I am nineteen, soon to be twenty."

"So, you are spoken for—am I correct in saying that? Your mama did mention this fact to me the first time I came here to let a room." She removed her palm from Jesse's rough hand and placed it back into her own lap.

"Yes, I am engaged, you might say, to Jackie Roberts. He is away at a school that teaches carpentry. If he ever finishes," she added with a big sigh, "we will get married."

"You sound so sad talking about your future. Why is that?"

"Well, he has been gone to Frisco City for months. He wants to learn how to build things, houses mostly. I am just plain tired of waiting. I want to be married now and get away from this place," she said, trying not to cry.

"You know I am sure it's hard for you, but what about him? I bet he can't wait to marry you, but it sounds like he is planning a great future for the two of you."

"Goodness, I hadn't really looked at it that way. I guess I should be more patient. He is coming home next week for a visit," she explained.

Realizing her good mood, Jesse felt that it was a good time to ask about her relationship with Rae. "Miss Amelia, may I ask you a few questions about a young lady I believe you went to school with?"

"I guess, who?"

"Do you know Rae Rogers?"

"Yes, we were friends at one time until she wanted to take my Jackie from me." She sat straight up and pushed her long hair back off her shoulders.

"So, you think that she wanted your boyfriend? Who told you that?"

"Well, Jackie did say that it wasn't true, but her stepfather told me. You know, Mr. Summers, the banker, the man you were talking to at the supper table."

"So, because of this false rumor, you stopped being her friend?"

"Well, I said some pretty ugly things about her to Mr. Summers, and I am sure he told her. I was too embarrassed to see her. Why are you asking about Rae?"

"I can't go into that now, but did you ever visit her after her mama married Mr. Summers and they had the baby?"

"Only once. I went with my mama to see Miss Claire and the new baby. Mama had knitted some booties. Miss Claire baked pies and cakes for Mama before she married the banker. You know, Rae is beautiful, but her mama—she looked like a princess lying in her bed. Something out of a storybook." She shook her head as she remembered Rae's mama. "She was a nice person, too."

"So, you never went back to see Rae when Mr. Summers was at home?"

Amelia shook her head *no*. "Have you been around him very much at all?"

"Like I said before, only that one time. He followed me from school to my gate and stopped me. He told me that Rae was after my beau, and I better keep a close eye on her because Rae liked him and she was jealous of me. I was so angry that I told him some ugly things to tell her, and I ran into the house."

"Later, I confronted Jackie. He said that he hadn't seen Rae in months, and that they really didn't even know each other. He couldn't understand why her stepfather would make up lies about Rae. He was really mad at me. He said that no one else would have believed such a wild story."

Chapter 14

Limason

Jesse had been gone for three days and nights, and everything at the ranch seemed to be running smoothly. All the men were pitching in to do the duties that Jesse did every day. This was a big load off Will's shoulders because Jesse had left him in charge. Will was finding out that being the boss carried a lot of responsibility. He had been left in charge before, but he had never been responsible for anyone's life.

Jesse stressed to him the importance of protecting Rae and Hope from strangers who may come around. Jesse's last words to him were not to let the baby out of his sight. Will didn't think Jesse knew what he was asking. The only time Hope was still was when she was sleeping.

Ollie kept busy with the cooking and cleaning. Rae helped her as much as possible. She really needed to stay busy. With Jesse gone to get information about Herbert, and with everyone worrying that someone coming to the ranch might recognize Hope, she was a nervous wreck.

Rider had butchered a few more hogs, and Ollie requested that he bring her four large hams and some meat that she could slice for bacon.

She needed to prepare her sugar-cured hams so they would be ready for the Christmas dinner in several months.

Ollie told Rae that she was going to teach her to put up hams and some other pork to be eaten during the winter months. She instructed Rider to bring up two large crocks from the cellar and to prepare plenty of coals to be ready to start simmering in the smokehouse.

"Now, Rae, we want to prepare our hams by washing them real good and getting as much blood off the soft skin as we can. Pour a bucket of water in each of the crocks and add about four pounds of salt to that water. Stir that mixture good. Now we are going to drop two hams into each crock and seal the lids. We will let them sit in that salty water for a week. I always take me a piece of paper and write down the day that I did this.

Each day, I make a mark for seven days.

"After a week, we will drain the hams and take them out to the smokehouse and hang them from the rafters for another week. Then, we will wrap the hams in some really thin cloth and place them in the barrel of sugar that we keep stored in the cellar. Come Christmas, we will have the best hams this side of Texas," said Ollie proudly. "I always prepare an extra one for a family that may be in need at that time."

"Oh, Ollie, you are a jewel, but I don't know if I will ever learn how to do all these things you are teaching me," said Rae. "I can't believe all the food that you have put up in canning jars down in the cellar. And to think, all those vegetables will be enjoyed this winter."

"When you live on a farm or ranch, preparing food every day and planning ahead for the winter is necessary. Your family has got to eat, and those who work for you have to be fed too. Having plenty of good food sure helps to make a happy home!"

"Yes, that is so true." Rae smiled.

Rae and Hope had settled into ranch life pretty easily with all the love and understanding that they had received from the men. Hank had fallen head over heels in love with Hope and enjoyed spoiling her every day. There wasn't anything she wanted that she didn't get when Hank was around. If Hank was sitting in the rocking chair, he became her climbing tree. She climbed on his back and shoulders, rode horsey on his good leg, and cuddled in his arms for a nap. Hank had no peace, but he wouldn't have had it any other way.

Will carried Hope for a ride on his pinto horse every afternoon and took her on long walks that always ended with a race back to the house.

They picked flowers to place on the graves in the cemetery and picked small baskets of fresh apples for Rae to cook into a pie or cobbler.

The other men were always teaching her about the animals on the ranch. Rider seemed to be the keeper of the hogs. He loved to watch Hope try to catch a piglet. She would chase it until it would just give up and lie down. After getting a hug and kiss on its little pink nose, she would very gently put it down to run back to its mama.

John took her to the barn every morning to visit with her new puppy.

The little pup was growing and walking around in the barn. With Hope's help, they had to build a small pen to keep the puppies from getting under the feet of the other animals. John would pick up the mama dog and place her in the pen so she could feed her hungry pack. Hope loved watching the puppies suck their milk. She counted the puppies each morning to make sure they were all there.

Joseph took time after lunch to read Hope a short story before she had to lay down for a noon nap. He would tell her stories about his girlfriend and how they were going to get married. It was a wonderful fairy tale about a prince and princess.

Rae knew in her heart that she would have to leave this wonderful place, but she couldn't seem to prepare her mind to start making plans.

Mama was gone. She would have to accept that. She was alone except for her precious little sister and her Aunt Katie. She knew she couldn't go to her aunt's home. Herbert would look there, if he hadn't already. Poor Aunt Katie. She is probably so worried about us. Rae knew that she would have to stay on the ranch for at least another week. *I can't leave until Jesse returns. I promised him that I wouldn't run again, she thought to herself.*

*****

The days that followed, waiting for Jesse's return, seemed to last forever. One afternoon as she was walking out back to bring in the wash from the clotheslines, she heard a horse and carriage driving into the front of the house.

Walking slowly to the corner of the house and looking around it, she saw the doctor climbing down out of the carriage. Will had come out of the barn to greet him, while Rider was standing in the top of the barn looking down with a gun.

What a welcome sight the young doctor was. He was dressed in a two-piece dark suit with a bowler hat on his head. His blond hair was shiny from underneath it. She heard Will ask him if he had been to a funeral. She didn't hear his answer, but they both laughed.

Patting her hair and smoothing her apron with her hands as she walked, Rae called out a greeting. "Hello, Tim. It's so nice of you to drop by. I'm sorry that Jesse isn't here to see you. He went out of town for a week or so."

"That's fine. Really fine, actually." He grinned.

Gosh, there's that smile again, Rae thought.

Rider came out of the barn, walking slowly up to the horse. He said that he would take care of him.

"Come on in to the porch and sit a while. I will get some cold lemonade that Ollie made this morning. She still had ice packed in sawdust in the cellar, and the lemons had to be used."

"Sounds wonderful, thank you."

"Hank is taking a nap, Doc, but I can wake him up," said Will as he pulled up a chair and leaned back in it.

"Let me visit with Rae before you wake him up. I'm in no hurry this afternoon," said Tim, never taking his eyes away from Rae while she was in the kitchen.

Rae came out of the house carrying a tray, and both the doctor and Will jumped up to assist her.

"Thank you, gentleman," she said, laughing. "Will, I brought you a glass too and a slice of my pound cake that I made for supper tonight. Tim, I hope you like pound cake."

Will slammed his chair down, causing Rae to jump. He said that he had to go inside to see Ollie. Grabbing his cake and lemonade, he stomped off into the kitchen.

Ollie had sat down in the rocking chair that was now free from Hank's big body; she was almost asleep. "What in the world is the matter with you, baby boy?" asked Ollie, concerned over the way Will was snorting as he flopped down on the bench at the table.

"Ollie, you best get out on the porch and chaperone Rae and that so-called doctor. He is making cow eyes at her and talking so sweet—it's enough to make a person want to throw up. I know that Jess would have a fi t if he saw the way that Doc is looking at Rae right this minute. He came here to court her, all dressed up in his new duds. I tell you the God's truth, Ollie, Jess wouldn't have any of this." Will pointed to the porch.

Ollie couldn't help smiling at the way Will was carrying on. "Now, Will, you aren't sure how Jess would feel. Rae is a grown girl, and if she doesn't mind the doctor coming to visit her, then it's none of your business or Jess's. Besides, she is not walking out with him. Th ey are only sitting on the porch. If you are so concerned, go back out and sit with them. Jess did make you responsible for her."

Ollie was enjoying herself for the first time in a week. Watching Will trying to protect what he seemed to think was Jesse's property was hilarious. She was going to have to wake Hank up to share this funny story with him.

Alone on the porch, Tim was so pleased to have Rae to himself for a while. "Miss Rae, how are you enjoying your stay here with Jess and his men? It sure is quiet out here. Have you considered moving into town?"

"My goodness, Tim, please call me just Rae. You have asked me several questions, and you haven't given me a second to answer one of them." She scolded him with a sweet smile.

"I'm sorry, Rae. I like saying your name." He reached over and patted her hand ever so softly. "When I'm nervous, I just seem to rattle on. Please, forgive me?"

"What in the world do you have to be nervous about?"

"Well, it's not every day that I get to sit next to a beautiful girl and one that is as nice as you. I don't mean to be so forward, but I can't seem to help myself when I am near you."

"Thank you, Tim. You're a very sweet man. To answer your questions, I am enjoying being here. Ollie is wonderful to Hope and me, and all the men are kind and very helpful. It is quiet here, but that is what I am used to. As for moving into town, Jess said that there isn't a decent place for me to live."

Sitting quietly for a minute, she continued, "I will not be staying here much longer. Maybe a few more weeks. Then we will be moving on." Rae said with much sadness in her voice.

Then she looked over at Tim. "Listen, it's my turn to ask you some questions. I am a little curious. How come a nice man like you isn't married? I would have thought that you would have had a nice young wife with a couple of kids," teased Rae.

Tim laughed loudly. "Me, married with kids? I wish, but going to medical school and trying to build up a practice is very expensive. But I did work in Boston for a few years with my uncle."

"So, how did you get this far south?" asked Rae.

"Well, after I graduated, my uncle wanted me to work in his practice. I always wanted to be a good doctor, so, I thought working with my uncle I could learn a lot. I wanted to know my patients and help them in any way that I could. My uncle had another theory about the way a doctor behaved. He and I worked from sunup to sundown with an office full of patients, and then we would go on house calls all during the night.

"The patients were so quiet and distant, so I tried to change that. I wanted to know the people that I helped. But, if I took an extra few minutes with a patient, my uncle would exercise his power by threatening to fire me. One day, I had enough of my cold, impersonal uncle." Tim cringed a little as he remembered the expression on his uncle's face when he told him his reason for leaving his practice.

"My uncle told me that doctors aren't supposed to be social butterflies. I told him that he shouldn't worry about that, because he would never become one. I walked out, and I never looked back. So, here I am."

Tim looked at Rae, and they both leaned back in the swing and burst out laughing at the same time.

Chapter 15

Rosedale

After learning more about Herbert's strange behavior from Amelia, Jesse knew that he still needed actual proof that this man was a threat to Rae, and if possible, that he was more than a little crazy.

Strolling up the boardwalk, passing one of the saloons that was still closed, Jesse noticed Herbert driving down the center of the street in a small carriage heading out of town.

Now will be a good time for me to go into the bank and talk with some of the employees working there, Jesse said to himself. Maybe they know something about Herbert's strange behavior.

When Jesse entered the bank, he observed a young couple who were in a private conversation. They didn't notice him at first. When the young lady glanced up and saw Jesse, she jumped back from the young man and told him in no uncertain terms that she would see him at supper. "And don't be late," she said as firm as she could before exiting.

"Wow," Jesse commented to the young man. "Now, there goes a piece of dynamite walking out the door." He laughed at the expression on the young man's face.

"You are so right. Girls. They just don't understand when a fellow has to work late. It isn't something we choose to do. I would love to be home eating supper with her folks," replied the young bank clerk.

"Well, things have a way of working out. Just be patience with her. Say, young fellow, are you the bank teller?"

"Actually, my title is 'clerk,' but to hear my boss describe me, I am the bank idiot," mumbled Sawyer.

"Are you the only employee of Mr. Summers, the banker?"

"That's right. My name is James Sawyer, known as Sawyer to everyone in town. How can I help you, sir?"

"My name is Jess Maxwell. I am a friend of Rae Rogers and her little sister. Do you know who I am speaking of?"

"Mr. Maxwell, this town is still small enough that everyone knows everybody and all their business. Yes, I know that Rae's mother married Mr. Summers. People are stilling talking about that marriage. Rae's mother was a beauty. Of course, she was almost old enough to be my mama, but even wearing old faded dresses, she was something special to look upon. My mom and her friends still talk about her marrying the banker man. That crazy old man." Placing his hand up to cover his mouth, he said, "Oh pardon me, sir. I shouldn't speak that way of my boss."

Jesse laughed and asked, "When was the last time you saw Rae? At her mama's funeral?"

"Oh no. Mr. Summers would not allow the bank to be closed, even on the day his wife was buried. Do you believe that? I had to stay here and guard the 'people's money'. That man is as crazy as a loon."

"So, when was the last time you saw her?"

"I had to take some important papers out to their house. This is after the marriage, and Rae came to the door. She was a beauty, just like her mama. Well, Mr. Summers came to the door, and he wanted to know what I was looking at. He said something like, 'Give me those papers and get the hell back to work.' He told me I wasn't paid to gawk. I know he embarrassed Rae, because he sure did me."

"What has Mr. Summers told you about his missing child?"

"Nothing. I saw the poster on the wall outside the sheriff's office, and I told him that I had seen it. He told me to mind my own business, and he left the office for the day."

"Earlier you said that Mr. Summers is crazy. Rae has told me a few stories about when he gets upset—he talks to himself. Have your ever witnessed him doing that?" inquired Jesse ever so cautiously.

Sawyer walked over to the big front window and glanced outside. "You know, Mr. Maxwell, I could lose my position here. I really need this job, and I hope to advance in the banking business. If Mr. Summers ever found out that I was telling people about how he acts, well, if he didn't kill me, I would certainly lose my job."

"Listen Sawyer, Rae's in trouble. She has always been afraid of Mr. Summers, and since her mama died, he has been trying to force her to marry him. She is terrified of him. Now, I am pleading with you to help her prove that he is not a well man. Have you ever witnessed him acting strange?"

"Well, before his wife died, he would come in the office and slam the door closed. I could hear him muttering to himself about her being better. But, the strange part is, he wouldn't be happy about that. After his wife passed away, I heard that Rae and his daughter had gone over to Peamont for a few weeks. He stayed locked up in his office most of one day. I could hear him pacing and talking to himself. He wouldn't even answer the knock on his door when I told him that Mr. Duffy had come to see him on business. Later, I could hear opening and closing of the desk drawers like he was searching for something. I pulled up that chair and looked at him through that open window over his door." Jesse glanced up to where Sawyer had pointed, and it was a small window that pushed out for ventilation.

"He was holding a small gun, checking it out, and then he placed it in his vest pocket. All the while he was checking the gun, he was saying something about killing those nasty pigs. Then he sat down in his chair and laughed. I had seen enough."

"Do you have any idea who he was talking about killing?" Jesse asked, very concerned.

"No, but it sounded like he was speaking about some men. I left for the day before he came out of his office. The next day, he dropped by the bank and said that he would be gone for a couple of days. He acted perfectly normal."

"Mr. Sawyer, would you be willing to talk to the marshal in Frisco City if I find that your testimony about the banker's actions might help Rae?"

Holding up his hand to stop Sawyer from answering, Jesse said, "Listen to me. Mr. Summers is a dangerous man. He is a danger to Rae and his child. And to you, too. You know that you will not be able to continue working for an insane person. I really believe that he is obsessed with desire for Rae. If he cannot have her for a wife, then he could possibly harm her."

Sawyer was afraid to help Jesse, but he was more afraid not to. "Yes, I will do whatever I can to assist Rae's cause."

Jesse reached out and clasped his hand and gave it a good shake.

"Thanks, fellow. I will let you know if I need your help. I am staying over at the boardinghouse. If Mr. Summers comes back here acting crazy, try to send for me."

*****

When Herbert drove into the yard at his home, he noticed two horses tied up at his small barn. He didn't recognize the horses, so he felt a little uncomfortable as he got down and started to the front door. He reached up and patted his chest, making sure his gun was still in place. As he stepped upon the small porch, the door swung open.

"Welcome home, banker man," bellowed Virgil, the nasty cowpuncher that he had hired to bring Rae home. "You ain't got enough food in this shack to feed the rats we seen swarming around. We're starving." He looked over at his young partner for him to agree.

"If I had known that I was having company, I would have prepared a feast," said Herbert sarcastically. "Sit down at the table and let's get this business deal finalized."

Virgil bent over the table and leaned into Herbert's face. He challenged him to show them the money they were promised.

"We don't talk without seeing green first, fat man."

Herbert reached in his vest pocket, careful not to touch his gun, and pulled out $1,000 and laid it on the table. "There. Like I promised."

"Give us the name of who you want us to kill," said Virgil with a grin, spitting a wad of tobacco juice onto the floor.

"You idiot, I don't want the girl killed. She's to be my wife."

"Careful, you fat turd, who you are calling an idiot? Tell us what you want us to do and where we are supposed to meet up with you after we nab the woman. Oh, excuse me, I mean your bride-to-be."

Herbert decided to stay calm and just give them the information they would need to retrieve Rae and get them on their way.

He gave them the name of the small town where Jesse's ranch was located and a description of Rae and Hope. "Rae is a beautiful young lady. If someone had seen her, they will remember. I only want *her*, but she may not leave without the child. Bring the girl along if you must, but dispose of her on the trip. I don't want the child."

The idea of harming a child did not set well with Joe, but Virgil would kill his own mother for a shot of whiskey. As Joe listened to the other two men making plans, he decided that after this deal was over and the money was divided, he was going to part ways with Virgil.

After writing down the town, Rae's name, and the cavern's location where they would take the girl and collect the rest of the money, Joe was feeling better. The plan was for them to bring the girl to the cave, and one of them would go and notify the banker man. Sounded simple enough.

Chapter 16

The morning started out as an ordinary day, but the breeze in the air was very humid for this time of year. Black storm clouds were forming out in the distance.

The men were all gathered for the morning meal when John came in a little later and announced that it looked like a bad storm was headed their way.

Will sat drinking his milk, trying to decide what Jesse would do to prepare the ranch for a storm. *Being in charge is not as easy as it sounds,* thought Will.

"John, what do you think about us rounding up the cattle, especially the heifers and calves, and bring them into the east fenced area? We don't want them scattering over the countryside if the thunder and lightning start getting bad."

John was a big help with knowing what needed to be done. He had come to this farm almost twenty-five years before when Jesse's grandfather was still alive. He had been working on a trail drive when he met Jesse's pa in town. He needed a couple of men to help him build his house, and John was hired and never left.

"Good idea, son. The hogs and piglets need to be brought into the big barn and secured. We've got to do something with the bull. God help us all if something happens to that new prize animal of Jess's," said John.

"Joseph, you and Rider start bringing the cattle in, and John and I will secure the hogs. We will drive the bull into his new shelter, and we better make a rope fence in the front so he cannot get out," Will told John.

"We will take the wagon out to the hay fields and bring in as much of the hay bundles as we can and place them in the barn against the wall in the back. Jess talked about doing that before he left."

"Baby boy," Ollie said, "I will gather my eggs again this morning and put all my chickens in their coop. They are sure scared of storms. They might not lay for a few days afterwards if it gets real bad."

"Ollie, please place Betsy in a stall with plenty of hay. She doesn't like storms either," said Will. He had raised Betsy from a small calf, and she was his baby.

Rider spoke up and said that he and Joseph would corral the horses too, and bring in the two mares that were expecting foals soon.

"Can any of you think of anything else we need to do?" The men glanced around at each other and shook their heads *no*.

"I really appreciate your help this morning, and with that said, let's get busy. Oh, Ollie, sandwiches will be just fine for lunch today. You and Rae have enough to do around here getting prepared for the storm without cooking three large meals." Will gave her a big grin and backed out the screen door.

"My lands, Mr. John, baby boy is all grown up," said Ollie with tears choking her throat. "Wait 'til I tell Mr. Jess."

After Rae had helped Ollie as much as she could with the gathering of eggs and with Hope running wild in the chicken yard, she decided it would be best to take Hope back into the house. At least Ollie could complete her task of locking the chickens in the coop until after the storm passed over.

Ollie had already prepared several loaves of bread to be baked, so Rae removed the cloth that covered the bowls, placed the dough into the pans, and then arranged them in the oven to cook. Fresh bread for the sandwiches would be appreciated once the men had completed their chores.

Rae tiptoed over to Hank's door and looked in on him. He had finally gone to sleep. He had tried walking on his foot earlier that morning, and he fell and bruised his shoulder all over again. Ollie put a little pain medicine in his coffee so he would rest better. He was snoring up a breeze now. Rae closed his door ever so lightly as not to disturb him.

The wind was really blowing now. Rae was looking out the back when she heard the front door open. That's strange, she thought. *No one ever comes through the house that way.* She turned and walked around the kitchen table and glanced into the living area. Two dirty, rough-looking men stood looking around the room.

"Who are you and what are you doing just marching into this home uninvited?" she demanded as she tried to appear unafraid of them. "Hope, come here," said Rae.

Hope got up from the floor and started walking to Rae when the tall, ugly man grabbed and picked her up high in the air. "Well, what do we have here?" Before he knew what hit him, Hope started screaming and kicking at him with her little feet. She got him right below the belt, and he turned her loose. She scrambled to Rae as fast as she could.

Breathing hard, the mean cowpuncher growled, "We have come to fetch you. Your bridegroom is waiting sweetheart, and we are leaving now. We got our horses tied up on the side of the house. If any one of those men outside comes through that door, I am going to blow him to hell and back. Understand? So start moving your fanny over to the front door."

"What do you mean 'bridegroom'? I am not getting married to anyone. Who sent you here? I can't just walk out and leave my baby."

While the men were listening to Rae, Ollie opened the kitchen door and entered. Looking at the two strangers, she immediately demanded, "What's going on here? Who are you men, and what do you want?"

"Damn it to hell! We got to git out of here now. You. Get out of our way before I blow a hole in that black skull of yours. She is leaving with us, and you best back off." The tall nasty stranger waved his pistol toward Rae.

"This here child ain't leaving this place, and if she does, she ain't leaving without me, you low-down piece of scum. Go ahead and shoot me if you want. But when those men outside hear the noise, you'll be one sorry dead piece of white trash!"

Virgil pointed his pistol straight at Ollie's head, and she stood staring at him, never blinking an eye, daring him to shoot. Joe, his silent partner, stepped in front of Virgil and said, "There will be no gunfire now. Understand? We aren't paid enough to kill a dozen people. So back off, and let's grab these two ladies and that child and get the hell out of here. The bride can ride with you, and the other one can ride the mare. I will carry the kid."

As Joe was trying to keep Virgil from going off half-cocked, Rae whispered to Hope to leave the room, quiet as a mouse, and hide. "I will come and find you in a little bit. Don't come out no matter what you hear."

"Let's all move to the front door now, before I forget myself and shoot you. *Now,*" said Virgil through his black, tobacco-stained teeth.

"Ollie, please stay here. I will be fine. I am sure Herbert has sent these men, and he won't harm me."

"It's too late. This here hag is going!"

"Please don't take her. She is nothing to Herbert. I beg you to let her stay," pleaded Rae.

"Shut your trap and move." He waved his gun toward the front door.

As Ollie and Rae went out the front door with Virgil to the horses, Joe looked around the front room for the child. Where did she get off to? he said as he glanced around. He went to a closed bedroom door, and he could hear snoring coming from that room. He moved to the next room, and he saw a dolly lying next to the bed on the floor. He looked behind the door, glanced around the dressing screen, and lifted the bedspread from one of the two beds.

He remembered what banker man said about disposing of the child.

Hell, why even bring her along? If we leave her here, then there will not be a problem. I am not going to harm a baby, he thought. When he turned around to walk out of the room, the dolly had disappeared. Now he knew the child's hiding place, and he also knew that she would be safer left behind.

Joe hurried out the front door and couldn't believe his eyes at the sight Virgil was having to handle. He had tied Rae's hands together and gagged her with his dirty bandanna and pushed her to the ground. The old black woman was gagged too, but her hands were left free. Virgil was cussing a blue streak at her, demanding that she get on the horse. If not for the wind, Virgil's voice would have been heard by the men.

Ollie had taken the back of her skirt and pulled it through her legs to the front and tucked it into her apron. She was trying to place her left leg in the stirrup and pull herself up on the horse. The horse was too high for her foot to reach. The mare was very skittish and was taking side steps away from her. With the strong wind blowing in the horse's face and the smell of fear coming from this strange black person, the mare was not cooperating at all. Joe took all this in and rushed over to Ollie.

"Here, I will give you a boost. Grab the saddle horn and pull up. The saddle will not come off." It took two more attempts, but with Joe's assistance, Ollie finally straddled the horse.

Virgil rushed over to Ollie and wrapped a rope around her wrists several times as tight as he could. "You make a wrong move, and I will hurt her bad." He motioned his head toward Rae. "I don't want to disfigure that lovely piece of merchandise, but I will if you make me." Ollie nodded to let the scumbag know that she would cooperate.

Virgil threw Rae upon his prancing horse and leaped up behind her, giving her an added squeeze. When Joe reached for his bridle, Virgil moved his horse over to him and asked, "Where is the brat?" Rae was looking all around, praying that Hope had found a good hiding place.

"I couldn't find her—besides, she's not part of the deal. Let's ride."

Joe jumped up on his saddle and grabbed the bridle of Ollie's mare, and he motioned for Virgil to take the lead.

*****

Hank had a good nap and his shoulder wasn't hurting him like it did earlier that morning. He was going to have to keep his big butt off his bad ankle for a little longer. He sat up on the side of the bed, stretched real big, and smelled something in the air that was different. He reached for his crutches and after standing straight, he hopped over and opened the door. *Gosh oh mighty, smoke?* He thought as he continued into the kitchen.

Black smoke was boiling out of the oven door. Looking around the house, it was quiet and empty of people. *What's going on?* He hopped over to the oven and reached up and got two hand towels. Opening the door of the oven, the smoke rushed out, smelling of burned bread. He reached and removed the four burned loaves of bread, wondering where in the blazes Ollie and Rae were.

Hank decided he needed some help to get this mess outside before it smelled up the whole house. Hopping over to the door, he went out to the porch and looked toward the barn, chicken yard, and the corral. The little breeze that started before he took a nap now had the making of a hurricane, Hank thought. The clouds overhead made the day appear to be sundown, and it was only a little after noon.

Hank couldn't believe that the girls weren't in the house. They would *never be out in this weather.* Something is wrong. I feel it in my bones, he said to himself.

Reaching for the dinner bell, he gave it a good ringing. *Hell, where is everybody?* The place looked like a ghost town with the wind howling. He gave the bell another good swing.

John and Will were in the back of the barn unloading the bales of hay when they heard the bell ringing, thinking that it was Ollie getting ready to put lunch on the table. "Let's finish this before the rains starts," said John. After the second time they heard the bell, Will looked at John and said, "Let's go!"

Rounding the house on the run, Will jumped up on the porch with John right behind him.

"What's wrong?" yelled Will over the howling of the wind.

"Where are the girls?" asked Hank. "Ollie, Rae, and Sweetheart are not in the house, and the bread is all burned. The house is filled with smoke."

"How long you been awake, Hank? Ollie was headed back in the house when John and I took the wagon out to the pasture about an hour ago. Right, John?" Will had started brushing the hay off his clothes before he entered the house.

"Well, you may have seen her coming to the house, but she ain't in here! Neither is Rae or the baby. Something's wrong. Come and give me a hand getting that stinking bread out of the kitchen and start looking around outside for them. Maybe toward the apple orchard," directed Hank.

John grabbed up the pans of bread and took them out to the porch.

Rider held open the screen door for John so he could dispose of the bread in a barrel. "What happened with that?" asked Rider, pointing to the burned loaves.

"We aren't sure. Ollie, Rae, and Sweetheart are not in the house. It's hard to believe that they would be out in this storm," yelled John.

"Hold the door for me, Rider," said Joseph as he came across the yard carrying a wooden box filled with the new puppies and the mama dog running beside him. "These little buggers were crawling all around in the barn. The other animals will be stepping on them for sure. I'm going to place them in the corner of the kitchen where they will be safe until this storm blows over."

After putting the pups down, Joseph turned to Rider and said, "What's wrong?"

Will came in from Hank's room and said, "Everyone go in different directions around the house and barn area. Look for any clues that may tell us where the girls are. We have got to get them in the house before this storm breaks."

As Will turned to leave the kitchen, he noticed that the front door was ajar. That door was never used. "Hey fellows, look. This door is open. Did any one of you open this door?"

The others had all gathered at the front door, and Will went on out to the porch and down the steps to the yard. Looking down on the ground, he spotted Ollie's red bandanna. Reaching down to pick it up, he yelled, "Hey fellows. Come look. The ground is all torn up with horse tracks."

Will turned white as a sheet and grabbed John's arm. "John, someone has taken them. That man that is after Rae … damn, everyone come into the house."

Joseph went over to the stove and put on a pot of coffee. Will told them to all sit down, and he would tell them as much as he knew about Rae and the reason she came to be at the ranch. He finished by saying, "So you see that is why Jesse is out of town. He went to Rosedale to investigate this stepfather of hers. He will not be back for another three or four days. Oh, my goodness. We are going to have to wait out this storm before we can try to follow them. By then, the rain will have washed away their tracks."

As the men talked, the mama dog had gotten up and gone into the girls' bedroom and laid down with her nose under Hope's bed. She started whimpering and wagging her tail. Hope raised her head up a little bit and looked into the eyes of the animal. While hiding under the bed and being as still as a mouse, she had fallen asleep. Hearing the whimpering and remembering that she was playing a game with

Mama, she placed her finger to her little lips and said, "Go away, be quiet."

John had noticed that the dog had gone out of the room and told Joseph, "You better check on that dog. You know Ollie don't like animals in the house."

Joseph put his coffee cup down and wandered into the bedroom where he found the mama dog. "Come on, girl, let's go back to your pups." Mama dog just continued wagging her tail and whimpering louder. "What you got treed under that bed, girl?" Walking over and bending down on one knee to look under the bed, Joseph couldn't believe his eyes.

"Hey, guys. Come and see who mama dog has discovered under the bed."

Hope started giggling at Joseph's remark and began scooting out from under the bed. "Mama didn't find me," she yelled, happy to know that she had hid really well this time.

Hank reached down and picked up his little sweetheart and hugged her so tight that she pushed at him to turn her loose. He had tears in his eyes. "I gotto go find Mama now," she declared, thinking that they were still playing.

Will took Hope by the hand and said, "Please come and sit with us at the table. We need for you to tell us about the game you were playing with your mama. Do you know where your mama and Ollie are right now?"

Please, Lord, *Will prayed,* let her know something to help us.

John reached in the cookie jar and got a cookie for Hope and a cup of milk. "While you are eating, why don't you tell us what you were doing before you went and hid under the bed?" he said.

"Mama and me was going to cook something yummy. A dirty man came in that door." She pointed her little finger in the direction of the door.

"He can't do that, can he, Will? Ollie told me never use that door. Mama didn't like him. Told him to go away. Another man came in that door too.

They shouldn't do that! Anyway, that man wanted Mama to go on a trip."

"Did your mama know these men? Did you hear them call each other a name?" asked Will.

"One question at a time, Will. Be patient, she will tell us what she knows in her own way," John said.

"Can I have another cookie? I'm hungry," asked Hope.

"Did your mama know these men who came into the house?" asked Will again.

"I never seen them before. They acted ugly and talked dirty," Hope said like a grown-up. "Ollie didn't like them! She did like this." Hope started waving her arm over her head, shaking her finger. "Ollie told them to leave. She picked up her broom and yelled at Mr. Scumbag that she would hurt him real bad if they didn't leave. I was scared of them. Mama whispered in my ear to go and hide and she would come and find me. So, I did. I hid real well too, 'cause Mr. Scumbag, he came looking for me in that room," pointing to the bedroom as she was talking.

"So, after you hid and the man didn't find you, could you hear the men talking to Rae and Ollie?" quizzed Hank.

"I just laid real still, quiet as a mouse. I hid real well. I want to tell Mama!" Hope said as she was attempting to get down from the table.

"Sweetheart, we think that Rae and Ollie went away for a while with those men. So, I am going to take care of you while they are gone. You and I are going to take care of the young colt and puppies for a few days. Will you help me do that?" Hank gave Hope a sweet smile while patting her little hand.

"But I want to go with Rae. Please Hankie. I want my mama," screamed Hope at the top of her lungs. "Rae promised to never leave me."

"Come here, Sweetheart, and sit on my lap. We are all going to be fine, I promise you that. Please don't cry," said Hank as he pressed her little face into his chest, trying to reassure her.

Will nodded his head for the men to follow him into the bedroom.

"We have to make plans now. It looks like Rae's stepfather only wanted those men to nab Rae and not his child."

"But why did they take Ollie?" asked Rider. "I have never seen her on horseback as long as I have been here, and there aren't any wagon wheel tracks out there."

"All I can figure from the nasty talk Hope overheard, Ollie must have walked in on them trying to take Rae. I bet she did give them a piece of her mind. She probably wouldn't allow them to take Rae without taking her, too."

"She's lucky the men didn't kill her," said Joseph.

"They would've had to shoot her. Most white men won't kill a woman any other way. They knew if they fired their gun, one of us would have heard it," remarked John.

"In the morning, John, you and Joseph, start tracking their trail or what's left of it. Check all the empty barns, miners' shacks, caves, and anything else they could use for a hideout. They have to have a place to put the girls until they make contact with the man who hired them."

"Rider, I need for you to ride to Rosedale and find Jess. Plan to leave as soon as you think it is safe outside. Pack at least three days' supplies to have with you on the trail. Be sure to take a bag of oats. You should find plenty of water for yourself and your horse. On second thought, you best take an extra mare, like Jess did.

"I will ride over to see Mr. Downing and ask if he will let one of his boys come over and feed the livestock every day. I will tell him to come in the house and get his orders from Hank," said Will, glancing over at Hank to get an okay sign. "The cattle and bull are fine for now. Maybe Mr. Downing will ride over and check on everything out in the pastures, too. We will be gone for a few days, for sure. I will ask Mrs. Downing if she will cook dinner for Hank and Hope each day. Her boy can bring it when he comes to do the afternoon chores. Hank can handle some of the cooking, I know. Of course, Jess will pay this family for helping out."

Will was trying to remember everything that needed to be done while they would all be gone.

"After I finish at the Downing farm, I will catch up with you," said Will, looking at John and Joseph. "Let start packing tonight and be ready to leave at first light," he said as they were entering the front room. "Select the strongest packhorse we have to help carry our supplies. We *are* going to find those rotten … critters." Noticing Hope still sitting in Hank's lap, he cleaned up his language.

The rain was pounding down on the roof of the house like a drummer. The wind was blowing tree limbs down, and water was overflowing from the windmill because it had been forgotten with all of the excitement. Will stood looking out of the window at the storm and said a silent prayer: *Please God, don't let anything happen to my Ollie. Keep her from harm, because she's the only mama I ever have known.*

Chapter 17

"Damn it, man, we've got to find shelter!" yelled Virgil back at Joe. "There ain't a dry spot on my body, and I'm freezing."

Stupid man, I guess he thinks we ain't wet or cold, thought Ollie, glancing around Joe, trying to see Virgil and Rae.

"I am sure there is an old miner's shack not far from here. We will have to chance staying there tonight," said Joe. "Let me take the lead, and I will find it." In just a few minutes, Joe was as good as his word, and he rode up in front of an old shack that was leaning to one side.

Have mercy, thought Ollie. *At least, let it have a roof,* she prayed.

Joe jumped down off his horse and hurried over to the shack's door and pushed it open. A few birds flew out, giving Joe a fright. "Crap," he said under his breath.

Taking a few more steps inside, he saw that it was dry and had a fireplace with a chimney. Stepping outside, he waved to Virgil to come on in. Joe walked over and unwrapped Ollie's hands that had been tied to the saddle horn, "Get down," he yelled. "Go inside quickly." Ollie looked down at the ground and said, "You put me up here, sonny boy, so you gonna have to help me down."

Joe took the bridle to hold the horse still while reaching up to help balance Ollie as she lifted one leg over and slid down the side of the saddle. Her legs and backside were on fire from the pain of riding, and her legs were stiff and wobbly. She slid down on to the ground, landing on her wide backside.

Virgil had gotten off his horse and pulled Rae down with him, dragging her toward the shack. When Rae reached Ollie, she tried to help her up. Virgil screamed into the wind, "Let that big tub of lard stay on the ground. Didn't want her to come anyway."

Joe gave Ollie a hand, steadied her on her feet, and pointed to the shack for her to go. He led the three animals around the back and tied them under an old shed that only had three posts holding it up. "Sorry boy," Joe whispered to his horse. "At least you will be out of the rain."

When Joe went into the house, Ollie had walked over to Rae and was struggling to untie her hands and remove the gag tired over her mouth.

"Damn, Virgil. Can't you even start a fire? We are all freezing. Go out and get your saddlebags. I got mine here with some supplies." Looking around, he said, "Maybe we can find a pot or something to make coffee in."

Virgil looked at Joe like he wanted to kill him, but he stormed out of the shack.

"Look ladies, Virgil is a mean man so you don't want to do anything to cross him. All we want to do is hand you over to the banker man and collect our reward for bringing you to him. I don't want any harm to come to either of you, so walk cautiously."

The shack door was jerked open and slammed when Virgil returned, carrying his saddlebags and sucking on a fresh bottle of rye whiskey. "Now, I am getting warm from the inside out." He sneered at the ladies.

Ollie had untied Rae's hands and removed the gag from her mouth.

Both women decided if there was going to be a fire, they were going to have to build it. Looking around the shack for some dry wood and seeing none, Ollie said, "We are going to have to bust up some of this rotten, old furniture to burn. Everything outside is too wet."

Joe took an old rocker that had one part of the rocker leg missing and slammed it on the stone chimney until it broke into many small pieces.

Reaching into his saddlebags, he pulled out a piece of flint. After giving it several hard rubs, in just a few seconds, a fire ignited and the rotten wood blazed quickly.

"I have never seen anything look so pretty," mummed Rae to Ollie. "It's glittering and oh so warm," holding out her hands toward the warmth.

Rae was standing shoulder to shoulder with Ollie in front of the fire. She was holding her hair close to the fire hoping to get it a little dryer.

Noticing Ollie's hair without her red bandanna covering it, she reached up and placed her hand on it. "I have never seen you without your scarf. Your hair is so pretty."

Ollie smiled for the first time in hours. Her hair was snow-white with a mass of tiny little curls. She looked so much younger. As a young slave, she wasn't allowed to wear her hair uncovered, so she kept it cut short with a bandanna over it. It was so kinky that it would not grow long, just straight out.

As Ollie wandered around the room, she found several pots and pans and a coffeepot. "Thank you, Jesus," she murmured under her breath.

"Hey there, you get me some water and I will make coffee. I need enough to wash this dirty pot." Ollie was looking over at Joe.

Virgil had spread his bedroll over in the corner of the front room and was sprawled out on it, nursing his bottle.

"Virgil, you need to eat something, man, or you gonna be drunker than a skunk in a short while. Hold off on some of that booze," instructed Joe.

"Since when did you become my nursemaid? I don't need you telling me what I need to do, and besides, I don't smell anything cooking." He laughed and turned over on his side to face the wall. He was wet and exhausted.

Joe knew that he was going to have to tread lightly around Virgil because he was very close to being drunk . *Virgil is always really bad, but he turns into a monster when totally intoxicated.*

"You," Joe said, pointing at Rae, "come with me. We have got to go out and get some rainwater."

Ollie busied herself by going through Joe's saddlebags and sorting out some of the food that he had brought. She found two cans of beans, and a rope of sausage that had to be eaten soon since it wasn't smoked. Joe and Rae returned quickly and both rushed back over to the fireplace. It had stopped raining, but the wind was still blowing and with wet clothes on, it was freezing outside. Joe pointed to the bucket of water that he brought in. Ollie took some of the water and washed out the coffeepot and filled it to the brim. She put in the coffee beans and placed it in the fireplace to boil. They all needed something hot to drink to warm their insides. Then she prepared the food in one of the pans she had found.

After the hot coffee, beans, and sausages were eaten, Ollie asked Joe if she and Rae could have a few minutes of privacy outside. "Sure thing. One at a time."

When they had both come back inside, Virgil's snoring was rattling the walls of the poor structure that at one time had probably been a pretty nice place. Rae and Ollie cleaned a spot on the floor for them to try and rest for the night. Joe came over and tied their hands and feet.

"I'm sorry I have to do this, but I'm dead. We rode nearly fifty miles before we ever got to your place. I want to be able to sleep without worrying about you two trying to sneak away from this charming place. We will be leaving at first light."

Joe unrolled his bedroll and started to spread it out on the floor near the fire. When he glanced up and saw the women without any cover, he shook his blankets apart and tossed one to them.

Ollie and Rae were sitting up with their backs leaning against the wall. Both of them were exhausted, too. Ollie placed her left arm around Rae's shoulder and pulled her head down onto her lap. "Rest, baby, I am here," she said.

The next morning, with the fire gone out in the fireplace, a deep chill had spread in the shack. Virgil woke up first, shivering from the cold while trying to stand. A tiny bit of sunlight peeked in through a dirty window was the only light in the room. After getting to his feet, he took a giant step and kicked Joe in the back. "Wake up. We've got to get out of here, and I gotta go outside to take a pee. Get them women up and pack our saddlebags. I'll be back in a minute. Be ready to ride."

Ollie was already awake. She could hardly rest because her legs and backside hurt so bad from the rough horse ride she had endured. Now, there would be more of the same today.

"Come on, Ollie. Let me help you up," said Rae. "Today, don't pull your skirt up between your legs. Use it to protect the skin on your thighs and the side of your calves." Rae had seen the red abrasions on Ollie's legs. The skin had been rubbed raw from touching the horse's hair while riding. Hugging her close, Rae whispered, "We are going to be fine. Jess, Will, and the others will find us. I am sure of that." Ollie held Rae tight and gave her a reassuring pat on the back.

Virgil came storming back inside the cabin demanding something to eat. *Th*ank goodness Joe saved some of the sausages from last night for the pig to eat, thought Ollie.

After a trip to the bushes to relieve themselves, Virgil grabbed Rae and retied her hands and placed her up on his horse, then leaped up behind her.

"Good morning, beautiful," he said, nuzzling her ear. She had to turn her head to keep from vomiting from the smell of his body odor.

Joe gave Ollie another lift onto her mare and took the bridle. "Damn, boy, ain't you gonna tie her hands?" demanded Virgil.

"She's not going anywhere. Besides, she needs all the help she can have to stay on her horse," replied Joe.

"You better say your prayers she doesn't get away. Idiot," declared Virgil.

It seemed like hours before Virgil pulled his horse to a stop. "I'm sure the cave is just over there behind those trees. I'm going to walk over that way to make sure. Watch these ladies."

Joe turned to the girls when he was sure Virgil was out of hearing range and said, "Listen, we will be staying in this cave for a few days until your bridegroom comes. We have plenty of food, and there is a small stream running inside. At least we will be dry and warm. Be quiet and don't say anything where Virgil can hear you. He will kill us all if we cross him today. Understand?" Joe said as he looked at Rae and Ollie. He did not really expect an answer.

Joe heard a whistle, and he knew that was the all-clear signal from Virgil. Grabbing the horses' bridles, he headed toward the cave.

"This is a great setup," said Virgil. "A man could hole up here for days. Someone left a lot of firewood over in that section of the cave. In the back, there is a place where we can put the horses. I am sure glad I remembered this place. I must have been ten, maybe twelve, when I stayed here with my pa on our way to Mexico."

"This is a nice place. When are you leaving to go get the banker? There is still plenty of daylight left," said Joe.

"What do you mean? When am I going? Who made you chief of this here war party? I may not want to ride for two hard days there and then back. I'm thinking that I might rather hang around here with this pretty little princess. I bet she's a virgin." Moving close to Rae, he pulled her to him and said, "Am I right? This here gal, lil' Joe, is fresh off the vine, and I am thinking we could share her." Virgil looked at Joe, grinning like a fool. "Why let that fat banker have all the fun?" Nuzzling Rae's neck and leaving whisker burns on her white delicate skin, she tried pushing him away. Then she remembered what Joe had said about crossing Virgil. She stopped fighting and stood as still as she could, letting her mind flow in other directions, except how he pawed at her body.

"Cut it out, Virgil," demanded Joe. "Stop messing with her." Seeing the marks on her neck, he said very calmly, "If you rough her up, the banker man may not want to pay us. Now, if you don't want to go and tell him where we are, then I will. I will be happy to ride along with the banker and guard the rest of our reward money. Besides, there's that little gal I've been wanting to revisit outside of Rosedale one more time before returning here."

Rae and Ollie were both praying that Joe would be the one holding them hostage. At least he wasn't as disgusting as Virgil.

"The hell you say, sonny boy. That gal is mine, and I can't trust you with the banker. You'll probably kill the old man and take the rest of the money," Virgil said, thinking that wasn't a bad idea. "Next time I see you, it would be in Mexico where I would have to shoot you." Virgil laughed like a wild man.

"No, sonny boy. I am leaving right this minute. I will be back in three days. If I'm not back," he said, reaching out to grab Rae's hair and pulling her body into his, "just blow out her pretty little brains." He gave Rae a shove that sent her flying to the hard floor.

Ollie started toward Rae, but immediately she saw Rae shake her head *no*. She stood very still so as not to bring any attention her way. *Please Lord, get that trash out of here before I have to kill him with my bare hands,* prayed Ollie.

Joe went out of the cave with Virgil and came back in leading his horse. "Move on back into the cave and find yourself a place to settle."

Rae and Ollie walked toward the darkness of the cave and looked around for a comfortable place to sit down. Joe stood over the girls and retied Rae's hands, and ran the rope down her legs and wrapped her ankles tight with the same length of rope. Looking down at how she was tied reminded her of the way cowboys roped and tied calves at a rodeo. It made her think that this man must have worked on a farm or ranch before.

"Come with me, ma'am, and go refresh yourself outside. I know you can cook, so afterward, you can rustle up something for us to eat," said Joe to Ollie. "Afterward, I will give Rae a turn outside. Now, let's go."

*****

Rosedale

Jess sat on his bed in the rooming house after talking with Amelia on the porch. He really didn't get the kind of proof he needed about Herbert from her. She did confirm several things about Rae's past that Rae had already told him. Living with Herbert had to be hard for a young, pretty girl. But he still needed concrete evidence that Herbert was dangerous and posed a threat to the girls. Mr. Sawyer's testimony would be a great help, but for now, it would be his word against the banker's.

After rising from the bed and removing his clothes, Jesse was exhausted. He had traveled on horseback thirty miles, overeaten at dinner, and then talked for an hour with Amelia. Right now, he knew that he still had a lot to do in order to help Rae. Stretching out on the bed, he was asleep in just a few minutes.

Sheriff Miller was having his second cup of coffee this morning at his desk when a young stranger opened his office door. Removing his hat, the man inquired, "Sheriff?"

"That's me, young man. Miller is my name. What's yours?"

"Back home, they call me Rider, sir. I'm looking for a man, and I am hoping that you can help me locate him."

"Who might that be, sonny?"

"His name is Jess Maxwell. Have you met him?"

"Sure have. Nice young man, too. Why are you looking for him?" The sheriff noticed the gun belt with a Colt pistol in the holster, riding low on his hips.

"We've got trouble at home, and I need to let him know about it pronto."

"Jess took a room at the boardinghouse, but a few days ago, he went to Peamont to see someone. I'm not sure he has made it back. Check his room first."

As Rider turned to leave, the sheriff asked, "What kind of trouble you got at home, son?"

"I best tell Jess first," mumbled Rider as he hurried out the door.

After gaining entrance into the boardinghouse with Mrs. Blazes trailing on his heels, he knocked hard on Jesse's door. When he heard someone rattling the door handle and calling his name, Jesse sat up and rolled off the bed, grabbing his jeans.

"Hey. Give me a second." he yelled, hopping on one foot then the other to pull up his pants. Jesse jerked the door open wide.

"Rider. This is a surprise. Come in." Standing behind Rider stood Mrs. Blazes. "Thank you, Mrs. Blazes, for allowing Rider up here," he said and shut the door in her face.

"What's happened?" Seeing Rider meant bad news.

Rider didn't waste words telling Jesse what had taken place at the ranch, starting with the two strangers sneaking in the house and kidnapping Rae and Ollie.

Jesse was stunned. "Why, why did the men take Ollie? Don't get me wrong. I knew that Herbert was a bad man and hiring men to grab Rae is not surprising, but Ollie? She has never ridden a horse." Jesse was astonished.

"Just listening to the baby tell her story, we figured Ollie wouldn't allow the men to take Rae without taking her too. She called them some nasty names. Sweetheart repeated most of them."

Jesse was putting on the rest of his clothes as Rider told him the facts as to what took place and what the rest of the guys were doing now. "Will, John, and Joseph are out trailing the men. Man, we had one bad storm. The worst I have ever seen. Before the rain, we saw horse tracks all around the side of the house. Those thieves came into the house by the front door."

While listening to Rider, Jesse had dressed and repacked his saddlebags.

He was ready to walk out of the door, when he stopped. "Why didn't they take Hope? She's Herbert's child." He gave Rider a bewildered glance.

"She told us that Rae said for her to run and hide, and she did. Joseph had brought in mama dog and her pups from the barn 'cause they were wandering all over, under the feet of the other animals. Mama dog went into the bedroom and sniffed Hope out from under the bed. That's where we found her. Safe and sound, thank goodness."

Jesse wanted to leave Rosedale immediately, but he had to stop in and talk with the sherifftepping into the office, Jesse said as calm as possible,

"Sheriff , he has gone and done it. Herbert hired two men to kidnap Rae and her little sister. But, his plan didn't go exactly as planned. Those fools that he hired took Rae and my old nanny, Ollie. I can understand the idiots kidnapping Rae for a reward that Herbert has offered to pay them, but to take Ollie." He shook his head and tried not to appear shaken. "If they harm either one of them, they will pay dearly with their lives," Jesse said, while trying not to have a violent outburst.

The sheriff had not said a word. He really didn't want to believe what he was being told. He has suspected the banker wasn't playing with a full deck for quite a while, but he hadn't been able to put his finger on the problem.

"Look Jess, before you go rabbit ass crazy, let's talk about this. I know that you are eager to get home, but have you been out to Herbert's house or to the bank to see if he is there?"

"No, Rider got me out of bed just fifteen minutes ago."

"I will ride out to his house, and if he is there, I will arrest him. If he isn't, I will break into the house and have a look around. You go to the bank and talk with that Sawyer fellow and see what he knows. Don't leave town without talking with me first. I will have to send a note to the marshal in Frisco City and get you some help down your way. All right, boy?"

"Good plan, and thanks for your help. We will see you back here in a little while," said Jesse.

"Come on, Rider, let's go to the bank. When we get there, I want you to go around the back. There is a back entrance. Watch it, and if that idiot comes out the door well, bring him back in," said Jesse.

Jesse walked slowly up to the front of the bank and pushed on the door.

It was locked. "Damn, it's not time for the bank to be open."

After peeking into the bank window and walking around on the boardwalk for a few seconds, he looked up and saw Mr. Sawyer coming across the street with a shiny, round lunch bucket. "Good morning Mr. Maxwell. You're an early bird today. Do you need to see Mr. Summers?"

"Just open the door so we can go in and talk," said Jesse very sternly.

"Of course, but I wanted to say that Mr. Summers is out of town for a few days."

"When did he leave?"

"Yesterday morning, I think. Why?"

Looking around the bank, Jesse asked Sawyer how Herbert was acting the last time he saw him.

"Well, kinda strange as usual, as far as I am concerned. He told me not to go near the bank vault. If someone needed money, they would just have to wait for his return."

"Do you have the combination to the safe?" Before Sawyer could answer, he asked, "Had he ever given you those same instructions when he left for a few days?"

Sawyer was giving Jesse a funny look when he asked about the combination to the safe. "Yes, I can open the safe when he is not here; and no, he has never told me not to help our customers."

"Come on, Sawyer, let's have a look in that safe. I have a feeling the banker man has helped himself to your customers' money." Jesse was very curious as to what they may find.

"What? Oh please, God, no. He always said that if money came up missing, I would go to jail. I swear Mr. ... I swear, I've never taking one penny."

"Calm down," said Jesse.

Hearing all the commotion and becoming alarmed, Rider pushed in the rear door and came charging in with his pistol drawn. "What the hell?" he snarled as he regained his balance.

"It's all right, Rider, put away the gun. Herbert has already left town. Sawyer is going to open the safe to see if Summers helped himself to some traveling money."

Sawyer's hands were very unsteady. It took three attempts to open the safe because he was terrified that the money would be gone. Once he heard the clink that signaled the opening of the safe, he slowly pushed open the door. Sawyer went white as a sheet and panicked. He screamed louder than Jesse had ever heard a man scream. *"No!"*

Jesse walked into the safe and saw the cause for Sawyer's frustration. All the money was gone. Banker man had taken every last penny.

For a minute, Jesse was ecstatic that he had the proof that Herbert had embezzled all the money, and that he would be able to help Rae. But a feeling of sorrow came just as fast. These good people of Rosedale didn't deserve to have their life savings stolen from them.

"Rider, please go and get the sheriff and tell him what we have found here. Tell him to hurry because we have got to get on our way. Herbert's house is the first house that you will see about two miles out traveling east. I will wait here with Sawyer."

Jesse walked over to the pump and got Sawyer a tall glass of water. "Here, man, drink this. You have nothing to worry about. Herbert will be caught, I promise you."

"How can you be so sure?"

"Remember me telling you before that Herbert really is an evil person? I do believe he is obsessed with having Rae as his wife. He hired two men to kidnap her, and they did this a few days ago. Unfortunately, my nanny was there and they took her too."

"What about his little girl? Did they take her?"

"No, they couldn't find her or didn't want to. Thank God for that. I am going to be leaving as soon as the sheriff comes. I want to thank you for all your help, and I hate this for you and the townspeople. You are stronger than you know, Mr. Sawyer. You will make a good bank president one day. Don't let this bank fold. Hopefully, some of the money will be retrieved when Herbert is caught."

Rider and Sheriff Miller knocked on the front door. Sawyer let them in, and after a long discussion as to who would be notified about the kidnapping and robbery, Jesse said his good-byes. "Take care, Sheriff , and take care of my man here," patting Sawyer on the back as he exited.

Chapter 18

Limason

Will and the other men traveled many miles through the slush and mud that the rain storm had caused. The rain had let up, but the terrain was really dangerous for the animals. In the dark early hours, the riders had to be careful not to guide their horses into a gopher hole or a small cactus.

Once it was daylight and the sun had come out, they were able to cover more territory. They were all so frustrated because the earth had been washed clean of any horse tracks and they were wet, hungry and exhausted.

After the third day of searching with no trace of the girls, they knew it was time to return home. Will prayed that Rider had found Jesse and that they were on their way back to the ranch. Hopefully, Hank had been able to send word to the sheriff of Limason. There were many miles of country between home and Mexico. Those buzzards could have Rae and Ollie hidden anywhere.

*****

Rosedale

Before Jesse and Rider started on the trip home, Jesse purchased two more horses. He planned for the two of them to travel as far as they could without stopping. They would rest for a few hours and head out again.

Both men were worried because they knew Herbert had a day's ride ahead of them. The fact that the banker was traveling in a carriage, stopping to rest, and spending the night under the stars, would help shorten the distance between them. Herbert wasn't a young man, and he couldn't endure the fast pace because he had never worked outside and his fat body was in poor condition.

*****

Limason

Late in the afternoon, Herbert and Virgil arrived at the livery in Limason. Before this town had settled down with a sheriff and law-abiding citizens, it had a house of ill repute called Lilly's Palace. The cattle drives that Virgil worked as a drover made frequent stops outside of town, and he was one of Lilly's regular customers. He was welcomed with open arms, so the ladies could empty his pockets of his hard-earned money. Virgil was mean to the ladies, often slapping them around to get the pleasure he had demanded. He had been banned from the place, but with no law in town, that didn't stop him from returning. One night, the place burned down to the ground, and the ladies all moved on.

Virgil unsaddled his horse and told Herbert that he was going to the café and get a bite to eat. "We don't need to be seen together, old man," said Virgil. "If you come into the café, don't speak to me." He spit a wad of tobacco juice on Herbert's boots and strolled out the barn door.

Herbert looked down at his boots and mumbled to himself, "Like I want to be seen with you." The livery boy was watching the display between the two men who had come in together, but he didn't hear all of Herbert's comments.

Herbert glanced up and saw the boy for the first time. "Please take care of my horse and carriage for the night. Better rub the other horse down and give him some grain too, pointing over at Virgil's animal, and flipping the boy a new silver dollar.

Wow! First time I have ever seen a brand-new coin, thought the young man.

Walking over to a bucket of water, Herbert took the dipper from the pail and poured some water over his boots to remove Virgil's spit. Giving the young boy a salute, he walked out the door and headed to the café himself. He was starving.

Once entering the café, he knew immediately that Virgil was there. He had pulled the young waitress down onto his lap, trying to steal a kiss from her. She was pushing and clawing at him to get loose. It seemed that Virgil had been well remembered by the menfolk in the room, because no one came forth to help the young girl. After spotting Herbert, he let the girl go and demanded that she bring him the biggest, most expensive steak in the house. Giving her a push toward the kitchen, he laughed like a wild person, looking around at the other customers and asking, "What the hell you looking at?"

An older lady came out of the kitchen area and asked Herbert what he would like to eat. After giving her his order, he asked if this town had a sheriff 's office. "We do, mister, but he is out of town with most of the townsmen. He formed a posse, and they are looking for two men that kidnapped two people. A new girl that came to town a while back and one of our own, Miss Ollie, God bless her soul."

"Have mercy," declared Herbert. "How long has the sheriff been gone?"

"Maybe two days. I'm not sure when he left."

"Does this town have a rooming house that a man can get a room for lodging for the night?" asked Herbert.

"Sure thing, just right up the street on your right at the edge of town. Nice, clean place, too."

Early, the next morning, Virgil was all saddled and ready to head out.

Herbert came waltzing into the livery, his clothes all clean with shiny boots, and his saddlebags tossed over his arms. He was acting like he didn't have a care in the world.

"Is his majesty ready to travel?" sneered Virgil at Herbert.

The young boy had hitched up the carriage to his horse and it was all ready for him to travel. "Thank you, my fine young man," said Herbert tossing him yet another silver dollar. The boy raced to the double doors of the livery and opened them wide so Herbert could drive out safely.

Watching both men leave, the young boy thought, *I hope the older guy comes back soon.*

*****

Jesse and Rider had ridden all day and most of the night. They would reach the ranch that evening if all went well. Th e horses were still in good shape, and the food they had packed had been plentiful. There were several full streams for the animals to drink because of the storm a few nights ago.

Jesse couldn't keep his mind off Rae and Ollie. He was filled with all kinds of mixed emotions when it came to Rae. I have never been in love before. All my waking thoughts are of her, even before she was taken by her crazy stepfather. My insides get all twisted when she is near Tim, the doctor.

One day, I may break his neck! I have never experienced jealousy before. My palms break out with sweat and words never come off my tongue like I mean for them to. I sound like an idiot most of the time. I am usually a tyrant around her. I have heard that love can make you do and say foolish things, *he thought.* Well this must be love, and it hurts like hell. I can't wait to wrap my arms around her and tell her how I feel about her, *he thought as he almost fell out of his saddle.*

"Hey, man," yelled Rider, "are you all right? Do you need to rest?"

"No. I'm fine. Just thinking too much, I guess. I'm so worried about Ollie. Rae is young and strong, but Ollie ... well, I'm just concerned about her," said Jesse. "You know Ollie has been with Will and me forever."

Shaking his head, he continued, "I will kill somebody if they hurt her."

*****

Limason

Joe was getting very concerned that Virgil had not made it back to the cave with Mr. Summers. They should have been there by now. The girls had not given him too much fuss. Every time he had to go outside or one of them needed to have a minute of privacy, he would tie the other one up. He knew that they were loyal to each other, and one would never leave the other.

The old black woman had cooked real good for all three of them. She never complained about having to do anything.

Joe walked over to the women and told them that he needed to tie them again because he wanted to take two of the horses outside for a spell.

He walked into the back of the cave and brought out the horses and went through the opening, then he stopped and placed the bushes back in front of the doorway. The fire was still burning, which cast off a glow of light in the cave for the girls to be able to see.

Ollie looked at Rae and said, "I think that stepfather of yours and Virgil will be here sometime today. What do you think we can do to stop him from taking you with him?"

"I don't know." She sighed. "Let's pray that Jesse and the others find us soon."

Rae had finally rested her head back on the cave wall. She started looking at Ollie and wondering about her. "You know, Ollie, I have been thinking about you. How brave you have been throughout this madness. Have you always been such a strong, determined woman? What were you like as a child?" asked Rae as quietly as she could and still be heard.

"Oh, honey child. I ain't always been strong or brave, but determined ...

yes, I guess I have been that. As far as what I was like as a child, I don't really remember. I didn't have a childhood like you or even Sweetheart. Funny how the boys all call Hope 'Sweetheart.' You know they all loves her. Well, getting back to me and my childhood." Ollie laid her head back against the cave wall and looked up.

"As long as I can remember, I was at the Waverly farm with my folks. You know Waverly is not too far from the ranch. We lived in the back of the big house in a slave shack, like all the other darkies like me. There were hundreds of folks working master's fields and taking care of his cattle, livestock, and the likes. My folks were field hands. They worked from sunup to sundown out in those hot cotton fields. Ollie sighed remembering how tired her folks would be at the end of the day.

"I never seen them much because for some reason I was chosen to work in the big house. I had to watch over Patsy, the master's daughter. We were the same age, but if she got into trouble, I got whipped, not her. So, I learned early to watch her real good, and I wouldn't let her run away or hide from me. I tied our hands together. At first, she cried and kicked at me. I just kicked back harder."

Smiling, Ollie continued. "She soon learned that we could have a good time together. At night I slept on a pallet next to her bed. The best thing about watching after her was she had a tutor. He came every day for a few hours and taught Patsy to read words and cipher. I learned to read and cipher real well too, but nobody could ever know that I knew. Master would not allow his slaves any schooling. Teaching slaves to read would only make us feel 'uppity.' After a few years, the master sent Patsy away to a school up north."

Ollie sat still for a moment, reflecting on the day that her little white friend left for good. "You knows, I missed that little girl so much. I cried myself to sleep for weeks. The missus, she let me keep working in the house. I learned from the other house servants to clean, wash, and cook. I loved working in the kitchen, even though it was hot, and I washed lots of dishes, but I never went hungry." Ollie looked at Rae. "Funny, how I remember that."

Ollie's childhood was captivating to Rae. She wanted to learn more.

"So you never married and had a family of your own?"

"Oh, I had a man once." Ollie reached up and ran her hand through her white curls and patted them down. "I feel so funny without my rag on my hair," she said.

"Well, my man's name was Jacob. Lord, what a fine boy. Tall with bronze arms as big as tree trunks, white teeth, and the biggest brown eyes. He worked around the big house doing all types of chores inside and out. We got to be friendly and started meeting at the edge of the woods at night. I was fascinated with him. He told me he loved me. We asked my folks if we could jump the broom, you know, get married. But they wouldn't have any of that. I cried and begged. When I got in the family way, my papa tried to beat it out of me. One day, Jacob was gone, never to be seen or heard of again." Ollie sighed. "I was heartbroken."

"Oh my, Ollie, what did you do?" cried Rae.

"Do? There wasn't anything I could do. My folks disowned me, but I had no place to go. After my baby boy was born, I was so happy. I had never felt love before in my life. I experienced happiness for the first time in all my young years. Holding that babe in my arms at night and smelling the sweetness in his little body brought me the greatest joy."

"Where is your son now?"

"Typhoid fever swept through the farm taking so many of my people. My folks first, and then my baby. At times, I can still feel his little life slipping away from me as I rocked him."

Ollie could barely speak, but she continued. "There wasn't any medicine. Afterward, the ones that survived had to burn everything. All the fields, slave houses, clothes—everything had to be destroyed to help rid the place of that terrible fever. I didn't think that I could live after I buried my baby, but I did. One hour, one day, at a time. There was no time for grieving. Master wouldn't allow it anyways."

"How did you come to be at Jesse's home place?" Rae asked Ollie, choking on her words from tears.

Wiping her tears off her face, Ollie stared straight ahead at the walls of the cave. She had not thought about her past in a long time. Looking at Rae with a smile on her face that didn't reach her eyes, she answered.

"One day, the master called all the people that was left on the place together and told us that we could leave his farm. He wanted us to leave. He called our names, and the foreman handed us each a paper. The papers were called Freedom Papers. He said he wanted us to go because he couldn't care for us any longer. There was no money to replant the fields or rebuild shelters for us. No money or gardens left to feed everyone. He didn't have to tell the younger men twice, because they started running right down the road out the big gate. That was shore a sight to see. I wondered if they knew where they was going. I had only been off the farm once. I was very little when I went into town with the master and Patsy." Ollie smiled as she remember seeing the town for the first time.

"Well, some of the older people chose to stay even though they didn't have any place to live but under the stars. I had mixed emotions about the situation I found myself in. Just the anticipation of what laid beyond that gate of freedom was just about more than I could stand. My blood was bubbling under my skin with excitement. I was all alone, but staying wouldn't change that fact, so I started walking right down that road that led to town. I had walked miles in my bare feet. Then I sat down on a log beside the road to rest. I hadn't sat there long when a big wagon stopped right in front of me.

"A big white man sitting up high on the wagon seat looked down at me and asked, 'Girl, you from the Waverly farm?'

" I was so afraid, I didn't answer him." I lowered my head and looked at the ground.

"I am not going to do you any harm, girl. Do you already have a place to go?'

"I finally shook my head *no*. He said that his wife died from the fever, and he needed a woman to help him care for his son. Jake, here, is ten summers, but he needs a woman to care for him while I am out in the fields working. Can you cook?"

"Realizing that I might have a place to start a new life, I raised my head and looked him in the eyes and said, 'Yes, sir. I cook, clean, wash, read and write, and I have all of my teeth. Is that enough for you to know about me?"

Mr. Maxwell and his son Jake laughed. "You'll do, if you want to come home with me. Like I said earlier, I won't ever harm you or allow anyone else to either. You will have your own room at my place. It is a sod house, for now, but it will be bigger soon. Grab your stuff and jump in the back."

I looked down and all around. "I don't have anything. We had to burn everything because of the fever."

"Well, we can fix that," he said.

"Goodness! You just got in that wagon with a perfect stranger, and you have been at this ranch ever since?" asked Rae, shaking her head.

"You might say that was the luckiest day of my life. Mr. Maxwell, Jess's grandpa, was true to his word. He was always kind and gave me everything I needed. It is still that way here with his grandsons."

"Listen," said Ollie, "I hear voices. Oh my goodness. I think Virgil is back along with your stepfather."

*****

Limason

Jesse and Rider rode up into the front yard of the ranch. Will and John ran out of the house to greet them.

"Any news yet?" Jesse asked, anxiously looking at the two men.

"Afraid not," said Will. "But the sheriff has formed a posse, and they are searching the southern area. We were restocking our saddlebags and heading out to meet them. Joseph just rode in from checking on your new bull, and now is he looking over the mares in the barn. Mr. Downing's son, Luke, has been coming over twice daily to do our outside chores.

Mrs. Downing has been cooking supper for Hank and Hope. I had to hire them. I know that you would have expected me to take care of the ranch, and that is the only way I could do it and search for Ollie and Rae too."

Jesse reached out and rubbed his hand on Will's shoulder. "You done good, pal. I knew that I could count on you. Rider and I both need fresh horses and something to eat. I better go inside and see Hank and the baby before we head out."

As Joseph was coming out of the barn, he looked up at the sound of a carriage coming. The driver of the small, black carriage was his girlfriend, Rebecca.

"What a surprise, honey." Joseph said as he gave her a big smile. "But how did you know that I was back?"

"I didn't. Remember before you left, you told me and mom to look out for strangers that may come into town? Last night, two different men came into the café. One was a nasty-acting cowpuncher who grabbed me around the waist and tried to kiss me. But when this well-dressed old man came in, he let me go. Like he knew him, you know, but they didn't speak."

"Come with me, babe." Joseph lifted her out of the carriage and then led the horse over to the fence and tied him up.

"Jess," yelled Joseph. Looking at Rebecca, he said, "I believe that they might be the men we are looking for."

Jesse and John came out on the porch and saw Joseph talking to Rebecca. "Hello, pretty lady," said Jesse, nodding his head at her.

"Rebecca said that two strange men came into her mom's café last night. Tell him, honey, what they looked like."

After hearing the description of the older fat man, Jesse was sure it was Herbert. "Why do you think he was with the other man?" asked Jesse.

"It was the way he acted when he noticed the man coming in the door. He got all cocky and very bossy, staring at him while he ate. They left about the same time. The older man asked for a place to spend the night, and Mom told him where the rooming house was located."

"Maybe we can get more information about him from Flo and the livery stable. I bet he left his horse there overnight," said John as he was putting his boots back on.

"Thank you so much, Rebecca, for coming out to give us this information. I know now that we aren't too far behind them," said Jesse, very excited for the first time in days.

Joseph took Rebecca's arm and walked her back to her horse and carriage. "Gosh, honey, I love you," he said as he moved forward and captured a kiss.

"Joseph, what will the others think of me allowing kisses out here in the front yard?"

"If they are looking, they will be very envious of me," he said as he tried to catch her again. But she pulled back faster, laughing.

"Please be careful and hurry home. I will be praying for Ollie and Mrs. Rivers' safe return."

Hank was very happy to see the men return, but he was still upset that they had no idea where the women had been taken. Will had completed his packing and was sitting in the rocker holding Sweetheart while she chatted on about her puppy.

Jess and John came back into the house and told them the news about Rebecca seeing a man that fit the description of Herbert in the café last night. She was sure that they were staying the night in town.

"I feel that we aren't far behind them. We will head into town and stop at the rooming house and the livery stable. Maybe Herbert might have dropped a hint as to what he was doing in town and where he is headed."

"Hank, it is sure good to see you up and around on your foot. I hope Sweetheart hasn't been a handful for you. She looks fine. I will tell Rae what good care you have been giving the baby when we catch up with them. Hopefully, that will be sometime today."

Jesse walked over to Hope and rubbed the top of her head. Surprised, she didn't try to pull away from him.

"Can I ride your horse?" she asked so sweetly, looking up at him.

"Oh, Sweetheart. When I get back, I will ride you all over the ranch."

All the men filed out of the house, climbed up on their horses, and rode out of the yard, heading toward the town of Limason. When they rode up to the hitching rail at the rooming house, Jesse tossed his bridle to Will and said, "I won't be but a minute. John, you guys ride over to the livery stable and question Chester or whoever was working last night. We will be along in a few minutes."

Jesse knocked on the door, and Mary Lou answered all dressed in her Sunday best. "Well, look who has come knocking again."

"Good morning, Mary Lou. This isn't a social call. May I see Miss Flo?" asked Jesse as he glanced around her to look down toward the hallway.

"Sure, sugar. *Flo!* " she yelled at the top of her voice.

While Jesse was looking at Mary Lou, he couldn't imagine what he ever saw in her. Rae was so different, with her face clean from powder and paint, dressed in a plain dress with an apron, hair smelling of rose water, and very soft-spoken. Rae was a beauty compared to Mary Lou, even dressed in all of her feathers and ruffles. Rae was a lady in every way.

His lady.

Flo had heard her name called and came to the door. "Howdy, Jesse, what can I do for you this morning?"

"I know you have heard about Ollie and Mrs. Rivers being kidnapped from my place a few days ago."

"Yes … I sure am sorry. I have always thought a lot of Miss Ollie. I know she's like a mama to you and your little brother. How can I help?"

"I understand you may have let a room to an older fat man last night. Might have hair on his chin. Is this true?"

"Yes, he left early this morning. Came marching into the dining room, snatched two biscuits off the table, and laughed real loud. I asked him to sit and eat, but he shook his head, reached into his pocket, and pulled out this here dollar bill."

Flo reached in her apron pocket and pulled the money out as she talked.

"'For the biscuits, my lady,' he said. "He walked out the door humming under his breath. I was glad to see him leave. There was something very strange about him."

"So, he didn't mention what he was doing here or where he was going when he left?" asked Jesse.

"No, nothing. I am sorry I can't help you more," said Flo sadly.

When Mary Lou left the house, she walked down the front path to the gate and noticed a fine-looking young man sitting on a horse, waiting. "Well, who do we have here?"

Walking over very close to Will's horse, she reached out to Will and placed her palm on his leg. Will was surprised to have this beautiful lady talking to him, much less having her hand rubbing on his leg.

"I can see that you're not Jesse's little brother anymore." She batted her eyes up at him.

"I'm a grown man," squeaked Will, his voice cracking. "I will be glad to show you sometime," he boasted.

Mary Lou laughed and said, "Spoken like a real man. You come see me anytime, big boy." She backed her prissy little body away from him, turned, and walked toward town with a smile on her face.

Jesse came out the door of the rooming house and walked over to

Will.

"What was she saying to you?" he asked, nodding his head at Mary Lou.

Will glanced at Mary Lou as she walked down the street, but he didn't say anything.

"Well, you just stay away from that little piece of trash," growled Jesse.

"Let's go. I am sure Herbert was here last night. Let's get over to the livery and see what the others found out." They met John and Joseph outside the livery stable.

"The young boy at the livery remembered the banker man, Jess," said John. "He is traveling in a small black carriage with a large trunk loaded on the back of it. That boy," John nodded at the youngster standing over in the doorway, "said that Herbert gave him a brand-new silver dollar to care for his horse and watch over the carriage. This morning the man came in, and when he left, he gave him another one. Shore free with his money." John remarked as he was shaking his head.

"Does he remember the other fellow?" asked Jesse.

"Yep, he said he was a mean one. He and Herbert left together," replied John.

"Which way did they leave?" Jesse asked the boy, who was still standing in the doorway.

"They traveled to the end of the street and turned south," he said.

"Are you sure that they were traveling together?" asked Will.

"Oh, they were traveling together for sure. The nasty fellow was waiting in the barn for the man driving the carriage to get here, and boy, he was really angry that he was late. Called him all kinds of names. Then the older fellow, well, he started talking to himself, real funny like." Tapping his head at the temple and looking around at all the men, he said, "I'm thinking he is sick in the head."

"You may have just hit the nail on the head, young man. Thanks for your help," said Jesse as he turned his horse to lead the way out of town.

As Jesse and the others were headed out of town, they saw the posse riding with Sheriff Murphy. Jesse and his men sat and waited for the sheriff to pull up beside them.

"No luck, Jess. We covered a lot of ground. We came back to freshen up and get some decent food in us and the horses. We'll start out again in a few hours. What direction are you heading?"

"We are going to travel south. Herbert is traveling in a carriage, so he is going to have to stay on the road or a very good path. He should be fairly easy to track. He has about a two-hour head start, but we can catch up to them quickly. Our plan is to let them lead us to the girls. We will plan further once we size up the situation."

"Sounds good. We will be right behind you. If you get off the road, leave us a good sign so we don't miss your trail," responded the sheriff .

*****

Several times Herbert nearly turned his carriage over. Virgil just laughed, thinking it would be funny to see his fat behind tossed in the air and landing in a ditch.

Herbert continued to slow down, and this was causing Virgil to lose his patience.

"The cave is hidden in some pretty thick brush. You've got to leave this carriage and walk a ways. We are almost there," said Virgil.

"Great. I can't take much more of this rough terrain," replied Herbert, using his handkerchief to wipe the sweat off his forehead.

After riding a few more miles, Virgil led his horse off the main road. He motioned for Herbert to follow him with the horse and carriage. "Get down and lead your horse over behind those trees and tie him real good. You'll have to walk a little ways through those trees. I am going to ride on ahead and tell Joe to get ready. You follow my trail," commanded Virgil.

Once he arrived at the cave, he removed part of the bushes from the entrance and walked in. Joe had heard someone moving around outside, and he had pulled his pistol out and had it pointed at the opening.

"What kind of welcome is this, partner?" said Virgil, grinning widely.

*****

Back at the ranch house, Hank heard a commotion of some kind.
He limped over to the screen door and looked outside. Mr. Downing was laughing and shaking the hand of an old black man that Hank had never seen. Opening the door and slowly stepping down the steps, he saw the Negro man giving him the once-over.

"Hank, this is Jeremiah, an old, old friend of mine. And this is Katherine Brown. She is from Peamont, and they have come to visit Mrs. Rivers," said Mr. Downing.

"My goodness, you must be Rae's aunt that Jess told me about. Please get down and come into the house." Hank couldn't believe his eyes. This was a beautiful, mature woman. "Mr. Downing, will you please show your friend where he can water his animals?"

Katherine got down off her horse and walked onto the porch with Hank. About that time, Hope came running out of the house and stopped dead in her tracks. She had seen this lady that looked just like her mama, and she remembered her. "Aunt Katie! Aunt Katie!" screamed Hope.

Reaching down and lifting Hope in her arms, she said, "My little pumpkin, look how much you have grown in just a few weeks. My, we are going to have to place a rock on your head to keep you little," kissing Hope's face all over.

"Oh, Aunt Katie, you are funny. My mama went away with a nasty man and Mr. S.O.B. Oh, I can't say that ugly word again but Aunt Katie I miss her so much. I want her to come home. Please go get her."

Katie was in shock, hearing her beautiful niece using foul language. "Here, sweetie, why don't you go outside and watch for my friend Jeremiah. He went into the barn. When he comes out, please bring him inside."

As Hope ran outside and sat down on the steps, Katie turned to Hank and said, "What has happened? Mr. Hank?""Yes," said Hank. He began to tell her the story of how the men came into the house and took Rae and Ollie. He told her how brave Hope was to run and hide. Then he said Jesse had returned with information about Herbert embezzling the bank's money.

"Jess, along with all the men, and the sheriff's posse are out looking for them now. Jess feels that they will catch up with them today. Mr. Downing came from town a little while ago and said that the sheriff thinks that they may have the girls holed up in a cave several hours south of town. There are some big caves that the Indians used to live in before they moved on."

Katie was looking at Hank with a strange expression on her face. "Wait a minute, Hank. Claire and I used to play in one cave while our father fished. Our father would take us camping, and we stayed in a big cave. It was large with a stream running through it. A person could live there, and no one would ever know. I have this funny feeling. I bet that's where they are holding them."

She turned and practically ran out of the house shouting for her man. "Jeremiah! Get the horses and my saddlebags. Leave the packhorse here. We have got to go. Please hurry. I will tell you where we are going as we travel."

"Mrs. Brown, are you thinking of looking for Rae by yourself? What if those men are there? That is too dangerous for you!" said Hank, very concerned.

"She won't be alone. I'm here, and my old faithful friend is right beside me." Jeremiah patted his double-barrel shotgun. He gave him a salute as they rode out of the yard.

"What do you make of them, Hank?" asked Mr. Downing.

"Lord have mercy on whoever gets in front of his old faithful friend," said Hank. He shook his head as he reached down to take Sweetheart's hand and lead her into the house.

*****

"Virgil, you nearly made me shoot you," declared Joe. "Is the banker man with you?"

Virgil looked back in the cave and saw the two girls. "Why aren't they tied up? What you running here, a social club? That there is our bread and butter, and you're allowing them to waltz free around in here. You're stupid. Pure stupid, boy. You better be glad that they are still here," sneered Virgil.

"They are here, and you best be careful who you are calling names," said Joe, dismayed. "I asked you if the banker man was with you, and did he bring the money to pay us? I'm ready to get out of here and head on down to Mexico."

"Yes, the fool is walking this way as we speak. Get your gear together, and as soon as the blathering idiot gets in here, we will relieve him of our reward money and anything else of value that he may have."

Virgil strolled over to where Rae and Ollie had huddled toward the back of the cave. "You aren't trying to hide from old Virgil are you, pretty girl? You know that I want to get me a good-bye kiss before we have to leave," he said with a smile that showed his filthy yellowed teeth.

Just as he reached out and grabbed Rae's wrist, Herbert entered the cave. "Unhand her, good man, before I shoot you right between the eyes. She is my property, and no trash like you shall ever touch her."

Virgil turned around and saw Herbert's pistol pointed at him. Fury like he had never felt before went through Virgil's body. "You old crazy fool. Point that toy of yours somewhere else before I shove it down your throat and pull it out of your butt," yelled Virgil.

"All right, Mr. Summers," said Joe, "we will take our payment of $4,000 now. We have delivered your woman to you, and we are ready to move out."

"Of course, gentlemen. I am a man of my word."

Walking back to the front of the cave where there was better light, Herbert reached into his vest pocket and pulled out the money in one-hundred-dollar bills. "Here is the money that I promised you. I hope that we will never cross paths again," said Herbert gleefully.

Joe walked over to Herbert and took the money from him. "You can count on it, Mr. Banker Man," said Joe.

Virgil reached Joe in a flash, grabbed the money out of his hands, and shoved it all into his saddlebag. "I'm the banker in our little partnership."

"What was that noise?" Joe was alarmed as he moved over to the front of the cave and peeked through the brush that was covering the entrance. "Damn! There's several men outside behind the trees. We are trapped!"

Jesse, Rider, John, and Joseph had followed the carriage tracks until they moved off the road. They had to walk their horses through the underbrush for a short piece. There, sitting out in the opening, was Herbert's carriage and his horse untied. In the back of the carriage was a large trunk with a big lock on the front.

"Rider, scout on ahead while we see what's in the trunk. Will, look in my saddlebag and get me that ax. We can use it to get this lock open."

Getting the lock open on the trunk was no easy task, but they managed to chop around the edge of the lock and break it off. Their persistence paid off.

"Well, boys, just look at all of this money. Sawyer will be one happy fellow when he sees this. Here comes Rider," Jesse said as he jumped down from the carriage.

"John, take this trunk and hide it somewhere away from this carriage. What did you find, Rider?"

"They are in the cave all right. I could hear them talking, but I'm sorry, I didn't see the women."

"Let's surround the cave while we decide how we are going to get them out safely. They are going to try to use the girls as shields to get away, but that is not going to happen."

"What are we going to do?" asked Will, who was very skeptical.

"Over here, John," said Jesse. "We have got to make a plan to try to get the girls out before they try to leave with them. I'm not letting them take them a foot further."

Joseph was at the front of the cave leaning against the wall so he could hear the voices inside.

Rider came scurrying over to Jesse and said, "I hear two or three horses coming this way, traveling fast."

Jesse looked at him and said, "Man, that Indian blood of yours sure comes in handy at times, even if it is only a little bit."

Jesse walked out toward the road to see who was coming their way.

What in the world! he thought when he saw Katie and Jeremiah racing through the underbrush, trying to find them.

"Katie, Jeremiah, over here!" Jesse called out. "What are you doing here?"

"We came to visit, and Hank filled us in on the kidnapping. He told me where the sheriff thought they may be held up with Rae. As a child, I remember coming to this cave. Are you sure they are in there?"

"Yes, Joseph has heard voices inside the cave. We have Herbert's horse and carriage and his trunk—which by the way, is filled with the bank's money."

"Praise the Lord for that," said Katie.

"Come on with me back to the cave," said Jesse, reaching out to take Katie's hand.

"You know, Mr. Jess," said Jeremiah, "I knows this cave, too. Did you know that it has a back entrance?"

"No, I have walked all over the top of it, but I didn't see any kind of opening."

"You wouldn't if you don't know what you are looking for. It just has grass growing over a hollow hole. There's no dirt. A person could be walking up there, and if they step on the soft spot, fall down into the cave. It's not far from the front of the cave, but I believe you could get in without being seen by them."

"Let's go find it, and John can help lower me down," said Jesse. It didn't take Jeremiah but a few minutes to locate the top entrance. After removing the growth of weeds, a person could see the floor of the cave.

"I'm ready to be lowered down," whispered Jesse, looking at John.

"No, *I'm* going." Katie came walking up on the top of the cave wearing a long, white muslin nightgown with her hair hanging loose almost to her waist.

"We all believe that Herbert is insane and that he killed Claire. Seeing her ghost should make him go nuts for sure. In the darkness of the cave, I really will look like my sister to him," said Katie.

"Are you kidding? You look like her in broad daylight," said Jeremiah, laughing softy.

"Jesse, don't let her do this," said John, very upset that this beautiful woman would place herself in so much danger.

Katie walked over to John and placed her finger in the middle of his chest. She poked her finger at John and said, "Back up! He is not stopping me! I know that Herbert will believe that I am my sister, and it will totally confuse his mind."

Looking at her loyal old friend, she motioned for him to help her down the tunnel. Jeremiah stepped over to stand beside Katie, but John said,

"No, I am taller with a longer stretch. I will lower you down." Softy he whispered for Katie's ears only, "If you get hurt, I shall never forgive you."

Katie looked into his beautiful eyes and gave him a strange look. She just shook her head.

Katie eased herself into the hole as John held her wrists tight while lowering her almost to the floor, and then he whispered to her, "Get ready for me to let go." Nodding her head, John let loose and Katie landed on her backside on the hard, damp floor of the cave.

John looked at Jeremiah and told him that he was going to go to the front of the cave so he could be ready to go in if Katie got into trouble.

Inside the cave, Katie picked herself up off the floor. She noticed the bright shining light coming straight down after John had moved from the entrance of the hole. Sliding along the side of the wall of the cave, she could see the firelight ahead. As she approached the horses, they started moving around. Katie ran her hands over their noses and whispered softly in their ears. She reached for the bridles, untied them, and led them further back in the cave.

Once the animals had settled down, she walked past them and saw Ollie standing as far back in the cave as she could get and still see what was taking place. Rae was close to the entrance near one man and Herbert.

Herbert was talking to Rae about how they were going to be married.

Another man ran over to the entrance and looked out through the brush and yelled that he could see several men hiding behind some trees.

He yelled, "We're trapped."

"You may be trapped, but I'm not!" said Virgil, who was very aggravated.

He reached down and grabbed up his saddlebag with the reward money in it. Glancing around at everyone, he walked over and took Rae's wrist and twisted her right arm up high behind her back.

"Ow," she screamed, "you hurting me!"

"Shut up, we're going outside, and your friends are going to give me one of their horses. If they follow us, I will blow your brains out right in front of them."

With all this commotion going on, Katie slipped up behind Ollie and put her hand over her mouth and whispered, "Stand very still. You can't help Rae now. Walk slowly backward and lean into the cave's wall."

Ollie did as she was told, never taking her eyes off Rae. She wanted to run to her and slap that Virgil silly.

Herbert couldn't believe that Virgil had again put his filthy hands on his most prized possession. "Turn her loose. Now!" screamed Herbert. "I told you to never touch her again, you nasty, rotten scum." He blathered to himself, "I know I will have to kill that son of a--- for sure!"

"You hear that, Joe? Banker man is as crazy as a loon!" Virgil laughed with disgust in his voice. Still hanging on to Rae, he marched her to the entrance of the cave and peeked out through the brush.

Herbert was staring at Virgil's every move. Again he warned Virgil to turn her loose. "Let her go or prepare to meet your maker."

Virgil acted like he never heard Herbert. He yelled to the men outside,

"If you men don't want me to shoot this pretty little girl, you best get me a horse and get away from the front of the cave. Princess and me are leaving, and you better not follow. She ain't nothing to me but protection. If I feel threatened, I will blow her brains out! Got that?"

Virgil watched outside the cave as he said over his shoulder, "Joe, go get our horses from the back!"

Joseph was leaning his body into the outside wall of the entrance of the cave. He could see Rae and Virgil.

"Look at that man making a fool out of you. He has his hands all over your woman. Shoot the scrum," shouted the voice inside Herbert's head.

Herbert raised his small gun and pointed it again straight at Virgil. Virgil was busy shouting at the men outside and hurting Rae, his beautiful bride-to-be. Herbert took aim and shot Virgil in the back. The sound of the small pistol was like a little explosion. Small pieces of dirt fell from the ceiling of the cave. Virgil released Rae, turned, and stared right at Herbert. He raised his gun and said, "You crazy-ass old man" and he fell forward, flat on his face. Dead.

With the explosion of the gun, Rae stumbled backward with her hands covering her face. She was at the edge of the entrance to the cave. Joseph acted fast. He reached out and pulled Rae over to where he was standing.

She screamed, and he placed his hand over her mouth and motioned for her to be quiet. She shook her head *yes* to let him know that she understood.

Jesse appeared and placed his arms around Rae's waist and led her away toward safety in the surrounding trees.

"Jesse, I have to go back in! ... I have to get ... Ollie. Please! I can't leave Ollie," she cried. She was struggling with him to turn her loose so she could go back in the cave. Jesse gave her a little shake to get her attention.

"This will all be over soon. Your Aunt Katie is in the cave with Ollie now. Just be quiet and trust us," pleaded Jesse.

Rae was stunned to hear that Katie was in the cave. What does he mean?

How did my Aunt Katie get here?

Joe didn't know what to do. He glanced at Virgil and then at Herbert.

He knew Virgil needed killing, but he never thought the banker man would be the one to do it. He knew he was trapped, with all the men outside. He was just going to give himself up. Looking toward the back of the cave, he wondered where Ollie was hiding.

Herbert was talking to himself again and looking around for Rae. He couldn't find her in the darkness. He picked up more wood and tossed it on the fire. The wood blazed up into a roaring fire, making the cave as hot as hades.

"Rae!" called Herbert. "You will never get away from me. Come out, come out, wherever you are. I don't have time for games."

Joe started looking around the cave for Rae too. Where had she gone? Could she have run out of the cave?

This was the right time for Katie to step out and call to Herbert. "Herbie … come to me, Herbie. "

Herbert looked up from the fire. He couldn't believe his ears. He took a step forward and looked into the darkness of the cave and saw Claire in her white nightgown. She's calling me. She can't be calling me! She dead, but she's calling me that disgusting pet name that she gave me, he said to himself. "Herbie … come to me … let's have some of my special drink … come … I miss you so … come, Herbie. " Katie stepped out in just enough light for Herbert to get a good look at her this time.

Joe had heard the voice calling Herbert, and now he could see her too. He couldn't believe his eyes or his ears! *Oh my Lord, I am losing my mind,* Joe thought. *I don't believe in ghosts,* he said to himself as he let his body slide down the cave wall. He sat on the floor with his head between his raised knees.

"Rae is going to go with me, Herbert. … She doesn't want to go with you. … Come, Herbie. "

Don't listen to the sick old woman! She is trying to keep Rae from going with you, said Herbert's friend in his head.

"Go away! I have never wanted to be with you. Rae is not going to go with you. She is mine. We're going to be married. You best go away and stay away. I killed you once. I will do it again." He was walking closer to the darkest part of the cave as he spoke. Katie's plan was working. He was too crazy to realize that this couldn't possibly be real.

Katie was in plain view now. Herbert could easily see her outline. He was within ten feet of her. She lifted her hair and pulled it in front of her with one hand and holding her gown out with the other. Swaying and waving her gown to appear like she was floating, she continued speaking softly to Herbert.

"*Come, come … come … Herbie!* "

Jesse, John, and Rider had sneaked into the front entrance of the cave. Rider pointed his gun directly at Joe who was sitting down on the cave floor. He immediately raised his hands above his head. Rider placed his finger to his lips giving Joe a signal to be very quiet.

Jesse was very concerned because he had not seen Ollie since entering the cave. He was praying that she was in the back and out of danger from any possible gunfire. He had a lot of respect for that spunky old black woman, and he didn't want her to be hurt.

Herbert couldn't take his eyes away from the ghost of Claire, his dead wife.

"It took you long enough to die with my special toddy. I should have smothered you a lot sooner. *That was so much easier.* You're right, old boy, she was gone just like that. No more special drinks. No more having to sit by her bedside pretending to be the loving husband. She didn't even struggle! The voice in his head said.

"Now, I am going to get rid of you once and for all," he said as he raised his small derringer and took aim at Katie. He pulled the trigger, and the bullet went into the wall of the cave. Katie immediately fell over onto the damp floor.

Herbert's perfect aim had been distracted by the three bullets that went into his body. He never knew what hit him. Jesse, John, and Rider looked at each other and quickly replaced their guns in their holsters.

Dirt had been shaken loose from the top of the cavern and was falling all around them.

Jesse raced over to Katie to help her up. He knew immediately that something was wrong. She was too still. John rushed over and moved Jesse out of the way. He picked Katie up and carried her outside of the cave.

Stooping down on one knee, holding her in his arms, he could see the blood pouring down her left arm onto her hand. Rider lifted her arm and could see that she had been hit in the back part of her left arm.

Will and Jeremiah came running over to John and Katie. "Did Herbert shoot Katie?" asked Jeremiah, his voice shaking.

"No, his bullet hit the side of the cave and it ricocheted into her. He won't be bothering anyone anymore. He's dead," said John.

Rae came hurrying over to Katie. "We need to get her to the doctor as fast as possible. Rider, do you have a knife on you?" He reached in his boot and offered her what she requested. "My goodness," she said and reached down with the long, sharp blade to cut a large section of Katie's nightgown.

Rae wrapped Katie's arm to stop the flow of blood.

Katie opened her eyes and glanced around. "Is Ollie out of the cave?"

Rae shook her head, not able to speak for the tears of happiness that were choking her. Katie laid her head back into the chest of the man holding her and looked directly into his eyes—the same concerned eyes that she had seen right before entering the cave.

"Please forgive me," she said softly. "I really didn't mean to get hurt." John brushed her hair back and smiled.

Jesse had gone into the cave to search for Ollie. She was walking with Rider and Joe, who had his hands tied behind his back. Joe was telling Ollie how sorry he was, and that he never would have harmed her or Rae.

"That is the reason I didn't bring the baby. I knew where she was hiding, but I didn't trust Virgil or that crazy Herbert. I have never hurt a woman or child," he said, hanging his head low.

When Ollie saw Jesse, she held out her arms, and Jesse rushed over to her. He hugged her so tight and lifted her feet off the ground, turning around and around. "I love you so much," he whispered. "I was so afraid for you. All of us have been sick with worry. And Hank! Mercy! He is like a wild man with concern for you." He laughed with gladness in his voice.

Ollie beamed, but then she looked at Jesse with sadness in her eyes and said, "Jess, I am so glad that Rae wasn't in there to hear that crazy man talking about how he killed her mama. She didn't need to hear those things."

"I feel the same as you do, but if she asks, she must be told. Don't fret about it now. Will is outside, and he is worried to death. Come on, let's go find him." Reaching up and running his hand through her short white curls, he grinned at her and said, "I like it. You need to leave that rag off more often."

She smiled and said, "Oh, go on with yourself. I'm a mess, and I knows I smell just like those little piglets of ours. I shore am looking forward to a hot bath," she said, laughing. "Lord, I hopes somebody thought to bring a wagon to carry me home. My old butt—oh my goodness." She laughed as she covered her mouth. "I've been with that nasty-talking Virgil too long. I'm talking just like him! Well, anyways, I don't care to ride a horse ever again!" she said as she limped toward the entrance of the cave.

"Oh my baby boy, come to your old Ollie." Will practically leaped into Ollie's open arms, and before he knew it, he was openly crying. "There, there, baby, I'm fine, really. I knew that you would come for me."

Rubbing his running nose on Ollie's shoulder, Will looked into her face and whispered his love for her. "I was so afraid for you. … I never knew that you could ride a horse," he said with raised eyebrows.

She hugged him again and laughed. "I can't!" "If he hadn't been for Joe, I would probably be dead. He helped me on and off the mare that I had to ride. And he didn't tie my hands. The first day, I had all the skin rubbed off my thighs and calves of my legs. They are better now, but I was pretty sore for a while."

Ollie looked around for Jesse and waved him over to her. "Jesse, that young man, Joe, he helped the other fellow take us, but I don't want him treated badly. He did wrong for sure, but he saved me and Rae from that mean man. He took care of us and risked his life several times. The one called Virgil would have done harm to us if he hadn't intervened. I'm sure Rae will tell you the same thing."

"Ollie, I won't have any say as to what they will do to him, but I will pass on your wishes to Sheriff Murphy concerning him. Maybe you can tell him yourself."

John had placed Katie in the carriage and was covering her up with a blanket stored in the back of the carriage. Jesse, Ollie, and Will walked up to them. "John, please let Ollie get in the carriage and hold Katie on the drive back to town. Ollie is too sore to ride a horse."

"Of course, Miss Ollie. You let me help you in the carriage, and we'll get to the doctor as quickly as we can. We are all so happy that you are all right," said John, trying not to show his disappointment. He had been looking forward to holding this beautiful woman in his arms as he drove the carriage to the doctor's office.

Rae was holding the bridle to Jesse's horse, while Jeremiah had already gotten on his horse and was prepared to leave.

"Joseph, please ride ahead and tell the doc that we are on our way. Tell him to prepare to remove a bullet out of Miss Katie's arm and that she has lost a good bit of blood. We will be arriving at his office shortly," said Jesse. "Look around for the sheriff and let him know what has happened.

I'm sure he will be relieved."

When they arrived at Doctor Tim's office, Rae and Ollie insisted that they help him with the surgery on Katie's arm. Rae held the lamp close to the wound as he pushed and wiggled the fat around inside the back part of her upper arm. "There!" he stated, "I got it. Thank goodness it was a small bullet. A larger one could have shattered the bone, but she will recover from this wound nicely."

Rae was so thankful to have that ordeal over with. She was nauseated and felt faint while he was prodding around in the bullet hole. *I sure hoped that I would have been a better nurse than this,* she thought.

The doctor said, "Now, Ollie, please pass me some bandage material and we will wrap this up right away. She should sleep the rest of the day. I will send her with something for the pain, but she shouldn't need too much after a few days."

Rae went to the outer office where the men were waiting and announced that Aunt Katie was going to be fine. "She will sleep most of the day. You know, Jesse, if we had a wagon with some blankets, we could take her home with us."

John leaped up from his chair and said, "I will ride to the ranch now and get the wagon and plenty of clean blankets." Before anyone could respond, he was out the door and gone in a flash. Everyone looked around at each other and started laughing.

Jesse placed his arm around Rae's waist and gazed into her eyes. "I know just how John feels," he whispered.

Rae looked at him as if to say, "Really?" but she kept silent.

Tim came out of his office and said to Rae. "It's your turn. Please come back in my office. Ollie, I want to check both you and Rae over to make sure you are fine. I know that you say you are fine, but I want to make sure." Giving Jesse a look that brooked no interference, he said, "This is what needs to be done."

Jesse gave Rae a little push toward Tim, and he told Ollie to allow Tim to look at her scrapes and burns. Both of the ladies were hesitant, but they walked back into the examination room with him.

While Tim was looking at Ollie's legs, he said, "My goodness, Miss Ollie, how did you get these abrasions on your skin?"

"Well, I haven't been on a horse since I was a little girl. The first day, we didn't travel far but it was dark, windy, and raining something fierce. My legs was touching the horse's hide and rubbing on it. The next day, I kept my skirt between the horse's hide and my legs. That helped some. Mostly I was too afraid to be worrying about my skin. I just prayed those fools wouldn't kill us."

"This cream will help to heal those abrasions. Rub it on twice a day," said Tim.

While examining Rae, the doctor found bruises all over her delicate skin. She didn't have any open wounds, but her skin was more black-and-blue than creamy white.

"I know that you have to be very sore, Rae. I want you to go home and take it easy for a few days. Be careful picking up your baby." Rae give Ollie a funny glance. Tim picked up on something very quickly. "Did I say something wrong?" He looked from Rae to Ollie and back again.

"Doc … Tim, I mean. Hope is not my baby. She is my little sister, but I have cared for her like she was mine. It's a long story. You will have to come to dinner soon, and I will tell you all about it."

Smiling, he said overjoyed, "Now that's a date."

"Don't you fret over Rae, Doc. I will take good care of her. Just like she took great care of me while we were gone." Ollie reached out to take Rae's hand and gave it a loving squeeze.

Jesse was very glad to see Ollie and Rae come out of the doctor's examination room.

"How are my girls, Doc? Can I take them home now?" asked Jesse.

Before Tim could answer, Sheriff Murphy entered the doctor's office. "Jess, Doc, ladies." He nodded to all in the room. "I need to talk with Rae and Ollie before you take them home. Please bring them down to my office."

"Tim," said Rae as she smiled at him, "John will be back here soon with a wagon to take Aunt Katie to Jess's ranch. Jeremiah, please don't let him leave until we get back here."

Sheriff Murphy was waiting in his office with a fresh pot of coffee brewing. Jesse held the door for Ollie, Will, and Rae to enter. "Come in ladies, and please have a seat. This will not take long."

As Ollie prepared to sit, she looked through the open door leading to the cells in the back. She could see Joe sitting on a bunk bed with his head held with both hands. He appeared so sad. She walked into the cell area, and Sheriff Murphy called to her, "Now Miss Ollie, you don't need to go back there."

"I won't be but a minute," she said as Joe stood up and walked to the bars of the cell.

"Miss Ollie, what are you doing back here? I would think that you wouldn't ever want to see me again."

"Now, Joe, I don't want to hear any of that talk. I know that you ain't a bad sort. I am going to try to talk with the sheriff out there. I want him to let you go home were you belong. I can't promise, but maybe Jess will help me convince him. Just be a good boy now. I will see you later," said Ollie.

Sheriff Murphy had some paperwork laid out on his desk. He told Rae that all she needed to do was sign it, and Joe would be transferred to Frisco City to be held for trial.

Rae sat looking at him and then up at Ollie. "What if we don't sign this paper?" asked Rae. "Ollie and I are alive today because of Joe. I truly believe that. I know he helped Virgil kidnap us, but he never intended to hurt us."

Looking around at the four men and then back again at Ollie, Rae asked her, "How do you feel about Joe?"

"Like I told Jess before, I don't want that boy," pointing to the jail cells, "punished. I want you to let him go home. God had mercy on me and Rae by sending Joe along with that nasty, filthy creature Virgil! Without him, Rae would have suffered very badly. That scoundrel was drinking and grabbing at her all the time. I'm sure he would have killed me, because if he had hurt her again, I was going to try to kill him with my bare hands."

Ollie was getting worked up to the point that the men thought she may have a stroke if she didn't calm down.

"All right, Miss Ollie, calm down. I am beginning to see a clear picture of how that fellow back there protected you and Rae. With that said, I can't just turn him loose. We all know that he did a bad thing, and the law says that he must be punished."

"What does that paper say that you want us to sign?" asked Ollie.

"It states that he kidnapped you and held you for a sum of money, to be paid by Mr. Herbert Summers," read the sheriff . "Now, Jess, please have them sign this paper." He was losing all of his patience as he spoke.

Ollie shook her head *no*, and then glanced at Rae, who was shaking her head at the same time.

"You might as well turn the fellow lose and allow him to go home. These hardheads are not going to sign anything that will place him behind bars," declared Jesse. "As for how I feel, I am just thankful that he didn't allow that other fellow to harm them."

"Sheriff Murphy," said Rae, "we appreciate your concern and all the help you gave Jess in trying to locate us. Herbert is gone, the money is ready to be returned to Rosedale. Aunt Katie is going to be all right, and I will never have to worry again about anyone taking my sister away from me. We all want to go home. Please, please, let us put this behind us. I don't want to think of that young man in prison—he was our guardian angel. Please, I beg of you, allow him to go home to his folks and get a fresh start. I know he has learned his lesson."

Sheriff Murphy looked at the three men and Ollie. Looking back at Rae, he stood. "Well … damn. I guess I know when I am whipped. All right … he can go free. But he better not ever show his face in my territory again!."

"Thank you so much, Sheriff," said Rae, giving him a big hug. "Please open the cell door so we can see him off."

After all the tears were shed—including some of Joe's—he was saddled and ready to ride out toward his home in Dallas. Jesse walked over to Joe and extended his right hand up to him. Joe hesitated a moment and then reached down and took his hand.

"No, sir." Joe started shaking his head vigorously. "I couldn't take your money. I will be fine," said Joe, feeling the paper money in Jesse's palm.

"Look, boy, don't make me call the sheriff over here. You have got to eat and feed this animal on your journey. Don't start your new life being dumb." Jesse grinned at Joe. "Please, this is from Ollie. You are in her heart now. Make her proud. Drop a line or two and let her know how you are making out at home."

"Thanks." Swallowing hard, he added, "Thank Miss Ollie." Joe clicked his heels into the side of his horse and rode out of their lives forever.

*****

Once Katie had been placed in Rae's room on the bed that Hope had been sleeping in, everyone seemed to settle back to normal.

Jesse insisted that Rae and Ollie go lay down while he got the men to bring in buckets of water to heat for a nice tub bath for them in Rae's room. Rae would not hear about being the first to get into that wonderful tub of steaming water. She assisted Ollie into the tub, and Ollie let Rae help wash her hair.

"Oh Ollie, you are so pretty without that bandanna on your hair. Please leave it uncovered."

Ollie laughed and said that Jesse had said the same thing. "Maybe I will." She grinned, rubbing her hand over the short, nappy curls.

Rae rubbed the cream over Ollie's calves and thighs and wrapped a soft cloth over her right leg. "This is the worst one," Ollie said as she looked down at the raw place on her right calf. "That first night I kept rocking and swaying back and forth in that saddle. I really don't know how I stayed on," Ollie said with a laugh.

Rae completed her bath and had her long hair wrapped in a towel. She looked up at Ollie as she finished nursing her leg. "Ollie, I am so sorry that I got you involved in my troubles. I almost cried when I saw how bad your legs were rubbed raw. I will always be thankful to you for the help and care you gave me on our terrible journey. I was so afraid of Virgil and you were so brave, standing up to him."

"Oh, honey, I was scared to death. That was one mean son—man. As for being thankful to me, let's just be grateful that you have this behind you now. Please don't get in no hurry to leave here, but you know now that as soon as you are stronger, you can go home."

Letting go of Ollie's hand, Rae turned and walked over to the dressing area and said very quietly, "I know."

Hank had kept Sweetheart out of the room where the women were resting and bathing. With Katie still asleep from the surgery, he told her she had to help prepare dinner.

While the women were in the bedroom, the men all pitched in to get food on the table. Jesse, Will, and John had gone to the smokehouse and selected a small ham to make sandwiches for supper. John brought it to the kitchen and sliced it very thin. Will went to the cellar and brought up three jars of canned peaches, opened them, and poured the peaches in a large bowl. Joseph had stopped in at his future mother-in-law's café, and she gave him four large loaves of fresh bread. "This should hold Miss Ollie until she can bake her own," she had told Joseph. So, Jesse turned the job of slicing the bread over to Hank. Jeremiah came in with a fresh pail of water and filled the coffeepot with water and coffee beans. The smell of fresh brewing coffee and the wonderful aroma of fresh baked bread brought Ollie and Rae out of their room.

"Mercy sakes alive," said Ollie, smiling. "Smells wonderful in here. I can't believe all this. Look Rae, the table's all set. There are platters of food, and my wonderful boys are gathered here … together." Ollie sighed softly.

She was trying to hold herself together and not just sit down and bawl. She was so overwhelmed and thankful to be back home. "Please sit, please sit down," she motioned with her hands.

Jesse came over and took Ollie's arm and led her to the head of the table to have a seat. Rae was seated next to his place.

Making sure everyone was settled, Jesse began asking grace. "Lord, we are gathered here today to say thank you." No other words could pass by the lump he had in his throat.

Jeremiah looked around at the heads bowed and spoke loud and clear, "Amen!" Everyone laughed, and "Amen" was repeated all around.

Jesse blushed, but he leaned over and kissed Ollie on the cheek, smiling with mist in his eyes. At that moment, he didn't care if he was acting like a little boy, because he loved this old, scrappy black woman.

"This is the best food Rae and I have had in days," she said as she passed the platter of ham. "You boys have done more than I ever expected."

"Yes, it is," said Rae, slipping from the bench to stand. "I want to say something since we are all gathered. Hank, thanks for the care you gave Hope—or Sweetheart."

"That's me, my name is Sweetheart," said Hope loudly. Ollie whispered in Hope's ear to be quiet and let Mama speak.

"As I was saying, Hank, I will always be grateful to you. Will, Joseph, Rider, and John. I cannot thank you all enough for helping to search and rescue me and Ollie. You placed yourself in danger, and saying thank you will never be enough."

Rider spoke up and said, "Just keep making those delicious pies, and that will be enough thanks for me." Everyone laughed and nodded their heads in agreement.

"Jeremiah, you and Aunt Katie arriving when you did at the cave was wonderful. Aunt Katie was so brave to go into that cave. I don't know really what to think about what she did pretending to be a ghost. I love you both."

Looking down at Jesse, words wouldn't come out like she wanted them too. "Thank you is simply not enough. I am so grateful to you for all of your help since the day I fell out of that stagecoach!"

Everyone laughed as Rae sat back down. Jesse stood up and announced, "That's enough thank you' s for one meal. Let's eat!"

Chapter 19

The old rooster called the beginning of a new day, and everyone was glad to be back into their daily routine. Ollie was happy to be back in her kitchen with a new red bandanna wrapped around her short curly hair and wearing a freshly starched apron. She was humming as she mixed up a big bowl of biscuits. A small fire was burning in the fireplace, and the smell of fresh coffee was brewing.

Jesse came strolling out of his room in his stocking feet with his shirt unbuttoned. Ollie looked up at her oldest boy and gave him a warm smile.

"I know a bunch of guys that are going to be very happy this morning!" said Jesse as he poured himself a cup of coffee.

Smiling, Ollie said, "Rae is awake helping Miss Katie. She finally woke up and that shoulder is really paining her. Rae fixed her some medicine, but she would like her to drink some strong, beef broth before she sleeps again. The broth helps to rebuild the blood, and she did lose quite a bit. I guess Tim will be out around lunch or suppertime to check on her," Ollie laughed.

Jesse looked toward the bedroom door and said, "I just bet you're right." He headed out onto the porch to ring the bell and was nearly pushed down by John. "Well, good morning to you too, John. Where's the fire?" asked Jesse.

"Oh, morning, Jess. Hank came out to the bunkhouse and said that Miss Katie was awake. I wanted to speak to her this morning."

"Sure thing, just knock first," he said, pointing to the bedroom door.

Jesse rang the bell and started laughing. John was surely smitten. Who could blame him? Miss Katie was a beautiful woman, and they are just the right age for each other.

John walked quickly over to the door and knocked. Rae opened the door, and John nodded his head to her, asking softly, "How is Miss Katie this morning?"

"Is that you, John?" asked Katie.

"Yes, I wanted to speak with you for just a minute."

"Please, Rae, give us a minute," said Katie.

Rae raised her eyebrows as she turned and headed to the kitchen.

Ollie and Jesse both gave her a questioning glance, and she shrugged her shoulders with a grin on her face.

After Rae left the bedroom, John walked over to the edge of the bed. "I hope that you don't mind me coming to see you ... alone. I just had to see for myself if you were doing all right this morning. Are you in any pain?"

"A little," she answered. "But Rae has given me some medicine, so I may fall asleep while we're speaking."

"Sleep is good for you."

Katie reached out and took John's hand and smiled up at him. He stooped down on one knee, careful not to shake the bed. She looked directly into his eyes and said, "You never did say that you forgave me for getting shot."

John reached and took a strand of Katie's golden white hair between his fingers, rubbing it back and forth, while looking at her angelic face. "I do ... but I still can't believe I allowed you to go into that cave," he said quietly.

Slipping down onto her pillow, Katie said, "You ... don't really ... think you could ... have ... stopped ... me." Closing her eyes, she fell into a sound sleep.

John continued to sit and stare at this beautiful woman with her golden white hair flowing around her shoulders. She had the most delicate, flawless white skin that he had ever seen. "Yes, my lady, I do. I will never allow you to place yourself in harm's way again," he said, knowing that his words were for his ears only. Then he joined the others at the table.

After breakfast, Jesse told Rae and Ollie that he needed to go see the Downing family. "I want to thank them for all of their help that they gave us. I will probably have to hold my gun on Mr. Downing to make him take some money. I need to check on the herd and my new bull. I have to ride into town to have a talk with the sheriff, too. We will need to decide what to do with Herbert's body. After I talk to the sheriff, I am sure he can help us. See you girls at supper."

As Jesse walked away from the house, he couldn't help but think about Herbert's estate. His property, especially his house, would now be Rae's.

She would have a place in Rosedale to go back to. She would leave here ... leave him.

*****

Later in the afternoon, Hank came back into the house for a fresh cup of coffee. He looked tired and sad. "Well, ladies, I think I will gather up my belongings and drag them back out to the bunkhouse. It's time for me to give up all this wonderful hospitality and get back to taking care of those young whippersnappers outside."

"Oh Hank, I'm not sure you're ready to do that. Are you sure your ankle is strong enough for you to go back to work, roping and pulling on those cattle?"

Before he could answer, Ollie asked, "What does Jess think?"

"Oh now, Miss Ollie, I'm fine. Really. I'm just gonna miss rocking Sweetheart in the morning. I sure have gotten mighty fond of that baby girl," said Hank.

"I haven't been in that bunkhouse in a while. Do you men have enough room? Do you all have enough blankets? I need to take a turn out there and check the place over," said Ollie.

"I have to admit that I've gotten a little spoiled laying up here in the house with all this beautiful company. Being waited on hand and foot. It's sure gonna be hard getting back into my old routine," Hank said.

Jeremiah knocked on the porch's screen door. He was eager to see Miss Ollie and maybe have a cup of coffee with her without all the others around. Rae walked to the door and told him to please come in.

"Everybody is busy outside, and I wanted to check on Miss Katie."

Jeremiah glanced over at Ollie, frowning as he took in that bandanna on her head. He couldn't believe that she had covered up her soft white curls. "Woman, why have you wrapped your hair up in that rag?" he said. *Gosh! I can't believe I said that*, he thought.

Ollie turned slowly and looked across the room at him. "Are you speaking to me, old man?"

"There ain't nobody else in this here room with a red rag on their beautiful white curls," he growled.

"Listen to me, you old black mule! I'll wear what I want, when I want. Don't you come in here complaining about how I look. You have a lot of nerve."

Looking a little sheepish, he said, "I was trying to say you have pretty hair. Why do you want to go and hide it under that thing?" pointing at the top of her head. "I just don't know. You ain't no slave woman here!" said Jeremiah, trying hard to weasel out of his blunder.

"Of course I'm no man's slave! I have been freed since I was a young girl. I think you, Mr. Jeremiah, better get some lessons on how to sweet-talk a woman if that is what you were trying to do," remarked Ollie, giving her head and neck a little jerk.

"Jeremiah," said Rae, stepping in between the two bulldogs, "Aunt Katie is asleep. She was in a lot of pain this morning and after I got her to drink some beef broth, I gave her some medicine. It helps her to rest and ease the pain. Tim, will be out here sometime today to see her. When he arrives, I will come and get you. Would you like to sit and have a cup of coffee?"

"Well, I did, but I better come back later," looking over at Ollie with her back turned from him, "and start over," he said, grinning at Rae.

She smiled back and said, "Do that. Ollie, I am going to take Hope for a walk. I have got to tell her about her papa. She might hear the men talking, so I want to be the one to tell her about his death. I am going to take her up to the cemetery. I think that will be a good way to start," said Rae.

Hope held Rae by the hand as they strolled around the house and up the hillside to the small fenced cemetery. Rae had stopped and picked some wildflowers that the frost had not killed, while Hope chased several butterflies. Rae noticed that Hope had already gotten the bottom of her dress dirty, and one of her socks had slipped down and wouldn't stay up.

Hope was out of breath when they sat down between Jesse's parents' graves. She stretched out on the grass and started looking at the white clouds floating above. "Look Rae-Rae, there's an old man's face in the sky, look. There's a pig." She was giggling so hard.

Rae reached over and tickled her on her stomach and told her that she had something to tell her. "What? Do you have a surprise for me?"

"No, honey, not a surprise. I have to tell you something about Herbert, your papa." Rae sounded very serious.

"Shoot," said Hope, "I thought it was something good." She laid down on her back, looking at the sky again.

"Hope, honey, I have to tell you that your papa had been sick, and well, he died, sweetheart," Rae said very softly. "I am so sorry, baby."

Hope laid very still, not moving a muscle. Rae wasn't sure that she had heard her. Looking down at Hope, she had her eyes closed and tears were dripping down the sides of her little face into her ears. Rae gathered her up in her arms and hugged her as close as possible. "Oh, baby, I am so sorry. Please don't worry. You have me, and I promise to never leave you."

Rae continued to hold Hope. She rocked back and forth with her nestled on her lap.

"Mama ... Rae. Can I have another papa?"

Rae sat speechless for a minute. "Well, I don't know … not right now, sweetheart."

"Why not? I got two mamas," said Hope, not understanding.

"That is different, honey. You know that our mama was very ill, and I had to take care of you. I am your sister, but you called me 'mama' ever since you could talk. And you may call me that always, if you like."

"I want another papa," she said excitedly. Rae thought the best thing to do now was to play along with her.

"If you could have another papa, who would you want it to be?" said Rae, very seriously.

Wiping her nose on the hem of her dress before Rae could stop her, she looked up at Rae with big doe eyes and said, "Hankie. I want Hankie to be my new papa!"

"Oh, honey! You are something else," Rae said, covering her mouth to hold in her laughter. "I don't think Hank would want to marry me."

Realizing that Hope was only three, Rae wanted to make sure that she fully understood about Herbert. "Now, Hope, do you understand that your papa will be in heaven with our mama, and we will never see him again?"

"Rae?" Hope was looking at her so seriously, pondering what she had just been told.

"Yes?" answered Rae.

"Mama said that only good boys and girls get to go to heaven. Well, Papa wasn't good … sometimes."

With a knot in her throat, Rae took Hope back into her arms and whispered, "I think he was good enough, honey."

After a little while, Rae said, "Let's go and get some lunch and check on Aunt Katie.

Rae and Hope walked and skipped all the way back to the house. Hope saw Hank coming out of the bunkhouse and ran up to him. She grabbed his hand and starting pulling him toward the barn. "Hankie," Hope said as she stopped and started pulling him down onto one knee. "My papa has gone to heaven, and I will never see him again. Will you be my new papa?"

"Sweetheart," Hankie was so surprised by her question that he didn't know how to respond. Looking into the face of this truly innocent child, he said, "I have to get to work this morning. Those old hogs have got to have a larger fenced yard. You want to help me build a new pen for them?"

Rae went into the house and found Ollie sitting at the table peeling potatoes. She already had a hen boiling on the stove. "I'm so glad you are back, honey. Do you mind making me a couple of piecrusts? I want to make a big chicken pot pie for lunch. I will use that deep round pan I placed on the stove."

Rae looked around the warm kitchen, and it felt so good being back home. *Yes, this feels like home. But, it is not my home,* she suddenly realized.

She and Hope would be leaving in a few weeks. As soon as Katie was well enough to travel, they would have to catch the stagecoach and make that three-day trip back to Rosedale.

Surely I can find work there, she thought . *I do have many old friends. I guess I better pen a letter to Mr. Sigler, the lawyer in Rosedale and inform him that I will be coming back and to please watch after my home for a few weeks.*

But sadly, she thought as she looked at Ollie and around this warm, cozy room, *how will I ever be able to leave? I love it here. I love everybody here.*

"Rae, are you all right? You have turned white as a sheet. Sit down. I knew that you overdid yourself this morning!" said Ollie. "I declare, honey child. You have got to rest."

"Really, Ollie, I am fine. I just had some sad thoughts, that's all. Let me get busy making the piecrust."

After the preparations of the hearty lunch, everyone had eaten except Jesse. He had gone into town to see the sheriff. Jeremiah and John stayed and visited with Katie, who was awake and wanted to sit up a spell. John adjusted her pillows and made her as comfortable as he could. He wanted to visit with her without Jeremiah's company, but it looked like Jeremiah had sit in for a while. John had to go back to work, so he left with a promise to come back this evening to see her again.

"Shame on you, Jeremiah," said Katie. "You knew that John wanted to visit with me alone, and you sat in that chair like a big fat mother bear on guard."

"Shore did, and I ain't apologizing to either of you. You might not be a girl of twenty anymore, but it has been a long time since you had a man trying to court you. I'm just taking his measure for you, missy."

"Well, mister know-it-all, what decision have you come to about him?"

"It's too soon to tell, but when I know, you will know." Jeremiah laughed. "I'm going to try to have a cup of coffee with that old black woman in the kitchen. And *no*, we don't need a chaperone."

*****

Jesse arrived from town near supper time. He was out in the corral with the new foals that had been born while they were gone. Mr. Downing and his son had done a great job in helping to deliver them. Will had already chosen one to be his and was rubbing her down from head to toe. She was all brown except for some white hair just above her eyes in the shape of a star. There was never any doubt what name Will would chose for the new colt. She was a beauty for sure.

Jesse was feeling pretty good now that everything seemed to be back to normal. All the cattle were turned back into the larger pastures, the horses were out of the corral, and his new bull was roaming around after the heifers.

The two large sows had given birth to almost twenty new little piglets, and a new fenced yard was been constructed by Hank for them today.

Yes, things were looking good on the ranch. Now it was time for him to start working on a plan for his future, and he wanted Rae to share in his decisions. He knew that he wanted Rae to be his wife, the mother of his children.

Jesse didn't have to look up to know the sound of that rickety black carriage driving into the yard. *Damn it.* He kicked the dirt and turned to walk toward the young doctor as he got out of the carriage.

"Howdy, Jess. I came to check on Mrs. Brown. How are Ollie and Rae doing?"

"Come in the house and see for yourself. It is almost supper time, but I am guessing you knew that already."

Tim just laughed and followed Jesse into the house. Looking around the room, Tim spotted Ollie over at the stove frying chicken and Rae whipping some potatoes.

"How are my two favorite patients this evening?" asked Tim, using his doctor's voice.

"Speaking for myself, I'm as good as they get!" said Ollie.

"And Rae," asked Tim, "what do you have to say about yourself?"

"I'm very well, thank you," Rae answered as she poured the potatoes into a large bowl.

Wiping her hands on her apron, she said to Tim, "Come and I will take you to see Aunt Katie. She is doing very well."

Jesse didn't take his eyes off the two of them as they walked out of the room. "Dinner sure smells wonderful, Ollie. Are you ready for me to ring the bell? I know the guys can smell this chicken for a country mile."

Reaching up on the shelf, Ollie got another plate and set it on the table for the doctor. "You knows he's staying," she said with a big grin.

Jeremiah came in the house and eased over to Ollie, asking her if he could help. She smiled with a twinkle in her eye and shook her head *no*.

"Just take your seat at the table."

Damn, what's going on here? First, John's acting like a dog in heat, sniffing after Katie. And now Jeremiah, making cow eyes at Ollie? And Ollie is eating it up! And that fool of a doctor, talking sweet to Rae every chance he gets. It's not even spring, and they have all gone crazy. Shaking his head, Jesse wondered what in the hell was keeping him from making his move.

Rae fixed Katie a plate of food and placed it on a serving tray to take in to her room. John rushed over and took it out of her hands. He said that he would take it to her and come back and get his plate. He didn't want her to eat alone. Jeremiah got up from his seat with the intention of going into the room with them. Ollie placed her hand on his shoulder and said, "Let them be. She's in good hands with John."

The dinner was a success as always. The men all filed outside to do whatever they wanted. Joseph saddled up his horse and rode to town to see his fiancée. Hank was sitting in the rocker with Hope on his lap, while she interpreted the pictures of her favorite storybook. Will had taken Rider into the barn to introduce him to his new foal, which he named Star.

Jesse stayed in the house helping Rae and Ollie clean up the kitchen while the doctor sat at the table telling them about a new preacher coming to town on Sunday. He had been told that the preacher may stay and preach for several weeks.

"It will be nice to go to church and sing praises to the Lord," said Tim.

"Sundays seem so different when you can't attend church services. Rae, would you like to go to the Sunday service with me? I will be happy to ride out and pick you up."

"That won't be necessary. If she wants to go, she can go with all of us. We always attend church when the preacher is in town," said Jesse with a straight face.

Ollie burst out laughing and said that some good old-fashioned preaching of hell and brimstone surely wouldn't hurt any of them. Jesse gave her a hard stare, daring her to speak up about him never going to church.

"Thank you, Tim, for the invitation, but I will ride in with Ollie and the boys," said Rae, looking at Jesse as he was busying himself by placing the mugs on the shelf above the stove.

"Oh, honey, I won't be going with ya'll. I goes to my own church a few miles through the woods. Reverend Jones is a wonderful old man who sings praises to the Lord every week. He is a soft-spoken man who never shouts and tells us that we are all going to go to hell. Oh, how I love to hear him sing, too. He sings at all the weddings and burials in the area. I have missed these past few weeks, but he will understand when I goes back this Sunday."

Rae smiled at Ollie as she was talking about her church preacher, and she remembered when she was little and her mama took her every Sunday until she got sick.

"I haven't been to church in years. I had better make sure that Hope and I have our Sunday clothes all ready. It will be good to go into town and see all the people who live here," said Rae.

"Be sure to save me a seat on your pew," said Tim. Rae just smiled at him as he was sipping his coffee.

"Well, I better head on back to my office. I have gotten a few more patients. It seems the sheriff has been singing my praises to the good people, and they are listening to him. Miss Ollie that was a wonderful supper."

"Rae, will you walk outside with me for a minute?" asked Tim, purposely not looking Jesse's way.

Rae looked into the living room at Hank and Hope, and she reached for a wrap that was hanging by the door. She could feel Jesse's eyes upon her back as she walked outside with Tim.

Sunday finally came, and Rae could hardly contain herself. She walked out on the porch and felt the chill in the air—another sign that fall was in the air. She and Hope had picked some beautiful golden orange leaves as they walked to the cemetery and chased butterflies the day before.

Ollie has gotten up and put a large beef roast into the oven, and the house already smelled wonderful. She had make dough for rolls while Rae had prepared a large rectangular pan of apple cobbler. Sunday lunch was well on its way and ready for their return from church.

Breakfast was a hurried affair. Everyone gobbled down the bacon, eggs, and biscuits that Ollie had prepared along with the pot of corn grits that Rae had cooked.

Rae took extra care with her toilette. She brushed her hair until Aunt Katie told her she was going to go bald. "Leave your hair down, Rae. It is beautiful, and it makes you have a fresh, young look."

"But, Aunt Katie. I don't want to look like a schoolgirl. I want to look like a full-grown woman. You know that I am twenty already."

Katie laughed. "Yes, you are really old."

"Now listen, Jeremiah is going to stay home with you this morning.

We won't be gone but a couple of hours. Are you sure that you don't need any pain medicine this morning?"

"I'm sure, dear. Please don't worry about me. I am getting stronger every day, and I am ready to get out of this bed and sit in the living area. I can't stand these walls much longer."

Jesse had the carriage brought out front. Will, Rider, and Joseph were dressed in their best blue denim pants and western shirts with their string ties, and they were all set to ride along with them. Joseph had instructions from Ollie to invite Rebecca, his fiancée, to come for lunch.

Rae and Hope strolled out to the screen porch, and Jesse hurried over to assist them both down the steps. A hush came over the men as they witnessed a vision of beauty walk past them. Rider leaned over to Will and said, "Man, she is knock-down gorgeous."

Rae looked around at the three men and remarked how handsome they all looked.

Finally they were off to church after all the compliments were passed around to each other with lots of kidding and laughter.

As the wagon and horses headed away from the house, Katie looked up from her bed and there stood John, leaning against the doorframe. Giving him a surprised look, she asked, "Where's Jeremiah?"

"Ollie persuaded him to go to church with her, and now we are home alone." John raised his eyebrows like a wicked old man.

She burst out laughing and said, "I may be in more danger here than I was in that dark cave."

Entering the room, walking slowly toward her bed, he said, "You just might be."

*****

Arriving at the church, the new preacher was standing next to the front porch steps. He was greeting all of the townspeople as they approached before they entered the church. Rae had not seen the church, and she was so surprised how very quaint it looked. The building was painted white with black shutters next to the windows. The double doors held two grapevine wreaths with fresh fall flowers attached to them. The church had been kept up even though the town didn't have a regular minister.

The men had hobbled their horses out in the field behind the church while Jesse had tied his horse and carriage under a shade tree.

Walking up to the preacher, Jesse extended his hand to the man who had to be at least five or six inches taller than any of the other men standing around. The first thing Jesse noticed was his eyes. He looked like he could see straight into a person's soul. Scary. He had a beak-shaped nose with big bushy eyebrows that looked as though they might connect to the beard growing down both sides of his face. His face was not pleasant to look upon at all.

Rae was standing back a little as Jesse made the introduction. "So," he said with a booming voice loud enough for all around to hear, "I finally meet the lady that the whole county is buzzing about. And you are the man who has coveted her. I see that I have arrived just in time to save your reputations."

Turning and putting his large hand on Jesse's left elbow and grabbing Rae's right hand, he pulled them into the church, saying, "Come, children, hear my sermon and see if I may repair and save your souls. We can't have people living in sin, especially in front of children."

Rae was beside herself. She was trembling from her head to her toes with rage. Glancing at Jesse, she could tell he felt the same way. Every muscle in his body was held so tight that he was actually afraid to move.

He wanted to strangle the God-fearing man right here in front of all these damn busybodies. Every eye was directed on them as the preacher shoved them into the front pew and said very loud that he would "take them in hand" after church.

Jesse's leg was shaking up and down, and his palms were sweating. He didn't dare look at Rae, but he could feel her rage. Tim O'Riley came and slid into the pew next to Rae. "Good morning," he whispered to Rae, but she didn't even acknowledge him.

Rae wanted to cry, but she'd be damned before she would shed a tear in front of these so-called Christians. She and Jesse had done nothing wrong, but why did she feel so guilty? She had never been alone with Jesse, and Ollie had been the perfect chaperone. *I'll die before I let that so-called religious man have a discussion of any kind with me!*

Everyone stood to sing, and Rae pushed into Jesse's side to get his attention. "Let's get out of here before I die." She didn't have to repeat herself to him. He stepped into the aisle and let her out of the pew to pass by him. Both of them actually ran, dragging Hope in their wake.

"Mama," complained Hope, "you are hurting me."

"Honey, I am so sorry, but we have to get home." Jesse untied his horse and helped Rae and Hope into the seat of the carriage. Will and Rider came running out of the church, placing their hats on their heads.

"What's wrong?" asked Will.

"We have to leave. Please stay and visit with your friends, and we will see you at lunchtime. I will tell you about this later." Jesse drove out of the churchyard, leaving Will and Rider looking at each other.

Jess had driven the carriage out of the churchyard like someone was chasing after them. He was shaking with anger, but he knew he must slow down. It wasn't safe to drive the small carriage too fast. "I'm sorry if I scared you, Rae, driving so wild. I wanted to get away from those people as fast as I could."

"Oh, Jesse." Rae had relaxed a little and let down her defenses. "Can you believe what the preacher said about us? Living in sin? I couldn't believe my ears. And everybody talking about us. I guess the trouble with Herbert has really gotten around and now that it is over they are making something ugly out of your help to me.

"I know that your family has always been well thought of and now for me to bring ugly talk to your door is so sad. I am so sorry. I have been waiting until Aunt Katie is well to travel home before I left, but I better leave now, as soon as I can get tickets on the stagecoach to Rosedale."

"No, running away is not the answer, Rae. I don't want you to leave.

I was trying to give you a period of time to mourn your mama before I tried to court you. I never believed your story about being a widow, but I knew something sad had happened in your life. I never dreamed it was something like Herbert. Anyway, I have wanted so bad to get to know you and allow you to know me." Looking at Hope, who was listening to every word that they were saying, he said, "Let's wait until we are alone to finish this discussion. Little ears have big mouths." Jesse smiled at Rae, while looking at Hope.

When they finally reached the ranch, Jesse helped Rae and Hope down from the carriage, and he drove it off to the barn to attend to the horses.

Rae took Hope and went to the back room to check on Katie. Sitting in a chair as close to the bed as he could get was John. Katie and John were so intense with their conversation that they didn't hear Rae or Hope come into the room.

Realizing that they were not alone, Katie said, "Goodness is church service over so soon?"

Taking one look at Rae's face, John knew that something was very wrong. He excused himself with the pretense of going out to help Jesse with the horses and carriage.

Rae sat down on her bed, covered her face with her hands and started crying. "Oh, Aunt Katie, it was terrible, just terrible," she cried. She jumped up and wiped her eyes. She began to unbuttoned Hope's dress and remove her Sunday shoes. "Let's put this play dress on, sweetheart, and you can go on the porch. Maybe John will bring your puppy from the barn."

Katie was watching Rae and not understanding her mood swing. After sending Hope out of the room onto the porch, Rae started removing her lovely blue calico dress to be replaced with a soft, yellow-and-brown-striped day dress. She didn't feel pretty any longer.

"Rae, what in the world has happened? And don't say 'nothing.' Maybe I can help," encouraged Katie as she moved over a little on her bed to allow Rae to sit beside her.

"Aunt Katie, I am the talk of the county. I am no better than a jezebel, living here on this ranch in 'sin'."

"What? Who said those nasty things about you?" Katie couldn't believe what Rae had said.

"The traveling preacher. He had heard all about me from one end of this county to the other. People are talking about me and Jesse living here in sin. Can you believe that? Boy, those people don't know Miss Ollie. If they did, they would know that she wouldn't allow anything like that going on under her roof. But Aunt Katie," Rae said, "some of the people do know Miss Ollie, and they still believe the stories. I am sure of that. I could feel them looking at us like we were … I can't even think of a word, I'm so mad!"

"Oh, honey, I believe that is a ridiculous statement about you and Jess living in sin."

"You wouldn't think that if you had heard that loathsome creature who calls himself a preacher. He told me and Jess that he was going to try and save our souls. There were several of the townspeople outside who heard him say that. I really wanted to die right there on the spot. As soon as we stood for the first hymn, I punched Jess in his side and told him I wanted to leave. We practically ran out of the church, dragging poor little Hope."

"So, what did Jess say on the way home about all this?"

"He is angry. I can assure you of that. He had started to talk about us, but he didn't want to talk in front of Hope. We are going to talk in a little while. I told him that I am going to leave and go home to Rosedale.

I have Herbert's house, and I can get a job in town. I am sure I can get somebody to help me with Hope."

"Rae, what do you mean you will have Herbert's house? Do you think that it is yours and Hope's now that he is dead?"

"Well, yes, I do. Why shouldn't I think that? I haven't written Mr. Sigler a letter as yet telling him that we are coming home, but I intend to, today." Rae was looking at the expression on Aunt Katie's face.

"What is it, Aunt Katie? What's wrong?"

"Honey, I hate to be the one to tell you this, but Herbert didn't own that house and land. He leased it from Mr. Sigler before he married Claire. Jeremiah found out that information from Mr. Sigler himself. He came by our house for a visit while traveling to Peamont, right after Herbert and Claire married. You remember, I told you that Mr. Sigler and I knew each other as children."

Rae backed up and sat down on her bed. She just had the wind knocked out of her sails. Reality was setting in like never before. She had no place to go. Why go back to Rosedale with no home there? Aunt Katie's home was too small with only one room for sleeping. Besides, there was no work in Peamont. *I couldn't live there even if she had the room,* thought Rae.

After a few minutes, she said that she had better get up and start earning her keep here. Lunch needed to be finished before the men and guests arrived home after church.

Trying her best to pretend that she was all right, she asked, "Aunt Katie, would you like to try to sit up in the rocking chair in the living area today? I will get John to assist you."

"That would be just wonderful. Please help me change my gown and let me use that pretty robe of yours. Will you brush my hair in the back?"

"Golly, I just asked if you wanted to sit in the rocker, not go to a dance."

"Hush your mouth, girl, and help me look decent. I am getting out of this room," Katie said with a laugh. She was feeling great but still very concerned over Rae and what she had been put through at church.

By the time Ollie and Jeremiah had arrived home from church, Rae had lunch all ready. She had placed the rolls in the oven, and the house smelled wonderful. The table was all set, just waiting for the family to arrive and gather around it. This should have been a happy Sunday afternoon, but it was filled with disappointment for Rae, and she was trying to hold back her anger and tears.

Ollie wanted to ask Rae about her first visit to the Sunday service in town, but she could tell that something was very wrong. Rae was quiet and looked like she might cry any second. She expected that Rae and Jesse must have heard the rumors that had been spread through the community.

Rae stood next to the rocker that Katie occupied, nibbling on her bottom lip. She was trying to avoid conversation with Ollie. She just wanted to finish with lunch so she could close herself away from everyone.

"Miss Katie, it is so good to see you up and about. This is a good sign that you are better," said Ollie.

Jesse came in the house followed by Hank, Hope, Rider, and Joseph and Rebecca. It was a beautiful sunny afternoon, and it should have been a pleasant day. There was a chill in the room that had nothing to do with the weather. Rae forced a smile on her lovely face, while Jesse only spoke when spoken to. Will and the other men couldn't understand why Jesse and Rae had run out of the church. Will knew that the congregation was talking about them, but everyone would hush up when he got within earshot of any of the conversations.

After lunch, Rae, Ollie, and Rebecca made quick work of cleaning the kitchen. While Rebecca went for a stroll with Joseph into the barn to see the new animals, Katie insisted that John take her to the front porch swing. Rae took Hope into her room to read her a story and make her take an afternoon nap. Will and Hank stood around in the living area, hoping that Jesse would explain what had taken place at the church.

"Please fellows, let me talk with Rae. Afterward, I will tell you the reason Rae and I felt we needed to get away from that crazy preacher and leave the church like we did."

Will and Hank went out the door saying how they would "kick ass if anyone ever hurt Rae's feelings, you can count on that." Jesse knew how much those two loved his Rae. *His Rae,* he thought. *Yes, my Rae.* He liked the sound of that very much.

Jesse was waiting on Rae to come out of the house. He had already asked Ollie to please watch Hope while he took Rae on a ride where they could talk privately.

He drove to a secluded spot in the woods next to a slow moving stream.

Jesse stopped the horse, jumped down from the carriage, and offered Rae his hand. As he lifted her down, he held her tight and allowed her body to slide down the front of his hard body.

She was surprised and gave him a little push backward. "Just because some old straitlaced matrons are talking about me doesn't make it true, so don't get any idea that you can bring me out here and seduce me."

"What in hades are you talking about?" Jesse shot right back at her.

"Maybe I did hold you too close for a second, but you know that neither one of us is guilty of what those ladies are saying about us. Gossip is what they thrive on." Jesse had so much anger penned up inside that he wanted to hit something.

Rae walked away from Jesse to a shady spot near the stream. She sat down on a large, smooth rock that was a perfect place to sit and fish.

"Look, Rae, we are going to have to stop this fighting. We are in this together, and we can put a stop to this gossip," said Jesse, walking behind her and putting his hands on her shoulders.

"You are right. We can, and the sooner I leave, the sooner they will stop talking about us and start on some other poor fools." It was very obvious that Rae was still very angry and hurt.

"That's not what I meant. Please turn around and look at me. I don't want you to leave. I want you to stay here with Ollie, Will, and me. We all care about you and the baby. We have grown very fond of you both and well, it will break Ollie's heart if you just up and left."

"I care for ... Ollie and Will too. We have been very happy here, but I can't just remain in your home. Nothing will change or stop the busybodies from talking about us. That crazy preacher is liable to come out here. It's no telling what he ... might do," said Rae, just so confused.

Hanging her head down to her chest, fighting back tears, she said, "Oh, Jess, I have no place to go. Herbert did not own the house where we lived in Rosedale, like I thought. Even so, I can't stay here."

"Listen to me, Rae. You can stay here with us—with me, I mean. Marry me and your problems will be solved. You will have a permanent home—no money worries and no more old hens flapping their gums. Our souls and reputations will be saved." He smiled as he was mocking the preacher's words.

Rae couldn't believe Jesse. *Marry him? Oh yes! I love him so. I have dreamed of this moment, but wait ...* Looking at Jesse, she realized that he had not said that he loved her. Or did he?

"Do you love me, Jess?" asked Rae so seriously that Jesse froze and hesitated a moment too long before answering. "Well, thank you for your proposal of marriage, but I must decline. Besides, how can I marry a man that I am afraid of half the time? Come here! Do this! Do that! Marry me. Then what? Live the rest of my life with a man who doesn't love me?" Rae stood ramrod straight, not daring to move a muscle.

"Rae, you don't have any reason to be frightened of me. I told you before that I would never hurt you or Hope. I want only what is best for you both. For all of us. You must consider what I am asking."

"Jess, don't make an assumption that because I haven't a place to live that I would ever stay here and be in a loveless marriage." Still, no declaration of love came from Jesse's lips.

Rae, standing very still, looked down at the flow of the water and thought, *this is my life. Drifting ... flowing along ... no destination.*

Looking over at Jesse in his new denims, dark shirt, and brown leather vest, he looked so young and handsome. *He is offering me his home and security,* thought Rae.

"You must give me some time to consider your proposal. It is not just *my* future that I must think about. I have Hope. I am more than a sister to her. I am her mama now."

"I have known from the very first that Hope belongs with you. I know that I can take care of you both, and I feel that this marriage will be for the best," he stated matter-of-factly.

"How can you know what's best for me when I don't even know myself?" she asked, all choked up from disappointment. She wanted him to say that he loved her.

Jesse reached out to take Rae's hands. "Don't touch me, Jess," she said. "You have no right, at least for now."

Jesse backed away and asked, "How much time do you need to consider my proposal of marriage?"

She continued looking down at the water as it slowing moved along. "Give me two weeks. By then, Aunt Katie should be well enough to travel and if I decide to leave, I will go home with her."

"Is there anything I can do or say to convince you to remain here?"

Rae stood up and walked toward the horse and carriage. She stopped, turned around, and said, "You will have to figure that one out by yourself."

Katie seemed to be getting stronger every day with the help of John. But she was very concerned about Rae. She watched Rae work like a Trojan horse, cleaning house and cooking circles around Ollie. She barely went outside except to help the lady who came to do the washing. She had Hank or Will take Hope out to the barn or for a long walk each day. Jesse kept taking time out of his work schedule to give Hope rides on his horse, which she dearly loved.

Rae had baked several pies and made four dozen cookies. The house smelled so good that the men couldn't stay out of the kitchen. Everyone was enjoying her cookies with some hot coffee when they heard the doctor's carriage pull up to the front of the house. Rae walked slowly to the door, opened the screen, and invited him to come and join them.

"Am I in time for a party?" asked Tim. "Boy, it smells wonderful in here."

"What brings you out this way, Doc?" asked Will.

"I wanted to check on Miss Brown and make sure Miss Ollie was doing all right now. Also, I was wondering why you, Rae, and Jess, left the church service before it was over. I was afraid that something had happened, but then I saw you and Rider come back inside." Rae just looked away, not bothering to answer his question.

"Aunt Katie is doing very well, Tim. Follow me and I will take you to her room." Rae stopped and knocked on the door, saying, "Aunt Katie, the doctor is here to see you."

"Come in, Doctor. It is so good to see you. I want you to tell these nice people here that I am well enough to travel and go home. Jeremiah and I really need to get back and take care of my flower gardens and a few livestock."

"Well, you are going to have to let me look at that arm and shoulder of yours. Rae, help her undress so I can look at her wound, please. I will step out and be right back."

Tim went back into the kitchen to retrieve his cup of coffee. While he was taking a sip, Jesse came in the back door.

"Hi Tim, how are you doing? We haven't had the pleasure of your company lately," he said sarcastically.

"Fortunately for me, I have been busy at the office. But I had to come out and see Miss Brown. I best get in there and check her over. Rae is in the room with me."

Jesse looked at all the guys sitting around the table enjoying the fresh baked cookies and coffee. "What the hell do you all think you are doing when you know we have a room to complete?" growled Jesse.

"John," barked Jesse, "start on the trim around the window and make sure the window's edges are sealed tight. That loft can be really hot, but it can be freezing up there in the winter. Have Rider and Will bring in the new potbellied heater that I have in the wagon. We will need to cut a hole in the outside wall for the pipe. I want that sealed tight too. Have Will tell Joseph where he wants his bed to be and have some shelves built for the opposite wall. He will need a place to put some of his things, and shelves will be nice. Joseph can sand the boards and stain them before they go up on the wall. This room may be in the loft, but I want it to be nice."

"I'll be right on it. I was waiting for the doctor's report on Kate, if you don't mind, Jess."

"Lord help me." Jesse sighed as he went out of the house toward the barn.

John could hear the doctor arguing with Katie. He came out of her room, shaking his head.

"What the verdict, Doc?" asked John, who was very concerned.

"Her arm still has a little infection in it. I gave her a shot and told her to keep taking the pills that will help cure it. She is unhappy about being a burden and wants to go home, but she is not leaving here without my blessing. I am going to talk with Jeremiah now. He will not take her home until I give him the go-ahead," said Tim, very determined to make Miss Brown stay there.

After seeking Jeremiah out and giving him his report on Katie's health, he went in search of Rae. He found her sitting in the kitchen having a cup of coffee.

"Aunt Katie is fast asleep already. That shot put her out. She's not in any danger, is she, Tim?" asked Rae.

"Not if she will take care of herself and get as much rest as possible. She thinks that because she was allowed to get out of bed for a while that she is fine, but that is far from the case. This infection is very serious. I am not surprised about the infection because that cave was filthy. I could have missed something when I operated. But the good news is that we got it in time, and I am sure she will recovery nicely if we can hold her down." He gave Rae that sweet, charming smile of his.

"I am sure John will sit on her if he has too. He is quite taken with Aunt Katie."

"Really? I would never have guessed." His teasing and laughter was contagious. Rae couldn't help but smile at him.

"Please walk with me out to my carriage. I hate that I missed lunch, but Ollie packed me a piece of pie to take with me. She said that you made it."

As they got to the carriage, Tim turned to Rae and smiled so sweetly, and gave her a big grin. "Will you go on a picnic with me tomorrow afternoon? I will bring everything, and you can bring Hope too. I am taking tomorrow off, and I would love to spend some time with you away from your watchdog," he said while looking over his shoulder at Jesse.

Jesse was standing in the doorway of the barn watching their every move.

Rae lifted her head as to snub Jesse and said very firmly, "Yes, I would enjoy spending the afternoon with you. I may leave Hope here napping."

She turned her head to look Jesse's way again and said, "If Hope doesn't get a nap, she can be a holy terror before supper."

"Great. I will be here around two?"

"Wonderful, I look forward to it."

Watching Tim drive out of the ranch yard, Rae put her hand on her hip and swayed her backside as she strolled back into the house, ignoring Jesse completely.

"Damn!" said Jesse, and he turned back to his chore of washing down one of the new colts.

Ollie had put Hope down for a nap in the bed next to Katie. They were both sleeping sound. John came out of the room and said to Ollie and Rae that he would be in the loft if Kate needed him.

Rae asked Ollie to come and sit with her on the porch. They settled in the swing, and Rae told Ollie what had taken place at church. "I was mortified, Ollie. This man, this stranger, who doesn't even know Jess and me, said the nastiest things to us. Like it was the truth! He had judged us by the rumors that he had heard. I felt so ashamed. He scared me, too," said Rae looking at Ollie.

"Now you listen to me, child. You and God knows that you and Jess have never done anything to be ashamed of. Jeremiah and I were told about the rumors, but I wants you to know that the people who knows us, and cares, don't believe any of it."

"Oh Ollie, Jess feels that we can stop the gossip by marrying. He has it all figured out," she said with a little disgust in her voice. "We get married and all the talk about us will stop immediately. He knows that I have no place to go except with Aunt Katie. Truth be known, I can't stay at her home. It is small, and there is no place for me to get work. I have to support myself and Hope. ... But Ollie, I can't just marry Jess."

"Why not, honey? What is the real reason you are hesitating? I know that you love him."

"How do you know that?" whispered Rae, looking at Ollie with a frown on her face.

Throwing back her head and laughing, she said, "Honey child, a person would have to have their head stuck in a hole not to see or feel the attraction that you two have for each other. Jess is so crazy about you he can hardly stand to be around himself. He watches your every move, and we all watch him watch you!" She laughed again. "And Lord have mercy on that poor doctor. ... If looks could kill, that young man would be dead many times over."

"I wish I could believe that. I do love him, but please don't tell him. I want him to love me. Ollie, I asked him if he loved me. He never answered me, and that was my answer. I don't want to marry Jess because he feels responsible for me. I am not worried about saving my reputation. I can get a place to live and support myself—eventually. I don't need a high-handed man bossing me around like Jess tries to do."

"So, what answer did you give him about marriage?"

"I need time to think about his proposal. This is our lives that he has planned out. I told him that I would give him my answer in two weeks."

A lot can happen in two weeks, thought Ollie.

*****

The next morning started out with a little frost on the ground, but it turned into a sunny afternoon. Perfect for a picnic. Th e only problem with this picnic was the company. Rae would rather be spending her afternoon with Jesse. She knew that Jesse cared for her, but caring and loving were very different. She knew that he displayed jealous behavior when Tim was around, but she just wasn't sure why. Ollie said that Jesse was crazy about her, but that is not love. Just maybe if she spent more time with Tim, Jesse might show his true feelings toward her. *Th is just might be worth a try,* she thought.

Rae was hurrying to get the lunch dishes washed and put away. Jesse was lingering in the kitchen, drinking a glass of milk and eating an extra piece of Rae's apple pie.

"I love your desserts," Jesse said as he got up to carry his plate to the dishpan of dirty dishes. He brushed real close to Rae and actually touched her shoulder as he passed by her.

"Oh, Jess, I didn't mean to bump into you," she said very softly.

"You didn't," he said. "I love the way you call me Jess." Reaching up, he pushed a strand of hair behind her ear.

"Jess," her heart beat wildly as he touched her hair, "I have to hurry … I've got to get ready."

"Ready? Where are you going?"

"Just for a … ride. An outing. Excuse me, please, I need to get by."

Jesse continued to block her path from the kitchen to her room. "Just who are you going on this outing with, missy?"

"*Missy?*" she repeated under her breath. "I am going on a picnic with Tim, if you *must* know. Now let me pass my Lord and master!"

Pulling her close to him and looking straight in her eyes, he warned, "Don't play games with me, Rae."

She waited with her heart in her throat, hoping that he was going to say something more personal, but he didn't. She stood close to him until she began to feel very uncomfortable.

"Please, let me pass," she said very softly. Jesse stepped aside and gave her a low bow.

Rae skirted by him as fast as she could and went into her room to change into another shirtwaist and got her bonnet.

When Tim drove up in his carriage, he was as happy as he could be. A beautiful day, a beautiful girl, a delicious lunch packed from the café. Who could ask for anything more?

Rae heard the carriage and hurried to look in the bedroom one more time at Hope. She was sleeping like a rock. Aunt Katie was propped up on her pillows watching Rae's every move.

Rae gathered her bonnet and shawl and started to the door when Katie called her to come back and sit down on her bed. "Listen, child, I know that I am not your mama, but I am going to give you some motherly advice. Tim is a nice young man and he is wearing his feelings for you where everyone can see them. He can't see what I see."

"And what do you see?" asked Rae as she glanced out the window.

"You love Jesse. He is mad for you too."

"Oh, Aunt Katie, he may want me, but he doesn't love me," said Rae with so much disappointment in her voice.

"Listen to me." She shook Rae's arm hard. "You have had very little experience with men. You haven't been around many since you were grown. Men show their feelings different than we do. But Rae … you cannot play around with their emotions. Don't lead this nice young man to believe that he may have a future with you, when you know in your heart that is never going to happen."

"It's just a picnic for goodness sakes. We aren't eloping! We're just friends."

"Maybe you better set him straight before someone gets hurts in this love triangle," said Katie very firmly.

Chapter 20

Jesse, John, and Joseph were all up in the loft banging away with their hammers and saws. The room was almost completed except for bringing in some more furniture for Will. Rider and Will were outside building a larger bed for the room. The men had joked about Will sleeping on that small bunk bed and letting his feet hang off the end. He decided that he wanted a big bed like the one in Jesse's room.

Jess had told him to go into town and tell Mr. Smith at the general store to order two of the larger new mattresses that he advertised being sold in Frisco City. Jess decided that it was time to toss out that old mattress that had been Pa's for years. Ollie said she didn't want one of those new hard things. She would just keep her old soft one that her old bones were used to sleeping on.

Jess was very pleased with the outcome of Will's new room in the loft. The new mattresses should be in soon. Rider and Will used ropes to wrap the sides of the bedframe, weaving it to resemble latticework to hold the mattress tight. Ollie had sent up bed linens and two new quilts that she had made over the years. Will and Hope had gathered some of his belongings out of his old room and carried them up the loft ladder. This was an exciting room for her.

"Can I come up here anytime I want to, baby boy?" asked Hope.

Will laughed and picked her up over his head and swung her little body around. "No, you may not, little miss. This is my private castle, and I can't have a little mouse like you running in and out. Besides, this ladder is not the safest thing for you to be climbing on all by yourself."

*****

Rae and Tim had ridden several miles away from the ranch. Tim reined in the horse and jumped out of the carriage. He said that this was a lovely spot that he had been wanting to bring her. Rae looked around the area, and he was right. It was lovely. Big oak trees covered in golden orange leaves shaded a perfect green spot of grass. Th ere was a small stream that Rae was sure joined the one that Jesse had taken her to on one of their outings.

"Oh, Tim, this is nice. You have chosen well. And I must confess that I am starving. I didn't eat much lunch."

"I hope you were too excited to eat, thinking about us being together," said Tim as he reached to help Rae down from the carriage.

He had brought a blanket to spread on the ground for them to sit and have lunch. After settling down and getting comfortable, he laughed and said, "I can't believe that we are finally alone."

Rae laughed too, but she was beginning to feel very unsure of her decision to come on this outing. Aunt Katie's words were in her thoughts, and she was beginning to feel very guilty. She had agreed to have lunch with Tim to make Jesse jealous. Tim didn't deserve to be used in her scheme to make Jesse confess his feelings for her. Ollie and Aunt Katie had both said that Jesse cared for her, but she needed to hear the words from him.

"Rae, I wanted us to spend some time together to really get to know each other," he said as he took her hand in his. "You know I can't help but think that Jess is going to ride up on his horse and shoot me!" They both laughed, but he looked at Rae and asked, "What happened Sunday to cause you and Jess to run out of the church? Everyone started talking, and the preacher said that he would take care of you two later. What in the world did he mean by that?"

"Oh, my goodness! That awful man said that?" Tim nodded his head *yes* and gave her hand a big squeeze.

"I can't believe that you haven't heard the rumors about me and Jess."

Tim gave her a questioning look and said nothing.

"Oh Tim, it is just too embarrassing to repeat what the preacher said to us on the steps of the church. He said that Jess and I are the talk of the whole county. He said that Jess and I are living in sin. I thought I would die right there, and if Jess had not been in shock, he probably would have strangled him with his bare hands. The next thing we knew, the preacher was pulling us into the church, and he shoved us in a pew. Right in front of everyone. I was mortified, and Jesse's body was jerking. You came in and then we all stood to sing. That's when I told Jess to take me home!"

"I can't believe a preacher would treat people like that," Tim said.

"Well, believe it. He said that he was going to save our souls."

"What are you going to do to stop the gossip?"

"Jess has the problem all solved." Holding her head down and looking at her lap, she added, "He says that we should get married and then the busybodies won't have anything to talk about."

"Wow! That is one way to shut people up from talking, I guess. So, how do you feel about marrying Jess?" he asked very softly.

"Tim," reaching out to touch his arm, "I wanted to talk to you about this. I like you very much, and if Jesse ... Well, Tim, I love Jess and have for a good while. He just doesn't feel the same about me. I know that he is jealous of you. You can tell that." She laughed while looking at him. "But being jealous isn't the same as loving someone."

"Rae, I knew all along that you had feelings for him. I have seen how you look at him, and I've wished that it was me. You can't blame a fellow for trying. Any man would be proud to have you as his wife."

Sitting quietly for a minute, Tim asked Rae, "What makes you think that Jess doesn't love you?"

Rae looked up. His boyish smile and the breeze blowing his wheat blond hair just melted her heart. "Oh Tim, I don't want it to be true. I feel something when he looks at me, and but I can't figure out what he is thinking. When he touches me, I can't think." Embarrassed at how she sounded, she said, "Well, anyway I don't want to get married just to stop some lies."

"Listen to me," said Tim very sternly. "Men know when another man has marked his territory. And Jess has marked his territory in many small ways. He has taken you and Hope under his wing from the first day you arrived, and now he is offering you his home and himself for 'life.' Maybe he hasn't spoken the words out loud, but they are in his heart. Jess is not going to let a few rumors *force* him into doing something that he doesn't want to do."

"You really think that he loves me?"

"Yes, with all his heart. When you were kidnapped, we all thought he would die. I was sure that he loved you then, but I had to throw my hat into the ring just in case you didn't want that hardheaded beast!" He slapped his leg, and they both laughed together again.

"Tim, there will be some lucky lady to come into your life, I just know it."

As they rode home, Rae closed her eyes and listened to the birds singing and the wind blowing in the trees. After all the frustration, disappointment, and anger that she had experienced these past few days, she needed to have some peace in her life. Tim was so sweet. They had formed a bond of friendship that she would not allow Jesse to come between. Tim was like a big brother she never had.

After arriving home, Jesse was sitting on the screen porch with Ollie and Hope. Tim leaned over in the carriage, took Rae's hands into his, and whispered, "Let's put a fire under the big boy and do this again Saturday afternoon. We'll take Hope. I can already feel darts coming through the porch wall at us." Before she knew his intentions, Tim leaned over and kissed her on the mouth.

"Tim, what are you doing?" asked a very surprised Rae.

"Fanning the flames, Rae, fanning the flames." He laughed as he was getting out of the carriage to help her down. "See you Saturday," he said loud enough for the ones sitting on the porch to hear.

*****

The few days that followed were the same. Everyone had their routine and chores to do. Rae was up early each morning helping Ollie with breakfast. She assisted Katie with her toilettes and helped her dress for the day. Katie was getting stronger and able to get around with her arm in a sling. After breakfast, Katie would sit on the screen porch and watch the men go about their daily chores. She could watch Rider and Joseph training the new horses to break them to the saddle. It was entertaining to watch these young men ride—and sometimes get thrown off the horses.

Rider was the determined one. Up and down. He wouldn't give the poor animals a rest. In the end, Rider would succeed, and Jesse would be able to sell the horses that were now broken to the saddle.

After breakfast, Rae helped Ollie start lunch, and then she dressed Hope. Later she would take Hope and her puppy for a short walk. Hope loved it outside, and she enjoyed feeding the chickens and chasing the little fuzzy yellow baby chicks. She enjoyed feeding the little piglets, but the mama sow was protective of her babies so Hope couldn't get too close.

Her favorite pastime was riding with Jesse. He took her horseback riding every day. Sometimes he took her with him to check on the cattle in the pasture. He helped her practice her numbers by counting the new calves that they would see.

Rae had started spending time with Will. She noticed that he had difficulty with some of the words in Hope's storybooks. She took him aside and talked to him about allowing her to help improve his reading. They agreed to meet in his new room each day before lunch and have a lesson.

He was hardheaded, but he was also a smart young man. He realized that he needed to be able to read better and work on his ciphering too. And if he could sit next to a beautiful teacher like Rae for an hour each day, he was certainly willing.

Joseph came home one day from visiting Rebecca and told Jesse that the new mattresses would be arriving at the general store the next day around noon. "Mr. Smith asked that you bring your wagon and come into town tomorrow and pick them up. He said something about a new carpet would be here too."

"Thanks Joseph. The new carpet is a surprised for Will. I thought that his room would be warmer with a rug on the floor," said Jesse. After learning that the new items he ordered would be at the store, he went in search of Ollie.

Ollie was outside in the chicken coop cleaning out some of the hens' nests. She was putting in new straw. She had a fire outside with a big black pot filled with boiling hot water.

"Ollie," Jesse called to her, and she came out of the chicken coop. "What are you doing?"

"I'm getting my chicken house ready for winter. I do this every year. I guess you have never been around the house when I have done this before. I use that hot water to scrub down the floor. If I don't clean this place once a year, a body wouldn't be able to go in after the eggs."

"Well I never knew you did this. I will have the men do this for you from now on. You don't need to be doing this kind of work. I came out here to ask if you would give my room a spring cleaning in the morning.

"With Hank being in there for a month, the room needs airing and my new mattress will be here after lunch. Maybe you could donate me one of your new oversized quilts for a coverlet?" he asked sweetly while raising his eyebrows at her.

"My goodness, Mr. Jess, I will be pleased to clean your room and make it look like one of those fine fancy hotel rooms where honeymooners stays!" Ollie snickered as she went back inside the chicken coop.

"Good, that's what I want," he said under his breath.

*****

The town was buzzing with rumors about Jesse and Rae. There was a lot of speculating as to when the wedding would be. Surely with the order of the new mattresses arriving, the marriage would be taking place soon.

The preacher had told everyone that if he had anything to do with it, the wedding would be today!

Mr. Smith, the owner of the general store, had told the preacher that Jesse or one of his men would be in town today to pick up their special order.

"If Jesse comes in, this will be a good chance for you to insist that he do right by that girl! It is a crying shame that she was abducted by two men and held hostage for almost a week with only an old black woman with her. Then to be brought back here to a ranch full of nothing but men. Why, he should be horsewhipped for not marrying that girl right away. We can't have people in our community living the way they do. If the sheriff ain't going to put a stop to it, then you must, Preacher."

"What am I supposed to put a stop to, Smithy? Your voice can be heard all the way to my office." Sheriff Murphy stood in the doorway of the store, looking very unhappy at what he was hearing Mr. Smith saying to the preacher.

"Why, Sheriff, I was just telling the preacher he needs to look after Miss Rivers ... I mean Miss Rogers's welfare. We all know that she has no family left to care for her, and she is out there at that ranch with all those young single men," said Mr. Smith.

The sheriff glanced over at the preacher and then back at Mr. Smith. "Let me tell you something, Smithy. You and I both know that Miss Rogers has been well chaperoned by Miss Ollie. She has never been alone with any one man at any time. And you damn well better know that. Another thing, you crazy-acting horny fool, if Jesse gets wind that you have been talking about Miss Rogers and Miss Ollie the way you are doing today, I will feel right sorry for your behind. That boy will stomp you in the ground. He puts a lot of store in that old black woman you keep talking about like she ain't nothing. Oh, and one more thing. I will be looking the other way. Get my drift?" He grinned broadly and started out of the door.

"But ... but ... you know that what I am saying is the truth!" stuttered Mr. Smith.

Sheriff Murphy stopped dead in his tracks, turned, and pointed his finger at Mr. Smith. "You," and then turning to gaze upon the preacher, "and you, better keep your traps shut and mind your own damn business. Jess Maxwell is a good man, and he will do what is right for Miss Rogers and her sister. You, preacher man, have embarrassed them enough and if it happens again, you will not be welcome in this town. I will personally kick your God-fearing butt to the county line."

A group of townspeople had gathered at the doorway of the store to take in the scene between the sheriff, Mr. Smith, and the preacher. They parted ways, allowing the sheriff to march out to the boardwalk. He informed them that they should move on—the show was over!

Joseph and John had made the trip into town to get the new supplies. Several of the townspeople nodded their heads in greeting to them, but no one stopped to ask any questions about Jesse and Rae like they thought might happen. Joseph went into the café to see Rebecca for a few minutes, and she told him all about Sheriff Murphy chewing Mr. Smith and the preacher up one side and down the other. She assured him that he put the fear of God in them, and now maybe some of the talk should stop.

Joseph explained to John about what Rebecca had told him. They were not surprised that Sheriff Murphy had defended Jesse and Rae. But he wasn't going to be able to stop all the women from gossiping. John told Joseph that Rae would never be accepted in the community by the other women as long as she continued to live under Jess's roof without marriage.

"Something is going to have to happen to get those two together and soon," said John.

*****

When the two men arrived back at the ranch with the new items for the house, it was almost like Christmas for Will. He was ecstatic over his mattress and loved the new rug that he wasn't expecting. The men helped him move his furniture to lay down his new rug. They brought up the new mattress for the bed. Rae came up with clean sheets and a brand-new quilt that Ollie had made. She immediately made the bed and put the new pillows on top of the quilt that she and Ollie had stuff ed with goose feathers.

Will was one proud young man who now had his very own room, his private castle. Hope giggled and crawled up on his bed and started bouncing up and down. Will grabbed her and said, "Oh no, you don't, little miss smarty britches. This is my bed, and you will not be jumping up and down on it. Besides, you could get hurt!"

Everyone laughed and removed themselves from Will's new room to allow him a few minutes alone in his private domain.

Jesse watched everyone file down the ladder from the loft room. When Rae's feet touched the floor, he asked, "So, Rae, do you think he likes his new space?"

"Why don't you go up and ask him yourself?" she said as she slid past him.

Jesse climbed the stairs and found Will lying on his bed with his hands behind his head, staring up at the ceiling. "Well, what do you think? Like it?" asked Jesse?

"Oh, Jesse, I do. Very much. This rug is great. I wasn't expecting it, but it sure feels good to my feet," he said while wiggling his toes in his stocking feet. Jesse was proud that Will appeared happy.

"Good. I expect you to keep this room neat. Ollie won't be coming up here, so it will be your job to bring down the linens and your dirty clothes on washday. I understand that Rae has been helping you with your reading." Will tensed but didn't response to that statement. "I'm happy about that," said Jesse as he headed to the stairs.

"Jess?" called Will. "When are you going to marry her?"

Jesse turned and looked at Will and then looked down at the floor as if he were looking at the new rug. After what seemed like forever, he surprised Will by answering, "As soon as I can convince her that I love her."

As he headed down the stairs, he said, "Don't forget about your evening chores."

As Jesse made his way out of the house, he heard laughter and giggling coming from the men and Hope. He walked out to the chicken yard to see what the excitement was all about. Jesse couldn't believe his eyes, but he started laughing immediately. In the chicken yard, Hope was chasing after a big brownish turkey with white-tipped feathers. She had a rope and was trying to lasso the bird.

"Where did the turkey come from?" asked Jesse.

"We picked it up today at the general store. Old Smithy had about a dozen in crates in the back of the store that someone had brought in to sell for Thanksgiving. I didn't figure that you would mind if we got it so Ollie can fatten it up for the holiday dinner."

"That bird won't put on any weight if Hope continues to chase the poor soul," laughed Jesse. "No, I don't mind at all. Thanks for getting it for us."

Chapter 21

Saturday morning was a beautiful fall day. The weekends on the ranch were like any other day as for the chores—the livestock had to be checked and fed, and meals had to be prepared. But aside from those necessities, it was a welcome break. After the men had completed their chores, they were free to do as they pleased. Today was no exception. Will and Rider had gotten up before sunrise and gone fishing, promising Ollie that they would bring enough fish home for lunch. Joseph had ridden into town to help Rebecca and her mom with some needed repairs to the café.

Ollie and Rae were cleaning up the kitchen while Aunt Katie and Jeremiah were sitting in the front room close to the fireplace. They were making plans for their departure back to their home in Peamont. Tim was expected to come out today to give Katie permission to travel. She was doing fine and had removed the sling from her arm. John was still insisting that she needed to wear it for another week. He was looking for any excuse to keep Katie at the ranch.

Rae had gone out on the porch to give the tablecloth a good shake, when she saw Sheriff Murphy on his horse talking to Jesse. "Get down and come on in and have some coffee," invited Jesse. "There may be a biscuit or two left from breakfast if you are hungry."

"Thanks, I could use a good cup of coffee. Is Miss Rogers in the house?" asked the sheriff. "I have something to tell you both."

"Come in, Sheriff," said Ollie. "Let me whip you up some breakfast while Rae pours you some coffee."

"Coffee and a biscuit with some of that delicious ham will be plenty, Miss Ollie."

After getting everyone settled around the table, the sheriff pulled out an envelope that contained a letter from the sheriff in Rosedale. "I got this here letter yesterday informing me that the money that was recovered from your stepfather had made it safely to Rosedale. It is back in the bank where it belongs. Mr. Sawyer, the bank teller, is now the president of the bank." Looking at Jesse, he said, "You told me about him and how bad he was treated by Mr. Summers."

"That's right. I am pleased to hear that he got that job. He went to college to learn about banking, so I know he will do a great job."

"There is a note in here for you, Miss Rogers. It seems that the lawyer wants to lease the house and land that your family lived in and would like to know what he should do with your personal belongings." Rae immediately looked at Jesse with great concern.

"There is one other thing of great importance that I have yet to mention." The sheriff was acting very suspicious and seemed to enjoy having everyone sitting on the edge of their seats, waiting for him to reveal the information. Reaching down in the envelope again, he pulled out another paper. "This here is a draft in the amount of $2,000 payable to the men and women who helped capture Virgil. Jesse is to be the administrator over the money. That means that Jess will divide the reward money to the people who earned it."

There wasn't a sound in the room. Everyone was in total surprise and shock. The sheriff continued on, "Come to find out, Virgil was wanted for murdering two men. The marshal in Frisco City sent the reward money on the stage to me. Also, the bank in Rosedale had a small reward payable for the return of their stolen money. Altogether there is $2,500 to be divided."

Sheriff Murphy looked at Jesse, Rae, Ollie, Katie, and Jeremiah. "Well, what do you think?"

Jesse sat down at the table at the same time Rae sat across from him. "I never expected anything like this, to be honest with you. I am sure no one here did. The money is a pleasant surprise, and I am sure the men will appreciate it." Jesse never took his eyes off Rae. He could almost read her thoughts. *She now has money to start her new life somewhere away from here. Away from me.*

Ollie spoke up and said, "This calls for a celebration. We must have an extra special dinner this evening, Jesse, so you can tell the men the good news. I bet Joseph will be getting married sooner than he planned," Ollie said with a laugh.

"Now, Ollie, I don't want you and Rae having to go to any trouble cooking a big dinner. I can just call them in and tell them," Jesse said.

"You just hush that talk! Those boys, Katie, and Jeremiah helped save our lives. It will be pure pleasure to help make this a special celebration for them."

"Sheriff Murphy, you are more than welcome to stay for our dinner celebration or come back out this evening," said Rae.

Looking around the room, he placed his hat back on his head and said, "Wild horses couldn't keep me away. See you this evening."

*****

Jesse came back into the house and told Rae that they needed to talk about something very important.

"Sorry, Jess, I can't take the time to talk this morning. I have a celebration to prepare for, and I must get to my baking now." She said this with a smile on her face as she skirted by him to pull out the flour barrel. "You best go and figure out how you are going to divide the reward money."

Rae finished preparing two large peach-and-apple cobblers. They were ready to go in the oven. She helped Ollie clean up the breakfast dishes.

Jeremiah came into the kitchen to take his usual seat at the table for a second cup of coffee that he and Ollie had started enjoying together.

Rae went into her room and put it in order, and then she walked to the door of Jesse's room. This was the first time she had been in his room since Hank moved back to the bunkhouse. She was shocked to find it so neat and clean. The large bed had the new mattress on it, and it was covered with a double wedding ring pattern quilt with pillow covers to match. *This* is too lovely for a man, *thought Rae.*

Jesse's desk and chair sat in the corner next to the window. It was very well organized, just like the man himself. There was a small round table next to the bed with a chimney lantern and an open Bible sitting on a pretty, lacy scarf. *Lace, my. This must be Ollie's doings.* A rocking chair with a large footstool sat next to the old potbellied stove, and a round, colorful woven rug covered most of the open floor. She had wondered before why this room didn't have a large fireplace like the one in her room. Continuing to look around, she noticed a beautiful carved tri-fold screen in the corner of the room. It was an oak finish with flowers and birds carvings all over it. *Goodness, this room is certainly not decorated just for a man,* she thought. *All this room needs to be complete is a beautiful bouquet of fresh flowers.*

As Rae came back in the kitchen, satisfied that the rest of the house was neat and in order, she asked Ollie what she could do to help with lunch.

Ollie glanced at Jeremiah and told her that she needed more new, red potatoes that were in the cellar. "I only want the little ones, so you may have to dig around under the bottom of that pile of potatoes. I need this bowl filled if you don't mind?" said Ollie.

"Goodness, Ollie, how many people are we going to feed for lunch?"

"Oh, these potatoes are for the celebration supper tonight," replied Ollie.

"Oh, in that case." She gave Ollie a questioning look, thinking that this would still be a lot of potatoes. Rae walked out of the kitchen and around to the side of the porch. She bent over and lifted the large door leading down to the cellar. Then she leaned it back and used a big stick to prop it open. She eased herself down the ladder into the dim light of the room. Feeling her way over to the table where the candles and matches where, she lit two of the tall candles and walked over to the pile of potatoes and started sorting the bigger ones out of the way.

As Jesse came into the house to start working on the paperwork that the sheriff brought out earlier, Ollie called to him.

"Jess, Rae has been down in the cellar for a good while getting me some potatoes. Will you go down and check on her? Maybe you can give her a hand to bring them back up the ladder." After she said this to Jesse, she turned and looked at Jeremiah with a grin on her shiny black face.

"Sure thing," said Jesse, nearly leaping over a straight chair as he raced out the kitchen door.

"So, Ollie, when did you start playing matchmaker?" Jeremiah asked.

"Sometimes you just have to put two lovebirds in the same cage together. Come on, old man, and help me." She laughed while walking out the door with Jeremiah following close behind. When Ollie got to the cellar door, she could hear raised voices. Pointing to the cellar door, she and Jeremiah lifted the prop that was holding the door and gave it a push.

Slam went the door as it closed.

Rae was so focused on sorting through the potatoes to get just the right ones, that when Jesse practically jumped down into the cellar, it gave her enough of a fright to cause her to scream.

"Sorry, sweetheart, I didn't mean to spook you." Just as he started to tell her that Ollie sent him to help her, the cellar door slammed closed and the wind blew out the candles, placing them in total darkness. Rae leaped into his arms.

"Whatever caused that door to do that?" asked Rae, feeling very anxious.

"I don't know, but I am thankful. I've been wanting to hold you like this for days," he said as he nuzzled his face into the side of her neck, smelling the fragrance in her hair.

"Stop, Jess!" Rae said as she gave him a good shove backward. "Light the candles so we can see to get the door open."

"I don't need to see you, honey. You feel just right in my arms. Stop fighting me and let me hold you," he said as he was trying to steal a kiss from her.

Rae jerked away from him and said, "Stop, Jesse. You have no right to touch my person." As she was trying to locate the candles and matches, she tripped and fell over a small barrel of flour, and it spilled open onto the floor.

Jesse was walking softly with his hands out like a blind man, teasing her. "You cannot hide from me, honey. This room is only about a ten-by-ten space."

Just as he said that, his boot slipped into the open barrel of flour. He jerked his boot back too quickly, causing him to get off balance. He went down right on top of Rae, and she screamed, "Get off me you ... lunatic! Let me up off this floor," she pleaded, close to tears.

He started laughing and said, "Now, I have you." She shoved and pushed at him as f our went flying up in the air. Her eyes had adjusted to the dark, and she grabbed up a handful of flour and threw it on him, hitting his mouth and neck.

Spitting and wiping the flour, he said, "So, the lady wants to play, does she?" Laughing, he reached into the barrel and got his hand full of flour and started rubbing it all over her face.

Rae reared up and tried to get way. Suddenly she felt panic rise within herself. She yanked and slapped at his hands, but he had her by the skirt.

Finally she lowered her head and bit the back of his hand, and he turned her loose. "No fair!" he yelled.

Feeling free, she jumped up and knocked some jars off the shelf behind her, and they broke and rolled all over the floor. "Oh my, Ollie is going to be so mad at you, honey child!" Jesse said, mocking the way Ollie spoke.

"Me? Let me go!" she yelled. He had her around her waist and turned her back to face him. He pulled her up against him and pressed her thighs into his, trying to kiss her again.

Once more, she yanked herself away from him and shouted, "No, Jess, you can't do these things to me. You don't love me, and I will never give myself to a brute of a man who doesn't want me for life!" She scrambled up the ladder and was pushing on the door, when he reached up and snatched a handful of her skirt. She struggled, but he grabbed her around her small waist and lifted her back down. Stepping and stumbling on one of the jars that didn't break, he flopped down on the floor, still holding Rae in his arms.

"You idiot. You're going to kill us!" gasped Rae.

"What ... do you ... mean ... I don't love you?" he asked her as he was trying to catch his breath from the fall backward. Turning her onto her back while leaning over her and glaring into her face, he asked, "How can you say that?"

"It's easy!" she said as she was slapping his hands away. "You have never told me!" Still trying to get loose from him, she pinched his arm and he yelled, "Ouch!" Having the advantage, she reached up and clutched a handful of hair at his temple and pulled until he released her. She scrambled up onto his thighs, and just as she stood, the cellar door opened.

Light flooded into the dark room. There in the middle of the floor stood Rae, while Jesse was still sitting on the floor. Both were covered with flour from head to toes. From up at the top of the ladder, there stood Ollie and Jeremiah gazing down at both of them.

"What's you two doing down in my cellar?" Ollie asked so innocently. "How did this door get closed?"

Rae hurried up the ladder as Ollie and Jeremiah took in her appearance. She ran around them and went into the house with flour flying everywhere.

Jesse came up the ladder, dusting off some of the dirt-and-flour combination. He stopped and looked at Ollie. "That's a good question, Ollie, dear. How did the door slam shut?" Standing with flour covering his face, hair, and clothes, he glared at her. He had already figured out the answer.

"Excuse me, but I have a wildcat to catch!" he said as he ran into the house, letting the screen door slam behind him.

Ollie looked at Jeremiah and smiled as she held up her hand with her two fingers crossed. "Just maybe this little trick of ours worked," she said.

"If it doesn't, I had no part in it," he said very firm.

Jess stormed into the house following the trail of white flour to Rae's room. "Rae." He tapped on her door. "Let me in. We have to finish our conversation that we were having in the cellar," he demanded.

"As far as I am concerned, we have finished. Go away!" she yelled through the door.

"Open this damn door, or I will kick it in!" yelled Jesse as he had lost all patience.

"Go away. We have nothing to talk about!" Before the words were out of her mouth, the door slammed back into the wall with a bang. Jesse stood in the open doorway with both hands on his hips. Rae had removed her dress, so she reached and grabbed up her wrapper. "Are you crazy? Get out!"

Marching forward into the room, he walked up to her as she started backing up. With each step he took, she took one backward. "You are going to listen to me if we have to stand here all day long!" He reached for her, and this time she stood very still.

"Rae," he spoke very forcefully, "you said down in the cellar that I didn't love you. You couldn't be more wrong. I do love you." Pulling her into his arms, he said, "I have loved you a very long time, and I can't see my future without you. I love you with all my heart and I adore Hope, Sweetheart, whatever she chooses to answer to," he said.

"Oh Jess, really? I love you too. I have loved you almost from the very start of coming here, but I tried not to. You have been so cantankerous and insufferable! Half the time I was afraid of you."

"Oh, honey, are you really afraid of me? All I want to do is make you happy, make you laugh, and make you want me more than anything else," he said as he held her tight. Pulling her closer to him, he closed her eyes with his kisses. He trailed his lips down her nose to her cheek, along her jaw to her chin, and finally touched her lips with his.

"I have waited all my life for you. When you were kidnapped, I thought I may have lost you—I nearly died. I knew then that I loved you with all my heart. I promised the Lord if I got you home safe and sound, that I would never let you go. And that is one promise I intend to keep."

Looking at Rae as he gave her a sweet smile, Jesse lowered himself down onto one knee. Taking both of her hands in his, he looked up into those beautiful soft brown eyes of hers and said, "Rae Rogers, will you do me the honor of becoming my wife?"

"Oh, Jesse." Suddenly her arms clung to him as he stood and kissed her until they were both breathless. He kissed her neck and buried his face in her hair. "I thought you would never ask. Yes!" she cried. "I want to be your wife more than anything in the world."

After kissing her over and over, he pushed away and said, while holding her at arm's length, "I better stop kissing you. Th at old preacher man might be right. We could be living in sin," he said as he raised his eyebrows up and down.

*****

After Jesse and Rae told Ollie that there was going to be a real special announcement at the celebration that night, Ollie declared that she wouldn't be surprised at all. She circled Jesse and Rae and pulled both into her warm, loving arms and said she couldn't be happier. Jesse and Will were her boys, and all she ever wanted for them was to grow up and be happy and find a sweet girl who would love them as much as she does.

"Child, I love you and Hope so much. I believe that I would have just died if you had to leave this home," said Ollie. "What a happy celebration we are going to have tonight."

Later that afternoon, the dinner preparation was well on its way with a big pot of beef stew simmering on the back of the stove. Large pork chops were all seasoned and ready to go into the oven for baking. Ollie had sat down in the rocking chair to rest while holding Hope as she had drifted off to sleep. Jeremiah walked over to the rocker and removed Hope out of Ollie's arms and carried her to bed for a long afternoon nap.

"Thank you, Jeremiah," said Ollie. "Now you come and sit a spell with me while those young folks sit out on the porch."

While Jesse and Rae were sitting in the swing on the porch whispering sweet words about their future, they looked up at the familiar black carriage coming into the ranch yard. "Oh my goodness, it's Tim! He is here to take me and Hope on a picnic," she whispered loudly to Jesse.

As she rose to get out of the swing and greet Tim, Jesse grabbed her arm at the elbow and said very sternly, "Your picnic outings with Tim or anybody else are over! If you want to go on an outing, it will be with me!"

Rae's temper flared for just a second, and then she started laughing. "Of course, don't be silly. We will give Tim our good news together."

Rae and Jesse stared at Tim with their mouths hanging open. They were so surprised to see him without his Sunday three-piece suit on. As Tim stood before them holding the reins of the horse, Rae and Jesse took in his new attire. He was a mirror image of Jesse. His new western denims, plaid shirt, brown leather vest, and new shiny leather boots were the same as Jesse wore every day.

Jesse jumped off the porch and circled Tim, looking at his new duds.

"What are you all decked out for?" Jesse asked. Tim watched Jesse closely as he walked around him, inspecting his new wardrobe.

"What do you mean? I just wanted to be more comfortable on the picnic. What is wrong with the way I am dressed?" Tim was feeling confident that just maybe he was already making Jesse a little jealous.

Looking up at Rae, Tim asked, "Hey, pretty girl, are you and Hope ready to go for a nice ride?"

Before Rae could answer, Jesse slapped Tim on his back and said, "Pal, old buddy, I'm afraid there has been a little change of plans. Pull your horse and carriage over to the barn and come sit a spell with us on the porch. We have some news we would like to share with you."

Watching Tim lead his old mare over to the barn, limping in his new boots and stiff denims, Jesse smiled up at Rae on the porch. "I will get us all something cool to drink while we wait on him to finish," said Rae, smiling.

*****

Tim and Sheriff Murphy were special guests at the dinner celebration.

Everyone anticipated the wonderful announcement. All the men had placed a little wager on what the announcement would be tonight. They were poking, shoving, and grinning at each other all the while they were being seated around the table. "Come on, out with it," said Hank, hoping to get Jesse to go ahead and make the wedding announcement.

Jesse had planned to make that announcement first before they ate, but he was feeling playful, so he decided that it could wait a while longer.

Taking his knife, he tapped on his coffee mug to get everyone's attention. "Now that I have your attention, let's say grace, and then I have a very important announcement that hopefully will please everyone.

"Lord, bless this wonderful dinner that Ollie and Rae have prepared for us, and thank you for this wonderful family and friends. Amen."

"Rae, look who has gotten up from her long nap," said Hank, pointing at Hope as she walked slowly into the room and eased up to him.

"Come on up here, Sweetheart, and sit next to old Hankie. Jess is going to give us some good news," he said as he picked her up and placed her on the bench seat.

"Now as I was starting to say, I have some great news that concerns all of you. Sheriff Murphy," Jesse said, flashing a big grin at the sheriff, "came out this morning and brought me a letter from the marshal in Frisco City.

It seems after some investigation, Virgil was a wanted man, and there was a reward of $2,000 on his head. Also, the bank in Rosedale was pleased to have the money back that was stolen by *someone*." Looking at Hope, he avoided using Herbert's name. "They have sent a bank draft for $500 to me. This reward money has been given to me to divide among all that had a part in capturing Virgil and retrieving the money."

Glancing at everyone sitting around the dinner table, Jesse said, "I feel each of you deserves an equal part of the reward money."

Hank spoke up and said that he didn't do anything but hop around on the crutches and care for Sweetheart. Tim said that he didn't help in the capturing of Virgil—he just patched up Miss Katie.

Jesse held his hands up in front of him and said, "Hold on. I know what everyone did. I know that you, Hank, help keep this ranch running. We were very fortunate to have you here. Tim, Aunt Katie could have bled to death without your knowledge and the care you have given her. So, you see, I know the importance of what each of you did. I feel that everyone here played an important part in earning the money. It is my decision, and I want everyone to take their part and do whatever you want with it. So what do you think?"

"Let's eat!" said Sheriff Murphy. "I have waited all day to dive into Ollie's good food!"

Everyone laughed, and the platters of food were passed around with a lot of joyful laughter.

Jeremiah looked at Ollie and smiled at his new friend with her big brown eyes and lovely white curls and asked, "So, Ollie, now that you are a lady of means, what are you going to do with your money? Buy some more rags to cover that pretty hair?"

Ollie started to lay into him for his smart remarks about her bandannas, but she was too happy to ruin the mood. "Well, I can tell you this. There won't be no youngster in my church without new shoes and a nice warm coat this winter. My heart is so full just thinking about those babies strutting around with those new shoes and coats," she declared.

Ollie glanced over at Joseph and quizzed him. "Joseph, what does this windfall mean to you?"

"Well, it may mean that Rebecca and I can tie the knot sooner than planned!"

"Oh, that is wonderful, just wonderful," said Ollie while the others smiled and offered him congratulations.

Will looked over at Rider and grinned. "Well, Rider, old boy, what gal are you going to spend your fortune on?"

"I'm not," he said, with his voice cracking. "I mean, I'm not going to throw this money away. I am going to open me an account at the bank and save it for my future." Sounding so mature, he looked at the older adults who were all nodding their heads in agreement.

"Good plan," said John, pleased with Rider's decision.

"Aunt Katie, what are your plans? I mean with your part of the money," asked Rae.

All heads turned to look at her, and some peeked over at John. "Well, I don't rightly know for sure. This is such a wonderful surprise. There are some things that need fixing at my cottage. I have always wanted a pump placed in the kitchen. I think that would be just wonderful!"

Will said, "I think I am going to do like Rider and hold on to mine for a while. It is sort of funny. Now that I have money, I find that I don't really want anything."

Jeremiah and John, when asked about what they would like to spend their money on, remarked that they were going to put it up for the time being, too.

Rae got up and placed the cobblers on the table to be served. Will couldn't contain himself any longer, and he asked Rae if she still planned to leave now that she had the funds to live somewhere else. The mood of the room became very quiet, and all eyes focused on her and Jesse.

Jesse motioned for Rae to stop what she was doing and come to him.

He was sitting at the head of the table. She placed the spoon down into the cobbler and strolled over to take his hand. Jesse pulled her down to sit on his left leg, leaned into her, and kissed her on the neck. She tried to get up, but he laughed and held her tighter. Every eye in the room was on them.

Laughing, Jesse said, "Ladies and gentlemen, I am proud to announce that Rae has consented to be my wife. We are going to be married as soon as we can make the arrangements!"

Aunt Katie jumped up and grabbed Rae around the neck, hugging and squeezing her. Ollie joined in on the hugs, and in just a minute Ollie, Rae, and Katie were all crying and laughing. Will grabbed up Sweetheart and kissed her on the cheek and said that he was going to be her uncle.

Rae took Hope from Will and told her that she was going to marry Jesse. "Isn't this wonderful, Hope? We won't ever have to leave here," she whispered to her. "We will live here with Ollie, Jess, and Will always, and you can have all the pets you want!"

Rae noticed that Hope had a funny expression on her face. "Aren't you happy, darling?"

Hope studied Rae for a minute and said, "But Mama … I want you to marry Hankie! Remember? I done told you that at the cem'tary."

Everyone laughed and returned to their seats at the table when they heard Hope's announcement. Jesse hugged Hank and said, "Hey, I didn't know *you* were my competition too."

Hank held on to Jesse's arm and said just as seriously as he could, "I couldn't be more pleased with this marriage. You have been like my own son, and now I will have a daughter and a granddaughter who I already love." He reached in his pocket and took out his handkerchief to wipe his eyes.

After the dessert was devoured by the men, Hank headed to the bunkhouse with Rider and Will on his heels, poking fun at him. "So you are going to be the groom in the wedding instead of Jess!"

"Yep!" he replied. "And you two knot heads are going to be the flower girls dressed in pink silk and ruffled pantaloons." Will and Rider doubled over with more hysterics as they continued to trail after Hank.

Chapter 22

After the celebration dinner, everyone headed their separate ways. Standing at his carriage, Tim expressed to Rae how happy he was for her, even though she had broken his heart. Together, they laughed.

"Oh Tim, you always make me laugh when no one else can. You are a dear man, and I want you, me, and Jess to be friends forever. Jess does like you very much, you know," she said, grinning.

"I know and I like him too. But if you ever change your mind, I will only be a whistle away," he said as he tapped her nose Just at that moment, Jesse walked out the door and said, "Unhand my woman, man," laughing as he joined them.

"Well, I guess the best man won," said Tim.

"I wouldn't go so far as to say that. Let's just say I found her first," replied Jesse.

"If you gentlemen will excuse me while you discuss me like I am not even here, I will check on Hope. Good night, Tim," said Rae.

Tim grinned at Jesse and said good night to him too. "Don't be a stranger, Tim. You are always welcome here."

*****

The sun was coming up, casting a glow across the breakfast table. Ollie and Katie sat at the table having their first cup of coffee while discussing her plans to leave and go home back to Peamont.

"I tell you, honey, you sure are going to be missed. Rae will be really upset if you don't come back for the ceremony," said Ollie.

"Thanksgiving is about three weeks away. We are going to have to travel to Rosedale and get a wedding dress. There is no way we can make one in that short of time. Claire's dress was beautiful, and I believe that we can make it over for Rae."

Ollie raised her brows when she mentioned Claire's dress. Katie took in that look and said quickly, "Not the dress she wore when she married Herbert! No, no. That would never happen. When Claire married Rae's father, she had a lovely white silk dress with a white overlay that just flowed. Rae will love it, but it is in Rosedale, in her mama's trunk."

"Sounds wonderful. So I guess Rae had better prepare to go home with you and get her dress made over, and she can get her other personal things from Herbert's home. I will go into town and get some pretty soft material and make Hope's dress. She will be a beautiful flower girl," said Ollie.

"Where do you think we should have the ceremony? In the chapel in town? I know that Rae will never let that preacher perform the ceremony."

Katie laughed at the thought.

"Here comes the bride now. Good morning, honey child. Katie and I have been discussing plans for your dress and the ceremony," said Ollie as Rae walked to the stove to pour herself a cup of coffee.

"Wonderful. I need all the help I can get. Thanksgiving is only a few weeks away, and I don't think we have time to make a dress," said Rae.

Katie told Rae about her mama's first wedding dress and how lovely it would look on her. Rae got so excited just thinking about being able to wear her mama's dress. It would be like Mama was with her. "Oh Aunt Katie, do you think we will have time to remake it to fit me?"

"Yes, I do, but we need to pack up and leave tomorrow. Jeremiah can pack our things today, and we will borrow the flatbed wagon so we will have a nice dry bed to sleep on while we travel. You can use the wagon to bring your personal items home," said Katie.

"How long do you think it will take to get to Rosedale?" asked Ollie.

"Who is going to Rosedale?" asked Jesse as he came through the screen door.

"Morning, Jess," said Katie. "We are discussing Rae's dress and other arrangements for the wedding. We don't have much time, so we will be leaving tomorrow morning to go to Rosedale."

"Who is 'we'? Who will be traveling to Rosedale?" asked Jesse, already knowing the answer.

After a long discussion with Rae, Jesse finally agreed to the trip. He wanted to go with her, but in order to take time away from the ranch for a honeymoon trip, he needed to stay home.

Jesse asked Rider to go with them, and after much pleading by Will, he finally agreed to allow him to go too. The two girls would be safe enough with Rider, Will, and Jeremiah.

Ollie had agreed to keep Hope. She told Rae that she needed her to be at the ranch so she could fi t her flower girl dress on her. After much more discussion, the guest list for the wedding was prepared, and the day after Thanksgiving was set for the wedding date. Ollie suggested that they have the wedding at the ranch and allow her minister to perform the ceremony.

Everything was all set.

*****

The travelers were all ready to drive out of the ranch yard, when John hailed them to stop. "Can I speak to you privately, Kate? I only need a minute of your time."

"But John, we are leaving!" Katie looked around at all the others. Will and Rider gave her a nod to go ahead and speak with him.

Katie stood up in the wagon. John walked over and helped her down and led her into the barn, out of sight of the others.

"John, what is so important that couldn't wait until I return?" Before she could complete that question, he grabbed her arms and pulled her into him, capturing her mouth with a hard, deep kiss. "John," she exclaimed.

"What ...?" He kissed her again.

"Kate, I couldn't allow you to leave without telling you how I feel. I fought this all night. I want you, Kate, more than I have ever wanted anything. I don't have the right to ask you to come back to me. I have very little to offer a woman. I do have money saved, but I have no land or home. All I have is what you see."

Katie started to talk, but he stopped her again with another steamy kiss. "John, are you ... asking me ... to marry you?" she said, out of breath.

"I want you to think about me and our future while you are gone. You can tell me when you get back. Please think seriously about us." Then he led her back out of the barn to the wagon where everyone was waiting patiently. He lifted her onto the wagon and whispered for her ears only, "I love you, Kate."

Jeremiah walked up to the two mares that were hitched to the wagon and said, "Gee, gee, girls." They were finally off, but Katie was still in shock. She kept looking back over her shoulder at John, standing straight and tall in the yard. Rae started laughing, and that finally got Katie's attention back to earth.

"It looks like love is really in the air," said Rae to Will as he rode beside her on his pinto pony.

After arriving in Rosedale, Rae walked over to the rooming house and requested rooms for them. Mrs. Blazes and Amelia were so glad to see that Rae had recovered from her bad experience with the kidnappers. They were still in shock to learn that Rae's stepfather had killed her mama, embezzled the money from the bank, and then tried to kidnap her. Things like this just didn't happen in the nice town of Rosedale.

"Come on in, child, and tell me how you and your darling sister are doing. Is she all right?" asked a very concerned Mrs. Blazes.

"Yes, we are all fine now, and I am here to collect my personal goods out of Mr. Summers's house. I especially want to get my mama's wedding dress because I am getting married Thanksgiving weekend," she said excitedly.

Both Mrs. Blazes and Amelia started clapping their hands, laughing and smiling. This was a joyous occasion in a young girl's life, and they were pleased that she shared the good news with them.

Once they were all settled into the rooming house, Rae notified Mr. Sigler, the lawyer, that she was in town to collect her things. They agreed to meet at the house in two hours. Will and Rider took their horse to the horse stable to bed them down for the night. Rae, Katie, and Jeremiah walked to the Rosedale bank to see the young new president, Mr. Sawyer.

As they entered the bank, Mr. Sawyer was coming out of his office. He looked up and saw Rae. "My goodness! What a wonderful surprise. Miss Rae, you look … wonderful!"

"Oh, Mr. Sawyer, you are too kind. And yes, I feel wonderful, thank you. I would like you to meet my Aunt Katie and our friend, Jeremiah."

After introductions were made, Rae told him that she and Jesse would be getting married in a few weeks. "Jess asked me to come here and personally invite you and your girlfriend, Mae, to our wedding. You would be our honored guests, and you can stay at the ranch."

"Well, I would love to come. Be honored to come, I should say. But I can't bring my girlfriend." He blushed and continued, "I would love to bring my wife!"

Rae, Jeremiah, and Katie looked at him in surprise. "We got married as soon as I got this promotion with the bank," he declared with joy and happiness reflecting all over him.

"Oh, how wonderful for both of you!" said Rae. "Let me write down the date for you and the directions to our ranch. Jess will be so happy to see you again."

After meeting with Mr. Sigler and gathering her belongings from the house, Rae went through the trunk and recovered her mama's wedding gown. It was in perfect condition. The silk material had yellowed a little, but with new overlay material, it would look like new.

Mrs. Blazes confessed that she was a seamstress in her spare time, making all of her and Amelia's clothes. She volunteered to help remake Claire's gown for Rae. "Your mama was a lovely lady, and I have missed her so much. She was the best pie maker in this county! This is the least I could do for her daughter," she said as she wiped her misty eyes.

"First thing after breakfast, we will get the material and spend all day remaking this lovely gown," she said, turning to Rae and Katie. "Amelia will need help in the kitchen preparing meals for these hungry folks that let from me. If you help her with the preparations, then I can sew all day if need be."

"Mrs. Blazes, you are a dear. Of course, we will be glad to help Amelia, and I will even make a couple of pies for your dinner meal. Just like Mama!" Rae said.

The gown turned out to be as lovely as any a person could order out of the mail-order catalogs. Mrs. Blazes worked diligently and completed the gown in one day. Rae told Will and Rider that they could head home the next day. She was pleased that they were one day ahead of the scheduled time for the trip.

Katie and Jeremiah told them that they were not going to make the trip home with them. They needed to go on to Peamont and check on her cottage and the few livestock that they had. A friend of Jeremiah's has been taking care of everything for them.

"But Aunt Katie, you never said that you weren't coming back to the ranch with us," Rae said, very disappointed. "What about the wedding? Surely you will be there. I couldn't get married without you!"

"Honey, I will be there. Jeremiah and I need to go home for a while.

We will return to the ranch in a couple of weeks. We will be there for Thanksgiving and the ceremony, if not a few days before. We have things to do to prepare for winter. Please understand," Katie explained.

As Rae hugged Katie, she whispered in her ear, "What shall I tell John? He will be so disappointed that you didn't come back with me."

"You leave John to me, honey. Now go and prepare your things for the trip back to your new home."

*****

Back at the ranch, Jesse and the men were very busy. Jesse and John had ridden out to the western range of the ranch to check on the bull. Jesse was so proud of the new animal, and he was filling out and growing larger every day. Jesse was sure that there would be many new calves come spring.

Jesse and John stopped at a small stream to let their horses get some water. They got down off the animals and stood to let them drink.

"All right, John, out with it. I have known you too long not to recognize the signs that you have something on your mind," remarked Jesse.

"Well, I do, but I'm not sure if I have the right to ask."

"You'll never know if you don't try it out on me."

"You're not the only one that has been bitten by the old love bug as Ollie calls it," said John, laughing.

"No kidding!" Jesse snickered as he slapped John on the back. "None of us would have ever guessed that you were smitten with Katie. How do you think she feels about you?"

"Before she left, I told her that I loved her and I wanted her to think seriously about us while she was gone with Rae."

"So, what are you planning for your future together?"

"I have money. I have saved for years and always intended to buy a small spread, but I never had the desire to live alone. I have never found someone that I cared about like I do Kate. I was hoping that I could get you to sell me about twenty acres of land where I could build a small house and have space enough for a garden and a place for some livestock. I would like to continue working for you and still have my own little farm where Kate and I could live in comfort. I know that Kate and Jeremiah would enjoy being close to Rae and Hope."

"John, what you just told me couldn't please me more. Rae will be so happy to have her Aunt Katie and Jeremiah close by. What section of my land have you had your eye on?"

"There is a section near the fence line that is fairly close to Mr. Downing's farm. I though Kate would like it very much. It has a small stream running across the back of the property line. I think it would be fairly easy to put a well down and have a pump put in the house."

"Saddle up, old man, and show me the land that you are speaking about. I believe we can work out some kind of deal. I'm thinking that this land might make a great wedding present from me and Rae." Jesse kicked his horse a little in his side and said, "Let's go, boy!"

*****

Ollie had already been into town and purchased material for Hope's dress for the wedding. For herself, she picked out a soft, shiny blue material with white material to make a large collar to go on it. She also wanted to make herself a very pretty white apron to go over her new dress since she would be serving food and drinks, and she wanted to look her best.

After lunch, while Sweetheart was taking her nap, Ollie cut the dresses out and started hand stitching them together. She wanted to have all the sewing done before Rae returned because there would be many other things to do to prepare for the wedding. While in town, she asked Rebecca to help her prepare the wedding invitations and announcements. Handwritten small posters would be placed at the post office and the general store.

Special announcements would be handed out to a chosen few.

"This will be the wedding of the century," declared Ollie.

Jesse's family had been in the community for many years and was well thought of by everyone. Most of the older people had witnessed Jesse grow from a small boy to a fine young man. They wanted to help him rejoice in the beginning of a new life with a family.

Food preparations were ordered from Rebecca's mom's café. They would prepare cakes and cookies along with two dozen loaves of fresh bread. Rae had already confided in Ollie that she wanted to make her own wedding cake and decorate it, in remembrance of her mama.

Hank had ordered three large, dressed turkeys, already cooked, from Mrs. Smith at the general store. Mr. Downing had told Hank that he would donate a side of beef to be barbequed for the reception dinner. All the ladies who were invited would bring a covered dish to help feed the one-hundred-plus people who would be attending this wonderful celebration.

Between Ollie and Hank, they had handled almost all the preparations for the wedding reception.

Joseph asked a small group of men who played their musical instruments for an occasional barn dance if they would perform at the reception, and they readily agreed. He had ordered some two-by-fours and smooth planks of wood to make a dance floor to be placed in front of the barn. This platform would be the perfect place for the wedding ceremony.

He was already planning to build an arch for the wedding couple to stand under as they said their vows.

Between Ollie, Hank, and Joseph, most of the wedding preparations had been prepared. Jesse and Rae would have to get with Ollie's minister and discuss the wedding vows. Jesse's father had given him his mother's wedding ring to be passed on to his future bride. The ring was small, but

Rae's hands were very slender. Jesse knew that it would be a perfect fit for her. Jesse asked Will to be his best man, and Rae choose Hank to walk her down the aisle. Both men were very proud to have been asked to be a part of the wedding.

Each day, Hank would spend time playing with Sweetheart. Her puppy was now big enough to tag along behind her every step. She loved to visit the little piglets and help feed the small babies that the mama sows didn't have room for. She had gotten very good at holding one and giving it a bottle.

Now that Joseph had bought home "Mr. Gobbler," Sweetheart was quite taken with the large, strutting bird. She could hold out a few pieces of grain and the old bird would walk over and eat it out of her hand. In all his life, Hank declared he had never seen anyone make a pet out of a turkey. Turkeys, in his opinion, were stupid birds! Hank would remind Sweetheart every day, "Don't like that bird too much, because we are going to eat him come Thanksgiving."

Jesse's routine each afternoon included taking Hope for a horseback ride over the ranch. He pointed out the horses that were in the corral, and she knew all of their names. She would tell him when a mama cow was getting fat. Jesse would show her the wheat and hay fields and explain why they had planted these crops. At her young age, she was learning all about ranch life.

Jesse adored her and enjoyed spending time with her. He thought what it would be like to have a child of his own. Feeling the love for someone else's child, he could only imagine what loving his own would be like.

Looking down at Hope, he prayed that one day, she may even look upon him as her papa instead of just Jesse.

*****

It was late one afternoon while Jesse was out riding with Hope that he saw the wagon with Rae and Will. Rider was trailing beside them on his horse. "Look, there, Hope. It's Rae and the boys heading home. Let's catch up with them," he said as he kicked his heels in the side of his horse.

"Goodie," said Hope, "Ollie's baby boy is coming home too!"

Rae looked up at the sound of a rider coming up behind them. She jumped up in the wagon, nearly falling headfirst to the ground. Will grabbed her skirt and pulled her back down.

"Careful, Rae. We won't have a bride if you fall out of this wagon on your head," yelled Will.

"Oh, Jess!" yelled Rae. "It is so good to see you."

Still reaching for him with her arms held over her head, he rode up beside the wagon and passed Hope to Will. "Take this squirt while I get my bride and take her for a little ride," said Jesse.

Will had pulled the brake on the wagon before the exchange of the girls was made. "Did you miss me?" said Will to Hope.

She continued to stand in the wagon, looking him straight in the face, and said, "You know Ollie and me missed our baby boy!" Then she turned and waved to Rider.

*****

"Oh Jess, I missed you so much, and I have a lot to tell you," said Rae.

Nuzzling her ear and the side of her neck, he led the horse over to the stream with crystal clear water flowing.

"Come on," he said, "let's sit over here, and you can tell me all about the trip. Hey, where are Katie and Jeremiah?"

"That's part of what I have to tell you," she said as he continued to nibble on her neck.

"Honey, I have missed you so much. I've spent hours thinking of you while you were away. All I could think about was being able to hold you again in my arms like this. I have been nearly crazy thinking about our future together. I have never been so busy. My goodness, Ollie has been a slave driver giving all of us orders from sunup to sundown with the preparations for the wedding." Jesse looked into her face and saw an expression of pure pleasure.

"Jesse, don't ever stop. Don't ever stop loving me. I feel so wonderful when you are near. I could hardly wait to leave Rosedale to get back home to you."

As Jesse continued to kiss Rae, and his hands were roaming all over her body, the heat between them became almost uncontrollable. "Stop, Jess," Rae whispered.

"But you said to never stop!" He pulled back from her. "Which is it? Stop, or don't stop?" Laughing and looking into her eyes, she knew that he was playing with her.

"Oh, you! If we don't stop, we are going to really be the talk of the county. Let's get on home so I can see Hope and Ollie. Oh, how I missed everyone."

*****

John came out to meet Jess and Rae when they rode back to the ranch house. Will had already told him that Katie and Jeremiah would be returning before Thanksgiving.

"Welcome home, Miss Rae," shouted John. "Were you able to take care of all your business?"

"Yes, John," answered Rae.

"Good." John nodded his head.

As John started walking to the bunkhouse, Rae spoke to him. "John, Aunt Katie will be coming back for Thanksgiving. She said that she wouldn't miss our wedding."

"Did she have a message for me?" asked John with concern.

Rae wanted to just die. She knew he was going to be so hurt. "No message, John." Rae watched John walk away until he was out of her sight.

She felt so sorry for him, and she was angry at her beloved Aunt Katie. She could have sent him a note and not just leave him wondering. John was a fine man. *Oh, I could just spit!*

Ollie was in the kitchen placing food on the table for Rae and Jesse when Rae entered the door. "Oh my gracious, my Rae is home," Ollie said as she grabbed up the tail her of big apron and started wiping her eyes.

"Child, I shore have missed you. Come and sit down and let me serve you some supper. I knows you are hungry."

*****

As the days and weeks passed, Thanksgiving was drawing nearer and the wedding preparations were all completed. The dance floor and beautiful arch had been built and put into the barn until the wedding day. The barbeque pit had been dug, and the wood had been chopped and stacked, ready to start cooking and smoking Thanksgiving eve. Many of the guests had responded that they would be in attendance.

Rae was sitting at the table helping Ollie shell pecans. "You know, Ollie, I was sure that Aunt Katie and Jeremiah would be here by now. I am so worried that they may not come."

"Now child, don't get to looking for something to worry about. Your Aunt Katie will be here. I just bet they come driving in tomorrow."

"I want to thank you for making Hope's flower girl dress. She is going to be beautiful. I know that you spent many hours making it. I can hardly believe that Mrs. Blades took the time to make Hope a flower basket out of some of my white voile scraps and had it sent to us on the stage. There are some wonderful people in this world. I must do something special when Amelia gets married."

*****

Early next morning, the sun was shining and a cool breeze was finally in the air. Everyone had their morning meal and they were doing their daily chores when the sound of a child's shriek filled the air.

"Listen, what in the world is all that noise? It sounds like Hope," said Rae as she got up and walked over to the screen door.

"Oh, my goodness, Ollie. It is Hope—and Hank has a hatchet."

"No ... no ... no, no, no. You can't hurt Mr. Gobbler! Will! Help, help me," screamed Hope, barring the chicken yard with her little arms stretched across the wire gate. Hank was standing near the door to the chicken yard with a thunderous expression on his face.

"I told you, Sweetheart, not to get attached to that fat ugly, squawking bird. We are having him for Thanksgiving dinner!"

Rae and Jesse met up at the chicken yard at the same time, followed by Ollie, who was breathing fast. "What are you doing with that hatchet, Hank?" yelled Jesse over the raised voices of Hope and Hank.

"I am planning on getting this bird ready for the boiling pot! He is our Thanksgiving dinner. We have been feeding him for over a month, getting him ready to enjoy."

Will, Rider, Joseph, and John had finally arrived to Hope's rescue.

They were all staring at Hope squatting in the middle of the chicken yard with her little arms wrapped around Mr. Gobbler's neck, offering him all of her little body's protection. Hank turned to look around at everyone, pleading for help.

"How could you even think about killing the baby's pet, you bloodthirsty killer," said Will, teasing as he and Rider passed by Hank.

They jumped out of his reach as they laughed and ran back to continue their chores.

"Sorry, Hank. The turkey has been reprieved. He will not be on our table this year. Put that hatchet away and go in there and make up with Sweetheart. She is just a baby and doesn't understand about not making friends with the animals," said Jesse.

"When we all start eating nothing but turnips greens and corn bread, don't blame me," he said as he entered the chicken yard.

"What a morning," said Ollie, laughing as she instructed Hank to dress three of her plump hens.

Hank immediately passed that chore to Joseph. "I don't want to be called 'killer' again."

Rae was helping Ollie place the lunch on the table, when a wagon drove up in the yard. "Come, Ollie, it is Aunt Katie." Racing out to the yard, clapping her hands and bouncing up and down, Rae was thrilled beyond words. "Oh, Aunt Katie. I am so glad you are here."

"Well, I am here," she said as she climbed down from the wagon.

"Jeremiah brought all of our belongings. What we could fit in this wagon, that is. We are here to stay," she whispered for Rae's ears only.

"Oh, Aunt Katie, this is wonderful news," said Rae.

Jesse came out of the barn followed by Will and Rider. "Look who has finally arrived!"

"Oh Jess," said Rae, "they are here to stay. I can't believe it. Where can they unload their wagon?"

"Jeremiah, Katie, welcome! I couldn't be happier. Katie, I mean Aunt Katie," Jesse grinned at her as he continued, "go into the house and let Ollie get you settled in with Rae and Hope. Jeremiah, old man, we still have your bunk."

As the women ran into the house still hugging and laughing, Jesse instructed Jeremiah to drive their wagon over to the barn. "Just get a few personal things out of the wagon for now, and I will get the boys to make room for it in the older building beside the smokehouse. It is still very sturdy and doesn't leak."

"Thanks so much, Jess. We can wait until after the wedding is over and you are away on your honeymoon. We will start looking for a place to stay later," said Jeremiah.

Will and Rider came out to hear the news and both hugged and slapped Jeremiah on the back to welcome him back. Joseph had prepared to ride out to check on the cattle, when John rode up beside him and told him to stay.

"I will check the herd and the bull this afternoon," said John and then rode off .

"But John, what about Miss Katie?" yelled Joseph. With no answer, he stood in the front yard watching John ride away. He noticed Miss Katie standing in the doorway watching John's retreat, too. She looked sad to Joseph.

The supper meal was a hurried affair with chicken noodle soup and cold sliced ham sandwiches. There was so much food to be prepared for the Thanksgiving dinner the next day. Everybody was excited that Katie and Jeremiah had finally arrived and planned to stay in the area. She told them about the preparations that had to be made in order to leave Peamont.

The cottage was sold to the neighbor on the west side of her. The cow and two old mules were sold and promised a good home to one of

Jeremiah's friends. She had kept a few pieces of furniture but gave most of it to a newlywed couple in the area. They were thrilled to have her cast-off furniture as she called it.

Jeremiah told about having to dig up so many flower bulbs, small scrubs, and bushes to bring. "She told me that she wasn't going anywhere without her babies." Everyone laughed as Katie blushed.

The evening would have been perfect if John had made an appearance.

Chapter 23

Thanksgiving Day's weather was perfect. Several long tables were made and set on the screen porch where all the guests gathered around to enjoy the wonderful meal. Ollie had prepared the table in the kitchen for all the food to be placed. Everyone served themselves and then took their places at the long tables.

Tim O'Riley, Sheriff Murphy, and Rebecca were special guests. Jesse asked the blessing and the serious eating began. There were many jokes made about the upcoming wedding the next day, and several sly remarks were made about the honeymoon—for the men's ears only.

No one said anything about John's absence. Ollie had expressed her concern to Jesse because John was one of her boys.

"He has to work this problem out for himself," remarked Jesse.

*****

After all the guests had left, Jesse and Rae took their last walk together until they were man and wife. Jesse pulled Rae into his arms and kissed her breathless. "I can hardly wait until tomorrow, honey. Are you all packed and ready to spend a week away from the ranch?"

Rae nodded *yes*. Jesse kissed her and let his hands roam up and down her back. She could hardly think straight, but she did know that they had to stop this necking before it was too late.

"Please, Jess, let's just talk."

Jesse gave a big sigh and said, "We will take the small carriage into McBain and spend the night at the rooming house there. I have already requested their best room for tomorrow night. Then we will catch the stagecoach to Frisco City. It will take us about two days to get there. I have several special things planned for us to do while we're there, but mostly we will enjoy the honeymoon suite at a beautiful new hotel," he said as he kissed her long and hard again. "Oh honey, I can hardly wait." He was breathing fast and hard as he held her tight.

"Please Jess, we had better go back to the house. We have been away too long as it is."

"Oh shoot, you're no fun." Jesse said, and he grabbed her hand to lead her back toward the house, knowing that she was right about them being alone.

Jesse left Rae on the front porch with another long, breathless kiss and said he couldn't wait until they would start their lives together. "Dream about me, honey." He winked at her as he strolled away.

He walked out to the barbeque pit where Joseph and Rider were placing the side of beef on the rack that would be lowered into the smoking pit. They would take the first watch over the meat, and Mr. Downing and his son would arrive around three in the morning to take charge, because they had smoked many beef steers.

*****

The wedding day had finally arrived. It was a gorgeous sunny day with just enough cool air to make it enjoyable. Hank had prepared breakfast for the men, including Jesse, in the bunkhouse. There was no way Jesse could see Rae until the wedding ceremony.

It took about a dozen men to bring the dance floor out of the barn and put it in place. Joseph took a mop and cleaned the planks until they shined. The lovely arch was placed on the dance floor and decorated with greenery woven all through it. Sunflowers were added to the arch for the final touch. Tall stools were placed at one end of the dance floor for the few band members to rest upon as they played their instruments.

Guests had started to arrive and the earliest arrivals were put to work. The men helped the boys with their daily chores. Even on special days, the animals had to be fed and cared for.

A number of ladies were busy helping Ollie prepare the last-minute dishes, and some just sat and watched Rae place the final touches on her beautiful wedding cake. Rae was so thankful that she had learned so much about decorating from her mama. With each touch of decorations, her thoughts were of her mama—how she wished that she could be here to share this wonderful day with her.

The wedding cake had three large tiers with a soft white creamy icing. The icing was placed in a piece of cheesecloth with a tiny hole cut in the end. Rae would squeeze some icing out on a plate and then use a small pointed stick to make the shape of leaves and tiny flowers.

After the decorations got hard, she would place them on the cake. The ladies were in awe of this beautifully decorated cake.

It was time for Rae to get into her wedding dress. She was so proud of it. Mrs. Blades had done a fantastic job remaking her mama's dress to fit her. The silk material had a layer of white voile on the top of the skirt.

The neckline went straight across with a small, flower design embroidered at the top edge. It was very delicate. Rae's flower bouquet was designed by Katie. She had dug up one of her white rosebushes from her cottage and placed it in a pot. She planned to cut the roses at the last minute before the ceremony and place them with some soft greenery and white ribbons.

Aunt Katie made sure Hope was kept in her room until time for the wedding. The baby's blonde curls hung down her back with a large pink bow placed on the side of her hair. The white dress that Ollie had made her was lovely. Ollie had stayed up late at night embroidering tiny pink flowers on the bodice. Rae had purchased her new white Sunday shoes to wear just for this occasion. She looked like a living doll.

Time was drawing near to the wedding ceremony when Katie approached Ollie with much sadness in her voice. "Ollie, I can't believe that I have chased John away from taking a part in Jesse's wedding. He is a big part of this family, and he should be here with Jess. I know that he is upset with me, and I am sorry for that, but I never meant for him to feel that he had to stay away. I thought that he would be here waiting for my return. I guess I was wrong."

Ollie knew that John had waited, and that he was hurt when Katie didn't send him a single note with Rae's return. She knew how John felt about Katie, but it wasn't her place to tell her.

"Honey, you take care of Rae, and I will see about John. I'll be right back."

Ollie gave a pull or two on her new lovely dress that she had made.

It was a soft blue top and skirt. She had left her hair uncovered, and the white curls had a mind of their own.

"Ollie, you looked ten years younger without that bandanna on your head," said Jeremiah earlier that morning. She was feeling happier and younger than she had in a long time. She marched out the front porch, her destination being the bunkhouse. Stopping to greet guests as she made her way across the front yard, she entered the bunkhouse without knocking.

Jesse, Hank, and Will all looked at her in surprise as she motioned her head toward John, who lay upon a bunk bed facing the wall. Th e boys all made themselves scarce.

Ollie walked over to John's bunk and said with the authority of a general in battle, "John. Sit up!"

John was so shocked at hearing Ollie's voice that he immediately jumped straight up and shouted, "What wrong, Miss Ollie?"

"You tell me."

"I don't know what you mean," he said as he hung his head, looking down at the floor.

"John, I didn't come out here to mince words with you. This is Jesse's big day, and he needs you to be out there sharing in his celebration. You are family to us, and your presence has sorely been missed. Now, I have let you pout long enough over Miss Katie. You are the oldest of my boys, and you knows better than to lay around acting like a lovesick calf. Be the man that you are and go out there," pointing her finger toward the door, "and tell that woman how much you loves her, or so help me, I will get my wooden spoon after you!" She turned and marched out the door just like she came in.

*****

The wedding music started and the old minister from Ollie's church stepped in front of the lovely arch. Jesse and Will walked up and took their places on the right side of him, looking grand in their new identical black suits and shiny boots.

Rider assisted Hope up on the platform, and she strolled toward the front carrying her flower basket and sprinkling rose petals as she walked.

She was a vision of a perfect living doll. Everyone sighed as she took her place up front.

Katie's entrance onto the platform was one many would not soon forget. They were witnessing a beautiful woman who was an older version of the bride. She looked lovely in her baby blue dress that gathered in the back and flowed onto the platform as she walked. She held her head high, just like a royal princess, walking toward the wedding party.

As the band changed the tone of the wedding march, everyone knew that Rae had stepped out of the house onto the porch. Hank walked over with his chest puffed out, took her hand, and helped her down the three short steps. Leading her to the platform, Rae and Hank stepped up together and walked arm in arm to the front where Jesse was waiting for her.

Rae handed Aunt Katie her beautiful rose bouquet, then she turned and placed her hands into Jesse's. The words that the minister shared with Jesse and Rae were some of the sweetest words ever heard spoken during a wedding ceremony. He spoke from his heart about the differences of love and loving.

He told the young couple, "When you love someone, you want to care and nurture that person. Offer up your heart to them and lay your life down to guard and protect them in all ways. And when you accept their loving, you want to receive this love with an open heart and be the best person you can be for them. You must guard their love with your whole heart."

Hope started fidgeting, so Ollie waved for her to come to her, which she ignored. But Hope settled down quickly when Aunt Katie touched her shoulder.

As the minister called for a prayer, Katie closed her eyes, but she sensed someone watching her. She peeked out and saw John openly staring at her. She opened her eyes wide, surprised to see him. He continued staring at her, never blinking. After the prayers ended, the minister said to the couple, "Now I proudly pronounce you man and wife. You may kiss your bride!"

Jesse slowly pulled Rae into his arms and kissed her lightly. Before she knew what happened, he kissed her again until she was leaning backward.

The guests went wild with their applause and laughter. Ollie stood with tears in her large, brown eyes, trying not to burst out crying. She openly rejoiced. She had never been happier for her older boy.

Jesse and Will hugged, and Rae turned to Aunt Katie who was looking over Rae's shoulder as they hugged tightly.

Jesse had lifted up Hope, swinging her around as he told her, "I love you, squirt!"

John stepped around the wedding party and stood in front of Katie. His Kate. They both reached for each other at the same time.

"Oh John," she said.

Jesse slapped John on the back, and he turned and hugged Jesse, who whispered into John's ear, "Ask her, you jackass!" John laughed as he grabbed Katie's hand and led her away from the other guests.

Ollie and Hank walked over to Jesse and Rae. Looking at Hank, Ollie said, "Children, Hank and I are both very happy. We both lived with your papa for many years, Jess, and we know that he would have been very proud of your choice of Rae."

Wiping at her eyes, she continued, "Now while you are gone on your honeymoon, we will be the best two old grandparents in this world to Sweetheart. We both loves her like she was our real grandbaby. Enough of this talk! I got to get the spread of food out here for these guests to eat."

Ollie went into the house with several ladies from her church who had come over to help serve the guests, and they started bringing out the food.

There were more guests than the hundred they had planned for—maybe about 150 guests in total—but she wasn't worried. There was plenty of food.

The beautiful wedding cake had been brought out of the house on a large square board that Rae had decorated the cake upon. They were being very careful. After several toasts were made to the bride and groom, they cut the cake together. Rebecca took over the job of serving the cake, while another lady poured the punch. The musicians that Joseph had hired had already warmed up their instruments and taken their place on the dance platform. Several of the men had removed the lovely arch.

Jesse surprised Rae by dancing the foxtrot without missing a step. He confessed that Ollie had taught him when he was younger. After several rounds on the dance floor, he motioned for everyone to join them.

Katie and John had walked a short ways from the festivities when he stopped, turned her to face him, and kissed her soundly. "Kate, my Kate, I didn't think that you were coming back to me. With no word or note, I didn't know what to believe."

"Oh, John, I wanted to be sure. After I left Rae and traveled home to Peamont, I knew that I was coming back. I'm sorry if I hurt you. Please, forgive me?"

"On one condition, my Kate." Stooping down on one knee, he said, "I love you with all my heart, and I can't imagine my life without you. Kate, will you marry me?"

"Yes, oh yes!" She leaped into his arms, and they kissed and laughed like they were two youngsters. "John," Kate said breathlessly, "I'm so happy. I feel like a young schoolgirl."

"Come on. Schoolgirl, let's go join the others and tell them our great news. I am pretty sure most of them won't be surprised!"

*****

Hope had taken herself a plate and filled it to almost overflowing with goodies. Ollie scolded her and said that she had better eat all that food.

"These nice ladies have cooked most of this delicious food, and it shouldn't be wasted. You go and sit down and eat your dinner like the good little girl you are."

When she had eaten her fill, she still had a lot of food left on her plate. She looked at the food and decided that she would feed the rest to her farm pets. "My little piglets will love this, and I will give some to Mr. Gobbler," she said to herself.

After bending down and giving her little puppy a piece of her cake, Hope rounded the chicken yard and noticed that the gate had been left open. She raced into the chicken yard and there was no Mr. Gobbler. She peeked into the chicken coop and then ran around the hog pens, climbing onto the fence to get a better look. Running toward the corral, she stepped in a puddle of water and lost one of her new Sunday shoes. "Drat," she said.

Thank goodness! She finally spotted Hank coming toward her.

"Hankie, I can't find Mr. Gobbler! Help me find him, please!"

Hank couldn't believe his eyes. "Sweetheart, look at yourself. What have you been doing? Ollie is going to skin you when she sees what you have done to your pretty dress—and where is your shoe? Run along and get cleaned up, and I will find that old bird of yours."

Once Hank left her, she looked down at her dress and sighed. "Oh well," she said and continued with her own search for her pet. Inside the barn, she looked in the stalls, stepping into a fresh pile of cow manure.

Looking at her sock, she pulled it off and tossed it down on the ground as she wiped her hand clean down the front of her lovely dress. Then she raced back outside.

Her hair had come loose, and her large pink bow was hanging on to one strand of hair down her back. The sash of her dress was dangling loose, but she took no notice. Stopping to think where Mr. Gobbler could be, she remembered what Hankie said about "eating" him.

We didn't eat him, but with all these strangers doing the cooking ... oh gosh! Hope raced around the food tables, and there in the center of a table, was a big turkey, fried with the legs pointing up to the sky. "Mr. Gobbler?" she said. Behind the table stood Jesse.

"You mean man. You let them scumbags kill my pet turkey. I hate you! I hate all of you! " she screamed as she looked around at the guests. Everyone appeared to be in shock. Never had they heard a child so small talk so ugly to grown people.

"Sweetheart, Sweetheart, Hope baby, I have … your bird!"

Hearing a racket, everyone saw Hank running across the yard, limping and hopping with one boot on. His dress jacket had been discarded, and his white shirt was pulled out of his pants. A large scratch on his cheek dripped blood down his chin. He was trying to hold on to Hope's big fat bird.

With flapping wings, loud squawking sounds, and feathers flying, Hank was calling to Hope as he was cussing a blue streak. Just as he got to the center of the crowd, he stumbled over his own single boot, still clutching tightly to the bird. Everyone was pushing to get out of his way as he collapsed upon the hard ground with Mr. Gobbler nestled under one arm.

Hope stooped down over Hank, running her hand across his bloody cheek. "Oh Hankie, you found Mr. Gobbler. I love you so much," she said as she took her sash and started wiping the blood away from his cheek.

Jesse took Rae into his arms, giving her one of his sassy grins and said,

"She will be no trouble at all?"

Epilogue

Limason, 1897

"Jesse, what in the world has those chickens all stirred up and the dogs barking? That racket is not helping me get little Claire to sleep," Rae said with a sigh.

As Jesse stepped out onto the porch to investigate the noise, he witnessed eight-year-old Sweetheart racing around the chicken yard. With her long limbs and her beautiful blonde curls twisted into a rope flying down her back, she was jumping back and forth, dodging Will's hot pursuit.

"What's wrong, big baby boy? Mad because I caught you and Janie … kissing? You both needed cooling off!" she yelled as she jumped again out of his long reach.

"You're the one whose butt is going to need cooling off, you snot-nosed Peeping Tom. I'm going to blister your sassy behind until you can't sit for a week!"

"Get her, get her!" shouted little Jess who was racing around them, clapping his hands. "Dunk her head in the horse trough!"

"Stop that horsing around and shut those blasted animals up. Rae is trying to get the baby to sleep," shouted Jesse.

Will loved the new baby, and he knew that little Claire had the colic and was giving Rae and Ollie fits with her constant crying. He immediately stopped the chase and stood in the barn door watching Janie, his new girlfriend, ride away from the ranch.

"I'm not finished with you yet." He pointed his finger and gave Sweetheart a fair warning.

Jesse and Rae had been married for five years, and they couldn't be more pleased with their growing family. Ollie and her constant companion, Jeremiah, made the best babysitters in the world. Little Jess, now four, was the apple of his dad's eye. If he wasn't riding his pony in the corral with Jesse, he was on the back of Jeremiah or Hank. It seemed that his feet never touched the ground. Will had spoiled him until he was a little brat at times, but Ollie still had her wooden spoon hanging on the wall in the kitchen when it was needed.

Now after three years, little Claire was born, named after Rae's beloved mama. With her little blonde fuzz and big brown eyes, she was just as beautiful as Hope was as a baby. After only being several weeks old, she developed the colic, but with Doctor Tim's medicine and Ollie's old-fashioned remedies, she was improving.

Ollie was busy at the stove preparing lunch when Jeremiah arrived for his second cup of coffee. Now that Katie and John had married almost four years ago, Jeremiah was almost a fixture at Ollie's kitchen table. She gave him a fresh cup of coffee and sat a bowl of potatoes that needed to be peeled in front of him.

John and Katie had settled down on the twenty acres of land that Jesse and Rae had given them as a wedding present. After John and the boys had cleared a place to build their cottage, the community formed a barn-raising party and built the foundation, framed the house, and finished with the roof. Each afternoon and on weekends, John worked diligently at completing the house. He included a pump in the kitchen so Katie could have her dream of running water in the house. While John was working on the inside of the house, Katie was working on the outside, planting the flowers and bulbs that she had brought from her home in Peamont.

Now the grounds surrounding their cottage, driveway, and fences were covered with lovely flowers. It was a showplace for sure. John and Jeremiah had built several small houses for Katie to raise more bulbs, small vegetable plants, and blooming shrubs. People from miles around would come and buy flowers to plant from Katie. John surprised her one day by painting her a sign that read "Flowers by Katie."

"Joseph and Rider will be here for lunch with their girls, Jeremiah," said Ollie. "I hope that will be enough potatoes."

"I hope Rebecca brings some of her mama's cream pies. Since little Claire has been sick Rae hasn't made any," said Jeremiah.

"I believe Joseph and Rebecca are going to be making an announcement at lunch. I have noticed that Rebecca has been putting on a little weight around the middle."

"My goodness, I hope that is true. They've been married for almost three years!" said Jeremiah. "You know I like that gal of Rider's too. She is so cute and dainty."

"What you know about being dainty, old man?" Ollie laughed.

Ollie was placing the food on the table when John, Katie, Joseph, and Rebecca arrived at the same time. Rider and his girlfriend, along with Will, followed them in the door. After all the greetings were over, everyone prepared to sit down for a delicious lunch. Rae had finally gotten little Claire to sleep, and now she could enjoy her family.

Little Jess hurried over to Will and pulled on his arm. He whispered into Will's ear that Sweetheart was out in the barn washing her feet before she came into the house.

"Thanks, sprout," said Will as he jumped up from the table, rushing out the screen door. "I owe you a penny."

Rae walked over to the door and looked out at Will as he entered the barn. She looked at Jesse and said, "What do you think he is up too?"

"I would say that he and Hope are fixing to have a 'church house meeting,' and I don't believe that she will be forgiven."

The End.

Made in the
USA
Columbia, SC